ONE ON ONE

Ripley fell into the shallow water, grunted and jumped up into a crouch. She tried to look in all directions at once, managed one; there was no immediate danger.

She didn't believe that the drones would have left their queen unprotected, but the only motion around her was the gently swaying ocean.

Doesn't mean it's going to stay that way. . .

All of her senses were in overdrive. The putrid odor of the planet, combined with the heat and gravity made her dizzy. Along with the fading sound of the APC, there was only the slosh of the water against her legs. The fierce winds had suddenly dwindled to almost nothing.

An alien's cry echoed through the dead air, but it came from the direction of the retreating transport.

She turned and faced the cluster of nests.

"It's just you and me now," she said.

ALIENS™

THE FEMALE WAR

OMNIBUS EDITION

GENOCIDE

Steve Perry & Stephani Perry
David Bischoff

(Based on the Twentieth Century Fox motion pictures, the designs of
H.R. Giger, and the graphic novels by Mark Verheiden, Sam Kieth,
Mike Richardson, John Arcudi, Damon Willis and Karl C. Story)

A DARK HORSE SCIENCE FICTION NOVEL

MILLENNIUM

First published in Great Britain in 1995 by
Millennium
The Orion Publishing Group
5 Upper St Martin's Lane
London WC2H 9EA

ISBN: 1 85798 454 4

Printed and bound in Great Britain by
Clays Ltd, St Ives plc

ALIENS™

THE FEMALE WAR

"If you are captured by the Indians, don't let them give you to the women."

Attributed to U.S. frontier cavalrymen during the attempted extermination of the Dakota Sioux.

Ripley felt the little girl's arms tighten around her neck as she slammed the lift button repeatedly.

The queen was almost certainly right behind them. They were going to die down here. The thought filled her with a sudden dizzying wave of sickness and she hit the button again. They were going to die in this hellish, humid, artificial pit on a crumbling planet, a big piece of which was itself about to be blown into atomic dust.

"Come *on*, goddammit!"

She hiked the crying child up higher and looked back over her shoulder into the darkness. Steam hissed from a ruptured pipe, adding a hot fog to the dankness of the alien-spittle covering the walls. She could feel it coming, could almost hear the rapid steps of the approaching mother, even over the screaming alarms and sirens. She had destroyed its children, hundreds of its deadly offspring, and she had no doubt that it was on its way to rip her and the girl apart.

She looked up then, saw the bottom of the lift slowly descending, still a few floors up. Any second now ...

From behind them came a piercing scream, inhuman, full of rage. Ripley instinctively clutched her weapon tighter and ran to the ladder attached to the wall; maybe they could catch the elevator on the next level up. "Hold on to me!" she shouted.

And then *she* was there, like the others but larger, swollen even if no longer gravid.

The queen had a huge crown, a comb of glossy black that swept up and back from her misshapen head. A second set of arms, smaller, jutted from her chest. It—*she*—moved slowly toward them from around the corner a few meters away, hissing and drooling.

Ripley backed away; the girl tightened her small, sweaty hands in a finger lock to keep from falling.

The lift, it was here!

Ripley spun.

The door opened, the mesh gate slid away, and they jumped in. Ripley slapped the control button more frantically than before—

The queen ran toward them—

The wire gate closed ...

Shut a second before the alien got there.

Ripley put the girl down, pointed her flame-thrower at the creature, fired through the mesh. The fuel was low; only thin and weak spurts of flame came out, but it was enough to stop the alien.

The queen snarled; thick streams of slime dripped from her open jaws. She held back.

The outer door closed.

Safe! They were safe!

The ride up was rough; explosions rocked the building, falling pieces of debris slammed into their all-too-slowly-rising lift. But they made it to the flight deck.

As the outer door opened, a calm female voice informed them that they had two minutes to get the minimum safe distance from the site, before the whole processing plant blew itself into non-existence. They ran together from the lift, and—

Where the fuck was the ship?!

It was gone! Their ride had taken off; that god-damned *machine*, the android, had betrayed them!

Ripley screamed in anger, pulled the little girl toward her. Flames leaped all around, the building rocked and shook with deafening noise ... and now, another sound. Ripley looked at the lifts.

Another elevator coming up.

Oh, no. It couldn't be. The queen couldn't know how to operate an elevator! She *couldn't*!

But she is smart, a little voice said inside Ripley's head. You saw her when she realized you were going to burn her eggs, how she waved the drones off, kept them away from you. At first.

Ripley looked at her carbine. The counter said it was out of ammo. The flame-thrower taped to the gun was also dry. She dropped the weapon, picked up the child, backed away.

The lift came to a stop, the door slid open. Ripley hugged the girl tightly.

"Close your eyes, baby," she said, and closed her own.

"Ripley? Are you okay?"

Ripley opened her eyes and looked at Billie, the young woman sitting across from her. Billie looked concerned, a slight frown creasing her brow. Ripley liked her, had liked her in the first moment or so of meeting—unusual. Trust was hard to come by these days, at least for her. But Billie's account of her childhood rescue had stirred up some stories of Ripley's own....

"Yeah," she said, and then sighed. "Sorry. I got lost there for a minute. Anyway, the last thing I really remember is settling into sleep after LV-426, me and one of the soldiers and a civilian, a little girl. I—I guess the ship must have sustained some damage somewhere along the way. I don't remember anything else. I woke up in a crowd of refugees on Earth six weeks ago, and they were on their way here; it seemed like a good idea— everything was falling to shit down there. So I've only been here a month longer than you have."

Billie nodded. "So what did the medics say about the missing part? Physical or psych damage?"

"I don't do medics," she said, smiling a little. "Besides, I feel fine."

Ripley stood and stretched her arms over her head. "Want to walk with me to dinner?"

Billie glanced curiously at the older woman as they headed toward the cafeteria. She was the first survivor, so far as anyone knew, to have seen the aliens and gone back for more. Billie found herself intrigued by Ripley's relaxed, confident demeanor, a calmness that seemed unlikely after all she must have been through. Especially given her own experiences with the monsters. Even after only two weeks here, it seemed like a million years had passed.

They walked down C-corridor toward the nearest dining hall. There was a viewing plate adjacent to the hatchway that led them down another corridor; peering out the window was a young couple, both medtechs by the look of their IDs, holding hands and talking quietly. Billie saw one whole stretch of the station from her vantage point, long tubes set into spheres and cubes, assembled like a giant child's toy. She shivered slightly from the cold as they neared the hatch. The station was made from heavy plastic and cheap lunar metals; heat came from baseboard heaters set along each corridor, but the void outside kept the corridors from ever really getting warm.

Apparently the newer modules were worse, exposed plastic beams and cramped quarters with poor facilities and lights. They had been slapped together to field the incoming refugees from Earth, the flood of people that had finally tapered to a trickle. Gateway Orbital Station now held somewhere around 17,000, almost twice the number it had been intended for—but it wouldn't need to hold many more. As Ripley said, things were falling to shit down there.

Though it was early for dinner, the hall was crowded. There had been a midday shipment of real vegetables from one of the hydroponic gardens, and word had spread fast.

Billie and Ripley both got small salads of carrot and lettuce to go with their meals. They sat at one of the smaller tables near the entrance. In spite of the crowd, it was quiet; most of the people on Gateway had lost friends and family to the aliens on Earth. It was almost like people were embarrassed to laugh or have a good time. Billie could understand that.

She had spent much of her life in various psych wards, trying to convince medtechs that the aliens existed; the solemn atmosphere of the station was familiar, if not comforting. She didn't feel particularly at home here, but then she'd never really had a home. At least her life wasn't in danger; that was something. After the trip with Wilks, being safe seemed almost like a dream.

Ripley ate a bite of her heated soypro and made a face. "Tastes like insulation that's been dehydrated, frozen, and reheated. Then spit on."

Billie tasted her own, then nodded. "At least it's warm."

They ate quietly, each concentrating on her meal.

"So do you dream of her? The mother alien?"

Billie looked up from her tray, startled.

Ripley watched her intently. "*I* do," she continued. "At least I did, before my memory lapse." She took another bite of soypro.

"I—yeah. I do, too. I've heard that others have dreams. . . ." Billie trailed off. Yeah, she had heard stories, mostly about fanatics, people who had turned their dreams of the aliens into some kind of religion; the Chosen who had realized that Judgment Day had already come. She'd mostly kept quiet about her own dreams, but recently . . . "I have them often. Almost every night."

Ripley nodded. "It got that way with me, too. They started with her reaching out, expressing love, and turned into these. I felt a connection. They were transmissions. I knew where she was, that she wanted to gather her children to her. The queen of the queens, the driving force behind the whole goddamned species. I knew where to *find* her!"

She pushed her tray aside abruptly. "And I lost her."

Billie nodded. "I knew I wasn't the only one, but I haven't had a lot of time to think about it lately and this station doesn't offer a whole lot in the way of group therapy sessions."

Ripley smiled, a short, bitter expression. "I think I know what she's waiting for," she said, "and I have an idea. We need to find more dreamers . . . what about Wilks?"

Billie shrugged. "I know he dreams, but I don't think it's the same way I do. That doesn't mean much. He keeps to himself. We could ask him." She glanced around, although she figured he had gone for a workout. In their two weeks at the station, Wilks had spent most of his time in some gym or another. "I'm supposed to meet him later for a drink."

"I'd like to come along—if it's not intruding," Ripley said. It seemed she chose her words with care.

"No problem. You're welcome." Billie smiled, and Ripley smiled back, a much easier expression than before. Billie found herself liking this woman more and more.

Wilks had been cycling for the better part of an hour, working up a real good sweat, when he noticed the young boy sitting in the corner with his head resting on his hands. He had been concentrating on the vid screen in front of him, a level-nine cycle run that was going to make him hurt like hell tomorrow, or he might have seen the boy earlier.

It was one of the station's smaller gyms, and he liked it that way; the larger workout rooms could hold 200, and that many people sweating in one place wasn't particularly appealing, especially given the smell of recycled air. And he didn't care much for crowds.

The kid was maybe ten or eleven, a thin, pale boy with dark hair and a neutral expression. He stared at nothing, his chin resting on his knees.

Something about him reminded Wilks of himself at that age; maybe it was the build or the hair ... maybe the blankness. He could relate to that.

Wilks had grown up in a small town on Earth in the southern United States, raised by his aunt; his mother had died of breast cancer when he was five, after his father had left the two of them the year before. Aunt Carrie was nice enough, but didn't spend much time with him; she worked the night shift at a rest home and was rather indifferent to his life. Little Davey Arthur Wilks had enough to eat and clothes to wear, and that was her responsibility as she saw it, that and nothing else.

Carrie Greene did not understand much of anything, and sure as hell not little boys.

They didn't discuss his parents often; his mother was a saint who had nothing but love for Davey, his father a no-account bastard son of a bitch who had nothing but his own best interests at heart. David—who hated being called "Davey"—wasn't so sure. He couldn't really remember either of them, and although he knew his mother wasn't gonna come back, he did dream of his father coming to get him one day, standing on their weather-beaten porch with a smile for his son and things to play with and a new place to live. His dad was handsome and strong and smart and didn't take shit from *nobody*.

It was late summer, two days after his eleventh birthday. David lay on the floor of their small, stuffy living room with his newest Danno Kruise,

Action-Man comic. Danno was in the middle of kicking some serious bad-guy butt when there was a knock at the door. Aunt Carrie was "resting her eyes" in the back bedroom, so David answered, expecting a salesman.

A tall man holding a brightly wrapped box stood there.

"David?" The guy was badly in need of a shave and wore a shabby suit a few years out of date, the synlin frayed at the cuffs.

"Yeah, why?" David stepped back from the door a little; he didn't know this man. This man with bright blue eyes . . .

"Ah—well, hi. I knew it was your birthday, and—well, I was in town. Here." The stranger pushed the box toward him.

David took it and looked at him. "Who are you?"

"Oh, hell." The stranger smiled weakly. "I'm Ben. I am—was a friend of your mother's." Ben looked at his watch, then back at David. "Happy birthday, Davey. Listen, I gotta get going, I'm supposed to meet someone . . . you know how it is." He looked at David helplessly.

David stared, unable to speak. His *father's* name was Ben. He clutched the package tightly. The wrapping crinkled under his grip. Ben.

The man turned and walked away, without looking back. David stood there for a long time before he closed the door. He tried to tell himself that it wasn't true, that this Ben wasn't his dad. It couldn't be. He wouldn't just come here, drop this present off, and *leave*. He wouldn't do that.

"Davey?" His aunt, risen from her nap, padded toward him. "Was that somebody at the door? What have you got there?"

The boy stared at her. He shook his head. "It wasn't anybody important," he said. He tossed the present at the shiny copper ash bucket his aunt kept next to the antique wood stove.

In the gym, Wilks shook his head again. Jesus. Some of those old tapes were real fucking hard to get rid of. He stared at the boy. "Hey, kid, you won't build any muscle sitting on your butt like that."

The boy looked at him, like some kind of big-eyed bird.

"Here. Let me show you how that machine works."

It wasn't much, but it was something Wilks could do. Nobody had ever done it for him.

The smile on the boy's face was worth a million, easy. And it didn't cost Wilks anything at all.

2

Amy and the old man stood in front of a tunnel covered in alien secretion and littered with debris. The tunnel led off into thick darkness.

The old man ran a shaky hand through his dirty white hair and put his arm around the adolescent. Amy smiled up at him. She was a pretty girl, in spite of her grimy skin and tattered clothes. Her nervous smile made her look much younger.

"They're using the underground to move beneath the city," he said, keeping his voice quiet. "The tunnels and grids are still here, but changed. Transformed." He and Amy walked forward a few steps. The lighting was weak; long shadows danced and re-formed beyond them as they moved through the silent cavern.

The old man continued:

"It's—it's difficult to be sure, but the tunnels appear to converge into a central locus—like spokes on a wheel."

The dark, ropy alien construct surrounded them completely now. The walls were embedded with long-dead humans—a mostly rotted arm hanging down from above, a half skull jutting out to their left. To the right was something that might have been a dog once.

Amy moved closer to the old man.

"As far as I can tell, the creatures keep to one area at a time, use it up, and move to another. Our camp is set up nearby." He put a shaky hand on Amy's shoulder. "The aliens are a few klicks from here, as far as I can tell, so we're as safe as we can be."

"I wish we could go up," Amy said. "We can't, though."

The old man nodded. "There are those who feel the 'connection' and hunt for alien breeders above ground. We're better off down here."

They walked down through the tunnel, death all around them like obscene art, both breathing shallowly through their mouths. After a minute they stopped, and the old man began to speak again in his schoolteacher's voice.

"We're not far from the hub now, one of the central areas. That's why there are more breeders here, what's left of them. We don't dare go any farther."

Amy shuddered slightly. "Can we get out of here, Daddy? It doesn't feel right."

He looked around warily and then smiled at the child. "Yeah, okay. Let's get an early dinner." They turned back to the tunnel, the old man letting Amy take the lead.

"You know, I should've—" he began, when suddenly a hand shot out from the dark wall and grabbed his knee. Amy let out a single, high-pitched yelp. The old man fell.

Another voice came out of the darkness. "Oh, shit. Oh, *shit*!" A young man ran into view.

"Paul!" shouted the old man, and the younger one ran to help him. "Get it off me, get it off!"

Paul held a small lantern into the air over the old man. A breeder was strung into the black secretion there, close to death. It had once been a woman, and now was barely animal, its eyes insane. It held tight.

"Daddy," Amy breathed out, chest hitching. She started to sob.

Both Paul and the old man beat at the woman's hand with their fists, but she would not let go. Her face was bloated and almost black. Paul looked toward the hub; somewhere, maybe far away, there were clattering noises.

"Lisssen," she rasped out, her lips bleeding and cracked. "I am the mother . . ."

Paul stood and kicked at her hand. The thing's wrist snapped cleanly, and the old man scuttled backward, away from the dying creature. She didn't seem to notice that her hand was hanging off her wrist; she didn't seem to feel pain.

The old man stood, grabbed Amy by the arm, and they all backed away from the mad breeder.

She closed her awful eyes. "Soon," she whispered hoarsely. "Soon, soon." The terror was there on all of their faces as they moved back toward camp, her final words seeming to echo all around the trio.

The old man said, "Paul?"

The younger man nodded. "I'll take care of it." He pulled a knife from a sheath on his belt. A stray beam of light glittered from the blade. He moved back toward the breeder—

The screen went to static. Billie found her hands clamped to the arms of the chair so hard her tendons creaked when she managed to loosen her grip. She shook her head back and forth, almost without realizing that she was doing it. A denial of Amy's pain, of her own—

She was in Gateway's main broadcast room, alone; the tech had gone on his dinner break.

"Not again," she said, feeling like a little girl herself. Her own childhood of running and hiding on Rim had never seemed closer—everyone gone, dragged away screaming to be food for the creatures. A flood of memories hit her: crouched in a ventilation duct while a fat man with bleeding ears howled in fear and pain a few feet away; gunshots and shouts in the middle of the night; blood splattered in the dark hallways; and always the terror, the constant, aching terror and hopelessness, the certainty that she would be discovered by the monsters. And eaten. Or worse.

But Amy was alive! A few years older and still alive.

The tech, an elderly man named Boyd, had mentioned offhand that there were still a few things coming in from Earth. "Mostly those goddamn religious shitheads," he'd muttered, picking at one ear.

"Any 'casts of a family?" said Billie, not expecting it. That would have been a miracle. . . .

"Oh yeah. Comes in on various channels, pretty random signals. A girl and her dad, couple of others off and on. Sad."

Boyd had shrugged and left to eat, warning her not to touch anything while he was gone. Billie figured the old tech hadn't meant he didn't care, it was just that there was nothing to be done. Except—

Ripley. Maybe her plan, whatever it was, could mean helping Amy. The same child, now older, she had seen in the 'casts when she and Wilks had been trapped on that mad military asshole's base. Amy.

Billie took a deep breath and let it out slowly. She saw herself in that little girl on Earth and would do whatever she could to save her. Anything.

Billie was a few minutes late to the Four Sails, no doubt the sleaziest bar on Gateway—and of course the one that Wilks *would* come to. It was small and dark. Drinkers and chem-heads sat at round tables surrounding the tiny stage near the back; according to a schedule posted on the wall, there would be erotic dancers later, couples and threesomes crowded onto the platform performing to pulsing music.

Billie spotted Ripley by herself at a table in the corner, a pitcher of splash and a few glasses in front of her.

"Wilks isn't here yet," Ripley said, pouring pale straw-colored liquid into one of the glasses. "Drink?"

"Yeah, thanks," said Billie. She took the glass. She swallowed half of its contents before setting it down.

Ripley raised an eyebrow. "Hard day?"

"Some of my past catching up to me. There's a family on Earth that sends broadcasts out—I first saw them on Spears's planetoid. One of them is a little girl, maybe twelve or thirteen now. Watching is—" Billie stopped and sipped her splash. "It's hard."

"Is it Amy?"

Billie looked up, surprised.

Ripley said, "I saw one a few days ago. Do you know her?"

Billie shook her head. "I feel like I do."

"Yeah, I understand. Amy was my daughter's name, too." She drank.

Wilks stepped through the doorway, nodded to the bartender, and came to their table.

"Sorry I'm late," he said. "I was—uh, weight-training. Guess I lost track of time." He smiled and sat down, then poured himself a glass of splash.

Billie noticed that he seemed much more relaxed than usual, his scarred face almost calm.

" 'Lo, Ripley."

Ripley leaned forward. "We need some help, Wilks," she said. "No point in coating it—do you dream of the aliens?"

"Doesn't everybody?" he said.

"Not nightmares," Billie said, her voice quiet. "Signals. Transmissions. From a queen mother, a leader of queens. She's—she's in a dark place, a cave or something, and she *wants*. She's waiting, she's calling."

Billie closed her eyes, remembering. "She moves closer, and then she speaks. She says she loves you and wants you with her; you can feel it coming off of her in waves, her need . . ."

Billie opened her eyes. Ripley was nodding. Wilks wore a skeptical look.

"Maybe it's something you ate," he said.

"Listen, Wilks, remember the robot ship? The dream I had?"

Wilks nodded. "Yeah. I remember."

Billie had known there were aliens on that ship when there was no way she could have; that dream had saved their lives.

"So what do you want from me?"

"We need to know who's having dreams," said Ripley. "I had 'em for a while, but they stopped; if they're actually transmissions of some kind, we may be able to use them. But we have to find out if anybody else dreams them to be sure. Any ideas?"

Wilks stared into his splash. "Maybe. I can ask

some people I know. If you think it's really worth doing."

"I don't know if it is," Ripley said. "But it might be."

Wilks shrugged. "Fuck it." He took a big drink of his splash. "Not like I got a whole hell of a lot else to do on this bucket of rocks and plastic. What the hell. I'll ask around." He drained his glass. Stood. "Meet you in the B-2 conference room at 0900 tomorrow."

Ripley smiled and Billie let out a deep breath, relieved. Amy was still hiding on Earth, and there was probably nothing she could do; but they were going to do *something*.

The private conference room was military access only, but it was small and rarely used, so Wilks had no trouble signing it out. Ripley and Billie stood on either side of him in front of a small computer. He spoke as he tapped in codes.

"I looked up an old friend last night, Leslie Elliot. She used to go out with this guy I trained with, till she realized that she had about 50 IQ points on him. She's a pretty good hacker, but these days she's doing basic data entry. I figured she wouldn't mind rascaling up what we needed . . . she even edited. Wait, here we go."

A readout scrolled up the screen. Names, dates, places. Then vid images.

Quincy Gaunt, Ph.D./Subject: Nancy Zetter. It was a poor quality vid of two people sitting in an office, the woman speaking:

". . . and then she comes up to me and I hear

this voice in my head telling me that she cares about me. She says, 'I love you.' " The attractive middle-aged woman shook her head, disgusted. "That awful thing, telling me that."

"And that's where it ends?" said the doctor, a thin young man with a neutral expression.

"Yes. Except it *doesn't* end," she said. "I keep having them—"

Wilks pushed a button on the console. More names blipped across the screen, another office with different people. A well-built young man squirmed nervously in a cushioned chair while an older man looked on.

"It's like—I don't know, she *wants* me," he blurted out.

"Sexually?"

The young man colored visibly. "No, not like that. Like—aw, shit, I don't know, like she's my mother or something."

"Do you dream about your mother?" said the doctor, leaning forward.

Wilks hit a button. A Dr. Torchin was talking to a female Lieutenant Adcox.

". . . and you feel like she's calling you to come be with her in these dreams," Torchin said. "Interesting."

Wilks handled the keyboard swiftly.

". . . it's a recurring dream—"

". . . she loves me, wants me—"

". . . you say the creature is asking you to find it—"

"It wants me to find her—"

". . . she's calling me—"

Wilks hit the stop button and turned to look at the two women.

"How many?" said Billie, her mouth dry.

"Not sure," said Wilks. "But Les accessed a week of psych visits and she came up with thirty-seven."

"And there are a lot of people who don't go to psych," said Ripley. She looked thoughtful. "Good job, Wilks."

"Where the fuck is this headed, Ripley?" he said, leaning back in his chair. "Does this mean something?"

"That queen mother wants her children," said Ripley. "I don't know why she wants them, but she does. The signal is for them. The drones aren't smart enough to load themselves onto starships and fly home. But if we could find her, get her to Earth—"

"They would go to her," said Billie.

"Lemme get this straight: This queen of queens is in another *stellar* system? Christ, you're talking faster-than-light transmission of this fucking call. Voodoo stuff."

"But what if it's true?" Billie said. "What if somehow the superqueen *can* make that long-distance call? Think how it would work if she were here."

"They would head for her like lemmings," Ripley said. "Gather themselves in a big bunch all together, every one of them."

Wilks wasn't the brightest guy who ever lived, but he saw the possibilities of this scenario pretty damned fast. When he spoke, his voice was soft, but interested: "We could wait until they all got collected into a big bunch and then nuke 'em all to hell."

He looked back at the vid screen, where a patient with dark circles beneath her eyes was frozen in mid-sentence. Nice dream, but that's all it seemed to be. He'd drifted since his first contact with the monsters, lost a big chunk of time, until he'd rediscovered Billie in that psych ward, and a new purpose along with her: to destroy the aliens who had fucked up him—and mankind—royally. That was his goal, but he was a practical man.

To Ripley, he said, "What makes you so sure about this?"

She shook her head. "I'm not sure, at least not in any way you could lay out and measure with a rule or a scale."

"But you believe all this psych stuff means what you said? There's some kind of supermom alien somewhere who could draw these bastards like shit does flies?"

"That's what I believe, yeah."

Wilks stared at the screen. Billie had been able to tell about the aliens on the ship he and Bueller and she had stolen, that was a fact. And he'd had his own hunches, ducked when there wasn't any reason to do it, and saved his ass because of it. He wasn't much on religion or psyche stuff, but you didn't have to be a chemical engineer to start a fire, either. Pragmatic was the way to go, to hell with the theoretical crap. If Billie could dream the truth, maybe other people could do it too. Made sense.

"Okay. Let's suppose this scenario works," he said. "It's worth checking out a little more. If it's right, it gives us a big hammer we can use against the suckers. I'm willing to play along and see where it goes. I'll go talk to my friend."

"I'll go with you, if that's okay," said Ripley. "Billie? If you could dig through these files, pull out names of military personnel—"

Billie plucked the metal info sphere out of the reader and put it in her pocket.

Ripley grinned. "Fine. Why don't we meet this evening and see what we've got?"

Billie walked toward her quarters quickly. It was good to be in action, better to know that she shared her dreams with others, that she wasn't alone. Ripley was a strong woman, a leader.

She turned a corner and almost ran into a robotech adjusting a light panel. Billie stopped short and stood there, studying the design. It was simple machinery, made for only a few manual tasks; vaguely humanoid, about two meters tall. Basically a control box with arms and legs.

Not like an android that you could mistake for human ...

Billie was suddenly very near tears. Mitch. She wondered what had become of him, her android lover. As always, a mix of confused emotions came with the thought: anger, that he hadn't told her the truth; worry, sadness. The pity she had felt when he'd been "repaired" on Spears's planetoid, his lovely torso strapped to ugly metal legs—like the limbs of the robot moving past her. When the final realization had hit, it had been too late; she and Wilks were in space, headed away from the battle on the planetoid where Mitch had been trapped. The transmission to their ship was the last she had seen of him. The truth of it was that for whatever Mitch had come to be, he was the best person she had ever known. And she had loved him.

Yeah, okay, so, life was fucking unfair. It was a cold fact that she'd learned and relearned too many times to cry about now. You spent a lot of time in a hospital, you learned to suck it up and keep your face blank.

Billie wiped the tears from her face. Crying didn't get you anywhere. If she'd learned nothing else in her recent adventures with Wilks, she had learned that the best way to get things done was to do them. You wanted an ass kicked, best you wore your heavy boots. Then you could take care of business. Sitting around and whining didn't get it done.

Ripley knew. Ripley had a plan. What the plan was didn't matter as much as the fact that it existed. And if there was any chance at all that it would work, Billie was going to help make the damned aliens suffer for what they'd done.

And laugh while they burned.

3

Ripley rubbed at her temples, frowned slightly.

"Problem?" Wilks whispered. He didn't want to disturb the woman concentrating at the console a couple of meters away.

"Headache," she said. "I get 'em a lot lately." She gave up her self-massage and looked around the small cubicle. The tasteful paintings and prints seemed out of place next to the cheap, built-in furnishings.

The tech, Leslie Elliot, had agreed to help them, volunteering her lunch break to dig for their information. They sat now in her cube, watching her work. She was an attractive woman, tightly muscled, with an easy smile and reddish-brown hair that she wore in tiny braids. Ripley wondered how well she and Wilks were acquainted. . . .

"Maybe you should stop by medical," said Wilks, interrupting her thought.

Ripley looked at him blankly.

"Your headache."

"Oh. No. I'm fine. Besides, I don't do medics; most problems seem to fix themselves."

Wilks seemed about to say something else when Leslie turned in her chair and grinned. "You owe me for this, Sarge," she said.

"If you got something."

Leslie's grin widened. "Gold mine, what I got. Just gotta ask the right questions. Hold on a sec. Gotta store these where we can find them and nobody will stumble across 'em."

Ripley smiled at Wilks.

"Okay, so maybe you aren't totally crazy," he said.

Ripley and Wilks walked toward Ripley's quarters. The smell of canned air seemed particularly stale in this corridor, a metallic tang that you could almost taste.

Wilks thought about the conversation they'd just had with Les.

"Only a few of the dreamers seem to be linear-minded," Leslie had said, tapping the keys expertly as she talked. "You know, math-science, left-brain types. Guys like you, Sarge, no imagination."

"Fuck you."

"You wish. Um, anyway, it stands to reason that

they would have a better fix on charting a map. If you'd told me what you were looking for last night, you could have saved yourselves a trip."

"Actually, we're making this up as we go along," Ripley said.

Even so, they had the names of people who could describe the alien's planet, six in all. Their details were vague, but Leslie had cross-referenced a known-systems map and come up with several possible locations. Ripley said she figured they could narrow it down if they could talk to the six.

This telepathy-empathy stuff was tricky, but it was what they had to work with. Wilks was still willing to go along for the ride, given that something had turned up. Weird, but there it was.

"I thought we blew their goddamn planet out of space," Wilks said. "I dropped chain-linked nukes that should have scraped the fucking surface clean."

"Doesn't matter," said Ripley. "They spawn wherever they are, and a planet overrun is a planet overrun."

"Yeah. But this one, wherever it is, appears to be the core. Makes me wonder how many places are seeded ..." He trailed off, remembering the conversation with the old soldier in the bar.

"Something?" Ripley said.

"Yeah. A few days after Billie and I got here I met this old man at the bar, name of Crane. He was ex-military and very drunk, wanted to buy every uniform in the place a drink. He rambled, glory days and dead soldiers, shit like that, I didn't pay much attention—until he started talking about the aliens. He called them war toys; said that they were too good at surviving to be natural."

Ripley turned to look at Wilks.

"Interesting," she said, considering for a minute. "Rapid procreative ability, acid blood, vacuum-resistant—it would explain a hell of a lot if it were *designed* that way."

Wilks nodded. "Worth thinking about, anyway. 'Course then the questions get worse: Who designed the fucking things? Why? What do they have in mind?"

They stopped in front of Ripley's quarters. "I'll catch up to you and Billie later," he said. "I've got some things to check out."

Ripley shut the door and thought about Wilks's secondhand theory. War toys? What insane species could've come up with the alien design; what kind of war could have warranted it?

Her headache was coming back.

There was a knock at Ripley's door.

"Come in."

Billie stepped in and glanced around at the bare walls of the older woman's room. Efficient and practical, like Ripley, who sat at a desk staring at the console in front of her. She looked weary.

"Hey, Billie," she said, swiveling in her chair. "Anything?"

"Eighteen military-affiliated, maybe half of

them trained in combat," she said. She leaned on the desk. She was on the tired side herself.

"Good. Wilks and I got some stuff from his hacker friend that looks promising, so we can get started. We'll have to do background checks on some of these folks and get going on transport— sooner the better."

Billie smiled at Ripley's straightforward confidence in her plan. Must be nice to be so in control, so sure of yourself. "Just out of curiosity," she said, "how did this idea of yours come up?"

Ripley shifted in the chair and looked suddenly uncomfortable. "You remember I said I had a daughter?"

Billie nodded.

"Amanda. She was very young when I left to work on the *Nostromo*. I promised her I'd come back for her birthday. I didn't make it."

Billie nodded again. She knew that part of it. Ripley had spent decades in deep sleep—she held the record, as far as anybody knew. It had been a lucky accident that she had been found at all, drifting through dead space. Billie wondered what it must have been like, to leave a child and come back to find she had died as an old woman. A daughter older than your own grandmother. Awful.

"On the ship to Gateway, I thought a lot about her, her whole life passing by while I slept. And the dreams of another mother who wanted her children back."

Ripley shook her head and smiled. There was no humor in the expression. "Funny comparison.

Me and that monstrous creature both wishing for the same thing."

Billie needed to do something. Awkwardly, she reached out and took Ripley's hand. "I'm sorry," she said.

"Yeah." Ripley pulled her hand away, not accepting the gesture of comfort. "Anyway. I didn't have any kind of revelation about what to do, no brilliant inspiration. I just loved my daughter and I miss her and I blame that *thing* for taking her away."

She looked up at Billie, her eyes angry. "My idea didn't come from wanting to save anyone, no great love for humanity—I just hate her and her whole fucking brood and I want them *exterminated*."

She took a deep breath and dropped her gaze, then shrugged. "Enough history. We have a lot to do."

Billie wondered how old the child had been; Amy's age, perhaps? Something that all three of them had in common, then; Ripley, Billie, and the alien queen. Just wanting their children ... No. Amy wasn't her child. Just a face on a viewscreen. Don't think of her that way.

Billie moved a chair over to Ripley's desk and sat beside her. There would be time to sort through the reasons later. For now, Ripley was right—there was a lot of work to be done. After two weeks of hanging around, the idea didn't seem so bad. Doing nothing was always worse than doing just about anything.

4

Sergeant Kegan Bako was ten years younger than Wilks and looked years younger than that. He had a baby face and a blond's complexion, fair and unwrinkled. Wilks guessed that Bako only had to shave every other day, if that, to keep with military office standard.

The two men sat in Bako's office, separated by a desk covered with paper flimsies and plastic food wrappers. The small room was stuffy, the smell of soy sauce cloying in the air.

"Sure you don't want some of this? Better than that shit they serve in the dining rooms." Bako maneuvered his chopsticks clumsily to his mouth, losing at least half of his fried noodles in the process.

"Thanks, I already ate some of the dining room shit."

"Too bad. So what brings you here? Don't tell me you're looking for a rematch—?"

"What, you haven't suffered enough this week?" He'd met the younger man at a gym while looking for a handball partner. They'd played several times since; although Bako hadn't won yet, it was a good workout and okay company. "Actually, I wanted to check something. Who'd I talk with to requisition a transport?"

Bako swallowed a mouthful of noodles and grinned. "God, maybe. You're kidding, right?"

"Hypothetically, let's say I wanted to go pick up a ... weapon that might wipe out the infestation on Earth. Could I get a ship?"

"What kind of weapon?"

"A hypothetical one."

Bako tapped his chopsticks against the desk. "Well, first of all, you'd have to have proof of this weapon, no hypothetical about it. Take that to General Peters, or maybe Davison—get an okay, a volunteer crew, and fill out the forms." Bako made another attempt at his noodles as he spoke. "I gotta tell you, though, you'll have a fuck of a time, even with solid evidence."

"Why's that?"

"In the last four months there have been three attempts to get to and from Earth. Three *official* attempts, if you know what I mean."

Wilks nodded. That meant other times that nobody wanted to talk about.

"The first ship came back with a dozen or so

new civilians but four marines outright dead or
gone out of an eight-man crew. On the second, we
lost almost all the crew and got zip rescues to
show for it."

"And the third?"

"Didn't come back. It's like the things knew the
ships were coming and were laying for them. And
we really can't afford to lose any more hardware,
local manufacturing facilities being what they are.
Just about every crate that could get free of the
gravity well left during the final days of the infestation. Some of those ships are here; a whole
shitload more of them are far away, and nobody
knows where."

Bako set his chopsticks down and looked at
Wilks. "They're planning another mission soon;
you know how the brass hates to have its butt
kicked, although you didn't hear it from me. My
point is, getting a ship to do something that could
maybe help isn't high priority right now. Even
scout ships are worth more than diamonds these
days."

And all Wilks wanted was a fully loaded starship to take God knew where across the galaxy to
kidnap the mother of all aliens. Hypothetically
speaking.

He nodded, stood, and smiled at the baby-faced
sergeant. "Thanks, Dimples. You've been a help."

"Don't call me that. C-court tomorrow, 0800?"

"Sure. I'll tie both hands behind my back, even
things up a little."

Wilks exited on Bako's laugh, but stopped smiling as the door closed behind him. Bako's infor-

mation hadn't exactly been a surprise. And if it were just him, he'd fuck going through the proper channels and just take a ship. He'd done that and he knew how it worked. But he didn't exactly live in a void. Someone else was in charge, and if Ripley wanted to try and go by the book, he'd do what he could to help. But unless the general was dreaming of the alien superqueen, proving anything was going to be a bitch.

Charlene Adcox answered her door wearing a pale green kimono tied loosely at the waist. She was short and almost boyishly thin. Her close-cropped hair and sharp features made her look oddly masculine in spite of the gown she wore. Billie caught a scent of perfume, light and flowery.

"Fem Adcox?"

"Yes."

"My name is Billie. Could I speak to you for a moment?"

"Concerning . . . ?" Adcox smiled politely.

Billie took a deep breath. "It's about the dreams," she said.

Adcox paused, then moved back from the door, her smile gone.

Billie stepped in. The room was larger than her own, decorated with Japanese prints and sparse, simple furniture. Adcox motioned to a futon for Billie to sit down, and seated herself across from her on a small wooden bench.

"How did you get my name?"

Billie hesitated. The psych files were classified,

but an elaborate lie would eventually be found out
by anyone whose help they enlisted. "There are
others having the same dream," she said. "Some
of us rascaled the psychiatric files."

Adcox nodded. "Okay," she said. The young
lieutenant seemed more relieved than anything
else, which Billie understood. "How many others?"

"We can't tell for sure. Upwards of fifty, at least.
They're all the same—they're transmissions, not
dreams. The aliens are telepathic or empathic,
whatever. It ain't coincidence."

Adcox offered her a weak smile. "No, it doesn't
sound like it. What do you want from me?"

Billie pulled an info sphere from her pocket.
"You can tell me where you think she is," she
said. "There are several possibilities described in
these files. Only a few of us seem to be able to
see location in the dreams, and you're one of
them. We want to find her."

Adcox tensed slightly. "To kill her?"

"Yes. Her and her children."

Adcox reached out and took the sphere from
Billie. "Call me Char," she said.

Ripley wrapped the towel around her neck and
padded naked to her bed. She stretched her long
body across the pad, toes pointing and arms over
her head. The interview with John Chin had gone
well. He was an architect, one of the linear-
minded dreamers, and had agreed to look at their
map. Chin wasn't a fighting man, and she doubted
he would volunteer to come with them when the

time came—but she imagined that there would be enough soldiers willing to take the risks. . . .

She closed her eyes. She wasn't sleepy, but the shower had relaxed her to a meditative frame of mind. She wondered how Billie had made out with Lieutenant Adcox . . . how old was Billie? Twenty-three, wasn't it?

In October of Ripley's twenty-third year, she had given birth to a beautiful, squalling, perfect little girl, Amanda Tei. Amy . . .

Ripley let her mind fall deeper into the memory.

"Shhhh, Amanda. Little sweet Amanda." She repeated the words over and over, a soft, lulling mantra to the newborn she held. The hospital room was dimly lit and done in soft colors. She had never met, and would never meet, the father; she had gone to a clinic, safer and neater for her single life. Except now she was a mommy. . . .

When the nurse laid the tiny child in her arms, Ripley had wept. She was so beautiful, so quiet and sleepy and tiny! Perfect little fingers and nails, a headful of dark, silky hair.

The labor had been hard and long, but it was worth it.

"Shh, little baby, sweet Amanda," she crooned, wondering how she could ever show her daughter how much she loved her, with this love that could move mountains. . . .

A man's face suddenly appeared a few inches from her own, frowning, his hand reaching out to touch her—

• • •

Ripley yelped, sat up in bed, eyes wide. She covered herself with the towel and looked around the room. No one. But—that face, that was—

The man's face had been in her head, in her daydream. And it had been—

"Bishop?" Ripley shook her head. The android, the one with the soldiers, *decades* after her daughter had been born, years after her mother had failed to get home in time for her birthday.

Where had *that* come from? Bishop ... she hadn't thought of him for a long time; the last time was—she had seen him last—

No good. Her pleasant wanderings had gotten weird somewhere; maybe the strain of everything was getting to be too much to handle. Ripley sighed, confused and frustrated by her inability to know her own mind. Maybe she was tired after all. . . .

Ripley stood and reached for a coverall. She didn't feel like being naked anymore.

5

Wilks tapped on Leslie's door using the small bottle of whiskey he'd bought.

"Hold on a sec!"

He heard muffled footsteps coming toward him, and then a loud thump. "Shit!"

Wilks smiled. The door opened to a very redfaced Leslie rubbing her right knee. Behind her was an overturned chair.

"Wilks, you asshole," she said, straightening up. She wore a snug black bodysuit and matching headband; sweat dotted her tawny skin. In spite of her words, she grinned. "That for me?" She motioned at the bottle.

"Well, if you're busy—"

"Depends."

"I wanted to thank you for helping us out; thought we might have a drink, unless you're otherwise involved—?"

Leslie grinned wider and stepped back from the door. "You always were the subtle type," she said, and her voice softened slightly. "Come in, David."

Billie sat in the uncomfortable plastic chair and watched the vid screen flicker with the ruins of Earth. The scanner roamed, and it surprised her how much old data was still being broadcast. Mostly advertising for companies long dead, sometimes documentaries, the occasional fiction program; many were in different languages. Billie touched the command button from time to time, looking for something real, something current.

Something like Amy.

There was a flash of static and then a black screen. Suddenly a man's face appeared, a close-up. Middle-aged, he was handsome in a rugged way, sharp nose and strong jaw dominated by intense, dark eyes. His mouth was tightly set, deep lines etching the corners. He stared into the camera as if he were about to fight it, his gaze unwavering. Something about the bland determination on his face reminded Billie of—

"This is an exercise of faith," he said. "Of the new Christ and the power She commands." His voice was deep and compelling.

Spears, she thought. *Like Spears.*

The camera pulled back to show the man standing on a low platform in a poorly lit studio. He was tall and short-haired and wore a tight coverall that emphasized his biceps and chest. A large knife was strapped to one hip.

"I am Carter Dane," he said, "and I have seen the Truth."

Billie heard quiet murmurs of approval from offscreen.

"There is power in my hands. The Goddess has shown me the way."

He began to pace back and forth as he spoke. "The Goddess brings no fear. The Goddess has no fear. We are Her children, She our mother. We are not worthy of Her; it is the failing of humanity."

More mumbles of assent.

Dane continued, his voice rising. "When the cleansing began, I was afraid. I cried in self-pity and *fear*—afraid for my own life and the lives of the weak and unworthy all around me." He paused, for dramatic effect. "I was no more than a pile of shit," he said.

"Yes!" A hoarse cry from the unseen audience.

"Useless and impotent fear," he continued, "left me empty. Incapable of action. I *wallowed* in it; I was *crippled* by it!" He stopped moving, faced the listeners.

"And She spoke to me. She asked for my help. The Goddess, the creator of so much power, asking a cripple to aid Her. Like She asks of all Her Chosen. And I became *strong* for Her, I learned of Her love, I found that death is *shit*! It is *fear*! It is *nothing*!"

Billie sat transfixed, watching the screen; she

found herself unable to move, to hit the command button. Another of the dreamers, and completely insane.

Dane motioned to one side and a heavyset woman in ill-fitting soldier's gear dragged a young man onto the stage. His hands were tied behind him and his slow, stumbling movements suggested heavy sedation. The soldier pushed him to the floor next to Dane and stepped back into the shadows. The boy looked barely out of his teens, was thin and dressed in rags and dirt. He lay on his side, eyes closed.

Dane pointed at the prisoner but kept his gaze on the listeners. "This," he said with disgust, "is humanity. Weak. Afraid. He is not fit to be the giver of Divine life, not when so many of the willing stand strong and proud in front of me." Dane made a sweeping gesture toward the crowd, and put his hand on his hip.

Put his hand on the hilt of the knife.

He pulled it out slowly and held it up. "The old humanity has outlived its usefulness," he said.

He knelt beside the boy. The youth gave no sign of having heard the speech and did not struggle as Dane pushed the blade without apparent effort deep into the bound boy's throat.

Blood erupted out across the platform.

The boy opened his eyes and his mouth, as if to speak. A horrible, wet gurgle was all that came out, a look of confused pain on his pale face. He rolled onto his back, his eyes fluttering. More blood spewed from the wound to mat his dark hair and white skin. His thin body shuddered in one final spasm. His eyes remained open.

Dane ran the back of the knife across his forehead, smearing red across his brow. Swiftly he ran the point of the blade from the groin to the sternum of the dead youth, cutting deeply. He turned to face his listeners, a wild grin on his face.

"Come and feed!" he shouted. "Eat of the flesh! Devour the old, become one with the Goddess!" He dropped the knife to the floor and thrust one bloodied hand into the boy's gut, then lifted it to his own mouth. Dark figures stepped onto the stage, tattered men and women converging on the corpse, a dozen or more, faces crazed, laughing loudly, reaching, pulling—

Dane ranted on, his mouth dripping blood, his voice cracking. "We are the Chosen! We will become! We will—"

Billie hit the command button convulsively, breaking the trance. The screen went to static and dimly, as if from another place, she heard a commercial for a retirement complex begin. She shivered all over. She stood, knocked over her chair. She ran blindly away from the madness, her hand over her mouth. There was a waste bin in the corner of the room; she stumbled to it and vomited. Retched again and again.

Slowly her surroundings came back into focus. Her spasms subsided into hitching, ragged breaths. "Okay," she said, "okay, okay." She brushed at her watering eyes. The dreams had been too much for their minds to bear on top of watching their world crumble, their families killed. But not her. They were sick, demented; she was here, and would change things.

"Okay," she said again, and straightened up. The smell of vomit was overpowering and sour, and she stepped away from the bin. She felt a sudden fury at what the queen had done. Her and her goddamn calling, urging those people into madness. Giving the unbalanced a reason to kill . . .

Billie sniffled and wiped her mouth with the back of one shaky hand, then took a deep breath. The boy's dying face would come back to her later, she knew; there was nothing she could do to change that. For now, she would concentrate on what she *could* change.

Wilks gently cupped his hand over one of Leslie's soft, small breasts; she stretched leisurely and covered his hand with her own, smiling.

They lay nude in a tangle of sweaty sheets, the musk of recent sex in the air. Wilks propped himself on one elbow beside her. He felt relaxed and at peace with his body. Leslie was a good lover, confident in her abilities without being assuming.

"Mmm," she said, and opened her eyes to look at him. "Not bad, Sarge. You should be promoted."

Wilks smiled. "Yeah, I think I make a pretty good drill sergeant. Drill, drill, drill . . ."

Leslie made a face. "On the other hand, your jokes leave something to be desired. Like humor."

"What? Hey, I'm funny."

"Sheeit."

They lay still for a moment, preoccupied with their own thoughts.

Wilks remembered his conversation with Bako. The evidence of the mother queen's existence was not overwhelming in his own mind, so proving it to somebody who didn't know Billie—specifically, to the general—would take a lot more than what they had.

"When are you leaving, David?"

"Hmm?"

"The dream alien. You're going to wherever she is. To get her."

It was a statement, not a question.

"I don't know," he said. "There's still a question of how—official backing is iffy." He shook his head. "We're not even sure of where she is yet. Ask me when I know more."

"And you're going with nothing more solid than a psychic vision?"

"Less—I don't even dream the dream. But you do. Do you believe it?"

"Yeah, I think she's real." She nuzzled her head against his bare chest. "I'll do whatever I can to help."

Wilks stroked the palm of his hand across her smooth belly in small circles, then moved lower, lightly touching the edge of her pubic mound. "Yeah? Anything?"

She pushed up against him, eyes closed. His penis stirred, pressed against her leg. She rolled toward him, a sly smile raising a corner of her parted lips.

"You *are* pretty good as a drill sergeant," she said. "Now which is for shooting and which is for fun ... ?"

Alone in her quarters, Ripley shut down the computer and rolled her head forward, yawning. Her thoughts had started running into each other. It was late and the pills she had swallowed for an earlier headache didn't seem to be working. Stronger medication would require a prescription, and her intrinsic mistrust of medtechs—

She frowned. How had that come about, anyway? Must have happened after the long sleep, some incident in the hospital that had lodged in her subconscious. She couldn't recall caring either way before that. . . .

It didn't really matter; headaches were not a major problem. Besides, it was most likely the stress of getting this action together that caused them.

She felt satisfied that they had their planet. Both of the dreamers she and Billie had talked to had fingered the same system, and Leslie had listed it as the most probable.

She walked to the bed, knuckled her tired eyes, and lay down, not bothering to undress. She hadn't seen Wilks for a while and wondered if he had gotten the information about military transport. It would be best to get the go from the power on Gateway, but if they couldn't—well, there were other ways.

She thought about the daydream she had experienced earlier, of Bishop's face surprising her back to reality. She had liked the android, an exception to her negative feelings for synthetics—but his appearance in her mind had seemed wrong. Out of place, not of her own memory.

Medtechs and artificial humans, the world of science and personal demons. Maybe they were all crazy. Maybe the idea was nothing more than a madwoman's nightmare and Ripley had stumbled into it. Maybe ...

Ripley fell asleep.

6

Peter Schell was a heavy-
set older man whose natural expression was a
slight scowl; even when he smiled his brow
creased downward. Ripley thought he looked like
he had bitten into something sour.

The man next to him, Keith Dunston, was
much younger, around Billie's age. He was small-
boned and wiry, a martial arts teacher. Dunston
had listened to Wilks outline the situation with a
placid interest, as if he were watching a 'cast of a
tennis match.

Ripley had let Wilks do most of the talking to
the two men. They had met in the private dojo
where Dunston taught classes. After brief introductions, Wilks had quickly laid out their theory
and research; Schell had interrupted several

times with questions while Dunston remained silent, occasionally running a small hand through his short red hair. Both men looked tired.

"So what if you don't get a transport?" said Schell.

Wilks shrugged. "Right now we're trying to get a crew. The more people who have faith in this, the better the chance we *will* get a ship."

"Yeah, but what if you don't?"

Schell's open skepticism was getting on Ripley's nerves. She didn't think he was going to end up working on this. . . .

Wilks took that one: "We'll burn that bridge when we come to it. Any more questions?"

There was a moment of silence. Wilks glanced at Ripley and back to the two men, who sat thinking.

Schell scowled at his watch. He stood and reached out to shake hands with Wilks.

"I appreciate your inviting me to this discussion. The dreams will be easier to live with knowing what you've told me—but I'll have to think about it and get back to you."

Wilks started to say something, but must have thought better of it; he shook hands with Schell.

Schell nodded at Ripley and Dunston, and exited.

Ripley sighed. Not everyone they spoke to was going to jump at the chance to risk their lives, of course.

"I'm in," Dunston said.

Ripley looked over at the man, surprised. He

had been so quiet through the presentation that she had guessed he wasn't interested.

Dunston didn't look as if he had said anything important; he sat with the same unreadable expression on his unlined face. "Let me know what I can do to help you prepare."

Wilks and Ripley both grinned. The sergeant explained the proposal they planned to give to General Peters. Ripley watched Dunston absorb the information. The teacher seemed to radiate calmness and strength; he would be a good man to have with them.

Billie sat on Char Adcox's futon and sipped a mug of black tea, waiting for her response. The lieutenant had seemed enthusiastic enough at the beginning of Billie's speech, but now looked apprehensive; she tapped her fingers against her own cup, frowning. Billie remained quiet, not wanting to pressure her.

"I don't know," Char said finally. "It sounds good, but I'm not really in a position—" She hesitated. "I had family on Earth," she said. "It's taken me a long time to deal with losing them, and I've worked hard to get where I am now as it is. Some mornings, I'm still barely able to get out of bed." She looked at Billie, searched her face for understanding.

Billie nodded.

"I just don't ... look, I can't, I'm sorry."

Billie tried not to look disappointed, but it must have shown.

Char sipped her tea, her eyes troubled. Billie

set her mug down and stood to go. "It's okay, Char," she said. "Really. We couldn't have gotten this far without your help. I understand."

Billie walked to the door. Damn. She liked the lieutenant, had been certain that she would volunteer.

She turned. "If you change your mind . . ."

Char nodded, but her forced smile said that her decision was firm. Billie walked out and stood in the corridor for a moment. She shook her head. She did understand. Given that the last couple of weeks had been the only time she'd been able to catch her breath since Wilks had come back into her life, she could see how peace and quiet had a lot of appeal. Then again, she realized she'd spent too much of her life in an enforced peace and quiet to want to sit still very long. Even if there were monsters out there waiting for her.

"Well, McQuade is in," Wilks said. "And Brewster. Did you get to Falk?"

Ripley nodded. "Yeah, but he lost interest when the question of payment came up. He said he'd *consider* it if we wanted to buy his time."

Wilks shrugged. "Not everyone has cause," he said. Too bad, though. He had run into Falk a few times on the station. Tall and heavily muscled, he was one of those guys whose loud voice and laugh could be heard in the midst of every card game. Not a real social adept, maybe, but he had the feel of somebody who'd be good to have covering your ass in a firefight.

They sat in Ripley's room, going over possible

crew members. McQuade, Brewster, Dunston, and Jones so far. Jon Jones was a young medic who seemed too serious for his age. Ripley had seemed tense when Wilks had mentioned the black doctor, but had not objected. A medtech would be a necessity, they both knew that.

Billie had stopped by earlier to say that Adcox wouldn't be going. She had seemed unhappy about it and hadn't stayed to discuss the trip. Wilks guessed that she was at the 'casting room looking for Amy; it had become an obsession of hers, looking for Amy. He understood why.

"What about Carvey? And Moto, she's had experience—"

Wilks returned his attention to the screen. A light flashed in the upper corner, accompanied by a muted tone, signaling a call.

Ripley tapped the receiver. It was Billie.

"Ripley, Wilks," she said, her voice strained, "tune in military channel, ten-vee, quick!" She discommed before either of them had a chance to reply.

Ripley hit the controls that would switch them to vid.

The image on the screen was confused, jumbled; Wilks recognized the inside of an armored personnel carrier. A pair of legs from the knees down ran by, then another set; apparently, the camera was on the floor. There were shouts and gunfire in the background. A man's voice, near hysteria, called out orders that were barely audible above the din.

"Broillet, Reiter, fall back! Hornoff, Anders,

Sites, respond! Respond! Fuck! There's no—" the voice was cut off.

Wilks started. Hornoff was one of the men listed in the psych files. . . .

There was nothing on the screen now except a dim shot of a storage compartment. The picture jerked slightly, as if the APC were being hit. Occasional bursts of gunfire could be heard in the distance, but no more voices.

"What—?" Ripley glanced at Wilks and looked back to the picture. Her expression was part dread and part anger; she knew what she was watching, if not the circumstances.

"Earth mission," said Wilks tightly. His knuckles were white. Bako had said there was going to be another.

"Old 'cast?"

"I don't think so. I was going to look up Hornoff tomorrow." He watched realization flood Ripley's face. She chewed at her lower lip. There was no reason for this to be on, unless—

"Somebody fucked up," he said.

Suddenly there came an alien's hoarse shriek, loud enough that it had to be inside the APC. There was no sound of a weapon to answer its cry.

A thick, spidery shape moved across the screen, too close to see clearly—but Wilks knew.

Ripley groaned. "Oh, shit."

The screen cut to static, then black. Neither of them said anything for a moment, just watched the darkness. A mechanical, unisex voice chimed on, informing them that there were technical difficulties.

"It was a mistake," said Wilks. The 'cast had played for less than two minutes, if Billie had caught the beginning; the voice meant that it had been pulled on purpose. Ten-vee was a consistently boring channel dedicated to pro-military information programs, propaganda. He could almost see some vidtech private sweating in his boots right now. A colossal fuck-up. The wrong tape switched to at the wrong time; everyone on Gateway tuned in would have seen it.

A harried-looking man stepped on to the screen and faced the camera. His brow and upper lip were dotted with sweat. His face and hair looked military, but he was dressed in a rumpled coverall.

"It's weasel time," said Wilks softly.

"You're *on*," a voice stage-whispered offscreen. Live, of course.

"We, uh, apologize for the interruption in regular programming," he said. "Due to an error in our video room, a transmission of the ... Earth mission from five weeks ago was ... put on." The PR man fumbled his way through a rationalization, obviously unprepared.

"What bullshit," Wilks said. "No way that was ever supposed to see air."

"We now return to, ah, the program. Ten-vee will issue a formal statement at a later time." The screen cut to a space walk, some minor fix-it operation on the station. Ripley hit the command, blacking the picture. She turned to Wilks, her face pale and numb.

"Won't people know?"

Wilks shook his head. "Maybe friends of the dead soldiers. But who will they talk to before command gets to them?" He realized his hands were still in fists and let them relax, taking a deep breath. "This was supposed to be a secret, and they're going to step on it hard. Believe that."

Ripley looked at him. "What do you think this is going to do to our mission?"

Wilks returned her look, frowning. What *would* it do? The military couldn't keep people from talking ... it could swing the transport problem either way.

"I don't know," he said. "I guess we'll find out soon enough."

Billie was getting ready for bed when her 'com *chinged*. She almost ignored it; whoever it was would try back at another time. She was exhausted and it was very late—she had gone back to the 'casting room after meeting with Wilks and Ripley and watched for Amy for another few hours.

All three of them had agreed it was an accident; someone had their ass in a sling by now for that little technical error. She *had* caught the beginning of the transmission and had called the others within ten seconds; they hadn't really missed anything, except the camera hitting the floor.

Billie sighed and stretched. There had been no

sign of Amy, and now someone was calling in the middle of the night.

She hit receive. "Yes?"

"Billie? This is Char Adcox. I didn't wake you, did I? I'm sorry to be calling so late—"

Billie felt her sleepiness slip away. "No, I was up. What's going on?"

"Did you see the ten-vee fubar this afternoon?"

"Yeah, I saw it."

Adcox sounded exhausted, too. "I've been thinking about what I saw. It brought back a lot of history—I'm sure it did for others—" She stopped, then laughed weakly at herself. "I'm sorry, I'm kind of a mess."

"You don't have to apologize, Char, it's fine."

There was a pause at the other end so long that Billie was about to speak again, when she heard the lieutenant take a deep breath. "I want to go with you," she said. Any trace of hesitation was gone. "If you still want me along, that is. I—need to go."

This was the voice of the woman she had seen on the tape of the psych files, strong and unafraid. "Good. Welcome aboard."

They made arrangements for the next day and discommed.

Billie lay down to try to sleep. She instinctively liked and trusted Char Adcox, and was happy the woman would be coming along. And having one of the linear dreamers on board wouldn't hurt.

Billie drifted off to a deep sleep. If the queen mother haunted her dreams, the next morning brought no memory of it.

7

Ripley opened her door and found Falk standing there, his face solemn. He had one hand raised to knock and dropped it; the big man looked as if he had slept badly. He smelled of stale alcohol and sour sweat.

"Falk," she said, "what a treat. I was just on my way to breakfast."

She saw that the sarcasm in her voice didn't escape him. He reddened slightly. "Yeah. Well, I wanted to talk to you for a minute, I—about the trip. I want to go."

Ripley stepped back, surprised. Falk obviously took it as an invitation; he walked over to the desk and leaned against it. He kept his gaze on the floor.

She looked him up and down. He had been sitting when she had met him the day before and she hadn't realized how huge the man was. At least 195 centimeters and 100 kilos, barrel-chested and long-legged. His receding hair was worn long in a blond ponytail, his mustache was slightly darker. Embarrassment didn't rest well on his hard face, and he looked as if it were an unfamiliar emotion; one corner of his mouth twitched, and his heavy brows were drawn together.

"We aren't offering money," she said finally.

His expression didn't change. "Yeah, that's fine. You still need help, don't you? I'm sorry I was such an asshole. I want to go."

Ripley frowned. This wasn't the man she had met yesterday, the loud, wise-cracking, up-yours pirate. He had admitted to having the dreams easily enough but treated them lightly. He said his woman had insisted on the psych visits and he had called them a waste of time.

"Why?" she said.

Falk sighed and looked up, but not at Ripley. "The military channel," he said, focusing his attention on the ceiling. "You heard about their little fuck-up yesterday?"

"I saw it."

"I was in the middle of a card game at a bar when it played. I almost had to beat the shit out of the 'tender to turn it up—" He seemed out of breath and paused for a few seconds.

Ripley waited.

"Marla was one of those soldiers," he said. "She told me that she would be gone a while, said it was standard drill shit. She told me not to worry."

Falk finally looked at Ripley. She saw that his eyes were bloodshot and rimmed in red. "Last night some asshole dressed in a captain's uniform told me that there had been an 'unfortunate accident' on her ship and that it'd be a good idea for me to keep quiet about it. The bastard stood there and *lied* to me; I heard her name on that 'cast, I heard somebody yelling it—"

Falk stopped and took a shuddery breath. All of Ripley's earlier dislike for the man evaporated. He was obviously in great pain.

"I'm sorry," she said, "I wish there was something I could do. . . ."

"I want to go," said Falk. "I want to kill them." He didn't sound angry or desperate; his voice was calm and matter-of-fact, as if he were discussing the weather. "I loved her."

"We're meeting at 0800 tomorrow in the dojo on C," she said.

He straightened up at that and nodded, his expression unreadable. Ripley understood what it was like to lose someone close and knew there was nothing she could do to make it easier for him.

"Thanks," he said, walking to the door. "I'll be there."

She had no doubts about that.

Wilks watched General Peters scan the printout sheet of the psych files Leslie had pulled. To avoid problems with confidentiality and computer

rascaling, she had only included the names of the
dreamers they had spoken to, along with state-
ments from Billie and Ripley; twelve in all. Ten of
them had agreed to go.

"And you say that this dream is the same in all
of these cases, Sergeant?" The general spoke
without looking up.

"Yes, sir." Wilks stood in his office at ease,
hands behind his back. It was one of the more pa-
latial rooms on Gateway, well-lit and comfortably
warm. Pastel paintings were hung on the walls
and the stuffed chairs were a high-quality synthetic leather. Peters had not asked him to sit.

The general had not gotten as far as he had
through imaginative thinking. His stoic expression and hard eyes said as much—standard military right down the line. The man was also quite
fat, hadn't seen much hands-on combat lately.
Wilks had served under such men before,
assholes too closed-minded and by-the-numbers
to believe in anything outside their own experience. He was wasting his fucking time here, but
Ripley wanted to give it a shot. Fine . . .

"Well, this is very interesting," Peters said,
looking up, "but I'm afraid there's really no way I
can authorize such a trip on just this. We'll have to
look into it further." His tone was dismissive.

Wilks said, "Is there somebody else I can
speak to about this, sir?"

"Excuse me?"

Wilks shrugged. He was still a marine, sort of.
They hadn't been able to pull all his records, so
his status was pretty much in limbo until they did.

That gave him a little leeway when talking to officers. He said, "Well, sir, there are civilians in the governing board. They might be interested in this."

Peters looked at Wilks with his piggy eyes. "Are you trying to be smart, Sergeant?"

"No, sir." Not with this clown. Say something smart and it would sail right past.

"Yes, there are civilians in power here, but when it comes to military missions using *my hardware*, I am *God*."

Wilks said nothing, waiting.

"I've read your record, Sergeant, and you've got a long history of being a troublemaker. I don't need any more trouble than I've got." Peters set the proposal aside and motioned toward the door.

Wilks could see that there was no chance. If he thought kissing ass here would work, well, fuck, he'd done worse, but he knew it was a waste of time. Had known it all along, but at least he'd held his temper in check. There was a time when he would have popped fatso here right in the mouth and smiled as he waited for the MPs to come get him.

"Thank you for your time, sir."

The general grunted but didn't look up from his desk, where he was already looking through other papers.

The temptation to slam the door on the way out was one that Wilks was only barely able to resist.

Billie met Wilks at the Four Sails. He sat at his table staring at his drink, his scarred face tense.

"Ripley 'commed, said she'd be a few minutes late," said Billie, and sat down. "How'd it go with the general?"

"About like I expected. Head was jammed too far up his ass for him to begin to hear me." He sipped at his drink. "Fucking officers."

Billie felt her stomach clutch at itself. This had become important to her. How could she get to Amy, how could she still hope that the child would be alive?

"What's the matter with you two?" Ripley said. She slid into the booth and sat across from them. "Are we ready for our meeting tomorrow?"

Wilks said, "Yeah, if we can fly without a ship. The general thinks we're crazy. No surprise."

Billie's heart felt heavy. "It looks like the game is over," she said. "Unless you want to *steal* a ship."

Ripley grinned. "I thought you'd never ask," she said.

Wilks returned the grin. "I knew it. I fucking knew it."

"You didn't really think some fat old general was going to *give* us a ship, did you? That was a long shot at best."

Wilks nodded. "Gonna make us criminals again."

"Well, sure, it would've been nice, but we don't always get what we want, do we? Time to go to plan B," Ripley said. "Which was really plan A all along: We swipe what we need."

"Makes sense to me," Wilks said. He raised his glass in salute. "Here's to crime."

Billie smiled and nodded. Well. It wasn't as if they'd never done it before. Christ, they were getting to be old hands at stealing ships. The one from Earth to Spears's military base, the one from there to here, the escape pod. It did make sense. What the hell.

What the hell.

8

Wilks looked over the group they had assembled and nodded. Everyone here had field experience, with the exceptions of Jones, the medic, and Dunston—although he taught hand-to-hand combat in the dojo where they all now stood or sat in small groups, talking. And Dunston looked as if he knew how to handle himself.

Brewster, Carvey, Moto, Adcox, and Captain McQuade were all marines and had fought on Earth at the beginning of the infestation.

Ana Moto was a thin, sad-looking woman with long features and a bright laugh. She was also the only surviving member of a special task force assigned to spot alien nests on Earth before things had gotten bad. She laughed at something Adcox said to her and Billie; the three young women stood together in one corner of the room.

Everyone had arrived early, with the exception of Falk, who walked into the dojo exactly on time. Ripley hadn't mentioned why he had changed his mind, just that he would be coming after all.

Wilks watched Falk nod at Ripley when he entered, and noted that the big man looked exhausted. He suspected that Falk had decided to go after watching the military 'cast, and figured that he had known one of the soldiers. Just a hunch. Falk sat apart from the others in one of the plastic chairs and stared at the scuffed foam floor. He looked like a man in pain.

Leslie smiled at him from across the room, where she was talking to Ripley and Maria Tully, a friend of hers. Tully was skilled with computers and had lost family on Earth; she would be the electronics tech.

Wilks had mixed emotions about Leslie. On the one hand, he wouldn't have minded having her along, for personal reasons. On the other hand, his expectations of surviving the mission weren't all that high. Ultimately he was glad she wasn't going; he didn't want anything to happen to her.

Wilks smiled back at her. After meeting with Billie and Ripley in the bar, he had gone to Leslie's quarters to discuss her part in their mission. Although she wouldn't be making the trip, her role would still be a major one in helping them get transport.

The room grew quiet as Ripley walked to the front to stand next to him. Billie left her group to join them, although they had both agreed to let Ripley run the session; she was a natural leader, and it was her idea anyhow. Wilks was glad somebody else was in charge for a change. Made things easier on him.

"Well," she began, "you all know why you're here. I'm Ellen Ripley, this is Wilks and Billie. Each of you has had certain useful experience, which is why you among the dreamers have been chosen. You have felt the alien presence, the queen—and it's time we did something about it."

Ripley had everyone's full attention; Wilks hoped that they'd still be listening after they heard the bad news.

"Before we work on the specifics of our mission, we need to let you know some of the obstacles we're looking at here. Wilks?"

He cleared his throat. "Yeah. I talked to General Peters yesterday, and he refused our request for transport." He paused. "Actually, the man thinks we're bugfuck."

Captain McQuade broke in. "Peters is an asshole," he said. The two marines with him nodded. "I'm surprised you bothered—the man's so full of shit he farts instead of burping."

Several people laughed.

Wilks grinned. "Yeah, well, be that as it may, we don't have the official green light. We can try again, but I think the general is a waste of time."

Ripley took over. "Which is why we've decided to borrow a ship," she said, "and that makes this an entirely different game. I want you all to understand what you're agreeing to before you make a final decision. If we get caught, we're in deep. If we fail, coming back here means consequences— maybe even if we succeed."

She met the eyes of each person as she spoke. "We didn't tell Peters where we were headed specifically, so we probably won't be chased if we get clear—but stealing a transport wasn't part of the plan when you agreed to go, and if you want to walk, now's the time. We'll understand."

There was a pause.

"Fuck it," said Falk from the back of the room in a hoarse voice. "Not doing anything would be worse."

There were several murmured affirmations from the group.

Wilks looked around the dojo and saw the same kind of determined look on everyone's face. No one moved.

After a moment, Ripley went on. "Good. Thanks. We want to leave here in a few days, and there's a lot to do to get ready. We're looking at ships now, and Leslie"—Ripley nodded at the hacker—"is getting us a read on the security system we're dealing with. We've got a list of shit that needs to be thought out, supplies and weapons to begin with, and we need to work out details of taking the ship. . . ."

As Ripley continued, Wilks watched the expressions of the people they would be working with. Several of them threw out suggestions as the discussion continued, and all of them looked as though they had been bestowed a special privilege in being included on this trip—this trip that could cost them their lives and probably would. Yeah, they were a good crew.

Not too bright, maybe, but he didn't have any room to talk.

Billie checked the supply list for the third time, cross-referenced with what was stocked on the *Kurtz*. The military freighter had been chosen for its large hold, designed to haul toxic liquid by-products. The containment area could hold up to 10,000 cubic liters of radioactive sludge, was airtight, had interleaved durasteel-and-lead walls half a meter thick, with hatches to match. Anyway, the hold was more than big enough to carry a queen alien. And to keep her from wandering around the ship, too. If they could catch her, if they could get her on board, *if* they could steal the ship in the first place. . . .

Billie rubbed her eyes and looked around her room. It was late; she knew she should get some sleep. In the morning they would meet back in the dojo to run down the details of taking the ship. Security looked to be minimal, but there was some, and they didn't want to get caught.

She and Doc Jones had been put in charge of provisions, although the list Leslie had rascaled seemed pretty complete. The *Kurtz* was built to quarter twenty people comfortably; it carried an APC and the food dispensers were stocked with pastes and concentrates that would be good for another ten years. "Good" being a relative term; they would taste like shit, but they would be edible. The ship was currently fueled and ready to go. All the comforts of home. More than she had here, actually.

In spite of her exhaustion, Billie felt too wired to sleep. Her thoughts were a jumbled mess of memories and hopes, all that she had been through and the people she had known. As awful as the dreams that she had experienced at the hospital on Earth had been, they were even worse these days. Wilks. Mitch. Now Ripley. And, of course, Amy.

It seemed to Billie she had been running and fighting her whole life. She was in a place where she didn't have to do that anymore; she could probably live out her life here on this station and maybe die of old age. But that thought didn't play. There were people down on Earth being eaten alive and that wasn't right. Especially since one of those at risk was Amy.

So, maybe she could go and do this thing and somehow survive, and maybe *that* would be the end of it.

Amy. The *Kurtz* probably wouldn't be equipped to receive Earth 'casts at the distance they would travel, so there would be no way to know if Amy and her family were still alive. The last transmission had been only a few days before, but there was no way to know if it had been on tape or live; Billie wanted to believe it was recent. She could feel that Amy was down there, perhaps praying for a way out.

Ripley's plan would be the answer.

Billie scanned back to the top of the list, yawned. She knew that there was nothing missing, but wanted to check once more. After all, there would be no second chance—when they got on board, there was no turning back.

Hell. It was already too late to turn back.

Ripley sat on the floor of the dimly lit dojo, alone. It was early morning. The crew wouldn't arrive for another half hour and then there would be no time to think.

She knew that they had planned the mission as thoroughly as possible, that they were as ready as they would be. They could probably spend another day or two working out details, but one could always wait; it was time to act. Too much planning raised too many doubts. You did what you could.

She ran down the list of crew members mentally: herself, Billie, and Wilks. Adcox and the other marines: Falk. Dunston. Tully, Leslie's hacker friend. And Jones . . .

They *were* a good group. The trial run had been successful; of course, it would be different in real time, but the crew seemed committed and confident enough to get past any trouble. The only part that worried her was getting past the guard ships—but they were watching for incoming transport mostly, had been posted to ward off a possibly infected ship or one manned by somebody dangerous, like the mad General Spears who had brought Billie and Wilks along as stowaways.

It should work. Ripley hoped it would be as

easy as it looked, but she knew from experience that things rarely were as easy as they looked.

She had concentrated so completely on getting the thing together that there hadn't been time to relax. Not that there had ever been time for that once she'd run into the aliens. For her, it hadn't been that long. In realtime, it had been the better part of a century. Now the fucking things owned Earth, and humankind was a third-class local power.

Her hatred for the creatures was as much a part of her as her hair color or height. It affected everything she did, was the force behind all she had gone through to get where she was. She smiled wryly. Where was she? Sitting in the dark preparing to lead a group of fighters to steal a ship, fly across the galaxy, capture the queen of queens. And, eventually, use their captive to lure and kill every one of the goddamned aliens.

Ripley sighed. The choices she had made were simple ones, of basic morality, right and wrong. But now it had gone beyond just her. This could cost lives, could mean the end of her own. She usually knew better than to try and take responsibility for the people around her, but this felt different.

Shit, it *always* felt different.

It helped to know one thing—she didn't want to die, but if it meant taking that queen bitch out, or taking the bitch's spawn, she would. That choice had been made after the *Nostromo*, and it had become everything to her. The things had cost her too much. Her crew. Her family. Her whole life. She had nothing else left.

Ripley closed her eyes and waited for the others.

9

Dunston and Tully walked down the corridor toward the entry of dock D6, loudly discussing station politics. When they turned the corner to the dock, they would be in a position to see any guard who might be present.

Dunston signaled to Ripley, Wilks, and Falk, who were following. No guard.

Wilks was close enough to see Tully pull a small keyboard from her pack and plug it into a panel set in the wall. She crouched down and quickly began to punch in codes.

"I don't know. I mean, it's one thing to *say* you're going to upgrade the conditions, but they've been saying that since I got here...."

Wilks and the others continued slowly toward the door while Tully checked for monitors.

Dunston droned on about the quality of the food served in the dining halls.

According to the deck layout in the computer, there wouldn't be any guard at this point. Ripley had insisted on a double check.

Tully looked up, grinning. "Clear," she said quietly.

Wilks felt himself loosen slightly. It was crucial to go unnoticed for as long as possible in order to get past the guard ships. Once an alarm was sounded, their chances fell damn fast.

The *Kurtz* was docked outside D6; to get to it they needed to open three doors—this one, the entry to the air lock, and the ship itself. All were computer-coded, and the complexity of the entry systems usually meant no human guards, a major selling point for their choice of transport.

They would get into the loading room and call in the rest of the crew; Captain McQuade's voiceprint would be the key to the *Kurtz*. A licensed military pilot and the proper codes were all they needed to get on board. The codes Leslie and Tully had rascaled up with little trouble.

Maybe too little . . .

While Tully set up her portable, Wilks moved to the nearest 'com to raise Billie and the others. They were waiting in Brewster's quarters. The marines had taken all of the carbines and grenades from the armory they could carry, signing them out with General Peters's personal access code. Wilks had laughed when Leslie had suggested using the general's code.

Looked like Peters had helped out after all.

Wilks walked quickly down D-corridor to a public 'com and tapped in Brewster's number.

"Yeah?"

"Hey, Brewster, it's Wilks. Why don't you pop on over and have a drink?"

"Sounds great. Meet you at the bar."

Wilks discommed and walked back down the empty hall. So far, so good. Billie and the marines would be there in two minutes or less, barring complications, and then they would be on their way—

"Hey," came a voice from behind him.

Wilks stopped and turned around. A burly young man in a security uniform approached him slowly, face grim. His hand rested lightly on the butt of his stunner.

"Where do you think *you're* going?"

Brewster nodded at the other marines and they stood, picking up assorted wrapped bundles. Weapons, ammo, various tools. No one spoke. Billie went to help Jones with his equipment, a few bags of med supplies and a small diagnostic unit. He smiled at her, teeth bright against his chocolate-colored skin.

"Guess we're about to be outlaws," he said. He looked nervous.

Billie returned his smile. "You get used to it after a while," she said. "Besides, you already *are* an outlaw. Conspiracy."

Adcox went first, as scout. She carried nothing, and would walk a half a minute ahead of the others.

Brewster and McQuade went next.

Billie counted silently to ten.

Carvey and Moto stepped out.

Finally, Billie and Jones walked to the door.

Billie's heart pounded and she felt a tiny trickle of sweat run between her breasts in spite of the cool air.

Amy, she thought. They stepped out into the corridor.

Wilks smiled at the guard. "I'm trying to find a biolab, D2—isn't it down here?"

The guard seemed to relax slightly, but didn't smile back. "Wrong direction. The labs are back that way," he said, pointing behind them, "and go left at the first tee."

Wilks shook his head, still smiling. "Thanks."

The guard nodded and stepped past him, headed toward D6. Where the others would be waiting for Wilks.

"Are you sure it's not to the right?" said Wilks loudly, when he had gotten but a few paces away.

"Yeah, I'm sure. Now—"

"Because I went left before, I think, and I think it's right. I mean, headed back to the lifts is right, right?" He spoke in what he hoped was a stupid but friendly tone. And he hoped the others would hear him.

The guard turned and moved closer to Wilks, as if proximity would somehow make his answer plainer.

"Look. Go back. When you get to the tee, go left. *Left*. Got it?"

"Left. Uh-huh. Got it."

The guard shook his head. And distracted by Wilks's stupidity, just as Wilks had hoped he'd be, he walked away from D6.

Which was good, since otherwise Wilks would've had to take him out.

Wilks let out a breath and waited for a few seconds before heading back. They were grouped in front of the door, all except for Falk; the large man stepped out from behind a turn farther down the hall, obviously prepared to deal with any interruptions. They had heard him working the guard.

Tully had her finger on the entry button and was waiting for the go.

Ripley arched an eyebrow at Wilks.

"Let's do it," he said.

But before Tully could move, the door slid open.

A man in a worker's coverall stood there, holding what looked like a weapon.

Billie and Jones walked down the hall side by side, not speaking. They came to the first turn, and Billie caught a glimpse of Moto and Carvey as they turned the corner ahead. She relaxed slightly. Everything seemed to be working as planned, so far. She wondered how Ripley's team was doing.

Dunston stepped forward as if to greet the surprised worker. The mechanical device apparently wasn't a weapon; the man dropped it and raised clenched hands, mouth set. He was surprised, but obviously combative. They weren't supposed to be here and he knew it.

Dunston reached out, holding his hands so the backs of his wrists faced the worker. Ripley saw the man blink, confused—

The martial arts teacher moved forward quickly on his right foot, almost crouching. He flicked his fingers at the man's eyes.

The worker raised his arms to cover his face, and—

Dunston dropped flat onto the deck, did something fast with his legs—

The worker squawked once, fell, hit the deck, hard.

Wilks dropped and clapped a hand over the man's mouth, but the guy wasn't moving. Apparently he'd hit his head and was out cold.

It all happened in the space of a few breaths.

"Nice move," Wilks said.

"No one else inside now," Dunston said. "But hurry. Somebody's coming."

Billie and the doctor were almost to the dock when they heard footsteps running toward them.

Billie froze, laying her free hand on the doctor's arm. He stopped and looked at her, his own dark features a mask of anxiety. She felt as though time had slowed to a crawl, but excuses ran through her head at lightning speed. *We're on our way to a medical emergency, I'm assisting, he's a doctor, we're teaching a class—*

Adcox appeared in front of them, out of breath. Billie and Jones let out shuddery sighs in unison, but the lieutenant's expression was frantic. She grabbed one of their bags.

"Trouble," she said, and turned back toward the dock.

Billie fell in beside Char and Jones at a jog. Adcox hadn't wasted any more air by telling them what had happened, and Billie didn't ask; they would find out soon enough.

Wilks dragged the worker inside before turning to Dunston. "Who's coming?" he said.

"Another worker."

"How—?" Wilks started to ask Dunston how he could possibly know, if he'd had some extrasensory flash or something, when he saw the evidence himself.

There was a table in one corner of the large room where the downed man had evidently been about to sit for breakfast. Except that there were two trays set out, two chairs, and two steaming cups of dark liquid.

"Pretty mystical," said Dunston. "Ancient secret of the Orient, multiple-coffee awareness."

Adcox arrived, trailed by Billie and Jones.

Wilks turned to her. "Get everyone in here, now. We're expecting company."

Tully was already working on the air lock; Falk had stepped back into the corridor to help the others bring in the equipment.

Wilks looked at Ripley and saw the same question on her face that he felt on his own: How much time?

• • •

Billie ran into the workroom, Falk shut the door behind her, and Carvey crouched to the floor with a welder. Light too bright to look at flashed. Carvey quickly melted part of the heavy plastic door to the frame and then stepped back.

Moto unpacked one of the carbines and pointed it at the now-jammed entry.

Tully tapped in codes at the air lock.

"Come *on*," said Ripley, jaw tight.

"Okay, okay . . ." said Tully, almost to herself. "And—got it!"

The air lock door slid open. Tully unplugged her portable and ran the few steps to the hatch of the *Kurtz*. She hooked the portable to the new hatch.

McQuade stepped in after her. The others stood tensed, ready to rush in—

Behind them, the door mechanism to the D6 entry buzzed. It buzzed again, longer this time, the sound edged with a high-pitched mechanical whine. It could have only been a second or two, but it seemed a lot longer. Then someone pounded at the door.

"Diestler!" called a female voice, muffled through the thick plastic. "Hey, open up!"

The man on the floor groaned slightly and rolled his head to one side. Diestler, apparently.

Moto pointed her weapon at him, but he didn't move again.

Ripley turned to look at Wilks, but he was already headed to the entryway.

The pounding continued. "You asshole! This shit's getting cold, open *up*!"

Wilks punched the entry button. The mechanism whined again, but the door remained closed.

"Hold on!" shouted Wilks. "Door's stuck!"

There was a pause. Ripley gritted her teeth and hoped that Wilks sounded at least remotely like the unconscious worker.

"Well, no shit," said the woman on the other side. "Come on, wonder-tech, fix the goddamn thing, my breakfast is dying out here."

Ripley could see the crew members relax a little. Wilks had just bought them a little time.

Tully stopped typing and motioned for McQuade to step forward. A quiet computerized voice came from the monitor at face level.

"Command pilot please enter vocal access code now."

"McQuade, Eric D., captain. A-seven-zero-five-oh-B," he said.

"Thank you."

Tully input the final code, a grin spreading across her face. With a triumphant flourish, she pressed "enter."

Ripley grinned. Almost there—

Nothing happened.

"Invalid code. Access denied. Please enter new code now."

Wilks picked up the tool that Diestler had dropped and stared at it. It was some kind of computer hookup, an oblong box with several conductors and prongs on one side.

The woman called impatiently from the other side. "Come on, Diestler, or I'm going to sit on the fucking floor and eat it all—yours, too. Don't tell me you did this door all by yourself while I was gone."

Wilks looked at the box in his hands and stopped. Of course, of *course*!

"Diestler? Say something." The woman sounded suspicious now. "What are you doing, anyway? You beating off in there or something?"

"Just a sec," said Wilks. "I'm trying the code on this one." It would have to hold her. He turned and ran, as quietly as he could, back to the air lock.

"I don't *have* any new codes!" said Tully. "This is it! They must have changed them since yesterday!"

The crew stood around her, tense.

"Can we blow the door?" said Jones.

"Not without alarms," said Falk. The big man looked angry. "And that wouldn't do us much good, to have a big fucking *hole* in our escape ship."

Billie felt despair rise inside her. To be stopped by a fucking *door*—

Wilks shoved past her and handed a box to Tully. "Plug this in," he said. "Quick!"

She grabbed it and jammed the conductor into the opening of her portable.

Ripley looked at Wilks. "What—"

"New access codes, got to be. The general is more paranoid than we thought."

The hatch of the *Kurtz* popped open.

•   •   •

McQuade and Ripley strapped themselves in at the console while the others moved around behind them, preparing for flight. Wilks stood next to the two pilots. With any luck, the female tech hadn't alerted anyone yet. If she had, they would be thoroughly fucked.

As McQuade punched the disengage controls, a voice crackled out over the intercom.

"Ah, *Kurtz* pilot, identify yourself, please."

"This is Captain Eric McQuade. And who is this?" He spoke gruffly, impatiently.

"Sir. This is Lieutenant Dunn, sir, of the *Kirkland*. Please state purpose and authorization. Sir."

"Operation Arrowhead," said McQuade. He sounded bored. "Access P-two-one-four-oh-two." General Peters's code.

There was a pause. "Sir? We have no missions scheduled from this sector." Dunn sounded very young and very nervous. "Could you please wait while I raise the general—sir?"

"Jesus Christ! Peters schedules another bughunt without telling some dumbshit lieutenant and now we have to wait until you drag him out of bed to okay it *again*? Think, son! Why would we want to go on this trip? For *fun*?" McQuade paused. "Fine. Go ahead. But you better hope the general is in a good mood. Lieutenant."

There was another pause, and Dunn spoke again, obviously cowed. "I'm sorry, sir. Um. Go ahead, access cleared and verified. Good luck, sir."

Wilks and Ripley grinned at one another and Wilks slapped McQuade on the back. From behind them, Wilks could hear the others laughing. He walked back to strap himself in, feeling vaguely sorry for Lieutenant Dunn; by the time he got hold of the general for verification, they'd be way out of range. And there would be hell to pay for it. Too bad.

Billie smiled at him when he sat down. "Score one for the good guys," she said.

He adjusted his seat before he answered. "That was the easy part."

She nodded, and her smile faltered slightly. Wilks leaned his head against the back of his chair and let out a deep breath.

They were in it all the way now.

10

Ripley was the last one awake on the *Kurtz*. She double-checked the course setting in the dimly lit room, shivering slightly from the cold. She wore only a tank top and underwear, fine for the sleep chamber but little protection from the frigid stillness of the ship; the air warmers and recyclers had already been dialed down to minimum. The system would kick back on a couple of hours before they woke up—or before *she* woke up. She had reset the controls on her chamber to rouse her an hour before the others. No good reason, really, just instinct.

The last of the preparations made, she turned away from the computer and padded barefoot to her chamber. All around her, the crew members rested, already in their own dreamworlds. Ripley hoped they slept well; so far, the men and women of the *Kurtz* had done okay, and she was glad to have their help.

She looked around the room a final time before climbing into her own sleep-box, and wondered if she would dream during the sleep that was so like a shadow of death. . . .

Ripley shivered again as she triggered the mechanism, but not so much from the cold as before.

Wilks had been here before, he was sure of it. He was standing in a dark place, the air around him alive with fear and tension.

"—they're all around us!" Someone yelled behind him. Familiar, like the rest of it. A warning horn screamed somewhere ahead of him in the hot, wet darkness. Huge coils of glistening black covered the walls all around him.

"No," he said softly.

It couldn't be. He, they were on Rim. Where the aliens had killed his unit, where he was going to die—

"Shut the fuck up!" Wilks yelled out. He knew what had to be done. He'd done it before. "Maintain your field of fire, we're gonna be fine!"

Eight of the squad were dead; as a corporal, he was ranking noncom, he had to stay in control—

He heard shots in the alien den; the sound of a caseless carbine pounded his ears.

A little girl clung to his arm, crying. Billie.

"Easy, honey," he said. As he picked her up she turned her tear-streaked face up to look at him while all around the creatures screamed and weapons screamed back at them. "We're gonna be fine. We're going back to the ship, everything is gonna be okay."

He was trying to run but his legs had been dipped in plastecrete. Everything was happening too fast and he couldn't *move*. He shouted more orders, unable to see who he called out to. Who was left?

"Shoot for targets, triplets only! We don't have enough ammo to waste on full auto suppressive fire!"

There was a sealed door ahead. They would have to cut their way out, fast. The reactor was approaching meltdown and a swarm of the killing things was right behind—

Billie screamed when he tried to put her down. God, she was so small, so helpless! "I gotta open the door," he said.

Someone stepped out of the darkness to hold her. He turned, grateful, and—

"Leslie?" She was dressed in camo, a carbine slung over one shoulder.

"Got her," she said. She smiled easily.

Wrong, this part was wrong—

No time to think. He pulled a plasma cutter from his belt, triggered it. The stacked carbon lock melted and ran like water as he waved the cutter back and forth.

The door slid up.

He knew what was coming, knew that the queen would be there, waiting to take him. He had dreamed it before. . . .

But—no.

He stepped forward into a black, empty corridor and the sounds behind him fell away. It was dead quiet.

Billie stood there. Not the little girl she had been only a minute before. She was grown, a woman, wearing an untabbed soldier's uniform. He could see one of her small breasts exposed, glistening with sweat. She walked toward him, her face calm and beautiful.

"David," she whispered, and pressed up against him.

His lower belly tingled, penis suddenly hard and straining.

He felt dizzy. No, this was wrong. But he went with it. "Billie," he said, "we have to get out of here, there's no time—"

She silenced his mouth with hers, traced his lips with her soft tongue. He closed his eyes as she moved her hands over his chest and downward, circling....

As he gave himself over to the pleasure, the noise behind them suddenly washed back over him. Alarms and gunfire and screams—

He jerked himself away from Billie and grabbed at his belt, opening his eyes. Quickly, a weapon, something—!

He was alone, unarmed. He spun around in a circle, looking for Billie, looking for anybody—

He heard the aliens getting closer, but couldn't see anything.

A computer-chip voice informed him that meltdown would occur in five seconds.

"No!" he cried out, fell to his knees. "No, no, no—"

"Three seconds. Two. One. Meltdown—"

The world turned white.

Billie and Ripley walked side by side down a dark, debris-littered tunnel on Earth. It was neither warm nor cold; the air was still and silent. Billie turned to look at Ripley several times, but the older woman kept her eyes straight ahead.

They were looking for Amy. Billie guessed that they were in some kind of transportation shaft; she wanted to ask Ripley, but couldn't find the words. She said nothing.

Billie felt anxious, scared that they would miss Amy somehow. She was reassured that Ripley was with her, knew that if anyone could find the little girl, it would be her. Besides, it didn't matter who found her, as long as she was okay. . . .

They came to a fork in the tunnel, both of the corridors leading off into darkness. Without speaking, Ripley started down the one to the left. Billie wanted to go with her, but Amy could be in either one. She walked into the other tunnel alone.

She kept up a steady pace for what seemed like hours, headed in a straight line. The only sounds were her footsteps and breathing, echoing off into nothing. She knew she shouldn't be able to see at all, there being no lights, but for some reason she could make out each section of the tunnel for a few feet in front of her. She walked on.

Suddenly, she heard a sound ahead of her. She

stopped and listened. A child was crying, the lonely wail carrying through the dark corridor and surrounding her. The acoustics were distorted; she couldn't tell how far away she was. . . .

"Amy!" She called out.

The crying continued.

Billie started to run, certain that it was her. "Hold on, Amy! I'm coming!" The sound of her voice was strange and somehow flat in the echoey chamber.

She ran for a long time until she saw a bend in the tunnel. She knew that Amy would be around the corner, and cried out, happy. After all this time, finally—

"Amy!" She ran around the corner. Stopped, heart pounding. Dark despair fell onto her, a hard rain, cold and awful.

The tunnel forked again into five spokes. Far away she could hear Amy crying, and try as she might she couldn't tell which tunnel it came from.

"Where *are* you?" She called out, but there was no answer except for the sobs of the lost little girl.

Billie sank to the floor, feeling more alone than she ever had in her life, cradling her head in her arms. She began to cry herself, feeling as lost and scared as the unseen child.

From somewhere distant, she heard someone call her name, but it wasn't Amy. She didn't have the strength to reply, and she didn't care. She would never find Amy, she knew that now.

She wept until she was awash in tears. There was no hope.

No hope at all.

11

Ripley slipped her feet into a pair of boots and yawned widely. She felt grainy and exhausted, hung over from sleep. She knew that it would eventually wear off once she got moving, but that didn't stop her from a vague, wistful feeling as she looked around at the slumbering crew members. There were times when just staying asleep seemed infinitely better than getting up.

She sighed, stood, stretched her arms over her head, then bent to touch her toes. A half-remembered line occurred to her as she flexed her arms—something about an early bird getting the jump on others. The air cyclers had kicked on as scheduled, a low mechanical hum in the quiet sleep area, but the room was still cold enough for her breath to show. It would be warmer by the time the others got up—apparently early birds were hot-blooded creatures.

Her sleep had been deep and dreamless and she had awakened, though not refreshed, at least ready to get on with things. Her general plan to get the queen to Earth was okay, if perhaps not altogether reasonable. The specifics were still hazy. Like getting the goddamned thing onboard, for one—the creature probably wasn't going to just hop into the hold if they asked politely: *Excuse me, bitch, would you step this way?*

Well, one thing at a time; they had three days before they reached the queen's planet, plenty of time to come up with something.

Ripley had seen the layout of the *Kurtz* onscreen back at Gateway, but maybe walking it would trigger some ideas.

She went out into the chilled corridor.

The *Kurtz* was a two-function freighter, built not only for deepspace but also to enter a planet's gravity and land. It was shaped like an old-style bullet with fins—flat on the bottom, with rudimentary wings—and was aerodynamic, more or less. She'd learned to fly in similar vessels, had gotten her ticket as a pilot in a ship not too different from this one.

The upper level where she now stood was a series of rooms bisected by a main corridor that ran the length of the vessel. The command control room was forward and to her left. Across from her were a series of doors running down the hall: crew's quarters.

So, let's take a little tour, shall we?

She began to walk to the rear of the ship.

Each room would have its own 'fresher, but the shower was communal to help regulate water supply. It stood in between the last cubicle and a small workout room. Beyond the gym and aft was the med center, which looked cold and sterile behind the clear plexiflex door. With any luck, they'd have no need for the facility. . . .

She reached the corridor's end, then turned back toward the front. To her left now was a large supply area where the marines had stored their equipment before hitting the sleep chambers. Past that, the mess. Ripley's stomach growled noisily at the thought of food. She stopped and looked in at the bolted-down tables and chairs. It would also serve as a conference room. She reluctantly walked on, deciding to wait and eat with the others.

Adjacent to the eating area she was back where she started, at the sleep chambers. All in all, a good enough ship. It was a bit larger than they really needed, but that wasn't a handicap; besides, she reminded herself, thieves can't always be choosy.

She shook her head. She was in trouble again, win or lose.

She walked into the command area and past the twenty-plus seats for crew takeoffs and landings, into the partitioned-off pilot's room. She stood for a moment and watched the console, its colored lights blinking or glowing in the dim chamber. No problems, of course. An alarm would have gone off. She stepped away from the board and to one of the ship's five stairwells, to check out the lower deck.

Ripley walked through the computer room and the APC bay without really looking. She felt her heart speed up a bit as she came to a stop in front of the double hatch to the cargo area. This was what she had wanted to see, the queen's new home. She took a deep breath of the frigid air and stepped inside.

It was a huge chamber, coated heavily with carbslip on every exposed surface except the work lights; those were behind thick plates of kleersteel. The acid-resistant gray coating of the carbslip made the chamber seem like what she imagined a giant intestine might look like from the inside. The coating was dry, but it had a greasy, almost slimy shine to it. There were two stairwells, leading to the sleep chambers and mess, respectively. Both sets of stairs ended at airtight and extra-thick pressure doors. They would want to reinforce those before admitting their cargo, just to be sure. This place would safely hold the most noxious biochemical and radioactive wastes men could produce. The engineers who designed the hold knew the vile cargo would normally be glass-crated solids or liquid in insulated barrels, but in a pinch, the doors could be sealed and the stuff pumped in through special piping so the whole chamber could be turned into something like a giant toxic aquarium.

The only sound in the room was her own breathing. She looked around the chamber and nodded slowly: a suitable place for the bitch queen. Let her dull her teeth and claws on the impervious carbslip; let her sit like a bug in a jar, wondering what her fate was to be. Fuck her.

She had seen what she'd needed to, and the crew would be waking shortly. What she really needed was something to eat and a hot shower. She'd had no startling revelations, but perhaps one of the others had dreamed something up—

She started back to the open stairs in the computer room. Maybe their closer proximity to the planet would offer more detailed dreams, ideas that they could use. It was just a thought—but then, their mission wasn't exactly based on solid facts so far, she thought as the thick treadplate steps rang hollowly under her boots.

She grinned to herself as she moved through the slowly warming rooms, back toward the sleep chambers. Maybe the queen *would* tell them how to trap her if they asked politely. It wouldn't be much crazier than the rest of this trip.

Wilks heard a few muttered groans from the other crew members as they climbed from their sleep chambers and stretched, put on clothes, came back to life. He swiveled his head and tried to relieve the tightness deep between his shoulder blades. He'd had worse hangovers, but coming out of cold sleep always left him feeling disoriented and spacey. He'd dreamed, although he couldn't quite remember—

"Good morning, Wilks." Billie.

She walked over to stand by him, clenched and

unclenched her fingers slowly. She looked pale. "You seen Ripley?"

Part of his dream came back to him when he looked at her, more of a feeling than a picture. Something sexual about Billie. He turned away from her slightly, uncomfortable.

"No. I hope she's making coffee, though." He hoped he sounded more at ease than he felt.

She nodded and walked toward the showers.

Wilks tabbed his boots. Maybe he'd shower after breakfast.

He yawned. Then he followed several of the others down the corridor and into the mess.

Ripley had indeed made coffee, in addition to putting out several trays of food packets and utensils. She sat at one of the long cafeteria tables, poking at her plate of steaming gray muck.

Wilks poured a cup of coffee and grabbed a tray with a foil pouch labeled "stir-fry." He sat down across from Ripley.

"Hey, Ripley. You're up early."

She nodded and watched him pour the contents of his activated packet onto his tray. It smelled like stir-fry, but was the same mottled soypro-gray as Ripley's. He grimaced.

"You'd think they'd invest in some food coloring," she said. "Sleep okay?"

"As well as could be expected. It's the getting out of bed that's a bitch."

She nodded again and went back to eating. Respectful of her silence, Wilks turned and focused his attention on the other crew members who straggled in.

McQuade looked haggard and irritable, and Brewster started in on him.

"Buddha, Cap, you look like shit."

Brewster turned to Carvey. "You know, they say it's harder for the old to travel like this."

McQuade fixed Brewster with a cold stare. "Yeah, well, it would have helped if I could have slept better. The sound of you virgins jacking off the whole time next to me kept me awake."

Carvey snickered.

Brewster tried to think of a comeback and came up short. He stalled, said, "Aw, gee, sorry about that, Cap, I—"

McQuade cut him off. "Yeah, well, your mother's sorry, too. At least that's what she told me when her mouth wasn't full in my quarters back on Gateway."

Even Brewster laughed at this.

Wilks smiled. The corporal was outmatched.

Moto and Falk walked in together and picked up trays.

"What's this?" said Falk. He pointed at a plate of crumbly tan substance.

"Ah, the famed and much-loved military instant corn bread," said Moto, putting a piece on her tray. "You get used to it."

"Like Brewster's mother," said Adcox. She smiled sweetly at Brewster.

He stabbed a chunk of soypro off his plate. "Oh, funny, Adcox."

Wilks was amused by the banter but felt a pang of bitter nostalgia listening to it. Talking the talk was an integral part of the military life; some things hadn't changed. It had been a long time since he had been in a group like this—he could almost hear his old friends talking, their voices superimposed over the *Kurtz*'s crew's. Jasper, Cassady, Ellis, Quinn, Lewis—and as always, he felt the guilt. He was still alive and they were dead.

Billie walked in and pulled her damp hair into a ponytail as she considered the food choices.

Wilks started to call her over when Adcox motioned for her to join her group. Billie waved at Wilks and Ripley as she sat down and started chatting with the other three.

Wilks sipped his coffee and noticed that both of the male soldiers perked up considerably when Billie sat down, Brewster in particular. He grinned at her as Carvey recounted some story involving a trip to a bar on Gateway.

Wilks was surprised by a sudden feeling of protectiveness toward Billie. Brewster wasn't her type, he was sure. She needed someone more mature, she had been through a lot, she needed somebody who could appreciate that—

Like me, he thought uneasily.

Ridiculous. They'd had opportunities before and decided to let them go by. What he felt for Billie was friendship, shared experiences.

But that dream—

Wilks looked away from Billie's group. Good that she had found some people her own age to hang around, finally. And maybe he was just developing some paternal instincts for her. . . .

Yeah. Right.

• • • •

Billie found that she liked Dylan Brewster a lot. He was self-effacing in a mildly sarcastic way, had a bright smile, was very amiable. He and Tom Carvey played off of each other well; their affection for each other was obvious—and in spite of herself, she hoped that it was only brotherly.

She made herself think of Mitch as she listened to them talk, poking at an old wound that suddenly seemed important to feel. Yes, she still missed him, still hurt thinking of him. Ought not to be sitting here thinking about another man.

Jesus, she was having *breakfast* with him, not screwing him. And yet each time Brewster turned his eyes her way she felt a slight tingle in the pit of her stomach.

Billie looked over at Wilks, who stared moodily into his coffee. What was she to him, exactly? Or he to her? She felt bonded to him somehow, some kind of—

Too much to think about. She felt tired already, worrying about relationships not an hour out of sleep. Troubled sleep at that. She had looked for Amy, running through her dreams and never finding her. Amy, she reminded herself, was the important thing.

Ripley stood up and looked around the room. "Excuse me," she said. "Everyone is here, so I'd like to throw out a suggestion."

The room quieted. Billie laid down her fork.

"Thanks. I'm thinking that our dreams might tell us something new this close to the planet," she said. "Maybe a more exact location, maybe numbers of aliens, something. I'd like you all to see if you can remember what you dream tonight, so tomorrow we can talk about it.

"One thing that all of your files showed is that you're highly creative and sensitive people. Spend some time thinking about it. I'm open to ideas, so if you think of anything, let me know."

She sat down again and started talking quietly with Wilks.

"Think of anything like *what*?" said Carvey.

"Do you understand 'idea,' Carv? It's kind of like a thought, but it's newer." Brewster smiled, pleased with himself.

"You wipe. I understand that you're as 'sensitive' as my skivvies—"

Billie tuned out the soldiers' talk and thought about what Ripley had said. She dreaded the dreams, had tried all sorts of meds back on Gateway to avoid them—and now they were going to be stronger, more detailed. She shuddered slightly at the thought. Her earliest memories were of bad dreams. She'd never been able to keep them at bay for long, either. Damn.

Then again, she told herself as she looked around at the pallid faces of the crew, there were worse things than dreams. They'd all found that out; humanity as a whole knew it all too well.

Brewster gave her a smile and she returned it, noting the slight flush in his cheeks. Well. At least she wasn't alone anymore. They were all in this together.

12

Keith Dunston stood in the black lair of the queen. The air was moist and hot; somewhere water dripped and somewhere else it flowed. He was surrounded by soft clicking and chittering, like fingernails tapping upon glass, or impossible creatures rustling in the dark. He knew which it was, and he also knew it was a dream.

He held his hands up in front of his face and counted his fingers. He breathed slowly and evenly; the trick was one he had used before, and in his subconscious wanderings it had always placed him in control. Of course, this was different; this was not of his own mind. But command of the transmission was not necessary, merely command of *himself*.

A huge shadow shifted in front of him, moved closer.

He could just make out her shape—taller than the Earth breed, longer, more powerful and sturdy.

Come to me—

The voice in his mind was inflected with great love and longing. His brain translated her need into something he would understand, would know, had known before.

He closed his eyes and concentrated on a response as he had done before, always to no avail. Perhaps this time—

Where are you? I must find you.

Come to me, I love you, I am waiting—

Yes. Are there others?

Dunston waited, eyes closed. The sounds of the alien breed moving intensified, filled the air. All around him now, they moved closer. Her children. Hundreds, perhaps thousands answered his questions only with their shifting, sliding, greasy motions, making noises like some insane hybrid of locust and wild plains animal.

The dream was different from before, more vivid. He sensed the texture of the nest's floor beneath his feet, felt the heat emanating from the alien construct around him. The smell was overwhelming, rot and decay and vomit and a bathroom with a bad chemical recycler. Even so, the emotional impact of the queen's desire was far greater; it would overwhelm him were he to open himself to it. The mother's love enshrouded him, tried to enter him with all the subtlety of a rapist.

Dunston raised his hands in front of his chest and placed his palms together, index fingers extended. The first of the nine kanji, of Kuji Kiri; Tu Mo, the channel of control . . .

The queen beckoned, a repeated cycle of need as Dunston calmed his heart and mind with the simple gestures. Stillness, now. Motion, action—those would come later.

In the dreams, there was time to be still.

Falk was in the hot, stuffy shithole where *she* and her offspring dwelled. The fucking queen. He had been here before, but this time was different somehow. It looked the same, what he could see of it, but it was—*more*. The air was dank, sweaty, warm glue against his face. It was all alive, the place, the weird moving noises—like he was standing in the belly of some huge beast.

He waited, full of anger and dread, for her to speak.

Come to me—

The hulking darkness in front of him moved, started forward. He raised his arms, hands clenched, and waited for her to come closer. He wanted to destroy, to rip her fucking head off and dance on her bones. Her children had taken Marla away—

Falk felt sadness splash over him, felt it engulf him in its flow like a dark and lonely tide. These brainless, giant fucking insects had ripped his life apart, had made the universe smaller and colder. Why Marla? Why?

I understand—

The voice in his head was simple and calm, full of strength. Not the queen, not the whispery, strange androgynous sound of the queen ... He lowered his hands, suddenly unsure.

"Marla?" he said. His voice was thick and quavering, swallowed in the muggy air. It was impossible.

I love you.

It *was* her voice, the lilt of it familiar and emotional, with that husky undertone he thought he'd never hear again.

He tried to step forward, but his feet wouldn't move. He looked around wildly, but he couldn't see in the murky darkness. Couldn't see if maybe Marla had somehow made it to this hellish place.

Come to me, I'm waiting—

Falk suddenly realized that he wasn't hearing the words aloud, that they were in his mind only. And that his mind was where Marla existed, and nowhere else. The message was the queen's; it was a trick. For one minute he had actually hoped—

His grief and confusion dissipated, were replaced by a searing anger so great that his whole body shook. Everything was tinted red; the blackness rippled and flowed with the new heat of the color.

Falk drew in breath to scream, to cry, to vent his fury and seal the queen's fate, and all of it disappeared and went gray....

Charlene Adcox stood in the queen's steamy chamber and tried to damp down her fear. She was scared, but being scared, she admonished herself, shouldn't stop one from getting things done. Her own mother had told her that many times, and she believed it still. Although her psych visits with Dr. Torchin had helped her see that she suppressed her emotions, was cut off from her feelings. . . .

It wasn't important now. She took in her surroundings, careful to let no detail slip by.

The place she was in was like a sauna, but the heat was wet and foul, the warmth of rot. It was dark, the only light coming from a few cracks in the roof of the nest, far above. There were sounds of water and movement around her, but it was centered . . . behind and to the left, and again beyond her, past where the darkness was thicker.

I need you, I love you—

The queen moved forward, her words echoing in Adcox's mind. With it, as before, came hints of other things, information that was not human. Tangential reference points, telemetry data, star charts seen with tunneled vision and delivered with the strength of utter supremacy. And purpose. It was all much clearer now—

Adcox could feel the emotional force that the queen radiated, but was not pulled by it. The love was huge but impersonal; her own thoughts were stronger, controllable in the chaos of feelings.

I wait for you—

When the queen spoke, Adcox got a sense of where she was, a curving roundness in water. The design was alien, complex but organic, somewhere . . .

The lieutenant concentrated, tried to force the image into geographical planes, but it wouldn't come. The beckoning was meant for different instincts than she could claim, terrifying in its insane pattern.

Suddenly the queen stepped even closer, close enough for Adcox to reach out and touch. Her attempts to put aside her fear vanished.

This isn't supposed to happen—!

Adcox screamed, any illusion of control gone, as the queen lifted a wormy, clawed arm to stroke her. . . .

13

Billie sat in the dining hall next to Char and sipped black coffee. She watched as the others filed in; they all looked like she felt. Dark circles beneath the eyes, pale faces, wired on nervous tension.

She had awakened frightened and angry from the queen's message, amazed at how much more real it had been. She had learned nothing new, except that the planet they would reach the next day was the right one. It had to be—the difference in dream intensity was staggering.

Billie hadn't slept after her dream, and she'd heard Char scream sometime after dawn; their quarters were side by side. She glanced at her friend, worried, but the lieutenant seemed to be holding up. They had sat up together until it was time for the meeting, talking about anything but the dreams.

Wilks was the last to arrive. He looked like he had slept okay; Billie felt a mild surge of envy when she remembered that he wasn't one of the dreamers.

Ripley leaned against one of the tables, arms folded. After Wilks sat, she began to speak.

"Good morning. I can tell nobody slept well, and we all know why. Now I'd like to hear if any of you got anything new from it."

"Well, it's the right planet," said Billie. Everyone else nodded.

"Fuckin' A," said Carvey.

"Good to know," said Ripley. "Adcox—you were the only one who saw *where* before . . ."

"She's got her nest set up in a lake or a swamp," Char said. Her voice was unemotional, dead. "I couldn't tell you where exactly. Someplace warm, obviously. It's rounded, like a dome—at least part of it is. And she's much stronger than the Earth breed."

Dunston nodded. "More powerful in body and intellect," he said. "And she's got an entire legion with her. Hundreds."

Ripley sighed. "Yeah, I was afraid of that. Anyone else get a fix on location?"

Dr. Jones cleared his throat. "She's at the hottest part of the planet. I didn't see the shape of it, but it *is* in some body of shallow water and it's wherever the temperature is most consistently warm."

"Good," said Ripley. "That's good. What else?"

It was quiet. Billie looked around the room. Brewster caught her gaze for a moment and smiled tiredly at her. She wondered how he was doing. He and Carvey remained silent. Falk stared at his hands, expression unreadable. Moto and Tully also looked around and waited for someone to speak.

Wilks stood and broke the tension. "We're close enough to get a good read on planet type, maybe find the hot spots. Tully, you want to do some checking?"

The woman nodded and picked up her coffee cup.

"Okay," Ripley said. "I know it's been rough, but we're going to be there tomorrow and we still need to get ready for a few things. McQuade and I are going to work on some mechanical suits after breakfast and we could use help. Meet down in the loading dock in half an hour."

The meeting was over. Billie didn't feel particularly hungry, but she went to a food dispenser and scanned the selection anyway. Maybe eating would wake her up a little. She punched in some mad scientist's version of eggs and bread. Char followed her.

"So current crisis aside, what are we going to do when we get her to Earth?" Char said. "Anyone thought that far ahead?"

"I don't know. I guess we'll worry about it if we make it that far."

Char chewed at her lip but didn't say anything else.

The food arrived in little sealed biodegradable packages, hot, but ugly.

As Billie choked down her order of scrambled soypro, she thought about Char's question. What were they going to do? Knowing the answers hadn't been a major part of this whole business so far, had it?

Ripley was surprised by McQuade's query.

"Orona's bombs," she said. "Isn't it obvious? They were never set off."

McQuade shrugged. "I don't know about anybody named 'Orona.'"

They had started on the loader suits; the others would be down in a few minutes. They were taking apart the *Kurtz*'s two power loaders in an attempt to make four new ones. Smaller, lighter, less overall protection, but better armor than none. The sounds of their work echoed in the big chamber.

Ripley laid down her wrench and turned to McQuade. "Orona was a government scientist. He conceived a plan to detonate nuclear bombs in the infested areas. He got it set up but then died before they could be triggered."

"Why didn't somebody else do it?"

It was Ripley's turn to shrug. "Some malfunction, maybe. Maybe somebody got cold feet when it came time to push the button. Probably anybody who could say is dead."

McQuade snorted.

"Well, that's why we're here, Captain." She

picked up the wrench and started in on one of the loader's clamps.

"So how did you find out about Orona?" said McQuade.

Ripley unhooked the mechanical arm and set it on the floor. "Common knowledge, or so I thought."

"Yeah. It just seems that the corps would have access to that information, and I never heard of it...."

Ripley gave him a tight grin. "That's the military for you. A group dedicated to making sure nobody gets to know what they know. They hoard little bits of trivia like diamonds and shit steel bricks if anyone finds out—when most people couldn't care less, much less use it for some diabolical purpose." She suddenly remembered who she was talking to. "No offense meant."

"None taken. I agree with you. The marine involvement in this crisis has been poorly organized from the start. Bunch of generals running around and flapping their arms and basically achieving zero. Why I'm here."

They went back to work, setting aside the pieces of machinery to be reassembled later. Ripley liked McQuade. He knew what he was doing and worked quickly and efficiently. At this rate, they'd be half done before anyone showed up. That McQuade didn't know about the bombs, though ...

She tried to recall who had told her about Orona's plan and drew a blank. She had heard it

sometime after the second LV-426 trip but before
Gateway—

Brewster, Carvey, Adcox, and Billie arrived at
the dock and headed toward them.

McQuade raised an eyebrow at Ripley.

"Go ahead," she said. "They *are* marines."

She watched as McQuade gave orders. Billie
sat on the floor and sorted out different-sized
holding pins and screws while the three soldiers
set to work on cannibalizing the second loader.
Power wrenches hummed, the smell of lube and
reluctant-to-move metal hung in the air.

Funny, that McQuade had looked to her before
he ordered the marines. She knew that the crew
thought of her as the leader, but was vaguely surprised that it felt so . . . natural.

She turned her mind back to the project and
made a mental note to ask the others about Orona
after lunch.

Wilks leaned over Tully's shoulder and scanned
the readout on the planet.

"Atmosphere's breathable, but just barely," she
said. "High in contaminants, low in oxygen."

"Could be worse," said Wilks. "Bulking around
out there in a climate suit would be a bitch."

"Plenty of water. Almost eighty percent ocean
and plenty of lakes—nasty, too. Full of trace elements and probably local bugs. Drinking it
wouldn't do you any good."

Wilks leaned closer. Gravity was almost half a
gee higher than Earth's; good thing their crew

was a strong group physically. "Don't drink the water, don't breathe the air?"

"Huh?"

"Old joke. What else?" he said. "Weather, plants, animals—?"

"It's windy," said Tully, "at least in the mountainous regions. Landing should be a thrill. Vegetation must live on heat and poison, 'cause the sun don't shine much through the cloud cover. It won't be pretty. Got to be some animals, though I haven't seen any."

Wilks heard that. Fucking monsters had to eat something. It could be worse—but they were about to set down on a hot, wet, poisoned planet where jogging would be an effort for the strongest of them. To try and overpower the almighty-top-of-the-heap-queen-fucking-head alien on her own ground. Great.

Well, hey. No problem, the marines were lean, mean, and obscene.

Yeah. Right.

"Okay," he said. "See if you can pinpoint the warmest areas for the flyby tomorrow."

He leaned against the wall and watched Tully dig for the information. The mother queen had no doubt picked a charming spot to build her home, and she probably wouldn't want to move without a fight.

Another bad place to die. And as he had thought so many times before, it was probably going to happen this trip. The universe could only pass out so much luck to any one guy and he'd sure as shit gone through his share a long while ago.

Well. What the hell. If it was your turn, there wasn't anything you could do. If it wasn't, he guessed he would find out soon enough.

14

Billie stroked Dylan's hair and watched him sleep; his legs were warm and smooth against her own. She wasn't scared to go to sleep—her fear of the dream lessened with a partner in her bed. Interesting, that sex instilled such a sense of peace. She felt relaxed and calm, but just too introspective to doze off.

He murmured in his sleep and rolled away from her. Dylan Brewster. He had shown up at her door a few hours before and asked if she wanted company. She felt a tiny, delicious shiver run down her spine as she looked at him now, the way he had asked politely to stay the night. Quite the gentleman ... at first, anyway. The sex had been passionate and wild.

Billie remembered having read somewhere that

sex was a normal reaction in threatening circumstances, a life-affirming instinct. That was probably so; she liked the young soldier a lot and was glad to have him there. But she was not in love with him—

She thought of Mitch and was surprised that it didn't hurt so much anymore. Whatever regrets she had over their short time together, it wasn't connected to having made love with Dylan. Mitch had only wanted her to feel loved and whole, whether or not he could be there; she doubted that he would begrudge her some peace of mind now.

In the morning, the crew would meet to discuss final plans for carrying out their mission. They would be dropping onto the planet in a little less than twelve hours. Her stomach tightened at the thought; if everything went perfectly, they could be on their way back to Earth soon afterward. She was nervous, but excited, too. It felt good to be on the offensive for a change, to fight actively instead of always running away. And maybe to make a difference for the people left on Earth ...

Billie moved down beneath the cover, snuggling against her new lover for warmth. He turned toward her and opened his eyes halfway.

"Hey," he said, voice heavy with sleep. "You okay?"

"Yeah. Just thinking."

He yawned and closed his eyes, but smiled slightly.

"What about?" he said, and slid one hand between her legs. She parted them and leaned back.

"I thought you were out for the night," she said, and inhaled sharply as he slipped a finger into her.

"I am. Just ignore me," he said.

Billie laughed and touched his erection, moved her hand up and down the silky-textured skin. He moaned as she crawled over him, covering his body with hers. She felt him slide deep inside, thrust herself against him to find her own pleasure, felt her climax build and stretch toward release.

This is life, she thought, and cried out.

Ripley stood in the loading dock and looked at the people assembled in front of her, watched them absorb the information that Tully and Wilks laid out. They were in orbit around what sounded like hell.

The *Kurtz* would land and drop off the APC, in which some of them would go check things out, then report back. Everyone agreed that it was the best action before coming up with a final plan. To be certain of what they were up against.

Must be getting mellow with age, she thought. There was a time there when waiting to do anything would have been out of the question.

Moto had suggested sending a robot probe first, but the motion had been vetoed. Not a bad idea, but what probes they had were severely limited. It wouldn't pay to get the wrong idea, and if the bot you sent couldn't see very well or smell the alien stink, that might give you a false sense of security.

Ripley had to smile at that. Security. Right.

Wilks and Tully wrapped up their presentation and turned to look at Ripley. She knew what was expected of her.

"Well," she said. "Anyone dream of the queen last night?"

The crew members looked at each other and shook their heads. Apparently nobody had.

"Does that mean she knows we're here?" said Adcox.

"Maybe so. Or it could just mean that she overshot us. Hard to say."

Adcox nodded, as did several of the others.

"You know about this place," Ripley said. "I wouldn't ask anyone to do anything I'm not prepared to do myself, so I'll be on that APC—and I'm asking for volunteers. Most of you have been in combat situations, but some of you are physically stronger and have a better chance out there. You need to make the decision, not me.

"However, some of you will have to stay onboard the ship. Tully—you're our computer whiz, you stay here."

"I figured as much," Tully said. She tried to sound disappointed, but Ripley could see her relax a little.

Ripley continued. "McQuade and Brewster—as pilots, I don't see how we can risk losing either of you, since I'll be down there—"

Brewster cut in. "Hey, I'm ready for this! McQuade can fly the ship, I—"

"Look, I'm not saying you're not capable, Brewster. We need you here. Besides, there has to be somebody to pick up the pieces if we fuck up. Got it?"

"Yeah," he said, in a tone of voice that said he didn't get it at all.

Tough shit, thought Ripley.

"Jones, you stay here, too."

The doctor shrugged. "You might need me there," he said.

"That's true. But if we get hurt, we can use the aid kits. Better you're here where you can do major repairs in relative safety when we get back." *If we get back*, Ripley said to herself.

Falk stood up. "I'm going," he said.

Ripley had assumed that he would volunteer. She nodded at him. "Okay, Falk. Welcome a-board."

Dunston and Carvey stood at the same time. Adcox rose, as did Billie. Wilks stepped away from Tully and joined the others, followed by Ana Moto.

Ripley held up a hand. "Stop there," she said. "Like I said, we need a backup crew in case anything happens to us. And if we all go, there's no room for weapons. Moto, you stay; you're probably the best strategist. Billie—"

"I'm going," she said, voice calm.

The determination in the young woman's eyes was firm. Ripley hesitated, then nodded.

"All right," she said.

She turned to McQuade and gave him the go-ahead. He walked to the front of the group and started to explain how the loader suits worked.

Ripley looked at her crew. Good people, all of them. This could work, it just might work.

It *had* to work.

Wilks stood in the control room with McQuade, Brewster, and Tully, and watched them look at the readings on landing sites. They were twenty minutes from drop and he could feel adrenaline seep into his system when he looked through the shield. Once more he was going to face off with the monsters. As long as there were any of them left, or he could still breathe, that was gonna keep happening, but it didn't seem to get any easier. You'd think he'd be used to it by now.

Brewster picked up a cluster of erratic movement in the southern hemisphere, which coincided with Tully's reading of warmest temperature. They would head there first. No one was betting whether or not *she* would be there; everyone seemed to know.

The meeting had continued for a while after the APC team selection had been made. McQuade demonstrated the makeshift suits and Ripley gave a rundown on the scientist, Orona. Wilks had known about Orona and his bombs, as had Ana Moto. Funny—Ripley had seemed relieved that they knew.

It looked like a rough ride going down, and it would be pretty stupid if one of them got whacked by a coffee cup someone forgot to put away, so they policed the ship and dogged down everything loose.

Wilks had seen how Billie and Brewster had

looked at each other during the meeting, and again during load. He couldn't ignore those glances, and he had a pretty good idea what they meant.

Well, it wasn't his business. Then again, he couldn't ignore how it made him feel. That Billie and the corporal had made love—the thought of it made him grit his teeth. It felt ... it was uncomfortable, although he couldn't pin down why exactly. Billie was a big girl, he didn't need to watch out for her—

That he thought about it now, a few minutes before they were to embark on the queen's home, was stupid. As if he didn't have enough to worry about. He shook his head a little and concentrated on the computer landscape in front of him. They were about to fly into a big fucking mess and he needed to be all the way there for it. Not concerned about Billie's sex life ...

With effort, he pushed everything else out of his mind and took a deep breath. It was time to get down to business here, time to do what had to be done. Everything else was secondary. It was gonna be kick ass or get it kicked and either way, he was ready.

Semper fi, motherfuckers, and the devil take the last guy out of the trenches.

15

Moto pulled off her protective goggles and turned to Ripley.

"If that doesn't hold it shut, nothing will," she said.

Moto had just finished welding braces around one of the hold's two exit hatches. McQuade was still working on the other one. Ripley stood with her arms crossed and waited for the alloy's glow to die down. The air stank of burned metal and plastic.

They were going in a few minutes and the tension of the crew showed in their tight expressions, but Ripley felt surprisingly calm.

McQuade snapped off his welder. "Done," he said, a little too loudly.

Ripley nodded at him. She had thought she

would be a lot jumpier by now; her relaxed state was almost disconcerting. But it wasn't a lack of concern, it was more like . . .

Fulfillment, she thought. *Being where I'm supposed to be.*

After she checked the hatches, Ripley followed the other two back to the upper deck. The hatches looked solid enough and were certainly the best they could do—but this wasn't some drone. She would have to hope that the queen bitch wasn't going to be too much for them to handle. She had dealt with ordinary queens, and they were bigger, stronger, and meaner than drones. She hoped the queen of queens wasn't that much worse.

No matter. It was what they had.

Now the crew strapped into their seats.

Billie offered her a quick and nervous smile as Ripley walked to the front and around the control area's partition.

Brewster sat in pilot one, Tully behind him.

Wilks adjusted a strap on one of the secondary chairs.

Ripley moved up to pilot two and sat.

Wilks looked at her. "Hey, Ripley. We ran a matrix on the movement in the southern hemisphere, in case we have to land there—"

"No, 'in case,'" she said. "She's there. You know it."

Wilks shook his head and grinned. "Okay, *probably*. We'll know soon enough. Anyway, Tully picked up rock formations like you wouldn't believe. It's going to be tricky. There's a little wind, too."

Brewster turned from the console and nodded at Wilks. "If it was easy, anybody could do it. Besides, topography's the APC's problem. All I gotta do is drop you off."

Ripley let the bitterness slip past. Brewster was obviously still pissed that he wasn't going to attend their scouting party.

"Yeah, but flying it's going to be a bitch. Glad you're at the helm, Brewster. Hotshot like you shouldn't have too many problems."

Brewster didn't reply, but Ripley saw him relax slightly. Good. They were going into harm's way and the last thing she needed was a smarmy pilot.

Tully spoke up. "Carvey and I sectored the APC's comlink," she said, "so you don't have to worry about scattering."

"Great," said Ripley. She looked at the readouts in front of her and felt her hands start to clench. The lack of tension she'd felt wasn't going to last now that there was nothing left to do but sit and wait.

"I guess we're ready," she said.

"Good thing," said Brewster, " 'cause here we go, bearing oh-six—"

The rest of his words seemed to fade as he punched a button and they fell out of space.

Billie gripped the armrests of her chair, eyes tightly closed. Her stomach was knotted in the usual lurch of free-fall. This was a feeling she didn't think she'd ever get used to. She imagined the *Kurtz* shooting through the heavy clouds, pummeled by the rains and—

Scratch that, she thought as she felt nausea rise up. She searched for a more pleasant thought. *Last night with Dylan, the closeness, the touching, the rolling and pumping, over and over, falling forever*—oh Lord, scratch that, too.

The ship suddenly seemed to catch up to her twisted belly. Not an easy drop, but the worst had to be over. She opened her eyes. She hoped the worst was over.

Char smiled at her shakily. "Not dead yet," she said.

Billie nodded and looked over at the nearest port. Nothing to see; they were still too high.

Wilks leaned his head around the partition, expression tense. "Local winds look to be pushing 130 knots," he said. "And that's down below the jet stream. Better button up before it gets rough."

At the sound of his voice, Billie felt her guts tighten. *So much for the worst being over.*

She fought down a rising sense of dread.

She felt that her entire life had been spent in preparation for this moment. She believed in this, was ready to risk her neck for it—for Amy, for Ripley and Wilks and the others. They all had their own reasons. Duty. Honor. She looked over at Falk, at his blank face—he had vengeance. It wasn't the thought of death that frightened her, it was the uncertainty.

The flight smoothed out, became almost calm.

Carvey and Falk unbuckled and moved to one of the ports.

What the hell, Billie thought, and stood to join them.

They broke out of the cloud cover into the most desolate place Billie had ever seen. The *Kurtz* moved too fast to get a good look, but as far as she could tell, it was all the same.

Pools of shallow gray water stretched for klicks, broken up and surrounded by dirty humps of rock. Clumps of colorless vegetation, much of it apparently fungal, towered at the edges of the water. Some strange variety of beige moss seemed to cover everything. They passed a copse of the bizarre plant life, which struck Billie as the work of an insane sculptor. Twisted limbs and vines branched off into the air and pulsed slightly in the winds that shook the ship. Off in the distance, Billie saw impossibly-tall stands of rock scattered randomly in the endless dark sea. Nice place. She turned away.

"We'd better head down to the APC," she said.

"Right," said Carvey. He started toward the stairs, followed by Falk and Dunston.

Jones walked back toward medical.

Billie stood still for a moment, tried to prepare herself.

"You okay?" Char asked.

Billie looked at her friend, saw the concern on the lieutenant's face.

"Yeah. Just getting my nerve up."

As Billie walked behind Char to the lower level, she couldn't stop the fear from welling up. That they were all just part of some huge plan; that their sense of purpose was fake. That maybe they hadn't really come of their own accord, but had been lured by the dreams ...

"Buddha, what a great place," said Brewster. "Maybe I'll take my vacation here." He navigated the *Kurtz* through the strange environment. Crosswinds buffeted the vessel hard enough to rock it.

Wilks stared. Yeah, this was without a doubt the most god-awful planet he'd ever seen. He could almost feel the thick wetness of the air around the ship, smell the dead chemical odor of the alkaline water. Just looking at this nightmare gave him the creeps.

Brewster interrupted his thoughts. "I got a spot scoped where it seems relatively calm, not far from the main cluster of movement."

No one spoke for a minute.

"Take it or leave it, folks—I can't dick around for long in this damn wind," said Brewster.

"Take it," said Ripley, and stood up. "Come on, Wilks, let's go back with the grunts."

Tully smiled at them as they headed down the stairs. "Luck," she said.

Brewster struggled with the controls but managed a thumbs-up.

The others were crowded around the APC in the dock. Wilks motioned for the rest of the crew to get on, and boarded last.

He watched everyone strap in before he moved to the front. Billie sat at the console; she would monitor outside activity as they got closer to the motion Brewster had picked up.

A voice crackled out over the intercom.

"Hey, kids, almost there," said Brewster. "Tully says the movement has stopped, but it seemed to be coming from a formation almost due west from where we're dropping you—that's a two-seven-two heading, to be exact."

"Rock formation?" said Billie.

"Negative. Looks organic. Listen, Carvey, you still owe me money, so be careful, okay? Goes for the rest of you, too."

"Got it," said Billie.

"Thanks, Brewster," Wilks said. "On your go."

Wilks keyed the controls for the machine and checked the navigational. Everything looked fine. The mobile unit was built like a chunk of lead on wheels, designed to move over any terrain, if not comfortably, at least efficiently. The front view-screen gave a good shot of the outside; currently, the inside of the dock. There was also a small kleersteel shield that offered a more limited view.

There were recoilless guns mounted on the pivotal up top, as well as in the front. This was supposed to be a check—with any luck, he wouldn't have to use them.

"Stand by," said Brewster, in a burst of static.

Wilks tensed, ready.

The *Kurtz* touched down. Wilks rolled his head with the sudden impact, felt the planet surface grind and crunch beneath the ship. The APC slid forward as the deck dropped out on metal struts, the hatch opening outward.

"Go!"

Wilks grabbed the control stick and eased the

APC off the extended ramp and into the water.
There were scattered rocks and weird vegetable
growths here and there, but essentially they were
looking at an ocean less than a meter deep. Here,
anyway. It surrounded them in every direction as
far as he could see. Wind rippled the surface into
a shifting washboard, occasional gusts blowing
spray from the tiny whitecaps.

The APC's rear wheels pulled off the deck and
they settled into the liquid with scarcely a bump.

"Good job," said Wilks. "We're down. And welcome to town, folks."

"And *we* are outta here," said Brewster.

The sounds of the ship as it lifted were loud
even inside the APC. Brewster and the others
would head back up, above the winds, and wait
for the pickup call.

If there's anybody left to send it, thought Wilks.
There was something wrong, he felt it in his gut;
but they were there, and it was time.

"Let's go see if the queen's home," he said.

The APC rumbled forward.

16

From the position of the cam on the APC, it was nearly impossible to tell exactly what it was they were headed toward. The screen showed nothing but water and sky, close enough in color to be nearly indistinguishable. It was like moving through a void.

Billie mostly kept her gaze on the motion sensors and the Doppler screen, where she had something to report: "We got six roughly spherical objects, approximately twenty meters apart and arranged in a circle. Largest measures maybe thirty meters high; it's centered inside the others," she said.

"Sounds like Adcox's nest," said Wilks.

"Yeah," Billie said. She pushed her hair off her sweaty forehead. The APC's coolers could only do so much against the wet heat of the planet that pressed in on them.

They wobbled and bumped as the APC made its way slowly through the water.

"Level, my ass," Wilks said. "I'd like to see Brewster's idea of rough terrain."

It all felt like a dream to Billie, and her heart thumped hard and loud enough she was surprised nobody noticed.

"Wilks—this is supposed to be a scouting trip, right? Why are we headed straight to her nest? Shouldn't we find somewhere safer, to observe—"

"Look around. Where would you suggest?"

"I'm just saying that we can scope things out a little more thoroughly, try a probe—"

"Listen, kid, we're not going to drive this thing into her front door, we're just going to pull up nearby and see what happens, okay? If the probes we had were worth a shit, I'd send one, but none of the robots we got can do the job."

Billie nodded, but continued to worry. "It doesn't feel good, Wilks," she said.

His lips tightened. "Yeah," he said. "I copy that."

Billie sighed. She and Wilks had been here before. Not this place, but this kind of situation. Somehow that felt a little comforting. Between the two of them, they'd pulled off some pretty scary deals. "ETA, two minutes," she said.

"We'll be ready," Ripley called out from behind her.

Billie wanted to go back and talk to Ripley

about her fear. Maybe there was some kind of psychic thing going on.

Suddenly the APC ground to a halt with a jarring crunch. The unit tilted to the left, throwing Billie back into her chair.

"What the fuck—?" began Falk.

Ripley held up her hand for silence. "Wilks, Billie, what do we have?"

Billie ran the diagnostic. "We bent one of the aft axle struts, but I think that's it," said Billie. Her voice sounded shaky.

"What did we hit?" said Adcox.

Wilks called out over his shoulder. "Don't know. Something underwater; treads lifted and we lost traction. Hang on, let me see if we can rock back off it."

The APC's engines rumbled. It took a few seconds, but Wilks managed to pull free of the obstruction. "Okay, we're clear." Then, "Take a look at the screen."

Ripley looked up at the vid screen and inhaled sharply as the picture panned left.

"Oh, my God," Adcox said.

They were less than a hundred meters from a huge, round orb sitting in the murky water, pinkish gray in color, with strange lines crisscrossing the surface.

Like veins, thought Ripley.

A long, thick cord connected it to another orb, larger. The one they were closest to was the length of the APC and maybe twice as high.

"I think we ran over something connected to that thing," said Wilks.

"Billie, is anybody home?" Ripley asked.

"No movement. If they're around, they must be asleep. Look, I think we should back off a little. I don't feel so great about this."

Ripley frowned. "We're here. If they heard that knock and they're still not coming, I think we'll be all right for a minute."

They all watched the screen with intense concentration.

Nothing happened.

Ripley half-expected to see a horde of the giant insects launch themselves from behind the weird orbs and attack. She looked at Billie; the girl was watching the sensor readouts closely.

No movement ...

It was Falk who broke the silence. "Let's go have a peek, what say?" He stood, picked up a comset, hooked it over the back of his head, and reached for a boot to one of the mechano suits.

Dunston also stood.

Ripley shook her head. "I think we should wait, maybe nudge one of them with the APC first," she said. "We don't know what we're dealing with here."

Falk continued to suit up. "Isn't that why we came?" he said. "To find out?"

Carvey got up and helped Dunston buckle on one of the lift boots before he grabbed a third suit.

"It's a good idea," said Carvey. "We'll just hop out and have a look. We've got weapons, we're armored, and the APC's right here. We're out there five minutes, tops."

Ripley thought about it. They knew what the aliens were capable of; they weren't going to be charging out there ignorant of what could happen. And Carvey had a point—they were as prepared as they were going to get. It was no crazier than the whole mission, which made less sense every time she thought about it.

"Okay," she said.

"No," said Billie from behind them. "Ripley, don't let them go, this isn't going to work. Can't you feel it?"

Dunston stepped forward, awkward in the suit. Hydraulics whined, the boots clumped heavily as he moved. "Billie," he said, his voice calm. "This is a choice. We made the decision to come here. This is part of it."

Something in his face, perhaps the acceptance of fate, stopped Billie from protesting any further. She turned and moved back to the front without another word.

The three men, fully suited, stood by the door and looked to Ripley for their cue. They each wore thick vests with head protectors, jointed metal running the length of their limbs. Each carried standard military carbines, the same 10mm caseless weapons Ripley had learned to use.

"Listen to your sets," she said. "Billie is monitoring the cluster. Any sign of trouble, get back here; we don't want any dead heroes. Good luck."

She paused for a moment. *What else is there to say?* Nothing.

"Go," she said.

The hatch slid open.

Wilks felt the blast of damp heat as the door slid shut. The smell was like he'd imagined, but worse—like rotten, poisoned food. The wind made the exposed edges of the hatch whistle.

He breathed through clenched teeth and watched the screen. Billie was pallid and tense beside him, but she also watched the readouts carefully.

Wilks wished he were out there with the others, but he tried to let it go. He was the best APC driver they had, and if anything went wrong they'd want to leave in a hurry.

"Falk, talk to me," he said.

"We're moving toward it, maybe thirty meters away now. We'll stay on this side of it." Falk's transmission was clear.

"Christo, it fucking *stinks*," said Carvey. "You're missing out, Sarge."

"What are you bitching about? At least you can breathe."

"Wish I'd thought to bring a kite. Wind must be gusting to a hundred klicks out here."

"One-fifteen," Wilks said.

He watched as the three men appeared at the bottom of the viewscreen. "Okay, now we got you on visual," he said.

One of the figures turned and waved. "Hi, Ma!"

Wilks grinned. "Knock that shit off, Carvey,

you're supposed to be part of a crack scouting team here."

Trying to be funny to break the tension seemed a little strained, but it was something.

The figures approached the sphere. Their boots rose and fell in the muck that came up to their knees, spatters of it blowing away in the gusts.

They separated a few meters from the orb; Falk remained in front while Dunston and Carvey moved to the sides.

"Don't get too far apart," said Wilks. The three men stopped. "Stay in sight of each other."

"There's goop all over this thing," said Carvey. "Like, uh—jelly."

"Seems to be emanating from the formation's core." That from Dunston.

"What *are* these things?" Carvey said. "They're too big to be egg sacs. . . . I *hope* they're too big to be egg sacs. Whatever the hell it is, it's oozing like a sonofabitch. I can almost see inside—" He raised a mechanical limb to touch it.

Billie gasped and Wilks felt his heart catch.

"Oh, fuck, movement!" she said.

"Everybody get out of there *now*!" Wilks shouted.

"It's coming from inside the pods!" said Billie into the com. "Move, get away!"

The three figures on the screen stumbled back as the nearest pod opened like a giant egg sac and a huge, glistening shape rose from out of it.

Adcox cried out from behind them. A queen-sized drone, bigger than any Wilks had ever seen, snapped out one powerful claw so fast Carvey hardly saw it move and latched on to his head protector.

The monster raised Carvey into the air like a child with a toy.

"Falk, Jesus, get it off, get it off me—!"

Carvey's cries were cut off abruptly as the drone used its other claw and ripped his throat out. The creature tossed the handful of flesh away and pulled one of Carvey's arms off. Tossed that away, too.

Oh, fuck—!

So goddamned fast!

Dunston and Falk had barely gotten their weapons raised.

"We're coming!" Ripley yelled into her 'com, but the two men were already slogging quickly backward toward the APC. "Go, Wilks! I'm on the guns!"

Falk blasted at the drone. It dropped Carvey, screamed, and started toward him, hissing, then fell into the water as Dunston's carbine joined the fire. They might be bigger and faster than normal drones, but they could die.

Wilks jammed the APC into full throttle.

Billie slammed her fist against the console. "Fuck, oh fuck, the other pods!"

Ripley was bringing the APC's guns online when she heard Billie.

"Come *on!*" she shouted to Wilks.

The APC lurched forward—only to hit another stop. The engine whined noisily.

"Dunston!" It was Falk yelling.

Ripley looked up at the viewscreen as an alien leaped *over* one of the pods and pounced at the teacher. He fell onto his back with a splash, absorbed the shock of the huge drone, and slammed his weapon into its belly—

Falk struggled to get a clear shot as the APC suddenly moved forward again—

"Die!" shouted Dunston.

Nothing happened. His weapon must have jammed. He raised his free arm, used the mechanical clamp to hold the alien's head away from his own—

It shrieked and opened its gigantic jaws. With a jerk, it shoved its head forward.

The steel armor crumpled like paper as its inner mouth snapped out and speared Dunston's face. Bright red splashed into the water and the teacher fell limp.

"Motherfucker!" yelled Falk, and opened up on the drone. The crash of gunfire shredded the alien. The area around the fallen creature hissed and bubbled as its blood ate the water. What fell on Dunston didn't matter.

Falk disappeared from the screen as the APC came to a stop.

"Wilks!" shouted Ripley.

"Don't make me knock, for Christ's sake!" said Falk through the 'com.

Adcox stood behind the door, weapon raised. Billie slammed the entry button and Falk fell inside, gasping.

"Close it!" he said.

Ripley caught a glimpse of one of the creatures

moving quickly through the muck. She put the gun tracker on it—

Billie slammed the hatch button again. "Come on—!"

The monster loped closer, its limbs splashing the foul water against the front of the APC—

Ripley said, "Too close to shoot, it'll spatter all over the APC—!"

The hatch closed.

"Emergency dustoff, now!" said Billie. She held her comlink headset in place with shaky fingers.

"We can't put down at your current position," said Brewster. His voice was anguished. "We got a force three hurricane wind aloft right there. Get away from the nest, get back closer to the initial drop point!"

"Shit!" Billie said.

"Billie, are you okay? Where's—"

"No time, Brewster," said Wilks. "Get moving. We'll be there ASAP."

Billie discommed and turned to Wilks. The aliens were so much bigger and stronger than before—

Before she could speak, something hammered against the APC wall, hard enough to dent metal.

Billie scanned the readouts. "Three of them," she said.

The entire unit was lifted and tipped backward, before it fell forward with a crash. The vid screen went black and mud splashed the kleersteel window. Metal groaned. Something snapped with a bell-like crack.

"Wilks," Billie said, in barely a whisper. She looked at the readout without blinking, hoped that it was wrong.

"Our internal cooling system just opened—" Even as she watched, the temperature was going up. "It's going to get hot in here. Crappy warranty on these things."

Wilks checked the monitor. "Ripley, we got some problems up here."

There was no answer.

Ripley belted the vest and nearly fell when the APC tipped. She picked up Falk's gun and checked the ammo read. Wilks shouted something at her as she searched the floor for additional magazines. Everything was rolling; the clips slid under the supply compartment.

"Ripley!" yelled Wilks again.

She walked to the front in the bulky suit. Falk and Adcox leaned against the wall that faced the door, weapons ready.

"Fuck this," said Falk. "Let's burn outta here."

Wilks turned around in his seat. He looked Ripley up and down. "Jesus," he said. "You're crazy."

"Just head for the drop site—"

"Can't. The manuals are shot, steering just about locked. Our reactor took a knock—we can go straight for about ten minutes and then we're talking meltdown. Got any ideas?"

"Yeah," said Ripley. "Use the APC's guns and hammer those three outside; won't matter if the acid damages the APC now. Seal the hatch and take off full speed as soon as I'm out. I need a couple minutes to get to her nest."

"And what are you going to do when you get there? Invite her to fucking tea?" said Wilks.

"I didn't come this far just to let her slip away," said Ripley. "If I can't capture her, I can kill her. I have to try. Listen, it's been good working with you—"

"You are fucking crazy," said Billie.

Ripley grinned and walked back to the rear hatch of the APC. Adcox followed, prepared to cover her.

Wilks triggered the APC's guns. One of them was still operable. The uranium slugs shattered the attacking aliens. "Clear," he said. "At the moment."

"Good luck," Ripley said.

The hatch opened and Ripley jumped out.

17

I'm showing several forms moving at high speed toward the APC," Billie said. Her mouth was dry. In spite of the heat, she felt cold all over. The blips on the screen wavered and jumped, moved closer.

"I guess that means Ripley's plan is working," she said.

Wilks didn't spare her a glance as he wrestled with the controls. "Reactor halfway to critical, APC's about to be overcome by superbugs—yeah, I'd say it's working. Any better and we could blow our brains out now and save those bastards the trouble."

"Should I call the *Kurtz* again?"

"Not yet. We give Ripley her five-plus and keep

going till this sucker suffers from a complete engine or axle lock."

"Then?" She turned to look at him. Her vision was blurred from sweat.

"Haven't gotten that far yet," he said.

The APC rocked. Billie looked back at the sensor and then screamed.

"Jesus—" said Wilks. A giant, dripping alien grin appeared on the other side of the kleersteel. The creature lifted huge, clawed hands up to the window, and with a muffled shriek plunged its head through the shield. The clear metal shattered inward, sprayed everywhere as the alien reached for Billie—

Ripley fell into the shallow water, grunted, and jumped up into a crouch. She tried to look in all directions at once, managed one; there was no immediate danger.

She didn't believe that the drones would have left their queen unprotected, but the only motion around her was the gently swaying ocean.

Doesn't mean it's going to stay that way . . .

All of her senses were in overdrive. The putrid odor of the planet, combined with the heat and gravity, made her dizzy. Along with the fading sound of the APC, there was only the slosh of the water against her legs. The fierce winds had suddenly dwindled to almost nothing.

An alien's cry echoed through the dead air, but it came from the direction of the retreating transport.

She turned and faced the cluster of nests.

"It's just you and me, now," she said.

Wilks grabbed for his weapon.

The creature already had its claws on Billie. It hissed, its decayed breath filling the air as Wilks came up with his carbine. Everything was mired in time, creaking forward in slow motion and thick gravity....

Too late, too late, his brain chanted.

The explosion thundered in his ears. The drone seemed to fly backward with a cry of rage and pain. Acid spattered, bubbled and smoked on the shards of kleersteel.

Adcox stepped forward, weapon extended. The alien was gone.

"Oh, *shit*," said Billie.

"Okay?" said Adcox.

Billie looked down at her ripped shirt and then back at the lieutenant. "Yeah."

Wilks exhaled heavily and checked the motion sensor. "One down," he said.

Hot, noxious air washed over them. Billie had a small cut on her left arm from the kleersteel, but that was it. That they hadn't been drenched with the bug's acid was amazing....

Time to think about it later, Wilks told himself. He glanced at the APC readout to see the core temperature still rising.

"Keep your eye on that thing," he said.

If there is a later, he thought.

• • •

Ripley slowly splashed toward the orbs. She heard shots in the distance.

"Bet we got one of your babies," she said. Her muscles were sore from the gravity; it felt like a hundred kilos had been strapped to each limb. Even breathing was an effort. But she could *feel* the queen, the powerful aura of the bitch—

Water splashed behind her. Ripley spun, raised her weapon—

The drone was still twenty meters away. It screamed, opened its jaws—

Ripley pulled the trigger, fired a quick burst at the massive target's chest. The running creature stopped dead, its abdomen peeled outward by the explosive force of the rounds. It fell into the water, hissing like a punctured air tank. The wave motion rocked Ripley's legs and she fought to maintain balance. The noise of the shots hurt her ears. Should have worn plugs—

Another shriek to her left. She turned again. This one was closer and moved at incredible speed, even in the heavy gravity.

She fired twice.

The giant alien fell backward, its taloned feet in the air for a second before it rolled over. The thing's jointed tail flailed up and then lashed into the water before it lay still. Speckles of liquid splashed Ripley's face.

She crouched for a minute and listened: only the sizzle of alien blood as it dispersed into the water.

She faced the nest.

"Is that the best you can do?" she said, breathing hard. "Those are your chosen protectors?"

Silence.

"Why don't you show yourself?" Ripley whacked the arm of her mechanical suit against one of the connecting cords. It rippled and swayed slightly. She felt a bitter anger rise up. . . .

"What the fuck is this? Why don't you come out here and tell me?"

She hit the cord again and moved closer to the center orb.

"Explain the crew of the *Nostromo*. The *Sulaco*. Explain Earth! Explain my *daughter*, you bitch!"

Ripley waited, breathing hard.

Suddenly, the huge sphere jerked. The translucent goo quivered. A long crack appeared at the top of the thing, pulsing slightly. It started opening.

Ripley tapped her 'com, never taking her eyes off of the nest. "*Kurtz*, this is Ripley," she said quickly. "Zero my position and get your asses here."

Brewster's fuzzy voice spoke into her ear. "I told Wilks, the wind—"

"The wind has died down. Get that ship over my coordinates, *now*."

As she spoke, a blackness started to move up from the orb. A glossy, elongated shape, a skull easily two meters in length, raised up. Three clawed digits wrapped over the lip of the crack, and then another three. The queen slowly pulled herself up. She hissed at Ripley, drool falling from her jaws as she unfurled herself from her home.

The queen. The mama of all mamas. Come to receive her visitor.

She was at least eight meters long, her whipping, bony tail making her eight more. Her comb was sleek and wet. Several of her vertebrae arched outward like spines, ran down her back like a row of fingers. She had four arms. She was the biggest living creature Ripley had ever seen, taller than the elephant she'd seen in the zoo as a kid. Jesus.

The queen ducked her head forward and down, craned her obscene skull to get a better look at what had disturbed her.

"That's right," said Ripley. She backed away from the advancing creature. "Come on out and have a look."

"Core temperature's going up. Meltdown in— seven minutes," said Billie. Her body was still shaking, but she had managed to control the worst of it.

"We're talking more than meltdown," said Wilks. "When that core burns through to the liquid fuel chamber, we're looking at an explosion."

"Gee, and everything's been going *great* so far," Char said.

Wilks pushed at the controls and then sighed. "Well, the engine and the wheels still work," he said. "That means this thing probably keeps rolling until it blows. Time to leave this party; we'll have to make the drop site on foot."

"That's *fucked*," Char said.

"Take all the ammunition you can carry and move out. Unless you want to cook here."

"New readings at the outer perimeter," Billie said.

She squinted at the motion sensor and then tapped the side of it, hard. "There's a *wall* of them, Wilks!"

Even as she spoke, a dozen or so lights flashed on the screen.

"What—?" Char said. "They're running past us!"

"Mama is calling her children," Wilks said.

Billie could barely fathom the number of moving creatures it would take to give that reading.

"There must be thousands," she said. Her stomach knotted tighter. "Ripley."

"She'll do what she has to," said Wilks. He stood and walked to the back.

Billie and Char both looked through the open shield for a few seconds, the choking air fetid against their faces. The army of drones moved toward them like a sheet of rain, closer and closer. Dozens ran past the APC, headed back to the queen. Billie could hear their shrieks over the rising whine of the transport.

"It's almost certain suicide to get out," Char said. "And what happened to the nice breeze we had?"

"We *know* it's suicide to stay," Billie said. "Maybe the bastards are on autopilot or something and they won't even notice us."

Without another word, they walked back to Falk and Wilks. The two men handed them loaded weapons and extra clips. They all moved to the rear hatch.

"Conserve ammo," said Wilks, "and fire only at targets coming at us. Stay close."

Billie searched for something to say, some last words, but there was nothing. Wilks hit the button and jumped, slipped, landed on his shoulder with a splash.

A chorus of howls went up all around the APC as Billie took a breath and leaped.

Ripley continued to back away from the hissing queen. It seemed like a long fucking time before she heard a noise that drowned the bitch out.

The sound of the *Kurtz* moving in overhead was sweet music.

"We'll bring her in as low as we can," crackled Brewster through her 'com, "and then—holy *shit.*"

"Quite the prize," said Ripley. "Open the containment chamber and get close to me."

"Yeah," said Brewster. "But if that wind picks up again . . ."

The queen refocused her attention on the thundering ship. She backed away from Ripley a step and let out a high-pitched, mewling noise.

"Pretty ship," said Ripley. "See the nice, pretty ship." She darted her gaze quickly to the descending *Kurtz* and then back to the queen. "Bitch want to go for a ride on the pretty ship?"

The queen didn't offer a reply.

"Closer, Brewster, come *on.*"

The queen took another step backward,

wagged her huge head, looked at Ripley, then the ship.

The *Kurtz*'s cargo bay was directly over her, the hatch open. Keeping her weapon pointed at the queen, Ripley held her other arm up. The clamp on the suit opened and then closed on metal.

She pulled herself up. It took a tremendous effort. Her arm felt like it was going to jerk out of its socket, even with the suit's augmentation.

The alien watched but didn't try to follow her.

As big as the ship was, Ripley couldn't believe the monster was afraid. Curious, perhaps, but the goddamned things never seemed to be afraid of anything.

Ripley sidled into the dock on her elbows, scrabbled forward on her knees.

She stood and looked down at the queen.

The creature hissed at her. All of her metallic teeth glinted wetly in the dim light.

Ripley smiled. "Perfect, Brewster. Hold here for a minute."

She retrained her weapon at the closest orb and fired.

The queen screamed as pieces of her nest flew. Ripley kept the trigger depressed, sent a steady stream of bullets into the orb. Bits of the weird, fleshy material dropped into the water and sank.

She released the trigger. The queen turned from the remains of her broken home and howled in anger. She looked at Ripley.

She knows I'm doing it, Ripley thought. Knows

what a gun is even though she's never seen one before.

Watch this.

Ripley aimed at the next orb and opened fire. With a shriek, the queen leaped at her.

Ripley stumbled backward as the queen extended her huge claws toward the slick alloy. The alien grasped at the edge of the door's frame and caught hold.

"Up, now, up!" Ripley screamed into the 'com.

The *Kurtz* lifted.

The queen pulled herself into the dock as Ripley ran toward the inner door.

"Seal the outer hatch!"

The queen screamed a sound of absolute fury as she started toward Ripley.

Ripley spun back to look at the queen and the nearly closed hatch. She had to be sure—

The queen's dark tail lashed out and the tip of it reached Ripley by the door. It thrashed down, thumped against the protecting bars of the mechano suit, bent the metal and stacked carbon fibers, smashed into Ripley's skull. The force of the blow knocked her sprawling.

The chamber washed out. Tiny bursts of light flashed around the howling alien. Ripley shook her head as the queen turned away from her, leaped at the hatch, and pounded on it. The trapped monster screamed for her freedom.

The shrill sound faded as Ripley scrabbled backward and the world went to gray.

●   ●   ●

Wilks, Billie, Adcox, and Falk stood in a circle and faced outward. Scores of the drones loped past them without stopping, splashed through the shallow water toward their mother. If the cloying, chemical stench of rot, the heavy air, and the heat weren't bad enough, hundreds of the nightmare creatures streamed past them, making it closer to hell than Wilks ever thought he'd be.

Someone fired from behind him. Aliens screamed and hissed and kept running.

One of the drones veered toward him, reached out, claws hooked—

Wilks squeezed the trigger and sprayed the alien with a short burst.

The thing fell into the water. Three or four of the bugs stumbled over the dead creature but kept running.

Another monster howled, lunged at Wilks. He fired again.

Falk cursed steadily behind him as more of the creatures stopped and were killed.

Wilks knew they would never make the drop site. There was no way they could move amidst the army of mindless bugs and keep themselves covered. He aimed at one of the grinning drones as it looked in their direction and squeezed off a single round. The alien's head exploded. It collapsed into the water, which bubbled madly now with the acidic blood of its brothers.

"We're not going to make it!" Billie shouted.

Wilks pointed his weapon at another one and fired. "Five more minutes and the APC will detonate," he called back. "We'll fucking take them with us!"

He squeezed the trigger over and over and hoped that their ammo would last until the white heat of the APC ended it all. . . .

The queen's tail lashed at Ripley's leg, slapped it hard enough to move the pain from her head. Her eyes snapped open. She had crumpled against the wall next to the door when—

My head, she thought. The queen still thrashed wildly at the outer hatch, but it wasn't giving.

Ripley hit the button that would get her out of danger. The door into the APC bay slid open.

At the sound, the queen turned. With her tail coiled behind her, she prepared to leap—

Ripley fell into the clean air of the dock and jerked her legs after her. Moto stood there, welder in hand.

"Quick!"

Moto slammed the control. The door closed a split second before the queen barreled into it. A muffled pounding started on the other side, but the reinforced metal held.

Ripley leaned against the wall and watched Moto seal the entry. She never thought she would think the canned air of the ship was sweet, but it was; she was alive—!

And the queen was *hers*!

"Going for a ride, bitch."

McQuade stepped forward and helped Ripley pull off the leggings of the suit. "Christo, Ripley, you did it!" he said.

Ripley winced as he pulled the metal boot off her left leg. "Yeah. Hurry, we have to go get the others!"

Moto finished the door and stood. She and McQuade exchanged a look.

"Can't," said McQuade. "Brewster says we're getting the hell out of here."

"What are you talking about?" said Ripley. "They're dead?" She suddenly felt dizzy and pressed a hand to her forehead.

"No. The APC's gone critical—it'll blow in a few minutes. The squad's pinned down in one of the narrow valleys, and Brewster said it's too tight for pickup—"

Ripley ran to the stairs before McQuade finished. Moto and the captain followed. She clambered up, ignored her body's mute cries of pain as she climbed into the control room.

Brewster and Tully sat at the console, expressions grim.

"Ripley," said Brewster. "Glad you're—"

"Get to those people, *now!*"

"Look, there's no way! I wish to God there was, but the wind is rising, there's no goddamn room, and no time!"

"Find a way," she said. "If we die, we die. What if it was you down there?"

Brewster frowned. "Listen—" he began.

"No, *you* listen. You take it back or I will." She was still in the top half of the suit and the servos whined as she snapped the grippers shut.

He blew out a big breath. "Fuck it." He nodded. "Okay," he said. "Hold on."

• • •

"Less than a hundred rounds here!" Char yelled.

Falk cursed and threw his weapon down. "Dry!"

Billie moved closer to him and covered. Her head ached and pounded with the endless sound of explosions and shrieks. The air beat down on her, the world had become screams and death and it was too much trouble just to stand up—

She hoped Ripley had made it, that it wasn't all for nothing. She felt tears roll down her cheeks. A huge emptiness opened inside her gut as she took out another of the slavering aliens. She had been here before and she hadn't gotten *used* to it, but she wasn't as afraid as she had been the last time. Fuck it.

The creatures suddenly scattered, backed away from their small group. Hundreds of them howled at once, reached their arms up to the sky. It was deafening. Billie turned to Wilks, confused—

He pointed upward, a tight grin on his scarred face.

The *Kurtz*! She hadn't heard the engines, her ears overwhelmed with the alien shrieks and gunfire.

Wilks grabbed her roughly, jerked her from under the drop path of the approaching ship.

The aliens screamed, ran toward the descending vessel. Dozens of them were crushed into the murky liquid, smashed into the mud under the weight.

The planet rumbled beneath her feet. A wave of

the foul ocean rose up, knocked into them at chest level. Char fell, but Falk caught her; Wilks kept an arm around Billie and leaned into the wave. He fired at a drone that ran toward them.

The APC bay door was open. Ripley and Moto stood on either side of the dock, holding on to metal struts. They pointed weapons past the four of them and fired continuously.

Billie and Wilks ran toward the dock. Billie saw Ripley, was relieved to see she was okay. But then Ripley's mouth formed into a scream. As they stumbled into the bay, Billie looked over her shoulder. The aliens were running into the suppressive fire and falling to the sides of the ship by the score. Falk was right behind them, but—

One of the drones had grabbed Char. She had fallen forward, with an alien right behind her. As in some vicious parody of sex, it pushed against her, shoved her face into the water. Billie saw it plunge a claw through the back of Char's neck, watched it force her head back up. Her blood was startlingly red against the gray water. Her head flopped to the side, hung by shreds of her flesh.

The alien's cry of triumph was short as bullets cut it in half—but Charlene Adcox was dead.

Hundreds of the drones threw themselves at the closing lock as Ripley and Moto hosed their fire through the narrowing gap. Just before it shut completely, a lunging creature stuck one clawed hand into the bay. The lock cycled shut and cut two of the drone's fingers off. They sizzled and hissed on the floor of the ship, burned smoking craters in the flooring.

They were all pressed to the floor of the dock as the ship suddenly bounced and rocketed upward.

"Brace yourselves—the APC will blow in a few seconds!" Ripley yelled. The words sounded far away. Wilks had hooked one arm around a metal beam and held tightly to Billie with the other.

Billie didn't hear the explosion, but the ship rocked violently around them. It tilted to one side, yawed impossibly. Billie and Wilks crashed sidelong into the wall.

And then it was over. The *Kurtz* straightened itself, smoothed out. Only the drone of the engines broke the silence.

Billie took a huge gulp of air and began to sob against Wilks's chest. He stroked her hair gently and didn't let go.

"It's okay. We made it. It's okay."

Once again they had outrun death.

18

Wilks pushed the gray bar up with a grunt and slowly lowered it to his chest. He exhaled, raised it again.

He was alone in the *Kurtz*'s small gym. Falk had been there when he had walked in; the big man had nodded at him once, acknowledged his presence without a word, and left for the showers. Wilks understood. Their success with the capture was overshadowed by the deaths of three good people. No one wanted to talk about it.

The decision to put off deepsleep for a few days hadn't needed discussion; they were only one day from the mother's planet and the crew needed time to digest what had happened. Time didn't move in sleep, after all.

Wilks set the bar back on lock and stood,

reached for the smaller hand weights to work his pecs. He was already on his second set; his muscles trembled slightly as he extended his arms and brought them in. But the body fatigue could be ignored. Concentrating on workouts helped, a little. The sweat that dripped from his skin washed away some of the feelings. Anger. Sorrow. The guilt that had chased him for so long, that he was still alive, for what it was worth. A career marine who would never make it past sergeant, who couldn't save the people who looked to him—

Billie had holed up in her quarters alone. Wilks had gone to see her the night before and again this morning and had brought her something to eat.

She had been listless, unresponsive. Her initial outburst of tears in the APC dock hadn't been repeated. He had searched for something to say to drive that haunted look from her eyes, but what? He could almost see her replay the death of the lieutenant over and over as she stared at the wall. Her friend. Her friend who she undoubtedly had felt responsible for.

Wilks had saved Billie's life more than once, and she his—but to save her from guilt? That was more than he could do for himself. So he sat and watched her until the frustration had been so great that he had excused himself, come here.

Coward, his mind whispered. *Fucking coward*.

Another part of him spoke up. *Hey, I'm not a shrink! I'm just a marine. . . .*

Yeah. Right.

He sighed heavily and moved back to the leg

machine. Maybe a third set would pound his brain into submission.

Billie sat on her bed and tried not to think. They were in space, the mother alien was quiet in the hold, they were on their way to kill the brood on Earth and save Amy—

—who is probably dead, like Char, like Carvey and Dunston, killed, murdered, dead—

She pressed her hands to her forehead and waited for tears to come. No chance. She didn't deserve the release, and the sadness was too big. That they had been so close to the *Kurtz*, inches from safety . . .

Carvey and Dunston, too. Brewster's best friend and the man who had been a teacher, who had convinced her that he had made a choice. To die. She hadn't known either of them as well as she had Char. Charlene. Billie had asked her on the trip that had cost her her life.

Wilks had been to see her, twice. She had tried to eat after he had gone, but the food stuck in her throat. Wilks's usually unreadable face had spoken plenty. She knew that he wanted to help, to make it better for her, but of course there was nothing to be said. They all had their own guilt.

Dylan Brewster had come last night after Wilks had gone, to explain that it should have been him, not Carvey. That Carvey had never been a "real" marine—his friend had been a kid at heart, eager to please. Hell, Carvey had only come on this trip *because* of Brewster—

Billie understood his pain, but was alone in her own.

She had not asked him to stay.

She tried to be objective, to tell herself that Char had made her own decision. That was true—and it didn't matter, because she was gone.

She'd thought she had come for Amy, but it was really about saving herself. Char Adcox had come to deal with her own loss, and Billie's reasons seemed selfish in comparison. Would the end justify the means? How could she know? Maybe the aliens were meant to have Earth; who was she to fuck with fate?

Billie lay down and pulled the coverlet up to her chin. Maybe later she would go talk to Ripley. But not now.

Ripley sat leaning against the dock wall next to the containment chamber and listened. Every now and then the queen rustled, a sliding, clicking noise as she moved her sharp body against the smooth, alloyed interior of her prison.

Ripley had spent most of the night here; the queen had eventually tired of pounding and screaming in the early hours of morning. Ripley checked the navigational comp and set McQuade to work on repairs—the damage to the *Kurtz* had been minimal. Jones tried to get her to medlab, but she was fine. And she had wanted to listen to the queen beat uselessly against the walls for a while.

Ripley was sorry about the deaths of Dunston and Carvey and Adcox; they had all died to get the queen to the *Kurtz*, and she knew that a large part of the responsibility was on her shoulders. But she would have died, too, had it been called for. To wipe out the murderous breed, the bitch queen who had caused the deaths of so many . . .

The fleeting desire she'd had to blow the queen into a million pieces when she could have was nothing compared to her hatred. The rage was hot and temporary; her hatred was cold and hard and forever. The bastards' extermination would vindicate all she had become.

She knew that living a life for revenge was not a healthy way to exist. She didn't care. This was right, she felt it stronger with every passing moment; each hour was a step closer to fulfillment.

The empty bay in front of her suddenly doubled. Ripley blinked several times. The double vision cleared.

Her head still ached where the bitch's tail had slapped her, but it was minor. The huge bruise on her leg already seemed to be fading. She was just tired, and hadn't eaten lately—

The thought of food and sleep was appealing. She stood and walked away from the door to the chamber.

"Later, you shit," she called out over her shoulder.

As she started toward the stairs, she noticed that the ship seemed to tilt slightly to the right. She frowned and paused, reached one hand out to touch the wall. The gravity wasn't supposed to flicker like that, she thought, taking another step toward the ladder. Suddenly, she felt like she was standing on the wall. She leaned into it, tried to right the effect.

"Tully!" she shouted.

No response.

Something was horribly wrong. She saw the alarm button on the wall and reached for it.

Why hasn't it gone off already—?

It was her last thought as she hit the button and the lights went out.

19

Billie sat silently in the mess hall with the others. After McQuade's short rundown of the *Kurtz* repairs, there didn't seem to be much to say.

They waited to hear Jones's voice over the 'com—or better, to see Ripley walk into the room.

An hour ago, the alert horn had snapped Billie awake and she had run into the corridor, prepared to hear the queen's fury erupting from the lower deck. The alarm had shut off seconds later, and Ana Moto had 'commed shipwide to report that she'd found Ripley unconscious and carried her to medical.

They had all gone to the mess hall to wait it out.

Moto appeared a few minutes later and told

them that the doctor was running a full diagnostic and would call when he knew.

Billie felt so tired that it was all she could do to keep her eyes open. The tension in the room only made her more exhausted. When would it stop? Now it was Ripley who could be dying, the woman she had grown to respect and admire and care about—

Wilks sat beside her and drank coffee. As usual, his expression revealed little. Billie was envious of his control. Nothing seemed to affect him for more than a few seconds; he reacted, then just dealt with what there was.

In comparison, she was a child, chronologically and emotionally. Her inner cries of unfairness were petty and pointless. And they changed nothing. . . .

Billie chewed at her lip and waited.

Wilks toyed with his coffee cup, aware that it was a good time to talk to Billie. He was concerned about Ripley, but Jones was the expert. There was nothing he could do there. Probably not a fuck of a lot he could do here, either.

Billie stared blankly at the table, as if watching a holo. Even when Bueller had been left on Spears's planetoid, she'd been able to talk about it. Sort of.

When Moto and Falk started a conversation across the room, he was ready.

"How are you doing?"

"Fine," she replied, voice dull.

"I'm sorry about Adcox," he said. No answer. "I

wish she were here. I wish I could've traded places with her."

Billie looked at him. "Why? It's not your fault."

"After Ripley left, I was in charge of the APC. I was responsible."

"You didn't make her come here, Wilks! I—" She stumbled on her words, stopped.

Wilks put his hand on her shoulder. "You didn't either," he said.

He felt out of place trying to comfort her, but he couldn't stand the look on her face—it reflected how he felt most of the time. He had learned how to hide it, but it was still there. She hurt. He knew.

She relaxed a little into his hand.

"It's really not your fault, Billie. You didn't make these things."

She looked away for a long time, and finally, she nodded. Her gaze turned to his, her eyes bright with tears, and she nodded again. "No," she said shakily. "I didn't."

Wilks felt his own tight gut loosen a bit. It was a start. Maybe he hadn't fucked up so bad after all—

"Hey, folks," the 'com crackled. "You there?"

It was Jones.

Tully called back. "What is it? How is she?"

Everyone in the room faced the wall 'com. Wilks tightened his hand on Billie's shoulder.

"She's okay," said Jones. "Good as new in no time."

Falk and Moto jumped up, grinning. McQuade

clapped his hand on the edge of his chair and laughed.

Wilks smiled at Billie, whose entire body relaxed as she started to cry. This crew hardly knew each other in real time, but Wilks was as relieved as anybody. Ripley was special. Hell, they were all special. He put his arm around her and she leaned on him, tears flowing. She would cry more about this, he understood. There was relief, and then there was letting go. Not something he had a lot of practice at himself.

Ripley swam up out of the murk slowly. Someone spoke nearby. She was tired, her head hurt—

"... now, in no time," said the voice. Far away, someone laughed. Ripley struggled to open her eyes.

"What happened?" That voice was distant, tinny—

The closer voice spoke again. "She sustained a head injury at some point, probably got hit by the queen."

Ripley faded out again. Too hard to concentrate. But then—"queen." Queen. She felt her hands clench, hard. *Wake up. Wake up.*

"... no cerebrospinal draining, no fracture. I was worried about hemorrhage, but there's no signs of that. Mostly fatigue, I think. Mild concussion. She's pretty tough. Tougher than she looks."

Jones. She was on the *Kurtz*, in medlab, and the queen—

Ripley groaned and rolled her head. She opened her eyes.

Jones stood by a wall 'com. He glanced at her and checked his watch.

"Oops. I have a patient to attend to. I'll let you know when she feels like visitors."

Ripley cringed as she looked around. Cold room, funny smell, shiny instruments. It scared her and she didn't know why.

"Where's the queen?" she said. Her throat was dry.

"Locked up in the containment area. Don't worry. Nothing happened, you just passed out," he said. "Everyone is fine." He got her a glass of water from the dispenser and held her head up so she could drink.

"How long?" she said, lying back.

"About twenty minutes since Moto found you."

Ripley started to sit up. "No offense, Jones, but I don't do doctors. I'd like to go back to my quarters."

"I'd rather you stay here—"

"I'd rather I didn't. I'm fine, right?" She swung her legs over the edge of the table and paused for a moment, head pounding. She had to get *out* of this awful room—

"All right," he said. "But let me help you. You're going to need to be looked at when we get back to Gateway; I don't have any training in your type. I mean, I wouldn't have even *known* without the blood sample."

Ripley stood and pulled away from Jones's outstretched hand.

"What are you talking about? I thought you said I was okay."

"Yeah, you're okay. I'm really impressed, in fact. So close, yet so far apart."

"Jones," she started, exasperated. "What's your point?"

"Don't upset yourself, Ripley. You're fine, but you do need to rest. I just don't understand why you never *told* me. I mean, what if I'd had to do an emergency procedure? Blood transfusion or like that?"

"A-positive," she said. "Don't you have it?"

Jones grinned at her. "Yeah, but you don't. And you don't have RH factors anyway. Although as advanced as you are, I wouldn't be surprised. I'd never have known without the microscope; even the color is perfect. Pretty amazing. Come on, let me help you to your—"

"What the hell *are* you talking about? 'Advanced as I am'?"

"Yeah, I'd heard they were pushing the envelope in the AP labs before the monsters landed, but you are so close it's hard to believe—"

She got it. It was a bad joke. She slapped his hand away, furious. "You're an asshole, Jones! This is not funny. Who the hell do you think you are? Not funny at *all*. Christ!"

His grin melted. "Ripley," he said, eyes wide. "Oh, God. You didn't know? You mean—how could you not know? Shit, I'm sorry—I thought—"

He faltered. His dark features were a mask of embarrassment. Ripley felt her own anger subside a little as she watched the truth on his face. She leaned heavily against the wall.

No, no, it, I—can't be, no, she thought. This is another bad dream, another nightmare. This can't be true. It can't be. I'm human! Not—not—

An android.

20

Wilks opened his door to an exhausted-looking Ripley.

"I know it's late, but can I talk to you for a minute?"

"Yeah, sure. How are you feeling? We thought ..." He trailed off as she brushed past him and sat on the edge of his bed, head down. She ran her hands through her mussed hair. Her shoulders were tense and there were dark smears beneath her eyes. Her face was ashen.

She looked up at Wilks with an expression that he couldn't quite place. Something like—fear? Shame?

"What's going on, Ripley?"

"I know that no one is officially in charge of this thing, but everyone has looked to me this far," she said. She seemed to stare through him, as if she were reciting to a wall.

"That's right," he said carefully. "And you've done a good job."

"Well, I quit. It's yours, Wilks. I want you to finish it."

She stood up as if the conversation was finished and stepped toward the door.

"Hold on a second, Ripley—what's going on here? You just got out of medical, you look like hell, and now you want to drop responsibility for our little stowaway on *me*? How hard did you get knocked on the skull?" He grinned to lighten the tone, but he was surprised.

"It's not open to discussion, Wilks. Look, if you don't want to do it, talk to McQuade, or Moto, or anyone. I don't care. But I'm *out*." Her cheeks were flushed, but Wilks still couldn't pin down the emotion.

"Why?" he said. "Can you tell me that? What happened?"

Ripley dropped her gaze and seemed to shrink. She didn't say anything, but she didn't move to leave, either.

Wilks waited, confused. Since day one this had been Ripley's baby. She'd brought the queen onboard single-handedly, and if it hadn't been for her, he and Billie and Falk would be atomic dust—if the aliens hadn't gotten to them first.

"I just had a long conversation with Jones," she said finally. Her voice was slow and measured and she wouldn't meet his eyes. "I'm a synthetic, Wilks. Fake." She crossed her arms and looked at him, face blank. "I'm not human, and I didn't even know it."

Wilks looked at her for a few beats as it sank in. An android? He took a deep breath. "Are you sure?"

"Jones showed me the blood samples; we ran through the tests. Yeah, I'm sure." She pressed the heel of her hand to her forehead, eyes closed.

"Not to make light of it, Ripley, but so fucking what? You've gotten us this far, and—"

"Don't you *get* it?" Her voice was high and shaky. "Who knows *what* my agenda is—I may have been programmed with this idea by some company that wants a specimen to *study*. What if I'm set up to kill all of you when we get to Earth?" She lowered her voice. "I'm not trustworthy."

"Can you, uh, access your program?"

"No. Apparently I'm too advanced. No mechanicals, no input or export jacks." Her voice was charged with bitter self-disgust. "Jones said he never would have known without a microscan. I can pass for human right down to the microscopic level."

Wilks frowned. "I see your point," he said. "But no shit, I don't think it makes a difference. You could've left us to die back there, you could have killed us already—and who's left on Earth to study anything?" He paused for a moment. "I think wherever your agenda came from, it's a good one. And if the only way to tell is with a microscan, what *is* the difference?"

Ripley walked to the door and pushed it open.

"The difference is me," she said. She stepped into the corridor.

Wilks looked at the half-open door. Jesus and Buddha. How would everyone else take this? Finding out that what they thought was human—

Billie, he thought. Ripley obviously wasn't dealing too well with this. Maybe Billie would have something to say about it; she had loved Bueller even after she had found out the truth. . . .

Wilks went to find her.

Billie knocked at Ripley's door and waited. There was no response. The *Kurtz's* heat had cycled down for the standard night; Billie folded her arms tightly against the chilly air. She knocked again, softer this time.

Maybe she's asleep, she thought. *Good.*

She waited another moment and then walked back to her quarters. Wilks stood up when she stepped into her room.

"She's asleep," said Billie.

"Or just not answering," he said. "Maybe you can talk to her tomorrow."

There didn't seem to be much else to say. He left, went back to his own cubicle. Billie went to hers.

Billie was tired, but there was too much going on to think about sleeping yet. She sat down on the edge of her bed.

What would she have said to Ripley? What *could* she say?

Oh, sorry, Ripley, that's tough. You know, I was in love with a soldier once, and it turned out he wasn't

*real either. I was hurt when I found out—I guess I
felt betrayed.* . . .

That would be very helpful.

Billie exhaled slowly and lay back. She stared
at the ceiling and tried to spot flaws in the smooth
plastic paneling as her mind wandered.

Mitch had been capable of love; she believed
that now. But by the time she had realized it, she
and Wilks had already been on Spears's ship.

Did knowing about Ripley change anything?
Billie thought about the mission so far. From the
start, Ripley had been totally committed to de-
stroying the creatures—no, her respect for Ripley
was solid.

Since Billie had known her, Ripley hadn't
seemed to need anyone. But it sounded like she
could use some support now. In a way, she suddenly seemed *more* real—

More *human*, she thought. The way Mitch had
been in that final transmission.

Billie knew all about the prejudices that people
still held about synthetics; it was hard for some to
talk to machines and feel comfortable.

Was Mitch just a machine? Is Ripley?

After Mitch, she had a different perspective on
things. And this was *about* perspective. Ripley
wasn't born in the usual way, but did that make
her soulless? Or any less valuable as a being?
Where could you draw the line?

Finally Billie slept. She dreamed of questions
with no answers.

•   •   •

Ripley finally acknowledged her hunger when it became apparent that it wasn't going to go away.

Fine, she thought, *I'm hungry. Big deal.*

It was late morning. She had slept for almost ten hours and had awakened still tired. She lay in bed, eyes closed.

It was all she could think about, and yet there was nothing to think. How *could* she feel? And what did it matter? Her feelings were simulated, false.

At least some things were clearer now. Her lapse of time after the *Sulaco*. The absence of dreams since then. And the intense distrust of doctors—obviously a programmed measure to avoid the truth. Can't let them go poking around in you, they'll figure it out.

The *why* was elusive, and maybe it was pointless besides. All of her beliefs were in question; androids were not to be trusted, they could betray themselves completely. It was their *nature*. The way she had been betrayed . . .

The synthetic on the *Nostromo* had been a murderer who had posed as a friend. Bishop had been okay, but—

Ripley frowned. There had even been something about Bishop that was all wrong, some duality, although she couldn't quite remember—

There was a knock at the door.

"Ripley? It's Billie. Can I come in?"

Ripley's heart tightened. *Billie*. The young woman had shown a lot of courage through all of this. Ripley had been proud of her.

Funny, she thought. *How human of me.*

"Not now, Billie."

"It'll only take a minute! Wilks wants to go into deepsleep tonight, and—"

"Go away, Billie. I don't want company." The mere thought of talking about it made Ripley more exhausted.

There was a hesitation. Ripley imagined Billie standing there, searching for magic words: *Nobody cares*, she would say, *really, it's okay—*

The idea of Billie pitying her made her feel sick. And the feeling wasn't even real.

Damn.

"Not now."

She heard Billie walk away. She was glad to hear that the others were going into deepsleep; she wanted to be left alone.

Ripley's stomach growled noisily; she pulled her knees to her chest and willed it all to go away.

21

Wilks felt great. He sat up in the chamber and looked around at the cold, sleeping forms of the others. He was surprised at the lack of usual side effects, but only vaguely. What mattered was how he felt.

He pulled on his clothes and grinned at the warm, easy strength in his body. He felt fucking terrific. But it was more than that. There was something—

Absolution, he thought. It was what he had wanted for so long that it had no longer seemed possible. And it didn't seem the slightest bit odd that he had awakened that way; it was about goddamned time. It was like a sense of peace had flowered in him in sleep, a knowledge that everything was finally as it should be. . . .

He laughed out loud as he walked to the stairs. For years he had carried so much, the guilt and torment of the past had weighed so heavy on his shoulders. And for what? It was gone, released into the void of space. There was nothing to wonder at; he was free!

A cool voice spoke gently in his mind, led him through this—revelation. *Freedom*, it said softly, *the key*—

Only one thing left to do. He descended the steps and walked through the APC dock; his feet barely touched the metal. So much of his life wasted! But everything was okay now....

He stepped to the door of the containment chamber and reached for the controls, as if in a dream.

Freedom, life, release—

A flood of warmth and peace washed over him as his hand hovered near the button. The feelings became insistent, stronger.

Let it go, let me go—

Wait. Wilks pulled his hand back, suddenly unsure. What mattered? Where was—

LET ME GO—

A sense of great power and awful dread coursed through him. He staggered back, away from the door. He was an empty space, overwhelmed abruptly with sorrow, despair.

But it was there! his mind screamed. That beautiful calm, that—

Release, freedom—The voice glittered softly with promise. And love.

All he had to do was punch the button.

Wilks crumpled against the wall and wept for the first time since he was a child.

Billie stood in the APC dock. It was cold and the lights were low. She was supposed to meet someone there, but she couldn't recall—

"Billie!"

The muffled voice came through the wall of the containment chamber. The voice that she had known and loved.

"Billie! It's me, Mitch!"

She started toward the door; an inkling of hope welled inside her chest.

"Mitch?" Her voice broke slightly.

"Yeah. Open up, Billie! I love you."

She stopped a few meters away. Her smile faded. No. There was no possible way—

"Billie! Billie, it's Char! Oh, God, don't let it get me, Billie, oh, please, no—"

How could she have thought it was Mitch? Char was in trouble, and Billie was responsible! She ran to the door and reached for the button. But—

Char is dead.

"Don't let it kill me, oh, Billie, don't do this to me, open the door!"

"You're dead," Billie said softly. "You aren't in there." She pulled her trembling hands away from the controls.

"You're right," said the voice on the other side. "And I might as well be dead. You don't give a shit, Billie; it's all about you. Leave me here. None of it matters."

It was Ripley.

"No," said Billie. This was all wrong! "Ripley, I care about you! I want to help, don't you know that? Let me help you—"

Ripley sounded hopeless, lost. "You won't even talk to me, Billie. I thought you were my friend, but, no, you would leave me to die in here—"

"No! I—" Why couldn't she open the door? "Ripley, I can't! There's something in there—"

The queen. The realization hit her full force. She fell back from the door as it all came clear and a chorus of voices called out, begging—

"Let me out—"

"I love you—"

"Please, no—"

Behind it all there was a screaming cry that harmonized with the pleadings of her lost friends. A powerful music, full of now-strident chords, pounding, thundering . . .

It surged over her like a soundful tide and washed everything with gelid darkness. . . .

Ripley sat with her back to the chamber door, the carbine locked and loaded across her lap. The crew had been asleep for two days. She would join them soon, but for now she sat. Waiting . . .

She had spent the first day alternately sleeping and eating. The idea of ending it had surfaced more than once, and she had considered it more carefully each time; who would give a shit about one less android? Just blow herself out of a lock, no great loss. She wasn't necessary to the survival of the plan. The others could get by. . . .

She had been aimlessly looking through the supply hold when the queen had screamed, the sound carrying well in the dead silence of the sleeping *Kurtz*. Ripley had grabbed a rifle almost by reflex and headed for the hold.

She'd run into the APC bay, heart racing wildly, afraid the queen had somehow managed to escape—but everything had been locked up tight. The queen was crying out and hammering at the walls, but she was pent.

The alien mother at her back had been silent for almost an hour now; the tantrum had only lasted a few minutes.

Ripley was glad she was still alive. She had ceased to care about much, but there was still *something*.

The bitch behind me is waiting to die and she is going to take her goddamned children with her when she goes.

Ripley wanted to see that. Had to know that it happened.

Right now, that was enough of a reason for Ripley to live. Whatever she was.

Wilks groaned as light assaulted him. The chamber door fanned open with a hiss and the warmth of his sleep-womb escaped into the cool air. His entire body ached.

He sat up slowly and remembered a great sadness—

The dreams.

"Everybody stay in here," he said. His voice

was a weak croak. He coughed and cleared his throat. "Nobody leaves until we talk!"

The others pulled themselves awake, expressions dazed and sour. Wilks ignored his body's aches as he grabbed his coverall and walked to the door. He dressed quickly in the chill air and waited for the others.

Some part of him relaxed when he saw that Ripley was among them. She had dressed quickly as well, and came to where he stood. She started to step past him.

"Hold on, Ripley. The queen was sending messages while we slept. I think we need to—"

"I don't dream," she said. "Excuse me."

He started to reply and thought better of it. He nodded at her as she stepped by.

Brewster tabbed his shirt and turned toward Wilks, scowling. "What the fuck, Wilks?" he said.

The others looked at him expectantly. He searched their faces for any change, but they all just looked tired and irritable, same as he felt.

"Anybody dream of letting the queen loose?" he said.

"Yes," said Billie.

Ana Moto nodded, as did McQuade and Jones. Brewster's face softened. "Yeah."

"Okay," he said. "We can talk about it over breakfast."

"The message *was* quite powerful," said Moto. "It was like an ongoing advertisement, 'Look what you win if you open the magic door.' It's no won-

der you wanted to check with us. You haven't had
to deal with it before."

Wilks nodded.

Billie swallowed a bit of soypro and looked at
Wilks, curious about what he had dreamed.

"Wanted to make sure none of us were going to
play, I suppose," said Brewster.

"Something like that."

"Welcome to the dreamers' club," Moto said.

They sat at one table and ate for the first time
in weeks. They would be in range of Gateway in
less than twenty hours. Billie's pulse quickened at
the thought of Earth. . . .

Ripley had walked by them on their way into
the mess hall as she'd carried a tray back to her
own room. Billie wished she would have at least
eaten with them; that there were three fewer crew
members was bad enough, but Ripley was *alive*.

"Hey, where's the boss?" said Brewster. "Why
isn't she eating with us?"

"Yeah," Tully added. "We need to go over what
we're going to do to get past Gateway."

Billie glanced over at Wilks. He laid down his
fork.

"Ripley is having some personal problems," Billie said.

"What kind of personal problems?" Falk asked.

Wilks nodded at Billie to continue. She stood.
Everyone stopped eating and looked at her.

"We need to talk about that," she began. "I'm
not sure—Ripley would probably rather not discuss it, but she would want you all to know." She
sounded much calmer than she felt.

"Ripley is an artificial person. An android. She apparently didn't find out until the medical check she just had, and the news has affected her badly."

She stopped and looked around the table. The room was uncomfortably silent.

"Ripley has asked if I would take over where she left off," said Wilks. "But it's going to have to be a combined effort. I'm not really the leader type, and—"

"How the fuck could she not *know*?" said McQuade. "Don't they all know what they are?"

"Not necessarily," said Jones. "Ripley didn't."

"We trusted her," said Tully quietly.

Billie felt a spark of anger.

"That explains how she managed the queen by herself," said Falk. He sounded depressed.

"If I had known," started McQuade, "I wouldn't—"

"If you had known, *shit*," Billie said. She remained standing; the cool dining hall had suddenly gotten very warm. "Ripley didn't *know*, do you get that?" She glared at Tully. "She trusted *herself*! How would you feel? Do you think she did this on *purpose*?"

She turned to Falk. "The last thing she needs is bigotry from this crew!"

She was losing it. Billie took a deep breath and forced herself to sit down. "Jones is better qualified to answer questions about it—"

"Not really," said Jones. "All I can tell you is that she's as close to human as I've ever seen.

And I think Billie is right. Ripley's a good leader."
He stopped and looked vaguely embarrassed.

The others absorbed the information.

Moto nodded slowly.

"Okay," said Wilks. "The more important issue
here is that we're getting closer to the station. I
think that there are a few people there who would
like to have a little chat with us...."

As Wilks discussed some possibilities, Billie
calmed herself. Tully and Falk both looked at her
in ways she thought were apologetic, although
McQuade still seemed pissed off.

She was surprised at herself, but not as much
as she would have thought, even a few months before. The outburst had felt good, and she thought
it might even have helped. Ripley hadn't done
anything *wrong*. It was distressing that any of
these people could overlook her strengths.

Billie yearned for the kind of courage that
Ripley possessed. She would need it to help Amy
... if Amy was still alive.

She refocused on the discussion, heart pounding.

22

Wilks sat in control with McQuade and Tully. In theory, the ship ought to be out of Gateway's visual and sensor range. Never knew but some technogeek with a telescope might be looking right at them, but that wasn't likely.

Wilks gripped the back of Tully's chair tightly and hoped that their shielded call would go through.

"Now we wait," said Tully as she finished tapping the keys. "If we're lucky, she'll catch her messages soon."

"And if she doesn't?" said McQuade.

"We wait longer," Wilks said. A coded direct signal could be channeled accurately if you knew what you were doing. In theory, outsiders wouldn't be able to collect it unless they were looking very carefully, and even then, they wouldn't be able to tap into it. There was some risk, but it ought to be minimal, and it was one they had to take.

Time passed.

A burst of static crackled over the 'com, a hum as compressed voxfiles expanded. And there was the time delay, but—

"About goddamn time. I expected you a week ago."

Tully smiled. "Hey there, Fem Elliot! How's life in the box?"

Once again the radio waves took their sweet and slow time and they waited for the reply.

"Maria? I should've known you'd still be around! Say, you reckon you got enough scramble on this signal? It's taking a hell of a lot of my comp's memory. The officials here aren't *that* smart, you know. Just how important do you think you are?"

Wilks leaned toward the 'com. "Thought we'd check in and see what *you* think."

"Ooh, my heart! Is that the infamous Sergeant Wilks? How's the action, Sarge?"

"Not bad, Leslie. We got what we were looking for."

"That's great, folks! Congratulations. And how is everyone?"

Wilks said, "We've had a few losses."

There was a longer pause than the waves needed. "I'm sorry to hear that."

"Yeah," said Wilks.

Tully spoke up. "Our immediate concern is who *else* has been expecting us. Whatcha got, Les?"

"Well. Y'all raised quite a fuss a few months back. I believe the terms were 'subversive' and 'mentally unstable.' Oh, and 'malicious intent.' To make a long story short, the official trickle-down was that a bunch of nuts stole a ship for no good reason except to fuck with the powers-that-be."

McQuade chuckled. "Not too far off," he said.

Wilks frowned. "Is that all?"

"You're kidding, right? *Unofficially*, General Peters got a very large boot jammed in his very tight ass for not recognizing the magnitude of your insanity. There are warrants out for all of you. The good news is that they think you're crackpots so maybe you'll get stuck in a nice clean hospital room and not a regular cell. And they're not expecting you for another six weeks, if then."

"Why's that?" said Wilks.

"Oh, they turned up a map in your quarters that placed your destination much farther away," she said.

Billie stepped forward, her pale face tensed and eager. Wilks hadn't even noticed her come in.

"Leslie, it's Billie. How are things on Earth?"

"Communication's been shot for weeks. Atmospheric static, sunspots acting up, something like that. But whatever the bugs are doing down there, it's gotten worse."

"What about the satellite uplinks?" said Billie.

She looked close to tears, but her voice was strong.

"The last signals we got are old news—and I have to tell you, it wasn't good. Anyone left on Earth probably belongs to the aliens now, one way or the other. I'm sorry."

Wilks put his hand on Billie's shoulder, but she shook it off. "Listen. Do me a favor and pipe the last few days of transmissions to us. Can you do that?"

"No problem."

"Thank you," Billie said. She walked out of the room.

"Listen, I'm glad to hear from you, but let's go easy with this. Even with the scramble—I'll let you know if anything important comes up. And take care, okay?"

"You too," Wilks said.

The 'com went silent. McQuade turned to Wilks. "Doesn't sound like we're going to win any votes here," he said.

Wilks shrugged. "To get to the bombs we're going to be in their gun sights at some point," he said. "And we've got the queen. I doubt we'll get any help from them, but maybe we can persuade them to let us have our shot. And even at worst case, they won't blow us out of space—they want the *Kurtz* back."

McQuade nodded, but looked uncertain. Wilks walked back to talk to the rest of the crew. The station wouldn't spot them for a few more hours, so they still had time to come up with alternate plans.

Wilks knew that he was good in tight situations; he was trained for it. But shit like this—

Dammit, why isn't Ripley doing this? Fuck her humanity, or lack of it—they were better off with her in charge. He knew his limits, and they were not far off.

Billie sat alone in the medlab at the small computer. The room was cold and gleaming white; it gave her a strange kind of nostalgia for the hospitals she had spent most of her life in. Right now there were more important things on her mind, however. . . .

She tapped in a short description of Amy and waited for a match.

The screen flickered. A fuzzy picture flashed onscreen of a young girl with a bad haircut. She stared at Billie for a few seconds, eyes too serious for a child. How old was she now? Thirteen? Fourteen maybe?

Oh, baby, thought Billie. Her heart tightened, but at the same time she felt a huge relief.

"Is it on?" Amy said. Her voice had deepened slightly, and it looked as if she had made an effort to wipe her face clean.

"Go ahead, honey," said a voice offscreen.

"Me and Daddy are in a factory that used to make microchips in Northern California. We're probably going to move soon. Uncle Paul is gone now. He went to look for food almost two weeks ago and I hope that he is just hiding, but we don't think so." Her face clouded as she spoke, but her young eyes didn't waver from the camera.

"It's getting warmer all the time. We have a new friend named Mordecai, and he says that he thinks the aliens have heated things up somehow with their nesting materials."

She smirked, a surprisingly adult gesture. "Mordecai also says that the goddamn religious fucks are as bad as the aliens now." She glanced past the camera sheepishly and then raised her eyebrows, obviously the recipient of a nasty look.

"Well, *he* said it!"

A sigh offscreen. "I know, honey. Go on."

"Anyway. We wanted to tell you that the aliens have been acting strange for a few weeks. They have been grouping together and staying quiet for days at a time, and no one knows why."

The little girl frowned. "I guess that's all," she said.

The old man's voice stated the date and coordinates as usual and the screen blanked.

Billie stared into the empty monitor for another moment and then laughed abruptly. She was still alive! The transmission was over a month old, but the family had survived for so long already that she *had* to be.

I would know if she was dead, she thought. *I would know.*

The connection that Billie felt was too intense for it to be otherwise. The coordinates listed were already etched into her mind.

Orona's bombs were part of an old-style military arsenal located in a remote area of the northwestern United States. Billie had been there once, when she and Wilks had escaped from Earth and ended up at Spears's planetoid. She and Wilks and Mitch ...

She shook the memory. Surely a military bunker would have some kind of transportation ...?

It wasn't impossible. Everything was falling into place; she was *meant* to save that family. To save Amy.

Billie felt fully awake for the first time since leaving the mother alien's planet. She had been a follower for a long time, had taken directions most of her life. This was her chance to make a difference. And it wasn't some distant dream anymore, it was *here*. Not on the scale of total extermination of the aliens—but it was hers, it was taking a stand that mattered most.

She sat and daydreamed of possible futures. Hang on, Amy. Just a little bit longer.

"This is Gateway Station calling. Please identify yourself."

Wilks looked at McQuade and nodded.

"This is Captain McQuade of the *Kurtz*," he said. "I would like to speak with your CO."

The time lag stretched past its limit. Wilks imagined the flurry of activity they had just caused and almost smiled.

"Bet we got some people pissing in their drawers right now," said McQuade.

"Sir," said a voice, "please stand by for Major Stone."

"Here we go," Wilks said.

"Captain McQuade, this is Major Stone." The

major's voice rang with authority. "Open your control modem for override."

"Actually, Major, we just wanted to talk for a minute. We have—"

"Captain, we'll be glad to talk to you when you get here. You know procedure. Now if you'll just let us help you arrive safely, I'm sure we can work this out." Major Stone spoke slowly and carefully, as if he was directing a child. Or a mental case.

"Major Stone, this is Sergeant Wilks. We *are not* coming to Gateway. We have the queen alien onboard the *Kurtz* and we're taking her to Earth. There is no need for Gateway military involvement; this is just to let you know." He attempted to sound calm and reasonable.

The major did not bite. "Sergeant, we are already sending people to fetch you. Now, you can come in like civilized men or we can drag you in kicking and screaming, but you *are* coming to this station! Do you copy?"

Wilks silenced the 'com. "Tully?"

"Station dispatched a ship," she said. "I got the drive signal spewing all over my long-range sensor array."

"Well, we gave it a shot. Okay, McQuade, get us out of here." He hit the 'com button and spoke quickly. "Gotta go, Major, nice talking to you."

"Wilks, you can't—"

He cut Stone off and switched on the shipwide. "Heads up, people. Looks like Gateway is coming to dinner and we don't have a lot of time. The shit is about to hit the fan."

•   •   •

Wilks's message echoed through the empty APC bay. Ripley ignored it. They would figure something out; it didn't matter as long as she still had the queen.

"Wouldn't want to miss the reunion," she whispered. "I gotta take you home to die with your babies, monster. *Every*body dies."

Nothing else mattered.

23

Can we outrun it?" said Falk.

"No," Brewster said. "That ship is more maneuverable and a lot faster."

"They won't fire at us, will they?" That from Jones.

"I don't think so," said Wilks. "They want us back in one piece. Well, at least they want the *ship* back in one piece. Same difference, far as we're concerned."

The crew stood in the dining hall nervously. They had about an hour before Gateway's ship would be in range. Billie noticed that for a change it was too warm. She wiped at her face and wondered where Ripley was.

Tully answered Jones: "They *could* try a gun or

laser-shot at our drives to damage us enough so we couldn't fly straight. But that's iffy—they might miss and punch a hole in us, accidentally destroy something they can't fix real easy. Or cheap. I'm with Wilks; I don't think they'll risk that."

"So what can they do?" said Jones. "Fly circles around us until we get dizzy and surrender?"

No one laughed.

Tully said, "They can disable the *Kurtz*'s control systems with an electromagnetic pulse and tow us in. That'd be the easiest—just get within range and push a button. That's what I would do."

"Our electronics aren't hardened?" said Falk.

"On this rust bucket? Sheeit."

Billie frowned. "Can't we do it to them first?"

"EMP capabilities in a *freighter*?" said Brewster. "Dream on. This ship isn't designed for combat of any kind. No shields, no weapons—basically, we're screwed."

But what about Amy? Billie wanted to shout. They couldn't just *quit*—

Moto sighed. "They won't *kill* us back on Gateway. I mean, once we get there, we could explain things. We do have the queen. The military could take her and finish the job for us—probably badly, but at least it'd get done."

No one replied and Billie watched acceptance start to settle on their faces. They might not like it, but what choice did they have?

It's not fair, she thought, and wiped at her brow again, frustrated. That after all of this, after people had *died* to make this work, they were just going to roll over and—

Suddenly, there was a grin on her face. Something Tully had said triggered it. "Wait. There's a way," she said. "I have an idea."

They all stared at her.

Engines idle, the *Kurtz* coasted toward Earth through the blackness, falling into the gravity well in a spiral that, if not interrupted, would end with whatever charred remains survived the reentry burn splashing down in the Indian Ocean.

"Everything is powered down," said Tully, "except lights and communications." Her voice sounded tinny over the headset, even though engineering was directly below them.

"Moto? Got your set on?" said Wilks.

"Yeah. Ready."

Wilks and McQuade waited for the call in the control room. The others would be strapped in behind them, in the crew area. Wilks hadn't spoken to Ripley, but had explained the plan over the shipwide; he hoped she had listened.

"*Kurtz* crew please acknowledge. This is Commander Hsu of the *Adams*."

"This is McQuade," the captain growled. "What the fuck do you want? I'm busy here."

"Sir," said Hsu politely, "we're here to escort you back to Gateway. There is no need to be unreasonable. Open your modem and we can avoid any unpleasantness—"

McQuade cut in. "No way. We're going to Earth and there's nothing you can do about it, Hsu.

Your weapons won't work on us—we're blessed!
You can't stop us! We're invulnerable!"

On his last words, the lights flickered and went
out.

A few seconds passed and the mechanical
emergency backups switched on.

They'd been EMPed. If their systems had been
running, half of the electronics would have probably been fried.

Wilks turned to McQuade. "Well, my guess is
that you are now more or less officially crazy,
Captain. Hsu probably has the med team on Gateway standing by with a full case of Trinomine
patches by now; you'll get doubles."

Wilks tapped his headset back to life. "Moto,
Tully. Let's get going."

It didn't take long. Twenty minutes or so. Then,
a dull thunk echoed through the ship and the
Kurtz slowed, finally stopped. After a moment, the
ship began to move in a new direction, toward
Gateway, though they couldn't see that from inside with all the systems off-line.

"They got their magnetic tow cable in place,"
Wilks said almost under his breath, as if those in
the other ship might somehow hear him.

McQuade nodded. "Fish on a line."

If this doesn't work, thought Wilks, *we're going to
be in* really *deep shit*.

Billie sat in the crew area with Jones, Falk, and
Brewster. Falk had laughed quietly at McQuade's
speech, which had carried to them through the
partition. They all waited silently now, tense.

Brewster unbuckled his strap and moved to the chair next to Billie's.

"Okay if I sit here?" he said.

She nodded and watched as he strapped back in and then turned to her. He seemed unsure of himself.

"How are you doing?" he said.

"I'm okay. I had a rough time for a while, but it's gotten better." She was glad that she meant what she said.

"Good to hear," he said. "I've been coming to terms with some of my own shit." He paused, obviously wanting to say more.

Billie smiled gently at him. "Dylan. We both have had a lot to deal with on this trip, and there's still a ways to go. But I consider us friends and I want you to know that no matter what happens, I wish you well."

"I don't regret it," he said quietly. Even in the dimly lit room, she could see that he had reddened slightly. He touched her hand.

"Neither do I." Their night together had been nice. She held his fingers in her own for a moment and squeezed lightly before letting go.

There were bigger things to be dealing with than a sexual encounter between them, and she felt like this was his acknowledgment of that; Dylan was okay. And so was she. More or less.

"Get ready," Wilks called back to them.

Billie leaned back in her seat and closed her eyes.

●　●　●

"Ready." Tully's voice crackled in Wilks's ears. He nodded at McQuade and held up his hand. The captain leaned to the controls and watched for the signal.

Billie's plan was almost embarrassingly simple. Play dead until they were being towed and then scoot forward and tap the other ship's drive control surfaces hard enough to damage them. By the time Gateway sent another ship, the *Kurtz* would be well on its way to Earth. What the hell, it was just goofy enough to have a chance.

"Stand by," Wilks called over his shoulder.

He pointed at McQuade. "Go!"

The *Kurtz* hummed back to life. McQuade hit the controls and the ship rocketed forward and to one side.

For an impossibly long time they hurtled through space. Wilks gritted his teeth.

The body of the ship shuddered with the impact, a loud crash. Even braced as he was, it jarred Wilks, hard. Then they were moving again, aslant to the ship they'd just hit.

The magnetic line snapped taut and the coupler was peeled off as the smaller ship was knocked away by the collision.

There goes the insurance, Wilks thought. He remembered an old joke about whiplash. *No time to dick around, now, Wilks.* "Shut it down *fast!*" he ordered.

The *Adams* could still trigger another pulse—

The system went dead; Tully and Moto had pulled everything off-line again. He hoped.

Wilks mentally counted to ten and then spoke into the set.

"Did they get us?"

"Nope," said Tully. She sounded out of breath.

"Hook up perimeter sensors," said Wilks. A few of the console lights blinked on. McQuade scanned the small screen and then laughed.

They were coasting, but moving at a good clip. Time passed, seemed to Wilks like a long chunk of it.

"Out of effective range," McQuade said. "And it looks like they're flying in circles."

Wilks grinned. "Good work down there," he said to engineering. "Get us back online."

"You know what to do, Captain," he said to McQuade.

As the *Kurtz* relit her systems, coming back to life, Wilks tapped the shipwide 'com. "Congratulations, Billie. Looks like we're going to Earth."

Ripley sat in her room alone. She wasn't particularly surprised that they were still on their way; the people onboard weren't stupid. Wilks had apparently turned into quite the leader—

Someone knocked at her door.

"Ripley? You home? It's Billie."

She considered not answering and then sighed. The *Kurtz* wasn't that big; where else could she be?

"Come back later," she said.

"No. I need to talk to you now."

Ripley sighed again. *May as well get it over with.* "Come in."

Billie walked in and sat on the edge of the bed. "How's it going?"

She looked different to Ripley somehow. Not as shy, perhaps, more self-assured. She had always thought of Billie as nervous in confrontative situations, but the young woman sitting on her bed looked anything but.

"How's it going? Why, everything's great. Wonderful. Couldn't be better."

"Really? I've gotten the impression that you don't like us much anymore."

Ripley raised her eyebrows. "Don't play games, Billie."

The younger woman shrugged. "Why not? You are."

Ripley was irritated. "This is what you needed to discuss with me? This is my business, you know, and—"

"—and you don't have to explain yourself to anyone. By all means, Ripley, don't worry about rationalizing on *my* account. But this excursion was *your* idea, and now you're leaving us hanging."

Ripley didn't respond. *So what?* she thought angrily. *You had your reasons for coming along.* Obviously she just wanted to bitch; fine. And she was right—Ripley didn't have to explain it.

"We need you, Ripley. I need you. You're important to me." She took a deep breath.

Here it comes, thought Ripley.

"I admire you," said Billie. "I guess that's what I needed to say. I wish that I had your strength in a lot of ways."

"Don't you mean that past tense?" said Ripley. She realized she sounded bitter, but who the fuck was Billie to come in and dump this on her? "It's not *me*, Billie! You admire a program, a machine."

Billie looked at her unwaveringly. "I was in love with a machine once," she said. Her voice softened. "His name was Mitch. Are you telling me that my love had no value because of what he was? That his love for me was some kind of trick, a—a glitch?"

Ripley turned away from Billie's gaze. This was not the pity she had expected.

"I'm not Mitch," she said.

"No," said Billie. "You're Ripley. I saw your broadcasts long before we ever met; I heard the stories. You act just like that Ellen did, far as I can tell. So what if you're an artificial person? My guess is that whoever made you used who you *were* to do it. So, you're a copy of yourself. So maybe you aren't perfect. So, who the fuck is? If you want to sit there and feel sorry for yourself because you aren't the woman you thought you were, go ahead. It won't change anything. And if we fuck this up because you won't help, you can blame that on yourself, too."

Billie stood, stared at her for a moment, then walked out without speaking again.

Ripley stared after her. Jesus.

Jesus.

24

They made it to Earth with no more trouble from Gateway.

That's something, at least, thought Wilks. They had achieved atmosphere without a hitch and now flew high over an ocean toward the North American continent. Brewster was at the controls; he was a better pilot in air than McQuade.

"ETA approximately ninety minutes," he said.

"Okay," said Wilks. He unstrapped from the co-pilot's chair and walked toward the dining hall. The others would be there in a few minutes. He moved slowly, lost in thought.

What next? They had made it to Earth with a psychic alien queen to—they hoped—obliterate the infestation there; they had lost three people, and their leader had developed an aversion to leading. Every bug on the planet would be after their asses once they set down. Aside from the fact that even if they succeeded at this point, going back to Gateway probably meant brainwipes and locktime as a reward.

Wilks grinned as he stepped out of the corridor. *All of that and the food's great, too*, he thought.

"What's so funny, Wilks?"

Ripley stood at a dispenser, a cup of coffee in hand. The room was empty except for the two of them.

"I was just thinking of all the fun we've been having so far," he said. "Hello, Ripley." He acted casual, but it was good to see her. He went to another dispenser and ordered a steak. Well, what passed for steak. The joy of soy.

Something that looked like a steaming, squashed-flat turd arrived. Wilks shook his head and picked up the tray.

Ripley walked with him to a table and sat across from him.

"Wilks," she began, "I want to thank you for stepping in to run this operation. And now that we're here, I'd like to offer my help—unless you've got everything under control. . . ." The last was almost a question.

He poked at the cutlet on his tray. "Actually, I was hoping you'd say something like that," he said. "Welcome back. I'm a crappy leader."

"Sounds like you've been doing fine," she said.

He shrugged. "What changed your mind?"

"Something Billie said. It pissed me off enough to start thinking about how I've been dealing with things." She stared at her hands for a minute and then looked up at him.

"Whatever my circumstances are, we still have a job to do, right?" She smiled, but there was no humor in the expression.

Falk and Moto walked into the room together, chatting. They stopped when they saw who was there.

"Hey, good to see you, Ripley," Moto said.

Falk grinned at her. "Yeah, you gonna stop Wilks from looking like an asshole?"

"I'll do my best," she said. "Miracles are difficult, you know?"

Wilks laughed. He felt better than he had since deepsleep.

Billie arrived. She waved to them and went to a dispenser for coffee. Wilks watched her smile brighten at the sight of Ripley, and felt a rush of warmth for her. She had changed so much since he'd broken her out of the hospital on Earth; she was stronger, braver, more beautiful—

Instead of immediately stifling the thought as he had in the past, he let it sit for a moment. Billie didn't need him to protect her anymore. She had demonstrated many times that she was more than capable of standing on her own. He felt comfortable working with her, he trusted her—she was really the closest thing he had to a friend. But a lover?

Why the fuck not? You're only old enough to be her father and you've got enough emotional trouble for two—bet she'd jump at the chance!

"You awake, Wilks?"

Billie waved a hand in front of him before she sat down. He blinked. Everyone was there now except the pilot.

... good time to daydream, Sarge, maybe you'd like to recite some fucking poetry to yourself while the crew takes care of things—

"Sorry," he said, and smiled at her. "Just thinking."

He suddenly recalled one of the sayings from boot camp that he hadn't thought of in decades: Don't be a fool for your tool.

He shook his head and put all those thoughts aside. Later.

"So how are we going to unload our cargo without getting eaten by it?" said Moto.

"Or getting our butts kicked by her unhappy children?" said McQuade.

Although the questions weren't necessarily directed at her, Ripley felt that they were waiting for her response.

"I've got a pretty good idea of the layout on where we're headed," she said. "We're going to have to do this quick; she'll be calling the creatures to her before we even land."

Billie broke in. "She's calling them already, I think. I watched some of the 'casts that Leslie sent over from about six weeks ago—the people on Earth said that the aliens have been gathering together and not attacking as often."

"Perhaps corresponding with when we abducted the mother," finished Moto. "Sounds like they're getting ready."

The crew watched Ripley, waited for her to speak. She was vaguely surprised that she had been accepted back with no confrontations, but didn't want to dwell on it. Her own problems were not a priority right now.

"This is going to be tight," she said. "The arsenal is set into the side of a mountain—we drop the queen on the other side and work fast enough to be done before the majority of her brood shows up. They might know about where she's landing, but not exactly."

"Not that it's important or anything, but does anyone know how to set up the bombs?" said Falk.

Ripley sighed. Sooner or later it was going to come up. "It's in my program," she said. She felt resigned as she looked at each of their faces and wondered what she would see. No one spoke for a moment.

Tully smiled. "Well, thank-fucking-Buddha," she said brightly. "That's something."

"Do you think the bunker will have been raided?" That from Jones.

Wilks shrugged. "Maybe. I'd say definitely, but it's an isolated area."

The whole topic had been glossed over as quickly as it had come up. Ripley suddenly realized that she wasn't going to get the response she had expected. For however the crew members felt about it, they seemed to have come to terms with her as a synthetic—at least on a working level.

Great, she thought, *if I don't glitch it and kill them all.*

Brewster's voice came over the 'com. "Hey, ya'll might want to come check this out—we're over land now. Looks like someone had a pretty wild party last night and wrecked the place." His attempt to sound casual was strained.

Several of them looked at Ripley. She nodded.

"We have as much of a plan as we're going to get," she said. "Let's go see what there is."

As Ripley followed the others into the corridor, Billie lagged back and put her hand on Ripley's arm. They walked slowly behind the others.

"Listen, what about Amy?" said Billie.

Ripley frowned. "The girl from the 'casts?"

Billie nodded. "We have to help her. She's not far from the site, an hour or two maybe, and I could take a flier to go get her."

"How do you know she's alive?"

"She is. I know." Billie looked anxious, her face tight.

Ripley remembered how important the girl had been to Billie back on the station. She stopped walking and faced the young woman. On the one hand, she knew exactly how she felt; on the other hand, there were bigger goals here.

"Billie," she said gently, "we can look at the situation when we get there, but we're not going to have much time. Whether she's alive or not, I don't know if we can afford to do it. I'm sorry."

For a second, a look of panic and frustration flashed across Billie's face, so intense that Ripley thought the girl would scream. Then she relaxed and dropped her gaze to the floor.

"I hear you," she said. She ran one hand

through her long hair. "But I won't give it up without trying." She looked up at Ripley, expression set.

"Well. We'll see what we can do."

Billie walked ahead of her, head still down. Ripley felt sorry for her, but they all had their own shit to work through. The important thing, the *only* thing, was their mission.

Billie stood with her arms crossed and watched Earth tell her story. The *Kurtz* flew high over the eastern states, too high to see unaided most of the destruction that the cameras fed to the ship's magnification screen. The men and women around her stood silently, their faces expressionless as they took in the ruins of the mother planet.

The midday sun spared nothing. The screen showed an overview of a dead city. Here, several blocks of burnt and crumbled buildings that had once towered. Filth littered the streets, parts of cars, vague splotches of blackness and greasy shadow that united the wreckage into a grim tapestry. Everywhere were exploded bits of plastecrete and wood, random pieces of melted metal and brick and bone.

The screen switched, cut to another shot. It was like the picture before, and the picture before that—ravaged and lifeless. This was an industrial area, a series of long, low buildings ripped apart. Billie could see where someone had tried to barricade one—huge crosses of some material covered one wall, right next to a giant hole through the building. An explosion, perhaps ...

Cut to a row of identical houses, windows smashed and doors open or gone. There was life here; Billie realized with disgust that the slight movement around the houses could only be an army of vermin.

The *Kurtz* grabbed random pictures of towns and cities and parks that were lost to humanity. The crew seemed stunned; there were no wisecracks, none of the usual banter that Billie had come to expect from the soldiers. She had grown up in hospitals, hadn't been a part of this world—but the thought that it had simply ceased to exist ...

Billie widened her eyes at the next shot.

"Hey," said Brewster excitedly. "Is that—" He shut up abruptly. There was a small group of people moving down a road. At first glance Billie had felt great hope—until she realized that the four or five figures were dragging another one in lengths of chains. The group stumbled along, tattered, holding weapons—they seemed to look up at the sky, at the ship. Billie remembered the vid she had seen back at the station, the human sacrifice—here were the fanatics, hunting for people to act as incubators. The last insane remnants of humanity.

She thought of what Ripley had said—not enough time to see about Amy—and felt her resolve strengthen. She would help Amy and her family or die trying, time or not. Fuck it.

Billie broke away from the screen and looked

around. The others all seemed lost in worlds of their own. She noticed that Moto and Falk had linked hands. Billie almost smiled at the small reminder that there were still good things. Not many, but some.

She noticed that Wilks's gaze also rested on Falk's and Moto's interlaced fingers. He looked up at her and smiled briefly, sadness heavy on his scarred face. She was surprised that he had let an emotion slip past his normally unshakable facade. As he looked away, she felt a strong urge to comfort him; Billie had never really thought about it before, but it occurred to her now that Wilks was very important to her.

David, she thought. The name sounded strange in her head, but then he was a strange man; so strong, yet so emotionally uncertain—

Billie turned back to the monitor. What was important was that they were here; one way or another, everything was building, coming to a head. . . .

From the hold, the unmistakable cries of the captive queen filtered out. She screamed and pounded in her chamber high over the silent Earth as they headed toward whatever fate held, almost as if she knew what her own end was to be.

If she did, she was ahead of them.

25

As if on cue, the on-screen pictures came to life. The queen howled uselessly and down on Earth, dark, loping figures began to appear. Only a few at first, but the numbers quickly increased. Each shot showed dozens of the creatures as they ran in one direction—after the path of the *Kurtz*.

Ripley felt a rush of cold triumph edged with worry. This was what she had expected, the beginning of the end, but if they fucked up now—

"Holy shit," said McQuade. "Looks like we got a riot coming up."

The monitor showed hundreds of the aliens as they raced through the blackened remains of some large city. Even as they watched, handfuls of the shiny insectile shapes erupted from the wreckage to join the advancing group.

"We'll never make it," Tully said. "There's too many."

Ripley glanced at the woman sharply. Tully didn't look so good—eyes wide, taking short breaths.

"*Tully*. We're headed toward a very isolated area, surrounded by mountains and water. It's going to take them longer than us to get there by land."

The hacker took a deep breath and then nodded at Ripley. "I—yeah, I hear you."

"Good. Start digging for topography maps, anything useful on Northern California and Oregon. Look at adjacent land as well. Go use medlab, okay?"

Tully nodded again and then stood. Having a job to do helped, Ripley knew. The woman looked more collected as she walked past the others.

Dr. Jones smiled at Ripley and then followed Tully.

"Brewster, how long we got?"

"Thirty minutes, give or take."

"Fine. Moto, why don't you and I go see what we can scrounge in the way of tools."

Moto let go of Falk's hand and went to the stairwell.

Captain McQuade sat down in the copilot's chair. "Guess I'll make sure Brewster doesn't crash us," he said.

"That leaves weapons detail to us," said Wilks. "Billie? Falk?"

Ripley nodded. Good. Seeing the planet's condition had been bad, but they all had something to do to keep the images of death at bay for a while. It would all be over before long.

"Tell Tully to call me as soon as she gets a fix on geography," she said. She directed this at Brewster as she followed Moto down the ladder.

The queen screamed in the hold below, sent her message to the Earth's breed.

Ripley grinned tightly as she took the steps. The bitch would have plenty to scream about soon enough.

Wilks watched the mountains grow as the *Kurtz* got closer to its destination. They had all regrouped around the control area and waited now while Brewster efficiently maneuvered the ship through the forested landscape. Thankfully, the monitor revealed less destruction out here.

The mother alien still beat at the walls downstairs, but there was no sign of her children through the blanket of trees. Yet.

There were several small peaks, all part of a range that ran through the Northwest. According to Tully's read, a few of them were volcanic, although none were currently active.

That'd be a kick, he thought, *we land and get buried in lava.*

They would drop the queen in a small, enclosed valley near the base of Orona's mountain and then fly to the arsenal a few minutes farther west. Since most of the creatures would come from inland, this would save the *Kurtz* from being trampled by them on their way to the queen; or so Wilks hoped.

The ship moved slowly over the treetops toward a towering mountain.

"We got a hole," said Tully quickly. "A big one." She listed the coordinates to Brewster.

Wilks grinned at Ripley. The queen might not take off running if they could find a cave to dump her into. There was no way to be sure, but Wilks had never seen one of the creatures traipse around in the open if there was somewhere dark to hide. They could only hope that the mother was similar to the other queens in that regard. When Ripley had mentioned the idea, he had once again been very glad that she was back in charge.

"Great," said McQuade. "That thing is starting to get on my nerves."

"Amen," said Falk.

The ship moved at a crawl. Wilks spotted the cavern, a dark opening in the rocks at ground level.

Perfect. He was ready. As soon as they dumped the alien, they would hurry to the bunker and get to work. Unless the setup was completely destroyed, they could fix it fast and get the fuck off the planet. It was probably just a rewire job—

"Ready, kids?" said Brewster. The *Kurtz* was in place.

"Do it," said Ripley.

They all watched Brewster push the button to open the outer hatch. A faint hum from the console, and a small red light flashed.

"*Shit*," said Ripley.

The hatch hadn't opened. The queen continued to scream.

"What the fuck is wrong?" said Wilks.

"I don't—mechanical failure somewhere," said Brewster. He touched the button again. The light blinked.

"EMP?" said Billie.

"No, we got off-line in time, I'm sure of it," said Moto.

Wilks looked over at Ripley. She chewed at her lip for a second and then slapped her hand against the console.

"She's pressing on the goddamn door!" said Ripley. "Stupid bitch is probably punching the pretty button, blocking her own goddamn exit."

She turned to the stairwell. "Open shipwide 'com and try it again when I say so, Brewster. Wilks, come with me."

He followed Ripley down the stairs. The roar of the engines was incredibly loud as they hurried through the APC bay together.

"The door from here is sealed!" he shouted to her. Ripley ignored him and jogged over to a tool cabinet set into the wall. She tossed a spanner to him and grabbed a second wrench, stepped to the wall and hit it. Wilks joined her, began to beat at the alloy with the spanner.

"Hey, asshole, over here!" Ripley shouted. "Come on, come *on!*"

Wilks hit the wall high, again and again. Between the engines, the queen, and the echoing crash of metal on metal, he was surprised that he heard the new sounds. Through the wall came an awful scraping noise, nails on kleersteel. Or rather, talons on alloy.

Ripley hit the door once more and then shouted to the 'com behind her. "Go!"

A few seconds passed, and the ship suddenly lifted slightly as the queen's cries faded to nothing. Wilks turned to face Ripley. She was still looking at the containment chamber.

"Not that smart, is she?" she said. She spoke loudly to be heard over the engines.

As they headed back upstairs, Wilks rephrased to himself an earlier thought; he was fucking *thrilled* that Ripley was back in charge.

The ship sped to the far side of the mountain in the early afternoon. Even as tense as she was, Billie felt some pleasure as she looked at the environment. It occurred to her that she had seen very little natural beauty in her life. She had grown up in cold, desolate places, had only seen green trees on holovids or in biolabs. Here were thousands, they covered the mountainous area in shades of emerald. All of it a waste ...

They skimmed another small peak and Billie saw the bunkers. The land was flat, wide enough to land two ships the size of the *Kurtz*, the trees cleared away. Directly ahead of them was a low hill, perhaps a tenth the height of the ice-capped mountain where they had left the queen. There were several buildings grouped around it, short and ugly blocks of plastecrete arranged in a semi-circle. A huge metal gate was set into the hill with yellow lines painted across it; the middle of the door had been blown apart.

Billie felt her breath catch in her throat when she spotted them, half hidden—two small fliers and an APC sat in between two of the buildings.

"It's dead," said Tully. "No activity on the sensors."

"Let's bring her in," said Ripley. "Keep an eye on the readings—it may not be as easy as it looks."

Dust swirled up around the ship as it settled to the ground with a rumble. After a moment, the air cleared. Billie had grown so accustomed to the drone of the engines that the silence seemed strange and empty.

"Tully?" said Ripley.

"Nada. If anyone's here, they're not moving."

"That door didn't explode by itself," said Brewster. "We should secure the area—"

"Me, take chances?" said Ripley. "Come on, folks, let's get armed."

Billie followed the others to the supply hold at the end of the corridor, heart pounding. One of those fliers was going to work. She was no pilot, but she had learned a lot watching Wilks; standard military fliers were designed to be operated by mainline field soldiers, not a particularly bright bunch on the average. They would be strictly automatic, coordinates and go. Billie had already borrowed the access code from the *Kurtz*'s computer and figured it should work; she would see what kind of timeline they had and take her chances.

Wilks passed out weapons to the crew while Ripley handed out extra clips and comsets.

"We start at the first building and work around," said Wilks, "marines up front—Moto, you're on point."

"Tully, I want you to stay onboard to monitor," said Ripley. "Jones, you watch the hatch. We're not going to be out of sight completely at any time, so just yell if you see anything Tully misses."

The doctor accepted his carbine tentatively.

"You know how to use it?" said Wilks.

"Yeah. Well, pretty much. I've never actually *fired* one, but we had a safety course in med school."

"Good enough," said Wilks.

"McQuade, Billie, you're covering our asses," said Ripley.

Billie and the captain nodded and slung their rifles.

"Once the area is secured, we'll come back for tools and then get to work on the detonator problem."

Tully walked back to control as the crew filed down to the APC dock. They stood at the hatch,

Moto, Wilks, and Brewster in front with their weapons ready.

Ripley put her hand on the door controls and looked at them. "Any questions?"

No one spoke. Billie took a deep breath as the deck fanned open.

26

ilks stepped into the bright sunlight, crouched, his carbine pointed to one side of the ship.

Nothing. Moto would be trained on the structure in front of them, Brewster to the other side.

"How's it look?" he said into the 'com. He scanned the area for movement.

"Clear," said Tully.

"*Go,*" said Wilks.

Moto jogged forward, weapon up, as Wilks and Brewster covered her. They were close enough to the dingy gray building that it only took half a minute. Moto leaned against the corner of the unit and crouched there.

"Go," said Wilks again. He and Brewster jogged across the dusty landing pad. Adrenaline

sparked his senses; his heart thumped. He knew
that Ripley and Falk had them covered, but that
didn't make a run through open space in unswept
territory any more comfortable. Then again, this
was what he knew how to do best. It almost felt
good.

They reached Moto and edged to the door of
the building. Wilks held up his hand for the others to stay put behind them.

"I'll kick," he said. "Moto, you're high, Brewster low—on my mark."

The three of them stepped to the entry.

"Now!"

Wilks kicked. The door crashed inward. Brewster sidled into the entry in a crouch, Moto standing. They swept the room left to right and Wilks
took in some air. It was a barracks and it looked
deserted. A row of cots lined the far wall, inter-
spaced with a series of tall cabinets that all stood
open and empty. There were no other exits.

The room was in disarray, with blankets and articles of clothing scattered about, and the air
smelled stale and musty. Dust motes swam in the
beams of sunlight and resettled. Whatever had
happened, they had missed it by weeks. Maybe
months.

"Looks clean," said Wilks. Better, it *felt* clean.

Brewster straightened up and motioned toward
the floor with his rifle. A series of bullet holes and
chipped plastecrete ran in a line up the wall behind them. A smashed cot lay nearby. It looked
like someone had tried unsuccessfully to barricade the door.

"Something went down, but it's old news," said Brewster quietly.

"Secured?" said Ripley through the 'com.

"Yeah." Wilks signed. "Only four more to go. And we should check the fliers and APC."

They backed out of the room.

Twenty minutes later, they were finished. There was a substantial amount of dried blood splashed in the mess hall, evidence of struggle in most of the structures, acid damage here and there, but no bodies and no apparent threat. Wilks felt the adrenaline seep from his system little by little, but he remained alert. Getting sloppy could cost.

As Ripley stood outside the ship and delegated responsibilities to the others, Wilks continued to scan the area. Not having a portable sensor was a bitch, although he found that as he got older, he didn't like to depend on mechanical augmentation as much. Earth had fallen to shit from too much greed and not enough humanity; the machines had just been fuel for the fire. As a young hotshot marine he had felt differently about things, but experience had taught him that nothing was infallible. . . .

Fucking middle age, he thought. *Maybe I should take up philosophy when this is over.*

If it was ever over. If they made it. The planet had become a dead end for billions of people; not so long ago, he had been a dead man walking on stolen time himself, but somewhere along the way that had changed. He was ready to play his part in the end, to finish it. . . .

"Ready," said Ripley. She started toward the hill.

"Ready," he replied, but not to anyone in particular. He started after her.

They stood at the base of the hill in front of the gate. The metal door looked as if it had been melted open with a welding device; it sported a huge gaping hole in the middle. Ripley had thought weapons fire when she had seen it from the *Kurtz*, but the edges of the hole were smooth. She wondered what exactly had gone on in the last hours here, before the scientists had been taken. . . .

Wilks stepped into the darkness first.

Ripley waited a few beats and then followed, pulled herself through the hole and took a breath. The air was thick with moisture and the smell of mold. Grayish-green moss and lichens had developed in scraggly patches along the inside of the gate. Nice place.

The small room she had stepped into led to a dark corridor; a mechanical door, stuck halfway open, separated the two.

"Talk to me, Wilks," she said.

"Got a straight walk ahead of you for ten meters, then a tee—the sign says 'armory' on the right and 'control' left. No sign of infestation, and the mold is pretty thick on either branch. I think we're alone."

Ripley let out her air and stepped around the broken door. "You heard him," she said. Moto and Tully came in behind her with the equipment cases.

"Let us know, Falk," she said softly. He would keep watch at the gate. Billie, McQuade, and the doctor were back at the *Kurtz.*

"Gotcha."

She directed her light forward as she moved down the dank hall. Wilks stood at the tee, weapon up, his face distorted in the swaying light.

"You stay here," he said. "I'll check control." His voice echoed with a faintly metallic ring.

Wilks moved off down the hall.

Ripley kept her weapon trained toward the armory, although Wilks was right—it didn't look like anyone had been here in months.

Anyone or any*thing,* she added mentally.

Moto and Tully waited with her. "Maybe the firing sequence was interrupted by some natural phenomenon," said Moto. She poked at a strand of damp moss on the wall. "These weapons were never meant to withstand exposure to the elements."

Wilks rejoined them. "Clear," he said. "Not a real complicated maze. Hall runs straight twenty meters and then elbows into control. Let me check the other side and we're set."

"I'll cover," said Ripley. "Tully, Moto, you go ahead."

Ripley clutched her weapon with damp palms— androids could sweat, after all—and waited for Wilks in the murky stillness. She was ready for this to be over with; she was tired of being looked to for answers. Billie was right—she *did* need to finish what she had started. But when it was done, she had a lot more shit to deal with. It seemed as though it would never end....

Wilks moved back to join her.

"That didn't take long," she said.

"Same setup on this side, only the door is locked and sealed. Hasn't been opened in a while, either. I think the bombs are safe."

She smiled. "Great—safe bombs."

Wilks chuckled. "Yeah, funny. I—"

"Hey," Moto crackled into their ears, "looks like we got a little more than corrosion down here." She sounded worried. "I think someone tried to put a stop to this countdown permanently."

Billie sat in the control room of the *Kurtz* and listened to Ripley's report.

"... we've localized the problem, but it's going to take longer than I'd hoped. Everything has been dislinked, and as far as we can tell, the main set of hardwiring was bollixed." Her voice was punctuated with heavy static; the 'coms weren't designed to send or receive through so many tons of rock.

"How long?" said Billie.

"We'll be lucky to get out of here by dark."

She continued to outline the situation, but Billie tuned it out. The sun was still high above; night was a good six hours away. Plenty of time.

She stood and stretched leisurely as Ripley cut off. "I'm going to take some food packets over," Billie said. "That should cheer them up."

McQuade grinned. "Or they might decide to blow us all to hell."

"Just don't give them any of the stir-fry and we're probably safe," said Jones. "Suicide *was* on my mind when I ate dinner."

Billie laughed.

"Want company?" said McQuade. "Jones could watch the sensors—"

"Nah." She hoped she sounded casual. "I'll only be a minute."

She walked back to the dining hall and gathered some of the self-heating packets and some utensils. She also stopped by the weapons stock for a few extra magazines before heading to the lower deck.

Taking a flier wouldn't jeopardize the mission; if she didn't make it back in time—well, she would just have to. She didn't expect them to wait for her.

Billie walked out of the APC dock and squinted in the bright light. The air was sweet and cool against her skin, a far cry from the canned recycled stuff that she was accustomed to. Insects and birds sang their songs in the trees around the compound. It was beautiful, what was left of it.

The firepower that the others were currently setting up would take out a big chunk of this entire region, as Ripley had explained it; but not right away.

"Six months?" Falk had said. "Why so fucking long?"

"It's a big planet. The aliens are all over it. Assuming they can swim—better, of course, if they can't and they drown—it'll take three or four months for them to *get* here. They could be 20,000 kilometers away, halfway around the planet. Allowing time for them to stop and eat and pee, six months should be plenty."

That had brought up a bunch of other questions: Why was the superqueen calling them? Maybe whoever made these war toys was coming to collect them, somebody—Wilks?—had said. Would they stay here once they arrived? Nobody knew. They had to go with what they had. They'd baited the trap and they had to allow time for the rats to get to the cheese. . . .

Billie shook the memory. Falk raised a hand as she approached.

"Brought you some lunch," she said.

"Oh, boy." He looked less than thrilled. "You gonna join us for the poisoning?"

"Nope. I thought I'd see if I could scavenge some supplies from a few of the buildings."

Falk took the assortment of foil pouches from her with a frown.

"I don't think that's such a good idea," he said. "Does Ripley know—?"

Billie shrugged. "Tell her if you want. I'm armed, the compound is empty, and McQuade is watching for activity." She tapped her headset. "Besides, I'm sick of sitting on my ass; thought I'd make myself useful."

"I hear that," said Falk. "Just be careful."

She smiled and walked away. The fliers were hidden from Falk's vantage point, two buildings away. She stepped out of view and picked up her pace a bit.

"What are you doing, Billie?" McQuade's voice spoke in her ear.

Falk spoke before she did. "Trying to find us some decent food instead of this swill," he said. "Surely you can't object to that?"

Thank you, Falk! She reached the first ship and looked inside; Wilks and the others had left the hatches popped open. The landhopper was tiny, made to accommodate a few people, with only minimal space and scant supplies. Her heart sank when she saw the ripped wires and broken plastic of the console.

"There's nothing in those ships but emergency rations," said McQuade. "Why don't you just get back here? I don't like the idea of you roaming around by yourself, and you could mess up my readings. The *Kurtz* isn't out of food—"

"I'm a big girl," said Billie as she moved to the second flier. She kept her movements casual; if McQuade saw her run, he'd sound an alarm. "I was actually looking for some more tools—"

"Billie, get back to the ship *now*," said Ripley. The edge in her voice was sharp, even through the static.

So much for playing it safe—

Billie stepped into the second flier and looked around. It seemed undamaged. She slid the hatch closed behind her and hurried to the pilot's seat. A few switches and the ship hummed to life.

"Dammit, Billie, talk to me! What the hell are

you doing? You can't *leave*; we don't have time for this!"

Billie ignored Ripley and fed the access codes and coordinates into the small computer. Thank Buddha for small favors, like nil security on the little ship. Plenty of fuel, automatic everything—

"Billie, wait!" It was Wilks. "I'll go with you, just hold on a minute—" At least he sounded more worried than angry.

"Sorry," she said. "This is the only way; I know she's not dead. I'll be back before dark if I can—"

Billie toggled the user-friendly controls and the flier began to lift. She understood most of the buttons and hoped that what she didn't know wouldn't hurt her. She yanked the headset off and threw it down as Ripley and the captain shouted at her and the small ship pivoted in the air.

She knew they were pissed, but they didn't need her to finish. Ripley's hatred was behind everything the older woman did; Billie was motivated by a feeling that seemed just as strong. Love?

She strapped in with a silent prayer as the flier rocketed south:

Please let this work.

27

Shit," Ripley said. "I should have known, she *told* me she was going to do this."

Tully and Moto continued to strip wires in the dimly lit control room.

"Nothing we can do about it now," Wilks said. An icy hand had gripped his heart; he felt as frustrated as Ripley and sick with fear for the young woman. He had known Billie longer, had known how the 'casts of the lost family had eaten at her; if anyone was responsible, he was.

If you had been thinking, you could have stopped her.

Then it was Billie's voice he heard: *Fuck off, Wilks, who do you think you are?*

Wilks gritted his teeth. There *wasn't* anything

he could do. Just hope that Billie was going
to come back. If anything happened to her,
he'd—

What?

Nothing.

Ripley said, "You're right. I just wish..."
She trailed off and absently picked up her spot
welder.

"Hey, everyone there?" McQuade's voice crackled from the set. "I got movement here, coming
from the west!"

Wilks unslung his rifle and started to the exit.

"Falk?" he said as he ran.

"Nothing yet."

"Can't get a number," said McQuade. "They're
moving in a group, five or six—"

Wilks reached the sliding door. Falk crouched
in the small anteroom, shielded by the thick
melted gate, weapon pointed out.

"They've stopped outside the compound,"
McQuade said. "Looks like—wait. Somebody's
coming."

Wilks and Falk stood together and waited.
"Everyone stay put," Wilks said.

A lone figure stumbled into view, halfway between the *Kurtz* and Orona's hill. A woman, unarmed. Her clothes were in rags, exposing one
dirty breast. Her face was a mask of fear.

"Hello?" she called out, voice quaking. "Is anyone here?" She pushed stringy, matted hair out of
her eyes and looked around nervously. "I'm safe!
We've been waiting for a ship to come—" She

turned and held outstretched arms toward the *Kurtz*, palms up. "Please!"

"Wilks?" Falk whispered. He lowered his rifle slightly.

"I dunno." He looked at the woman. Yelled: "Bring the others out into the open!"

She spun at the sound of his voice, but kept her arms up. Her face twisted and she began to sob. "Yes," she said, "of course!"

Two men and another woman walked into view, as tattered and grubby as the first person. They all looked frightened and unsure of themselves. None of them were armed.

"McQuade? Is that it?" Wilks asked.

A pause. "Can't tell. Nothing else moving."

The four stood in the open. They swayed slightly, as if holding themselves up was an effort.

"You catching this, Ripley?" said Wilks.

"Yeah." She sounded worried. "I don't like it; could be trouble."

"We got 'em covered," said Falk. "What say I step outside and see? If they got friends in the bushes, they won't fire on their own people—"

Wilks tightened his jaw. "They might."

"We could stay in here and talk about it all day," Falk said, "but eventually we're going to have to go back to the ship. Gotta do something with 'em."

Wilks nodded. He didn't like it either, but Falk was right. "Stay low and give me a clear sight," he said.

Falk raised his voice. "Okay, I'm coming out now! We have loaded weapons, so don't move!"

The first woman continued to sob, the only noise in the still air. Falk climbed through the gate, carbine trained on the ragged group. He moved toward them slowly and carefully.

Wilks put one leg through the gate and straddled it. He pointed his rifle at the clump of trees on the west—

The four people suddenly hit the ground as one, the quiet shattered as gunfire cracked across the compound.

Billie looked at the computer readings as the flier sped toward the state that had been Northern California, but she didn't touch anything. It all seemed fine; she would be at the coordinates in a little under two hours, provided nothing went wrong....

What could go wrong? I'm a top-notch pilot and Amy and her family will be standing by, waiting to jump onboard when I show up. Plus I have lots of time.

She smiled at herself. She had apparently gone insane at some point and hadn't noticed until now. When she had committed herself to saving the child back on Gateway, she'd never thought she'd be doing it this way—alone in a stolen ship. She couldn't remember *what* she had thought—

That it would be easy, maybe. That someone else would do it for me.

If she had learned anything from knowing Ripley, it was that to make something happen, *you* had to make it happen; silly and redundant, but

very true. She couldn't just sit and hope that
things would change by themselves.

Not anymore. The little girl's name was Amy,
but it was also Billie; they would make it together
or not at all.

Shit—
Wilks hit the ground. He didn't see the shooters, but he capped off a short burst into the trees
at chest level. The hillside provided partial protection; he didn't dare move—

McQuade shouted in his ear, most of it lost in
the noise. "... fuckin' two gunners, due—"

The metal gate clanged as bullets drilled into it.

Wilks fired again and spared a glance at Falk.
He was down—hit, or had he purposely dropped?
No way to know—

The four fanatics remained still, but one of the
men began to shout. "Don't kill them, we need
them, She demands them—"

The other three began to screech for salvation,
calling loudly on the Great Mother.

Oh, man! They were pinned down; they had to
do something to break this up.

Another barrage of fire *chinged* into the gate.
Wilks got an idea. He screamed and lay still, pre-
tending to be wounded.

Don't move, Falk, if you're alive, don't move!

Seconds ticked by. Wilks stared into the bushes
and waited. Sweat trickled down his neck as the
sun suddenly seemed to get much hotter. He
heard quiet movement behind him, from inside

the gate, and hoped that Ripley had the sense to stay put.

The four fanatics continued to pray in high, shaky voices.

Wilks heard twigs crackle and snap ahead of him. A dark shape moved through the woods.

"Not *yet*!" a voice tried to hiss from several meters farther into the trees. "Wait!"

Two gunners. Wilks aimed at the shape in front and fired a double tap.

The figure fell back into the shadows with a yelp.

Wilks retrained his rifle at the voice and squeezed the trigger again. The unseen sniper cried out in pain.

At the sound of the shots, the people lying next to Falk jumped up and ran toward Wilks. One of them tripped over Falk's body and smacked into the dirt.

Falk rolled over, sat up, and cracked the man's skull with the butt of his rifle.

Way to go, Falk!

Wilks fired twice more. Both of the women crumpled.

The last man stumbled onward, eyes crazed. He got close enough so that gore spattered Wilks as his final shot caught the runner in the chest. The man fell, coughed blood, and died.

"Hold it!" Wilks shouted.

Nothing moved. If the gunners were still alive, there was no sign. He came up slowly, rifle still aimed into the trees.

"Falk, you hit?" he said into the 'com.

The big man had lain back down. "Yeah. Not too bad, I don't think." His voice shook.

"Ripley?"

"Right here. Did you get them?" She didn't sound too steady either.

"Pretty sure." He wiped at the bits of tissue and blood on his skin. "That, or I shot a couple of innocent bystanders; let me check. Hang in there, Falk."

"I'm not going anywhere."

Wilks pulled into a crouch and ran low for the trees, weapon ready. If anybody moved, he or she was going to get pasted.

One of the shooters was dead, a middle-aged man with a shaved head. He'd been shot in the throat. The other was still alive, a few meters away, a small woman with a bad stomach wound. The bullets had ripped her gut to shreds. Amazingly, she was still conscious; she lay on her back and pushed at the dirt with her bare feet, trying to crawl away from the compound. She opened her eyes as Wilks approached, her face contorted with pain and rage, her abdomen a slick red tangle of exposed intestine.

"You'll—die—" she managed. "You'll—" She closed her eyes, exhausted.

It was cool in the shade of the trees; a light breeze stalled the sweat on Wilks's brow as he aimed carefully. "Yeah," he said.

The shot echoed for a long time.

Tully worked at her portable console while Ripley continued to hook the system back together in the dim light. The original detonator was set up on a sequential timer, too complicated to fix easily, so Tully worked on a chain-link relay. The hardwiring had to be clean; it had to last for a while.

Falk was okay. He had two wounds, a minor one high in the left shoulder and a slightly more serious one through the meat of his bicep. Jones had already patched him up and filled him with painkillers.

Ripley worked as quickly as she could, aware that this first trouble wouldn't be their last if they didn't hurry.

"Ready," Tully said. "We still have to tune Orona's dish to where we're gonna be when we reach a safe distance, but the program is set. In theory, we call the computer here and the clock starts running when we send the signal."

Ripley looked at the small console and nodded.

"Go try it," she said. "We don't want to count on theory."

"Right. I'll type in a command and send it. If the word shows on the screen, we have a clean signal."

"Go."

Tully grabbed a light and disappeared into the dark corridor.

Ripley stared at the jumble of wires and sighed. She didn't want to think about it, no time, but—

She had fired on the people who had run toward the gate. Meaning she wasn't First Lawed, a mandatory feature in synthetics. It was almost enough to make her believe that somehow it wasn't true, that Jones had misread the tests. Except she had never taken any kind of electronics course in her life and she knew exactly what went where; the knowledge was just *there*, like how to walk or speak. She wondered what else she knew. . . .

"Ripley?" It was Tully, her voice barely audible.

"Do it," she said into the set. She turned toward the portable and watched. A series of numbers ran across the screen and disappeared. A second passed, and the word "boom" appeared in the upper left corner in glowing green letters.

Ripley nodded. "It works."

Static intertwined with Tully's laughter, making Ripley suddenly feel very far away from everything. From humanity.

She got back to work.

Only a few minutes until landing. Billie watched the computer screen nervously and checked the action on her carbine for the hundredth time.

The ship began a gradual descent through the outskirts of an industrial town. She had flown over several small cities, had watched for signs of life all along the way; she'd seen plenty. Hundreds, thousands of aliens had run beneath her, headed north; there had been no people.

Billie hoped that the others were doing well. She also hoped that she wasn't about to crash. She rested her hands on the steering and pulled left a hair; the ship pulled left. She pushed forward and the ship nosed downward a bit.

Okay, got it—

The monitor blinked that the desired coordinates had been reached. If Amy's father had given out the wrong numbers in that last transmission, she was screwed. The flier's landing engines kicked on and it began to lower straight down. Billie maneuvered the ship over a strip of road. Rubble flew in the wake of the ship as it settled onto the pavement.

Billie unbuckled her safety straps and switched the engines off, amazed that it had been so easy. There was no movement outside the flier.

She patted the extra magazines and set of flaresticks in her hip pouch as she walked to the hatch and tried to ignore the fear. That the flying had been so simple somehow made it worse, like she had used up her luck.

Amy is the thing, she told herself firmly, *Amy and her father and Mordecai, and whoever else has become the girl's family.*

She stepped out of the flier, weapon raised, and immediately recoiled from the smell. The stench of burnt plastic and rot was overwhelming; maybe it was like that in all of the cities now. But the debris wasn't too bad, at least. Apparently there were still a few places that hadn't been destroyed completely by riots or infestation.

She walked around the ship. There was no sound, no motion; it was as if she were the only living being in an empty world. The buildings around her were all a uniform beige, and silent.

Where to start? She walked toward the structure to her right and read the lettering set above the smashed door frame. ENDOTECH MICRO. That sure sounded like a microchip company, and that's what the transmission had said, right? This had to be the place.

Unfortunately, the same lettering was on the building across the street. It was an entire complex, not one factory. Damn.

The silence was unnerving. Billie stepped through the door frame. Her boots crunched on bits of shattered plexi material as she looked up and down the entryway; halls led off into blackness in either direction.

Maybe she could find a control room of some kind with a working intercom system, or a speaker she could hook up to the flier. . . .

Brilliant. Except what the fuck do you know about wiring something like that up?

If she could fly a ship, she could figure it out. She sure as hell didn't have time to search each building—

Billie pulled a flarestick from her pocket and snapped it. The tip sizzled red—a dim light at best, but it'd have to do; if there had been a portable light onboard the flier, she hadn't seen it. She kicked herself for not thinking of it back at the compound as she stared into the pitch hallway, but there was nothing to be done about it now.

She started down the corridor to her left. Her

footsteps echoed loudly and hollowly in the cool, dead air—if anyone was in the building, she wasn't going to be a surprise to them.

Within seconds, the light from the outside had disappeared completely. The glow from the flare only illuminated the space a meter or two ahead. She walked close to one wall, held the light up to make out the words on the doors she passed—mostly names of employees, it seemed.

The hallway seemed to go on forever. She struggled to damp down a feeling of dread that threatened to rise up and bloom into panic. The stale air was clammy against her skin; she didn't know where she was headed; anything could be waiting for her, watching her—and it was dark. That was the worst; it was blacker than space—

She stopped. This was completely stupid. She would go back outside and reevaluate the situation, she was going to lose it in here—

Suddenly she heard a noise directly behind her. *Snick.*

She froze. Just a little sound, *could be anything, a shift of weight or—*

The sound of a door opening.

Billie threw the flarestick to the ground and stepped on it. It dimmed, but didn't go out entirely. The flickering glow made the shadows dance wildly. She gritted her teeth against a scream, her eyes wide and useless in the dark. She turned slowly, as quietly as she could, her brain yammering a thousand things at once.

*Human, not a drone, fanatic maybe, do I talk
or wait? Are they armed? Oh, shit, oh Amy—*

She pointed the carbine ahead of her and tried
to think clearly—

—until a pair of rough hands brushed against
her face—

28

The sound came up so gradually it took Wilks a while to realize he was hearing it and what it was.

He had taken over Falk's position outside the armory and watched as the shadows lengthened across the compound. Moto went back to work with the others after Jones assured them Falk was okay. Wilks couldn't seem to focus on much of anything except Billie; McQuade was still monitoring the sensor readings and Ripley had as much help as she needed, so Wilks leaned against the gate and waited for Billie to get back.

And wondered if she ever would.

McQuade picked up a ship to the east, too big

to be the landhopper that Billie had taken. It had
set down not far from where they had dropped
the mother queen. Apparently there were pilots in
the fanatic crowd, and none too smart. The bugs
weren't going to be separating the followers from
the baby food for long once they started arriving
in big numbers.

Now he focused on the sound. Kind of a high,
keening wail, a faint whine.

"Hurry, Ripley," he said into the 'com. "They're
coming."

Billie screamed and jerked the trigger. The
blackness broke and re-formed around the bursts
of gunfire, the sound deafening in the corridor as
the bullets hit the wall. She fell to the floor and
scrabbled backward on her elbows after catching
a glimpse of tattered clothing—

"Oh, God, don't shoot! Stop!" A man's voice.
"Please, I'm sane, I'm sane!"

He sounded as terrified as she felt. Billie held
still so that he wouldn't have a target and trained
her carbine at the voice. She held her fire as the
man babbled on.

"Please, I have to find her, don't kill me—"

Her. The word sank in and footsteps suddenly
crashed through the hallway as he ran away from
Billie, back toward the entry.

"Wait!" she shouted. "Amy!"

The footsteps stopped. He spoke again, pathet-
ically eager. "You've seen her? Please, where is
she? Who are you?"

Billie stood up. "Walk toward the exit," she said. "I've got my gun on you, so don't make any sudden moves."

As she followed his footsteps down the corridor, the full impact of his words sank in. He knew Amy.

An old, white-haired man with a ragged beard stepped into the light filtering in through the broken door. Deep lines of fear and worry creased his brow. Billie moved up to meet him.

"It's you," she said, "—your transmissions—where is Amy?"

His eyes widened. "You saw them? We had hoped that someone—" He broke off. Then: "They took her, two days ago. Mordecai was killed trying to stop them, the lunatics—she's gone. I don't even know if she's alive—" Tears welled in his eyes.

Billie felt sick. Two days! "Where did they take her?"

"There are underground tunnels throughout the complex," he said. "They have Amy with the others, part of their food or breeding stock, there's a nest at the east end—" He spoke quickly, tried to say everything at once. "I've been trying to get in but I *can't*, there were drone guards and today they started running away, north, and I heard ships, I heard your ship—"

"Take me there," said Billie. If Amy was still alive, maybe she'd be in the nest, waiting to be implanted ... maybe most of the guards would be on their way to the queen. True, there'd probably be a few left behind to guard the eggs that were still unhatched, but maybe it wasn't over yet.

Ripley had fucked up.

They pulled the control board from the wall and she worked over the dismantled pieces and stripped wires for hours. It had to go sequentially, A to B to C and so on, or the hidden bombs, some of them kilometers away, wouldn't all detonate; rewire the wrong way and the first explosion could knock the system apart. That wouldn't do at all.

It had been going fine. Tully and Moto had both finished their jobs and she was almost finished—when she suddenly discovered that something was missing. She was halfway through the seventh switch before she realized that she had run out of board to work on and she needed more.

"No," she said. She checked and rechecked; the third panel had been misdirected to the fifth. She would have to pull it loose and rewire it. It would take another two hours.

How long before the first group of drones reached the compound? Maybe long after dark. Or maybe five minutes from now . . .

She pulled the switch loose and started over. If she had to stay on Earth to finish it, she would. It didn't matter if she died—as long as the alien bitch and her children were destroyed along with her.

●　　●　　●

Billie and the old man crept down the stairwell together, the walls lined thickly with alien secretions. The main nest was in the basement of a structure only two blocks from the ship.

They had run in the dwindling light together through the empty streets, had stopped for him to tie a rag-torch before stepping into the silent building.

He held the torch high as they edged down the steps. The flame reflected off the dark, shiny substance and created a flickering illusion that the stairs themselves were alive. With each footfall the structure moved and shifted; it seemed as if they were stepping on alien bodies about to rise up—

It got hotter as they moved toward the nest; they rounded the landing and started the next flight down. A half-open door webbed with cobby spittle stood at the bottom.

A low moan, human, drifted up to greet them, followed by a chittering sigh. They stopped a few steps from the bottom. Sweat ran down Billie's spine.

"I never got this far," whispered the old man.

Billie kept her carbine trained on the door and willed her legs to move forward. The nest wouldn't be completely deserted, of course— someone had to watch the eggs—but Ripley had figured that into the time delay—

The door flung open and a drone leaped for them—

Billie fired. The thing screamed, its teeth

gnashing as its chest shattered. Acid hissed and bubbled, ate into the plastecrete.

A second howling creature catapulted over the first.

Billie's shots ripped open the long skull; its jaw dropped open and kept dropping as it fell onto the stairs. More alien blood spattered.

The old man cried out and there was a third—

It loomed in the doorway and hissed, kicked at the fallen sibling in front of it to get to them—

Billie depressed the trigger. One of the bullets hit at an angle and sparked, a tiny fire in the gloom.

The creature fell back and Billie stumbled over the dead drone at her feet to get to the door, the old man behind her.

"Don't step in the blood!" she said.

Billie lunged into the basement and fired; alien cries blended with the explosions of the carbine. The noise pounded her ears.

Dark figures darted toward her as she shot again and again—

Her left calf was on fire, the pain deep and intense—

The old man's light flickered on behind her, just in time for her to see a grinning drone clap a talon on her shoulder. Its inner set of teeth shot out of the gaping mouth and she screamed, jammed her carbine into its gut. The shots blew its abdomen out behind it. The thing's claw ripped at her flesh, tore her coverall and some of her skin, but released her and fell away. . . .

Billie panted, whipped her carbine left to right.

Nothing else came at her, nothing moved. Her skin was blistered from the blast of close gunfire; her ears rang. Acid had touched her leg and she felt her blood run from the chemical burn, but she was still standing.

The guards were all dead.

They were in a small room. The torch chased shadows in the slimy den, a dozen or so eggs in the center, most peeled open. Dim figures were strung to the walls in various stages of decay; a few looked alive, unconscious. Spidery dead larvae littered the floor and the place reeked of rotten flesh.

"Amy—" said the old man. He stepped past Billie. She felt a scream rise up when she saw what he moved toward.

A small figure roped to the wall, head down, short reddish hair—

What had been a person moaned, lifted its face to the light. . . .

An emaciated young man, his skin cracked, one eye swollen closed. Drool ran down his bearded chin.

He grinned at the old man, his puffy tongue hanging out. "I'm pregnant," he croaked, words slurred. Caked blood nestled in the corners of his mouth.

"Where are they?" said Billie, her voice shrill. "Where's Amy?"

The man's head lolled forward. Amy's father

grabbed his hair and jerked his head back, held the torch close to the dying man's face.

"Presents," he said. A bubble of pus in one nostril popped open; the liquid ran over his scabbed lips. "The Chosen—breeders flew away—serve the Mother"—the word came out *muder*—"flew to oneness . . . revelation. She waits—"

"No," Billie said. The ships that the old man had heard—

He turned to her, awful realization on his tired face.

". . . the holy land . . ." rasped the fanatic.

"She's lost," said the old man. His voice hitched.

"Stand back," said Billie. She rammed a new magazine into her rifle and tossed the empty to the floor. "I know where they went."

And they would go there: Orona's mountain, the holy land—

But first things first.

Billie pointed the carbine and pulled the trigger.

The howls of the closing army were nearer, more distinct now. He knew it took thousands of the bugs to make that kind of noise; Wilks scanned the skies as the minutes stretched by, the compound bathed in reddish twilight. If Billie didn't return soon—

The *Kurtz* could circle and wait for a while, but they only had so much fuel. And they couldn't stay put with that many aliens on their way.

Thinking about it, Wilks realized they had made a mistake. They should have wired the bombs first, parked the ship with the queen somewhere else to draw the brood, then dropped her off after things were ready. They hadn't thought it out right, hadn't expected the damned things to come so fast, for there to be so many of them from that direction—

Shit, shit, shit—

"Done!" Ripley said.

Wilks took a deep breath and let it out slowly. He knew Ripley would wait until the last possible second to pull out, but that second seemed much closer suddenly—and it was almost dark.

"Wilks! Company, due west, *now*!" McQuade shouted.

Wilks pointed his rifle at the trees and yelled through the gate. "Ripley, Moto, let's move!"

An unseen alien screamed from nearby as Moto and then Ripley stumbled through the hole in the door. They dropped the tool cases and unslung their carbines.

As a unit, the three of them moved toward the ship.

The woods crashed and crunched with the sounds of movement, but there was still nothing to see—

The first drone broke from the trees and ran into the compound, its long body hunched, arms extended. It was going to see the queen, but they were between it and her.

All three of them fired at once. The thing

shrieked and hit the ground, nearly cut in two by the armor-piercing bullets.

The forest suddenly erupted, spewed forth a handful of the drones at once. They loped for the threesome, howled as the rain of bullets found them.

"Come *on!*" someone shouted behind them.

It was Falk. He stood in the hatchway of the *Kurtz*, bandaged arm limp, rifle extended with his good arm.

"Go," Ripley said. She stood her ground, continued to fire as more of the drones ran into view.

Wilks and Moto ran the few meters to the ship as Ripley and Falk covered.

Wilks spun in the open hatch and fired. Dozens more of the bugs came out of the trees, their insane bodies moving at great speed—

"Ripley!" he yelled.

She backed to the *Kurtz* without looking and nearly tripped on the deck. Wilks took out three more of the creatures as she turned and stumbled inside.

Falk hit the button. The hatch slid up and in, too slow. Wilks crouched down and fired as several of the bugs scrabbled to get in. One of the drones grabbed at the barrel of his rifle just before the deck shut. He shot its glistening teeth through the back of its skull.

Tiny molten flecks peppered Wilks's cheeks.

But they were all inside. A score of aliens pounded at the closed hatch, their cries muffled through the alloy.

"McQuade, Brewster, get us out of here!"
Ripley yelled into her set.

Wilks slammed a fist against the hatch.

Billie was too late.

29

The flier descended slowly over the trees.

Despair washed over Billie at the sight of the empty compound—well, almost empty. Even in the heavy dusk she could see the dark, alien bodies strewn on the ground.

"Oh, no," she said softly.

The old man clenched his hands and said nothing. She had explained the situation on the way. Since the coordinates were preset and neither of them was a pilot, they'd had to return to the compound first; Billie had hoped that the *Kurtz*'s computer could help them locate Amy's ship, but now—

They'd had to leave, there'd been no choice, she told herself over and over.

In spite of what she knew to be the truth, a knot formed in her throat; she had been abandoned. Ripley had finished the detonator and the *Kurtz* had left. They would die.

Billie swallowed hard as the ship settled gently to the ground. She had made her decision and had no alternative but to accept the results.

"I'm sorry," she said. She didn't look at him, didn't want to see the pain on his face as their mutual hope died.

"It's not your fault," he said, his voice dull. "You tried. I—I'm glad it'll be over soon."

"We could try to escape the blast," she said, but disregarded the words as she spoke them. Where would they go? The planet would be dead, was already dead—

"Amy was all I had," he said. "It doesn't matter."

Tears finally spilled down Billie's cheeks and she nodded. She understood.

She turned to him, not certain of what to say—

And heard the sound of engines overhead.

Her heart pounded as she grabbed for the comset by her feet and held the plug to her ear.

"...in, Billie! Talk to me!" It was Brewster.

Her tears turned to relieved sobs as the old man put his arm around her and laughed out loud.

"No," said Ripley. "We have to get out of here, now. If the things come back and start poking around the compound, they could mess up the bombs. I'm sorry."

Jesus, what a shitty deal, she thought. She *was* sorry; but the truth was that someone had to keep the priorities straight.

The *Kurtz*'s engines were cycling. Ripley stood in the APC bay with Billie and the old man, had listened to their story with mixed emotions. The initial happiness that Billie had returned had been replaced by frustration and disbelief. And a horrible, dreadful sense of nostalgia.

"You don't have to wait for us," said Billie. She wiped at her tear-stained face roughly, like a child, but stood tall. "Just help us find the ship. You can do that with the computer in a minute."

"And then what?" said Ripley. "You're going to set down in the middle of 10,000 drones on the chance that she's alive? I understand *why,* I know how it feels, but that's suicide!"

Ripley knew that she was right, but suddenly didn't want to meet Billie's gaze. *Did* she remember how it felt?

Fucking hypocrite. What had happened to her? All she wanted now was to destroy the breed that had destroyed her life—by taking her daughter.

"Maybe you can leave without her," Billie said. "I can't."

Ripley didn't speak, her thoughts jumbled. Her goal was to kill the creatures. Once upon a time, there had been other goals. Back when she still cared . . .

She looked up at Billie and saw a very familiar face.

"A ship set down about ten klicks east a few

hours ago," she said. Her mind began to clear as she spoke.

Ripley turned to the old man. "Can you handle a military carbine?"

"My eyesight isn't so good," he said, "but I can probably hold my own."

Ripley shook her head. "This isn't going to be a few drones, and it won't be easy in the dark." She paused. "I guess I'll have to go with you," she said to Billie.

Wilks watched as Ripley gathered extra magazines and two portable lamps from supply and felt the anger build. Finally, he couldn't stand it.

"You're out of your fucking minds!" He searched for words, frustrated. "Think about it!"

Ripley spoke over her shoulder as if she hadn't heard him. "Stay here as long as you can, then put down somewhere safe nearby. We'll come back here. If we haven't shown on the sensors in an hour, you get to be in charge again."

She turned, faced him, expression set. "Don't fuck it up."

He wanted to scream. When McQuade had spotted Billie's flier, something inside of him had—*released*; that was the only word he could put to it. And now Billie *and* Ripley were about to go try and kill themselves.

No. Stop this.

"I'll come with you," he said. "At least let me do that—"

"No," said Ripley calmly. She shouldered her rifle. "Someone's got to make sure things get finished."

"You can start the timer going now," he said. "In six months it goes off, we don't have to wait—"

"Wilks—" Ripley began.

"She's not your kid!" he tried.

Billie and Ripley looked at each other and then at Wilks. "Yeah, she is," Billie said. "She's ours."

Ripley said, "Besides, we don't have any room."

"That's bullshit! There's—"

"Cut it, Wilks. We're going, you're not."

He followed them down the steps and into the APC bay and tried to think of something else to say. The old man waited there. Moto stood nearby with a rifle.

"Ready?" said Billie.

The old man touched her arm. "I wish I could be of more help," he said. He started to say something else, then fell silent.

Billie nodded. Ripley handed her a lamp as Moto stepped to the entry button.

Wilks looked at Billie. He wasn't sure how he felt, didn't know what could happen between them in the right circumstances, but—

She looked back at him, obviously prepared for some kind of plea. Defiant, strong—

"Please come back," he said to her. "You have to come back, kid, because ... because—"

She put her fingers on his lips. "I know, David."

Christ, he felt as if he were going to cry. He turned to Ripley. "Be careful," he said.

She nodded at him.

The door opened and they were gone.

They flew to the east without speaking. Billie was scared but determined, and she could see that Ripley felt the same way. There was nothing to say.

The flier's lights illuminated very little of the landscape, a blanket of trees and the peaks of the hills.

As they got closer to the queen's mountain, the noise increased, making the situation pretty damned clear. The combined hisses and howls of the monsters almost drowned out the ship's engines as they circled the peak.

Billie drew in a ragged breath as the flier's lights lit the ground. The circle of light was filled with moving black shapes.

"The ship is a little farther east," said Ripley. "Maybe it won't be so bad."

"Maybe," said Billie. She had never been much on gods, given her upbringing, but she prayed to any that might exist that Amy was still alive.

Ripley vaguely remembered some part of a quote as she maneuvered the ship toward the small peak in front of them. How did it go? Into the valley of death rode the six hundred...?

Below, maybe 100,000 of the queen's children screeched, a roiling sea of deadly, mindless monsters. She wondered what was on the agenda for their convention, if they had any idea what they were doing here or what was going to happen to them. And she wondered how many more there were to come.

They skimmed the peak and Ripley slowed the flier. They didn't have to search, at least. The land was flat here, some kind of recreational area gone to seed. The ship was in plain view, directly starboard.

Dozens of the drones ran west through the light of the descending ship. Ripley edged the hopper as close as she could to the larger ship and set it down.

The pounding started almost immediately. Through the shield dark figures continued to stream past, their cries Dopplering away.

Both of them stood and moved toward the hatch.

"We stick together," said Ripley. "Get inside, find her, back out."

Billie nodded, her cheeks flushed.

She's probably dead, thought Ripley, but didn't say it. After all, so where they.

She slid the hatch aside.

The doors of the ships faced one another, both open.

Billie leapt from the flier and faced east. She depressed the trigger without aiming; it wasn't necessary. A wall of creatures ran into the blasts and fell, sprayed acid and bits of exoskeleton behind them.

Ripley jumped with her and fired repeatedly into the oncoming tide of drones.

An alien skittered across the top of the flier and

prepared to lunge. Billie smashed in its chest with a short burst.

They sidestepped to the breeder ship, weapons on full auto. Enough of the things had dropped to create an obstacle; more monsters clambered over their fallen siblings to be slaughtered.

Billie ejected a spent magazine and slammed in another, just in time to pick another creature off the roof of the ship. The explosive bullets were shattering the things, and still they screamed and charged.

When they hit the entry of the breeder ship, Ripley covered as Billie moved inside.

A drone shrieked, reached for Billie from inside the doorway—

She sprayed it with steel and its acidic blood spewed and bubbled the wall—

The alien cries quieted abruptly as Ripley slammed the hatch closed.

Billie moved into the hold. Dim emergency lighting, two exits, there didn't seem—

A creature howled and emerged from one of the hallways in a crouch, cramped by the two-meter-high ceiling—

Ripley blasted it.

The monster's head blew apart; its arms flailed for another second before it realized it was dead and fell to the floor.

They scanned the room for more. Billie took in the human blood that painted the interior, the articles of shredded clothing that lay about. And the bodies.

"Amy!" she screamed.

It had been a massacre. Billie counted twenty humans, maybe more, in a tangled heap in a corner of the room. Some had been ripped apart—there she saw a naked arm separated from its torso, here a disembodied leg. . . .

She stepped over the serrated tail of one of the dead bugs and screamed again. "Amy!"

No response. There was only the pounding of her heart, matched by the pounding cries of the alien sea behind them.

Ripley took in the destruction, the wasted life that littered the ship, her mind in overdrive. She had been here before. . . .

Billie took a step toward what was probably the control area and called for the girl again. Nothing. The young woman approached the heap of corpses, searched for the lost child in their midst. Ripley kept her rifle trained on the door closest to Billie.

It's better if she's dead than taken—But her heart wrenched as Billie let out a cry and fell to her knees before the pile, her face gray.

"No, no, no—" Billie repeated the word again and again as she reached through the tangle of limbs—

—and the hatch behind them pulled loose with a metallic screech and monstrous cries filled the room—

Billie was nauseated. The people must have huddled together at the end as they attempted to fend off an attack. At least two of the dead still clutched weapons—had the breeders gotten control? Or had the fanatics finally understood that the creatures didn't give a shit about *any* human life?

It didn't matter, none of it. She felt a blind second of hope as she looked quickly at each body.

A small face, flecked with gore, eyes closed, half beneath the body of a tattered corpse. Billie felt her legs buckle; words of denial came from far away, from her.

Amy.

Billie shoved at the bodies, placed a shaky hand on the tiny brow. Oh, God, Amy—

The little girl's eyes flickered open.

Gunfire roared.

Ripley spun and fired. Two meters away, a drone's grin melted and ran. A speckle of burning acid hit Ripley's arm as she shot again; another bug's chest exploded into black shards. She backed up a step as a third creature ducked toward her from the stream outside—

"Billie!" she yelled. She opened fire; the blasts took the bug at its thighs, the limbs skittered away from its torso, and still it reached—

The thing's arms flew back as Billie stepped beside her and shot its abdomen to bits. A scream—

Amy?

The scream was human, a child's. A red-haired girl clung to Billie and cried out, the sound lost as the weapons thundered.

Ripley moved forward again. They had to get

back to the flier, back past the relentless wash of
death—

—her rifle clicked empty as a taloned claw shot
through the entry and grabbed at her—

—and Billie fired, sent alien shrapnel flying as
Ripley jammed a new magazine into her carbine—

It had to be now.

"I'll cover!" Ripley shouted. "Go!"

She jumped out into the darkness. She sprayed
bullets, cut at the things. She was dimly aware
that Billie and the girl were ducking behind her
toward the flier, was dimly aware that she was
screaming—a hoarse cry of rage from deep inside. All thought was gone, blotted out by the
hatred that controlled her, that pulled the
trigger—

They ran toward the flier, almost there—

Billie slapped at the external control. The hatch
opened.

The girl stumbled, fell into the flier. Billie was
right behind her, Ripley almost on top of them.
Ripley spun, hosed her weapon back and forth,
sleeting death on full auto—

The hatch closed as her weapon ran dry.

The ship rocked from side to side as the aliens
swarmed over and around it, howled and hit.

The girl huddled against the wall and sobbed.

Billie crooned at the girl: "It's okay, Amy, it's
okay, it's okay—"

Ripley ran to the pilot's seat and fumbled with
the controls. There was a splintering crash from
behind, then another.

They're tearing the goddamn walls—

"Hang on!" Ripley screamed.

The engine whined and groaned. And lifted the ship several meters before letting it crash back to the ground.

The impact dropped Billie to the floor. She turned to the child, who trembled and cried but didn't seem injured.

Too much weight—

The flier couldn't lift with the monsters still clinging to it, screaming—

There was a wrenching crack from the rear. A jagged, gaping hole appeared in the wall. Black taloned arms pulled at the edges, widened it. A strange, oily smell filled the small ship.

Billie aimed at the hole as a great black skull, teeth dripping, hissed and craned into the flier.

"Billie, no! Don't—"

Billie fired. The drone vanished—and the entire rear of the little ship exploded into flames.

Ripley smelled the fuel and turned; the fuckers must have ruptured the tank—

She saw Billie point her weapon.

"Billie, no! Don't shoot!"

The words were lost as a great flash of heat washed over Ripley. Billie was thrown backward; the little girl tumbled with her to the front.

Aliens shrieked outside.

Fuck—!

Ripley ran to the hatch, weapon extended, and hit the control. Nothing. Electrical and hydraulics were shot, the door jammed.

The fire spread toward them, licked up the walls as the air became thick with greasy smoke. They were going to fry, unless—

She triggered the explosive bolts and the hatch fell away. Cool air rushed in.

Billie staggered over, coughing, one arm around the child.

They had to make it back to the breeder ship and pray that it would make air—

Ripley raised her weapon and stepped back into the middle of the nightmare.

Billie hustled Amy out the door in front of her. She searched the darkness wildly for targets, but the creatures were preoccupied with the flames. A drone fell toward them with a scream, its spindly torso coated and consumed with fire. Bright orange crackled up its dark body as it writhed on the ground. Other aliens drenched in flaming fuel ran from the ship, living torches.

Amy screamed and pointed to the roof of the breeder ship. Billie aimed as a monster flung itself toward them, shot it. The creature clattered to the ground.

"Move!" shouted Ripley. She ran for the breeder ship, firing occasional bursts of ammo at the creatures that still ran at them.

There were at least a dozen caught in the explosion. The huge bugs danced and hissed, lit the night with their fire-soaked movements. The air had heated to blistering—and the creatures had ceased attacking.

They didn't like fire, Billie remembered.

She and Amy followed Ripley back onto the breeder ship.

Stupid, stupid—! Ripley had tried to warn her; she should have known the smell of fuel.

"Watch the door!" Ripley yelled. She ran for the control room. Billie aimed at the broken hatch, her vision blurred from the heat and sweat.

Amy screamed behind her—

Billie pivoted, saw the drone rise up from behind the form-chairs and reach for Amy—

The spray of bullets batted it down. Amy cried out again, looked past Billie—

—and Billie spun just in time to see a scrabbling shape, coated with fire and screeching, run into the entry and jump for her.

There was a dead man in the pilot's chair, his throat torn out.

Ripley kicked at him. The body slid to the floor with a thump. She dropped into the seat, stabbed at the controls, and the ship's engines coughed to life.

Relief, cool and welcome, flooded over her.

She heard the little girl scream, heard Billie's weapon rumble and roar as she continued to check the readings. Hardly enough fuel to take off, recyclers down, landing gear disabled, shields missing—they'd be lucky to move at all.

Just a little, just enough, just get us out of here—

Amazed, Ripley discovered she didn't want to die.

•   •   •

The creature fell toward Billie; its dying claws clutched at her torn coverall. Hot pain as the fire burned her arms and chest—

She rammed the weapon out, jerked the trigger—

The monster flew back, sprayed pieces of burning shell. Billie slapped at the fire on her clothes, the stench of burned flesh and hair her own. She dry-heaved once with pain and the odors of cooked skin—

The ship jerked suddenly beneath her feet. Billie stumbled backward and fell.

"Hold tight!" she shouted to Amy. She saw that the girl had grabbed on to the edge of a form-chair.

She turned back to the door, everything in slow motion now as the world shook—

—yet another monster scrabbled at the entry and Billie fired, blew it back. Strange, she had only seen its head—

She hiked herself up on one elbow and watched. The night was lit from the burning flier, monsters howled and ran past the doorway, the smell of burned materials gagged her—but—

Amy was alive.

It was her last thought before the darkness claimed her for itself.

The ship trembled as Ripley worked the lift controls. It rose at a slant, one of the mains out— but it did rise.

Fuck coordinates. Ripley grabbed the stick and

pushed, led the disabled ship up and away from the creatures, headed west.

"Got 'em!" Tully shouted.

Wilks felt a grin spread across his face.

The *Kurtz* was in the air, flying an eight pattern high over the compound. Wilks hadn't waited for the bugs to show—half an hour into Ripley's time limit, he'd had Brewster take the ship up. If they were coming back, better that they had a clear spot to land. . . .

Tully frowned. "Wait. It's not them—"

"Who else—?" Wilks began and then stopped. He leaned over her shoulder and checked the read. It was the other ship, the breeder. As he watched, the vessel got closer to the compound and started down—

"It's gonna crash," said Tully, her voice cracking.

It was them, it had to be, and they were about to smack down hard. Wilks clenched his fists and waited.

The ship was called the *Coleman*, according to the control board. Odd how she would notice a thing like that at a time like this. She navigated the landscape as best she could, but the crippled flier dipped and swayed alarmingly. She shouted Billie's name once, but no answer. She had no time to panic; alarm lights blinked across the console and told her that the flight would be a short one.

They were almost to the compound when the blinking overheat panel turned to solid red.

"We're going down!" she called back. Sweat dripped from her scalp and she lowered the ship, prayed that the drop wouldn't kill them when the engines cut out.

The ship sheared off the tops of a dozen trees and hit the ground in a steep slide.

"Get down there, now!" said Wilks. His body felt tight and shaky as Brewster took the *Kurtz* down.

Billie opened her eyes as something shook her awake. She hurt all over, her stomach swam and dived—

Everything was strange, tilted. She sat up sideways and shook her head, wondered—

"Amy?" Her throat felt dry as sand.

The little girl clutched at a bolted chair across the room and wept. At the sound of Billie's voice, she lifted her puffy face and looked at her.

"Your daddy sent us," said Billie. "He's safe."

"Really?" Amy's eyes widened.

"Yes," said Billie. "Really."

Amy's face changed, the look of despair swept away. Tears still running, the child stood and stumbled across the room toward Billie, who stretched out her arms. Amy fell into them and hugged her hard.

Billie felt no pain, in spite of her wounds.

In fact, she'd never felt better in her whole life.

• • •

Ripley limped into the room and saw the two of them embracing. The sound of the *Kurtz*'s engines overhead was beautiful, a perfect complement to the picture before her.

"Let's get out of here," she said. Tears trickled down her cheeks for the first time in as long as she could remember.

She could still cry.

Something else to live for.

30

The *Kurtz* lifted, up through the atmosphere to where Orona's dish would be aimed. The dark Earth fell away.

Wilks stood at the door of medlab.

Billie and Ripley had both been wounded, but not as badly as he'd first thought when they'd staggered out of the ship. Both had acid burns, and Billie had inhaled a good amount of chemical smoke, but they were going to be okay. Jones checked the child for implantation; she was clean.

It was over. *Almost*, he amended.

He felt—pretty good, actually. For a change. The way Billie had smiled at him in medlab had something to do with it. . . .

He'd thought that the end would leave him empty, but it was having an opposite effect. There was still a lot of universe out there. He was old, yeah, but not dead yet.

Not by a long fucking shot. For a burnout, for a dumbass marine who had wasted so much of his life waiting for it to be over, he had finally done something worth doing—and now, he decided, it was time to move on.

Yeah.

Billie lay in her cot and felt sleepy and warm. Whatever Jones had given her was doing her a world of good.

Amy and her father had just left for the dining hall, hands linked. They'd sat on the exam table next to her for an hour, exchanged stories, paused now and then for pats and hugs. Amy cried through much of it; the emotional wounds would be slow to heal, Billie knew. But she would be there to help.

Billie felt a sense of peace that she had never felt before. The hiding was over. She had set out with the others little more than a scared child herself, had faced fears that had plagued her entire life—and had survived.

No, better. *They* had survived. Ripley, Wilks, Amy and her father, the rest—now they could move on.

To what, she didn't know—and as she felt consciousness slip away, she found she didn't care. There was love in her ... for Amy, for David— hard to think of him that way and not as Wilks, but she could get used to it. Things were okay—

Billie slept.

• • •

Ripley touched the plastiskin on her arm absently and stared into the blank computer. She sat in front of the controls, Tully, Wilks, and McQuade nearby.

Seeing Amy and Billie together had reminded her of a few things from her past, emotions that were real and strong, synthetic or not. She had played a part in the lives of these people; and she had discovered something in herself that she'd thought was gone forever—self-respect. She was ready to give a shit about who she was—*what* she was. Somehow, it wasn't nearly so frightening anymore. . . .

"Whenever you're ready," Tully said.

Ripley put her fingers on the keys; a sudden rush of energy flowed through her. What word could she type in, what word would tell the story best? It didn't matter, of course—any four-letter command on the right frequency would send the signal that began the countdown, the pulse that would start the clock running—but it felt important anyway, some symbolic gesture of the finality. . . .

After a moment, she tapped in the word *Life* and looked at it for a few seconds. Yes. That was appropriate.

With a steady hand, Ripley reached for the send key.

ALIENS

GENOCIDE

For the Haldemans—
Jay and Vol
Joe and Gay
Thanks for everything, folks!

Prologue

The planet was not hell.

It just looked and smelled and tasted like it, according to the marines who had come there and raped it.

Its denizens were not demons.

They were far worse.

The marines simply called it Hiveworld, although the navigators of hyperspace had an obscure numbered tag for it. They had come here, to this blighted planet, and they had plundered it, stealing its queen mother.

Without the psychic bonds of the ruler to guide the lives of her minions, genetic drift occurred. Different queens, pretenders to the throne, developed and flourished.

All were killed by the most dominant of the bunch, a traditional creature who could have been

1

an identical twin to the queen mother who had perished in a nuclear blast in the Pacific Northwest of Earth.

Call them "black."

Call her the "black queen mother."

And the new group, the changelings.

Call them "red," though they were not red. To a casual observer, they looked identical. But to the "blacks," through touch and smell and morphic fields, they were anathema. Strangers, aliens. Freaks that had to be destroyed.

Leader of this new brood, living against all calculable probability, was the "red" queen mother.

Bearer of recessive genes, any sign of whose chromosomal changes had brought instant death in the hive before.

The red queen mother and her minions fled. In the confusion of reorganization, they escaped and they established a new hive far enough away to thrive.

The red queen mother spawned, using the herds of animals that roved this bleak planet.

A new rival kingdom was created and for years the kingdoms lived in peace.

But each knew instinctively that the other hive was the enemy, that this peace would not last long. And when war came, the principle weapons would be in the numbers of warriors.

And so the creatures bred . . . and bred. . . . and bred.

While others of their ilk were hunted under different suns . . .

1

The alien hive was exactly at Hollywood and Vine.

The god of the bugs alone knew if the sliming, sucking, skulking bastards knew the cultural significance of the intersection they'd chosen. In truth, that section of La-La land wasn't exactly what it had once been, but then nothing in Los Angeles was these days. And the fact that they chose to infest the old creaking bank building, in what after all was comparatively open territory, testified to the fact that this batch's IQ seemed rather low.

Still, thought Captain Alexandra Kozlowski as she stood a block away from the sun-faded concrete dialing the polarizing filter down on her faceplate against the grim and gritty southern California sun. You could count on each and every one of the merciless mother-killers being just as

mean and nasty and ornery as the worst of the last
hive she'd exterminated for Uncle Sam.

Who ya goin' to call?

Bug Busters!

Oddly enough, it felt good to be back in an
E-suit, clunky helmet and all.

She turned to the hunky lieutenant to her left,
already sweating in his armor.

"Got your jock strap on tight, Lieutenant Michaels?"

"You want to check?" The square jaws grinned
defiantly and the blue eyes crinkled.

"Maybe later." She winked and chinned her radio. "Approaching hive zero zero nine, LA sector B
forty-seven." She chinned her radio off and gave a
significant look to the platoon under her command: 69th platoon. AOE. Alien Occupation Eradication. The toughest soldiers in the biz. They all
looked back at her, smiles covering what she knew
was fear.

A fear she felt in her own heart.

A fear every time she got near the things.

"Roger, it's a go, Captain," crackled the command voice over her radio. "Commence explor-
atory and extermination. Backup targeted."

In Captain Alexandra Kozlowski's humble opinion, the "backup" should have been all that was necessary. A couple of borer missiles with multi-K
payloads, primed to go off when the sensors were
buried in alien hive musk. Just burn the bastards,
erase them, destroy. However, with the numbers of
aliens so significantly reduced on this, the eigh-
teenth year following the Alien-Earth War, scientists
and private interests wanted carcasses, pickled eggs,

photographs, and any royal jelly that could be scarfed up.

This meant Personal Delivery. Service with a Death Grin. Rock and roll and kill.

Well, it kept a lot of kids out of gangs, anyway.

The other twenty members of this assault squad had the same radios in their suits and heard the same message, but Kozlowski gave the hand signal anyway, just to reinforce her command—and to assure herself of it as much as to remind her "bug guys."

They rolled out. They were just foot soldiers marching alongside the anchor vehicle, a Mark 23 Access Tank. In this kind of operation, if you needed extra ammo or just a quick ham sandwich, not to mention a little close-up heavy artillery, it was nice to have a Big Metal Brother along. The metal treads chewed up old concrete and worn metal stars on the Walk of Fame as the troop approached their objective. Almost immediately they broke through the ribboned "perimeter" that had been staked out when the authorities for what was left of Los Angeles had determined the existence of the hive in the old Bank of America Building. Basically, this informed the natives that this was a danger zone, that if they trespassed—no sweat off legal backs—you were likely to become egg-fodder.

Even here, fifty meters from the objective, Kozlowski could see the hardened ooze of the hive stuff filling up the building's windows and frozen down the side.

"Hey, Koz!" said Lieutenant Michaels. "Why did the bug cross the road?"

"To get to the other side, wreak havoc, kill and

spread its kind, and generally give 'life' a bad name, you asshole," she barked back.

"You heard it before!"

"You know I hate jokes while I'm working."

"Just smart-ass remarks."

"As long as they're *mine*, subordinate officer Michaels."

He glared at her and she started defiantly as they marched along. It was a way they'd found they could get up for a heavy mission like this. Afterward, when the acid got sluiced from their suits and any wounds were mended, she and Michaels also had another tradition.

Strip and hump each other's sweaty bodies like bloody bunnies.

Ain't love grand? thought Kozlowski as she let her keening hormones blend with adrenaline and regulation Army boosters for what brewed up to be a regular Kamikaze Cocktail. She and Michaels had been an item for a year now, which in this Idiot's Army was just about a lifetime. The favorite gag around the barracks was that if the captain and the lieutenant ever got hitched and pregnant, the spawn would come charging out its birth parent (it was still up in the air in the minds of the privates as to who that would be) with a flamethrower in one hand, a missile launcher in the other—and a grenade in its mouth.

As for Kozlowski, she was always just glad that they could spend any time together at all.

They'd met in the service and he fit her like a hand in a glove. He was a couple years younger than her twenty-eight, an army brat who'd spent his younger years first in a safe area on Earth, then

offworld after the evacuation . He was smooth and
fit, a devotee of exercises and sports, a big blond
package of sexuality that she never grew tired of
unwrapping. Captain Alex's muscles—and scars—
had been earned in the field. Even before she'd
joined the army she'd been battling the aliens. Her
parents—landowners in Montana—had stayed and
battled the things. She'd lost her brothers to the
monsters, her mother had died of a broken heart—
and her pop . . . Well, her pop was a tangle of mean
gristle and bone and determination, eternally
guarding his ranch under the big blue sky against
the critters from beyond.

And Alex? Well, Alex was just a chip off the old
tendon, a small-breasted, big-hipped storm cloud of
a gal, feisty as an undefeated bantam-weight
fighter. She had a brunette haircut from the Bowl-
on-the-Head Salon, dark eyebrows like accents
over burning hazel eyes, and a pair of scars like pa-
rentheses over a classically cut face. She could
fight or make love with equal abandon. She just
wasn't sure which she liked better.

A burnt stench was hanging over the area, moving down from the Cahuenga Pass like a curse.
Smog hung over the rest of the city like a stubborn
spirit condemned to hell but staying put. The
squad rolled along with practiced ease to the hole
that was the principle entrance to the nest.

Ten meters from the entrance, she chinned her
radio and commanded a halt. "Okay. Main thrust
force. Double line. Let's move it."

However, before they could even assemble, the
defenders struck.

Five large bugs, the sun gleaming sickly on their

carapaces, their prehensile skeletal tails snapping
behind them, scuttled from the frontmost tunnel,
just below the crooked sign that read BANK OF AMER-
ICA.

"Jesus! Guns!" she cried, unstrapping her own
.45mm blaster. "Rodriguez . . . Swivel and fire.
Take cover!"

Like the crack team they were, the soldiers broke
ranks and took positions as though this were all in
the plan. Even as Kozlowski lowered her rifle, the
turreted guns of the tank angled and aimed. A
nanosecond later, they spoke, hurling a frenzied
hail of fire at the enemy.

Kozlowski found her crosshairs, aligned them on
the closest alien—a twisted thing with a burned or
deformed forelimb—and squeezed off a charge.

The stream of fiery energy tore off its feet at
what served as its kneecaps. The thing acted as
though losing its limbs was an everyday affair. Slavering as though in anticipation of burying its secondary jaws in Kozlowski's throat, the xeno raced
onward.

The others let loose with their own weapons,
only staggered beats behind Kozlowski and the
tank.

The resulting fire tore the X's apart. Arms and
heads and deadly acid blood flew and splattered.
Entrails blew across the street. One of the banana-
shaped heads rolled toward them like a lobbed
bomb.

Instinctively Kozlowski aimed and fired, crushing
and rendering the thing a charred, fragmented
skull.

She gave them a moment to play a little more

fire at the things, just in case, and then ordered a cease.

The smoke slowly cleared, revealing the scattered, steaming remains of the bugs.

"What the hell was *that*?" said Michaels, taking in a hoarse breath, sweat now pouring down his temples.

Ultimately, as always, it was their trained reflexes that saved them. This kind of offensive action in midday hardly ever happened with the aliens.

Kozlowski shook her head. "Don't know. These bugs . . . they're getting weird."

"Big sons of bitches," muttered Sergeant Garcia, lifting his helmet to spit onto the street.

"Yes," said Michaels. "Maybe we'd better send a robo in there."

"Right? You think the Army's going to waste good robots when they've got cheap soldiers?" Kozlowski snorted disgust, lifted her faceplate, hawked and spit out a gob of phlegm on one of the smoking bodies. "C'mon. These xenos have got something in there they don't want us to have. Which makes me want it!"

Michaels nodded, but Alex detected a glint of fear in his eyes, of vulnerability and foreboding. A pang of empathy sprang inside her: the poor guy. Spiking the X's wasn't second nature to Peter Michaels. He hadn't jammed his instinctive horror and terror of the things back into a rock-hard ball to use against them. For a moment she wanted to hold him. Hold him and tell him that it would be okay, that this was just a destructive game and when it was over, she'd soothe his hurts and make everything all right.

But she couldn't. She was in charge here. She was the dominant, and she had to pretend she'd left her femininity back in the makeup case in the locker.

"All right, groaners. Pop 'em if you got 'em, and let's get in there while their carapaces are around their ankles!"

A halfhearted cheer sounded in her earphones as she dialed out a pill for herself. One second, two seconds. Hold the nose, open the gums—look out, stomach, here it comes. She opened her mouth just in time to accept the dosage of Wail. Getting it intravenously was faster, but the designers of these suits hadn't figured out how to safeguard soldiers from accidentally getting jammed with drug-filled needles.

Pills were just fine with Koz. She had an oral fixation anyway. She took lots of pills. Oodles. The higher-ups not only didn't mind, they helped supply them. Yep, things were sure different in This Gal's Army.

"All right, assholes. Let's roll!"

Holding her gun at the ready, she waved them on and the mechanical pack kicked into motion again, heading for that door into X-land.

By the time they made it to the otherworldly entrance, the drugs had kicked in. Kozlowski felt a power, an elation—a sense of belonging and an Army urge to fuse her forces into a brilliant battering ram and crush out this threat to Earth. Primal territorial urges were tapped. She was the leader of a Neanderthal pack, guarding her tribe from sabertooths. She was the head of a village on the English coast, guarding her kin from marauding Vikings, broadsword gleaming in the lightning. She was Gaia, guarding her precious brood from cosmic crawly interlopers.

The suited soldiers entered the hole into the bank building without incident. They continued down the tunnel. It was like a tube through a cancer. Noxious drippings oozed along the sides. X-holes always had an acrid, unnerving stench. Alex had already kicked in her filters.

"Looks like a normal hive to me," said Michaels. "I hope this is a by-the-book."

"Only these xenos want to be stars. I bet they're all wearing sunglasses and sporting tans!" said Garcia.

"Well, this is the only take we're going to have on this production," said Alex, bringing up her rifle. "Lights, camera, action, guys."

They came up to a narrower passage that dived downward.

"The tank won't fit," barked the machine's operator into her ear.

"Yeah," said Alex. "I figured as much. Okay, you stay here. Sentinel duty. The rest of us—we go down. *Looks* routine to me, but expect the unexpected anyway. Got it?"

"Yes, sir!" chimed the voices of the units cacophonously in her ear.

"Good. I want the short rangers out on the horn tip."

Two men with Mark Five Crankers—the equivalent of high-tech sawed-off shotguns—trundled up to take the lead, and they were off to see the lizards.

Within twenty-five yards, the tunnel opened up

into a large underground chamber—the remains of
a huge vault basement, daubed with alien gunk.

"Gimme some light!" said Alex, and the guys
obliged her by turning up their suit lanterns. The
chamber blazed with incandescence, but as usual
in these kinds of places, Alex Kozlowski wasn't
crazy about what she saw.

Against one of the tenebrous walls hung people.

Alien egg sacks.

Live people, impregnated with alien young.
Chest-bursters that looked like they were about to
blow at any minute. The victims—ten men, five
women—hung at the edge of death, dangling like
corpses that had forgotten to rot.

"Agents," said Garcia.

"What?" said Kozlowski.

"Hollywood agents. That building got overrun by
bugs last week down the road." The dark-skinned
man nodded toward the ropy remains. "The Creative Talent Agency, one of the diehards of the en-
tertainment industry that stuck it out here in LA."
He walked forward to have a closer look, remaining
cautious.

"Yeah. Yeah, I remember," said Michaels. "Whole
building blew up. The assumption was that everyone was killed."

"Looks like they're still making deals," said
Kozlowski.

One of the agents, a woman in a shredded dark
black jumpsuit, her hair a mat of grease, slimy
green threads clamped into her skull, seemed in
some netherworld of delirium. She had on an ear-
tab that sprouted artfully into a thin microphone,
and she was mumbling dramatically into it.

Garcia stepped back into ranks, clucking his tongue. "Too far gone. All of them."

Kozlowski nodded. She'd suspected as much. If you caught on egger early, you had a pretty good chance of squeezing out the spark of new life in it. But this far along, a baby xeno was so linked up in its parasitic position amid vital tissue that even if you were able to yank the X out without it boring a hole in you, there was no way you could save the donor.

Kozlowski knew what had to be done. There were precedents. She'd done it before, and would probably do it again. She was just following orders. Orders that made sense.

That didn't mean that she liked it.

"Needles," she whispered.

There of the men were certified executioners in this kind of circumstance. They brought out their air pistols, tapped in cartridges of darts filled with a fast-acting poison that shut down the nervous system first, then destroyed the body. Two of the men had grim frowns as they aimed. The other man, Dickens, was an LA native. Dickens had been a writer and producer and actor in LA.

Dickens was grinning.

"Put the poor bastards out of their misery," commanded Kozlowski.

Thwip! Thwip! Thwip!

Three of the hanging bodies shuddered, and then were still.

Quickly, the executioners finished their task, then stepped back. "Okay, quick—before the bursters hit their ejection buttons!" Kozlowski screamed.

Two men had readied themselves. They stepped

forward. One sprayed a thick fluid on the bodies, stepped back. The other, with a high-density flamethrower, stepped forward and with fire condensed to incredibly high temperatures immolated the dangling egg sacks.

When the smoke cleared, all that was left was blackened, incinerated ashes.

"Good. Now let's go slag the Xes that did this!" barked Kozlowski.

"Amen," said Lieutenant Michaels, pale, with sweat shining on his brow.

Of course, they weren't just here to slag xenos.

Nope, that would be too easy.

In this day and age, in a disintegrating place like the City of Angels, theoretically you could just slip a limited nuke down a nest and skedaddle. Easy, quick, and a minimum of lost soldiers. However, although that nuclear holocaust up in the Pacific Northwest years back had certainly turned the tide in the Alien-Earth War, giving humanity a hope of getting its planet back, such extreme measures weren't used these days, for more reasons than just the glowing glands they tended to produce in neighboring villages.

No, these xenos had their uses these days.

And damn them for it.

"Okay. Fall out. The chamber's probably down that tunnel there," called Kozlowski. "Garcia?"

"You got it, sir," said the grizzled vet. "These bugs haven't changed that much, and this tunnel looks like the anteroom to where we're headed. What I ain't seen though is enough bugs. These hellhounds know we're here. I don't get why they didn't try and protect their progeny. Something stinks."

"Could be they're out somewhere," said Michaels. "Could be lots of things."

Garcia grunted. "Yeah. Lots."

"We're here, we'll do what we came to do, and second-guess later. We've got artillery guarding our asses, and we've got firepower. Now move it!" Kozlowski growled in a low, no-bullshit voice. She'd perfected it when she realized she had to order men around. Lowered voices worked well with dogs and human males.

The troop descended quickly but cautiously, illumination lamps picking out their direction for them down the foul, mucousy passageway.

Kozlowski would have liked these missions much better if she could just obliterate all the xenos. However, there were two things that the Army wanted her to haul out these days.

A couple of bug bodies, dead of course.

Random DNA samples.

And whatever royal jelly from the queen's chambers they could tap. Gold from outer space, some of the top brass were calling it these days. Bug juice. The lab coats were going absolutely nuts with it, and there was talk about all kinds of new possible uses for the stuff. With the U. S. government pretty much busted, private industry had suddenly become the main financial backer for the armed forces. Drug companies, mostly, along with other medical and scientific researchers. The government wanted their share, of course, but when push came to shove, the interest groups holding the biggest bucks in their outstretched hands got the biggest shovelsful of goop.

Alien royal jelly.

The stuff that made the right kind of drones into queens. Food of the xeno gods. Kozlowski wasn't entirely sure what they needed it for. Hell, it could just be gab, and they were collecting the stuff for nothing. But it was what the upper brass told them to do, and so they did it, without questioning.

The scuttlebutt that she heard was this:

Each hive was based around a queen. Queens bred drones. However, only a certain kind of bug could breed queens—the so-called queen mother. None of which existed on Earth now. Rumor had it that it was the queen mother royal jelly that was the primo stuff. Regular jelly had its uses, but it was nothing compared to the Q-M gunk. In truth, though, Kozlowski had other more important things to think about. Like staying alive.

There were all kinds of differences between alien hives and insect hives on Earth. Scientists didn't really understand the full activities of the beasties. Was their communication telepathic, or some weirder somatic buzz? It had already been established that the wavelengths of a queen's call could be picked up by human dreamers. One of the best ways of scoping out obscure hive locations was listening to these sensitive dreamers who acted as receivers, and in the best circumstances as locaters.

Just what did the monsters want? Where had they come from? What were they doing? Where were they going? What was their cosmic destiny?

Were they so grouchy because the race had gotten up on the wrong side of their galactic beds in some prehistoric starday?

Kozlowski had a theory.

They'd accidentally eaten all their males, and were on one hell of a PMS jag. The theory wasn't exactly scientific, but it did explain a lot. Here were all these hysterical bugs, with no men to scream at.

Anyway, the core truth of what they were doing down here was the tanks in the cart that Private Henderson drove. Of course, to get to the jelly, you had to off the royalty first, and this was probably the most onerous task anybody could want in this kind of situation.

Corporal Michelin's head snapped up from a radar set.

"Incoming!" he said. "Twenty-five yards ahead. Sensor range. Picking up five bogies, coming in at five klicks per hour. Same direction."

Kozlowski was almost relieved. This dead silence was getting to her. "Okay, dig in, and I want a man with his weapon trained on the ceiling. Adams— you can shoot skeet. I've seen them break through and jump down from above. If they do that, I want 'em dead before they hit the ground."

"Yes, sir!"

She didn't have to notify the front or rear guards. They were already down and dug in, ready for the attack. Kozlowski threw a beam of light down on the floor. Solid-looking enough, but she was ready if any of the bastards popped up from that direction. With bugs, you just didn't know *where* they could pop from. They couldn't teleport, that much was known. But for all of that, sometimes it seemed like they *could*. And the commanding officer who underestimated them usually ended up just as dead as her men . . .

Or worse.

In this case, though, what the sensors showed was all the hive was throwing at them.

Five bugs.

Plenty, though.

As soon as they scrabbled into view, the frontmost boys let loose a barrage of fire. Down here in the claustrophobic darkness, Kozlowski felt the familiar tug of total irrational fear. Trapped-in-a-coffin fear. Preternatural mammal-hiding-from-the-dinosaur fear. That was one of the unnerving intellectual aspects of the bugs. They seemed to have been designed specifically to grip those hard claws deep into the softest parts of your soul. And squeeze.

The bugs dodged the first bolts. Awareness of human weapons was either bred or trained into them by their maturity these days. These were Earth bugs and they were ready to scrap with Earth people.

However, the soldiers had also been trained, and better. Countless simulations gave them a sense of exactly where the things would hop in their erratic jumps.

A bolt hit one. The explosion shattered it, splattering its viscous blood over the whole corridor.

"Duck, dammit!" cried Kozlowski, hitting the dirt as the acid blood sprayed every which way. The stuff could bore through the best armor if you got enough on you. She peered up through the smoke. The boys were still firing away, but crouched low and off to the side. "Knees and head!" she cried. "Knees and head."

You hit the head, the things died with a minimum of acid splatter. You hit the knees, you had the bug on the ground and a good chance for the head.

Alex Kozlowski immediately saw that she was going to have a chance to show them. A bug minus a right arm had broken loose and was scampering along the side wall. Alex lifted her weapon and squeezed off two quick but carefully aimed shots. The first missed, exploding far away. But the second caught the left knee dead on, shattering the joint and causing the alien to go down.

Garcia's next shot caught it right in its banana brain with a satisfying thud and soft *ker-plow*, like an M-80 in a gourd.

With this guidance, the boys calmed down and picked off the rest of the things. The fire boys cleaned up the wiggling jaws and claws with a dose of concentrated high temp, and then applied a splash of acid-neutralizing spray to get through.

Kozlowski allowed herself a smile. They'd killed lots of aliens already, without so much as a stubbed toe. "Good work, chums, but don't get cocky. The toughest part is straight down there, in the general direction of hell."

"Hey, don't we know it!" said Michaels.

"Pretty dumb bunch of bugs, though," said Garcia.

"They're not exactly known for their high IQs," said Kozlowski. "But then neither are grunts, so I don't want any slackers. Move it! We're not exactly in unfamiliar territory now."

Chances were the xenos were about as ready as they could be for the attack, but that didn't mean it was good for the men to rest on their laurels. Best to use the adrenaline and the other performance-augmenting drugs while they were peaking.

They traipsed over the dead, crackling things in the tunnel, trundling into the darkness.

The corridor widened, and their lamps illuminated a chamber.

In the center, like a giant flower bulb of chitinous flesh, grew the "throne"—the storage place for the royal jelly and home of the spawning queen.

Kozlowski had been in these places before. That didn't mean she was used to them. The hole was like Death's uterus, with hubs and cordings and odds and ends of effluvia that while biological seemed antilife. Every cell in her body rebelled at the sight presented here. Training and experience and resolve fought with a deep instinct in her to turn and run.

A bent, insane frieze of alien sculpture, a mockery of life.

Otherwise the chamber was empty.

"What the hell?" said Michaels. "Where are they?"

Garcia looked like if he hadn't had a helmet, he would have very much liked to have scratched his head. "I don't understand. Where's the freakin' queen?"

"Off at the Hollywood high spots?" quipped a jokester.

"I don't like it," said Kozlowski. "Get back. The queen doesn't leave her chamber unless there's a damned good reason."

Michaels shook his head. "Look. We've got a pot full of royal jelly waiting to be tapped. Half the time, the stuff gets blown up or burnt." He grabbed a tapper and started walking toward the bulb. "I say let's get this stuff tanked right now and we're assured a good supply, no matter if we take out these bugs or not!"

"Michaels! Halt!" screeched Kozlowski. "I'm not certain that junk is all that valuable. It's certainly not worth the extra risk. You're not going anywhere—and that's an order."

Michaels stopped in his tracks. He turned around, his eyes flaming. Kozlowski could see the drugs in those eyes, and the male pride. Don't do this to me, Koz, said those eyes. Don't be so damned protective.

"Yeah! Lover boy might get himself a boo-boo!" said a veiled voice in baby talk.

"What have you got on the sensors?" Kozlowski demanded.

The private looked up from the telltale board. "Activity, but nothing close."

"Come on, Captain. I could have started tapping by now!"

"Yeah. We get our quota, we get extra leave!"

She didn't like it. Not one bit. But there wasn't any good reason to say no. And if she didn't let Michaels do this, the other jerks here would call favoritism, and she couldn't deny that.

"Okay, but I want the rest of you to back him up. And, Daniels . . . you go along."

"No problem," said the tough Army man.

Damn it, Peter. Why are you doing this to me?

"The rest of you. Fan out and check for other exits."

The men, grateful for action, spread out.

"What do you think, Garcia?" she asked the sergeant as Lt. Michaels strode for the huge bulb.

"I don't know, sir. It's not like the bugs to leave their jelly unguarded."

The soldier walking off to one side looked up from his instruments. "Sir! I'm reading lower rooms. They're chambers, sir, and just as big as—"

The lieutenant was just driving in the tap, connected to a couple of storage tanks. Daniels had slung his rifle in order to help with the tricky manipulation.

It came to her like thunder.

This wasn't the main chamber! And if it wasn't what they were really after, then it was a—

"Michaels! Daniels!" screamed Kozlowski. "Get away from—"

Trap!

The bulb split open like a pregnant belly. And the baby was deadly as death itself.

"Jesus!" cried Daniels, leaping back, pulling his rifle down.

The emerging bug struck with the speed that still was astonishing to see, even though Kozlowski had seen it many times before. It grabbed Lieutenant Michaels by the arms and pulled him up.

It had been hiding inside. The alien was just waiting for them to tap.

Michaels screamed as he was hoisted upward in the claws. The secondary jaws, slathering drool, rammed against the reinforced helmet, cracking it.

Michaels screamed again.

Automatically Daniels fired his rifle.

Only yards away, the shell hit its mark. The mark, though, was the torso of the beast. A gory hunk of creature was torn away, and like a burst vessel, alien blood pumped.

The secondary jaw whacked into Michaels's helmet again, cutting a hole before the thing began to crumple. Michaels fell under it, and Kozlowski, helpless, watched as the alien blood spouted into the interior of her lover's helmet.

Directly into his face.

The scream ratcheted through the radio, until the radio was killed. It seemed to grow louder and more horrible carried only by the fetid air.

The acid worked with amazing quickness upon the face. It was as though she were watching time-lapse photography. The skin sizzled off, snapping with gooey bubbles. The eyes boiled and melted.

The screaming stopped.

The skull began showing and then the acid began to eat through that, frying Lieutenant Peter Michaels's brain.

"Nooooooo!" cried Kozlowski. She grabbed up her rifle and was about to riddle the beast with slugs.

A hand on her suit's shoulder stopped her. Garcia. "Don't. You're in charge here, Captain. *Stay* in charge."

The alien slumped, twitching.

The burnt remains of her lover mixed into a liquid, unholy embrace.

"Check on him," she said tersely.

If only I hadn't let him go. I knew there was something wrong!

"He's gone."

"I said *check* on him!" she bellowed. "If he's not, I don't want him to suffer!"

Garcia nodded. He stepped over to the bodies, gingerly nudged the lieutenant with the butt of his rifle.

Acid mixed with smoking gore rivuleted out into a horrible puddle.

It burned straight through the floor, leaving a ragged, smoking hole.

"Dead."

"Right," said Kozlowski. She could feel the iron grip of control exert itself and she was in command again. "There's another chamber, and that's where we're going. No more heroics, you assholes." She took a breath. "No more carelessness. Or I swear to God, if the bugs don't kill you, *I* will."

The silent squad followed the telltale to their destination.

Lieutenant Alexandra Kozlowski tongued for another pill. She swallowed it and her tears.

2

Victory.

The smell of it was in the air, alongside the fading stench of the ruins of war.

Victory.

Domination.

Excellence.

He could feel the demand for it throbbing in his sinews, pulsing in his veins. He could feel the need in the stadium crowd outside, the impatient stamping of their feet, their calls and their applause. Its power and its glory electrified the air.

Now it was time to electrify some nerves. Goose some synapses. Nudge some neurons.

Jack Oriander stood in the shadows of the tunnel. Outside, his fellow contestants milled around, waiting for the officials to call for the beginning of the hundred-yard dash. He felt more secure here, away from the open space. He was slightly agoraphobic; anyway, that was what his dad had said. He wasn't so sure about that himself, since he didn't really have a *fear* of being outside. He just preferred walls around him.

Pop was dead now. He'd been a captain in the Alien-Earth War, and he was dead now. The Army had not supplied the details, nor did the Oriander family want details. Not when it came to the aliens.

Jack Oriander took a sip of cold water from a paper cup, swished it in his mouth, and spat it out. The Middle Eastern sun was hot out there. Jack wanted his mouth wet, but he didn't want his stomach bloated. He had his sunblocker lotion on, and he'd taken care to drink lots of fluids yesterday and today as well as "carbing up" for the contest. At twenty years old, he was in absolutely peak condition. His muscles, trained and corn-fed in Iowa, sang with health and speed and proportion. He'd run track and field in junior high and high school and now college at Iowa U, now that these kinds of things were getting back on track. The Earth had lost some time—and so had Jack, because of the war and reconstruction. But time didn't mean that much when you were young. There seemed lots of it behind you and lots of it ahead of you. Even though you saw people older than you with bald heads and paunches and lines around their eyes, the idea that *you'd* be like that one day seemed absurd.

"Win today, grow old tomorrow," Coach Donnell had said, his eyes glaring down like lasers into Jack. "We're counting on you, Jack, to put us on the map." That's what the graying, grizzled man said every day of the training.

He got his message across in more ways than one.

The tension in the air was thick. Jack's nerves seemed stretched as tight as violin strings. He knew that if he was going to get some help, he'd have to get it now. Around his waist was a light flesh-colored belt of synthetic material. Jack de-Velcroed a pouch, pulled out a small bottle. A fresh one. Best if fresh, his mom had always said, and though Jack wasn't sure if that applied to this stuff, his obsessive-compulsive nature made him use a fresh bottle even though there was a half-full one in his luggage.

Jack cracked open the safety seal and knocked out a pill.

Hell, why not?

He rattled out another one into his palm, then quickly screwed the top back on and stuffed it back into the pouch, readjusted his oversize shirt, tucking it into the elasticized top of his shorts.

He looked down at the capsules. They were a deep green, seemingly embedded with silver sparkles.

For a moment he heard the old man's voice at the back of his head. "Take it from me, Jack. You've got all the drugs you really need in you already. Learn to tap those first before you go for other ones." But he discounted it as he'd always done, listening to the voice of the coach instead. "Tell you what, Jack. You do what you got to do to *win*."

Jack slipped both capsules between his lips. He took the paper cup and used the small amount of water left to wash them down. Not too much. Didn't want to get too much moisture inside of him. Balance. That was the ticket. The old man was always keen on balance. Yin and yang. Now the old man was dead. So if what Jack swallowed tipped the scales a little to his favor, what did it matter?

Xeno-Zip.

Street name: Fire.

From Neo-Pharm.

Great stuff.

He'd been taking Fire ever since it first came out. He'd asked the coach about it and the guy had taken a few seconds to read the label. ALL NATURAL INGREDIENTS. That was okay with the coach. Just as long as there weren't any steroids in the mix. Not that the man had anything against steroids himself. Anything that could give you that extra edge was really okay by him. Judging committees were a lot more laissez-faire these days.

Besides, it wasn't any worse than a couple of extra cups of coffee in the morning. That's what the ads implied, anyway.

He hadn't looked into it very closely. Jack immediately noticed that not only was he more alert and self-confident after swallowing one, his athletic abilities improved. Concentration, agility, coordination: all jumped into higher levels. Not only that, he *felt* better. Fire gave a little more zing, a little more oomph.

The official line was that they made the stuff from alien queen mother royal jelly.

Rumor had it that they used ground-up alien bodies from the war.

Jack didn't care. He liked the stuff. The glow that it put on life's horizons was just the icing. What Jack liked was the edge it gave him in sports.

Jack waited for the glow to start, listening to the sounds outside, peeking into the light, shading his eyes.

The stadium was a spectacular tribute to the reconstruction of Earth, a wonder spawn of new technology and architecture. Lots of companies had tossed in contributions to build the thing, and not just demicreds. Big coin. A tubular confluence of lines and efficiency, of new and mighty alloys, centered around a traditional field. Wedding of the new and the old. Blimps and zeppelinlike hovercars hung in the sky, bristling with tracking devices and media sensor arrays. Field Humanitas was the name, and these competitions in which Jack Oriander participated had been dubbed the Goodwill Games.

Now that the Olympics had been destroyed, along with much of old Earth, you had to start with something, after all. Something to unite people, something to celebrate the New Humanity, something to take civilized minds off the savage past.

A sweeter conflict among nations.

A good-natured competition among athletes.

Jack Oriander leaned out into the sun a bit. He could smell the familiar humanity out there. He smelled the popcorn and the hot dogs, the spilled beer and the excitement in the air. He intended to be the center of that excitement now, yes, sirree bob.

He felt a lick of the drug playing around his nerves, and blinked.

Ah!

"Yo! Oreo! You want to get your ass out here!" called Fred Staton. Staton was the other guy from the States. He was clean-cut and slender like Oriander, only he had neatly clipped blond hair instead of black, with no widow's peak. A strapping young man. As Oriander's senses sharpened, squeezed into a fine focus by the tongues of fire, he smelled his friend's lemony deodorant and the talc on his hands. Caught a wisp of grape jam from today's breakfast, along with the astringent touch of Gatorade. "We're just about set to line up!"

"Uh . . . yeah, right."

"Hey, man. You okay?"

"Sure. Why?"

"I dunno. Your eyes . . . they're a little odd."

"This sun . . . it's kind of getting to me. That's why I'm staying in the shade as long as possible."

"And your hands. They're trembling some."

Oriander lifted his hands. He fancied he could feel special blood pouring into them now. Fiery blood.

But they'd never shaken before on Fire.

"Man, I just guess I'm a little nervous!"

"Aren't we all."

"I'll be fine. Just give me a sec."

"Sure. But seconds aren't mine to give. And those officials are oiling up their guns." He slapped his friend on the shoulder. "You'll be fine. Take a deep breath. You're only a few feet away from a hundred yards." He snapped his fingers. "It'll be all over like that and we'll go out and celebrate, huh?"

"Yeah. Right." Jack grinned.

Fred was right. He should move on out. He could see the milling racers not just lining up, but slotting themselves in their starting posts.

Yet the sun was not only hot, it looked terribly bright now, much too bright. Fire had never sharpened his vision up *this* much before. He felt like he had just been blessed with telescopic sight. Such incredible detail!

Maybe he shouldn't have taken two pills after all.

Squaring his shoulders, pushing back the razory feeling along his spine, Jack Oriander trotted out to assume his position.

As he slotted himself in line, he got the A-OK signal from Fred. "C'mon, Oreo. Let's show them that American sneakers can still kick butt."

Jack smiled and waved. He fitted his feet into the metal stirrups, leaned down onto his knuckles. A buzzing began to keen in his ear, like an amp feeding back. He cocked his ear, waiting for the starting pistol. The finish line loomed ahead like a magnificent promise.

Glory. Achievement.

Winning.

The crowd noise died down to a hush.

But the keening in his ear grew to a roar.

What was—

The chemical rush hit Jack Oriander like the hammer of Thor. Molten energy poured into his muscles and lightning exploded from his brain.

The signal pistol went off, and his legs answered as though they'd been waiting for this moment their entire life. They pushed him forward, shooting him off like a bullet down a rifle chamber. Suddenly he wasn't just Jack anymore. He could feel the atoms exploding in his sinews, he could feel a cosmic power gushing through his entire being.

He was a god!

The crowd went crazy.

The PA system rumbled with the announcer's astonishment. "Unbelievable! Jack Oriander of the USA is literally burning up the track!"

His face had grown a rictus of determination and sweat burst from his brow in riveting globules. His feet seemed to have grown wings. The air rushed past him like a wild river and the determination to win inside his breast burst into white-hot brilliance.

The yards streamed by in a flash.

Jack Oriander crossed over the finish line, well ahead of the others, his feet a blur and his mind hot as an incandescent filament in a megawatt bulb.

And Jack Oriander kept on going.

The crowd in the stadium and the millions watching the race would never forget the close-ups.

Jack Oriander's arms pumping.

His legs slamming onto the turf outside the track like John Henry's sledgehammers.

His eyes gazing into madness.

The young athlete from Iowa did not seem satisfied in shaving off a solid four seconds from the world record for the one-hundred-yard dash. As though eager to get on to yet another race, unseen by any but him, he loped over the finish line, covering the distance between the edge of the track and the wall in a couple of blinks of the eye, reason and sanity burned out in chemical conflagration in his cortex.

He smashed through the corrugated plastic of the wall.

Only the steel girder just beyond stopped his demented run.

And the blood . . .

The blood was *everywhere*.

You can buy black market videos from media vultures. You can see shreds of skin and veins and hair torn from the speeding body and hanging from the edges of the shattered plastic wall in clumps of gore. You can see the twisted remains of the rest of the body, lying akimbo under the harsh glare like road kill in a cleated tank run.

And, if you look closely in these tapes, you can see the medic take something from Oriander's blood-spattered pouch belt, and tuck it into his own pocket.

Xeno-Zip.

3

The sun shone down gently and pleasantly on Quantico Marine Base, Virginia. It wasn't often these days you got sun, not with some of the clouds that still hung in the atmosphere, not with the strange weather since the invasion. Colonel Leon Marshall had his drapes flung wide to let the warmth into his office.

He sat at his desk now, the report printout neatly encased in clear mylar before him. He glanced over the neatly listed facts and figures and smiled to himself, feeling a pleasant rush of anticipation.

Amazing.

Absolutely astonishing.

Puissance to the formerly powerless, power to the formerly impotent, is heady stuff indeed, and the close-cropped, burly colonel was feeling positively giddy with the prospects that lay before him.

The digital clock on his desk turned silently to 11:00 A.M. The general was a prompt man. He'd be here any moment. Colonel Leon Marshall had been preparing his demonstration since seven hundred hours this morning, and all was ready to go. Now he could afford to take a quick breather, relax and enjoy the prospects that lay before him, his career and, of course, the future of this battered country in its efforts to build a strong defense even as it rebuilt its cities and its economy.

The digital clock was just threatening to transmute to another number when his intercom chimed softly and the adenoidal voice of his secretary swept through.

"Colonel. General Burroughs is here."

"Excellent." Colonel Marshall slapped his desk and its thin burden lightly and stood up. "Send him in."

The door cycled open with a whir and the burly figure of General Delmore Burroughs marched in, his eyes turreting like offensive guns on a land carrier. They lighted on Marshall and a flicker of camaraderie shone in them below the grim and businesslike exterior. "Leon." Pudgy fingers were extended. The general's grip was certain and firm.

"General Burroughs. Thank you so much for coming."

"I believe the words 'urgent' and 'maximum importance' were used in your communication, Colonel. I tend to respond to those words. But I am a busy man." The eyes turned stony. "I hope that my time here is not misspent."

General Delmore Burroughs was a beefy black man with a bald pate rising up from grayed temples. He had a broad nose and a voice deep and full. He smelled strongly of bay rum and the Instistarch of his uniform. He was a general who had gotten where he'd gotten by taking no shit, and Marshall respected that. If he was a person who trifled with such things as mottos, then this general's motto would have been "The ends justify the means." That was why Colonel Marshall needed to get him in on the project.

"I'm not a man to waste time, you know that," said Marshall. "Tell you what—you think it's a waste of time, you get to use my ski chalet in Vermont for a weekend . . . complete with my little black book."

The general's eyes glimmered a bit. A hint of a smile played on his lips. Then his teeth clamped down, his face assumed its normal grim posture. "Fair enough."

"Good. Then lean back, drink some Kona, and have a cigar. This will take a couple of minutes and I might as well kiss your butt awhile as well."

The general couldn't help but chuckle. "Cigars? Where you getting cigars, Colonel?" He sat down.

Marshall stuck a cup of steaming java beside the general's elbow. Then he pulled out a humidor from one of the drawers. Smith y Ortegas. "They're just swinging into production again, and my sources dug up the best of the first batch."

The general rolled it, sniffing. "You know, soldier. It's been so long since I've had one of these, this might just kill me with pleasure." He chuckled and took up the clipper Marshall offered, dealt with the cigar end in an almost reverent fashion. "Now exactly what have you got on that scheming mind of yours?" He stuck the cigar in his mouth and allowed Marshall to play a flame over the end. He puffed, blew out bluish smoke. His eyes seemed to roll back with pleasure.

"General, do you recall that unfortunate incident last week with the Iowa boy at the Goodwill Games?"

"Sure. Put the world record in the American camp firmly. Probably for years to come." Puff. Spume. "Too bad about the accident."

"Colonel, did you know that drugs were involved?"

"Nonsense. Good American talent and muscle pulled that boy over the line."

"You didn't read the results of the autopsy? Oriander had Xeno-Zip in his blood."

"Xeno-Zip? Fire? What, that silly pick-me-up they're putting in the stores now? Marshall, he probably had caffeine and lots of good old-fashioned testosterone, too. Ain't nothing that great about those pills. Hell, I tried a couple. Goosed me a bit is all, but with no crash and burn. Nothing that would make me win a race!"

"That's exactly what everyone says. But I did a quick search of news cuts for the last couple of months. And then I had the boys at biochem do some quick testing. Came up with some remarkable findings."

He gave the general a moment to exhale his last puff of smoke, and then he tendered the plastic-enclosed paper to the man. General Burroughs grunted. He murmured a whiff of annoyance, and then dug into a side pocket for a pair of half-frame spectacles, which he put on. His eyes strafed the paper for several moments, then he shrugged and handed it back to Marshall.

"I've got a team of science boys to read this stuff for me and digest it. I don't get much out of it on my own, I'm afraid."

"That's all right, General. I had to have most of it explained to me. Just a few items of jargon, some facts and figures to illustrate the fact that I've done some serious work on this."

"Right, Colonel. I believe you, but I still don't see where you're coming from." The general tapped off some ash from the cigar, then left the smoking thing sitting in the tray. He folded his arms. A sure sign of impatience. Time to cut to the chase.

"You're aware of the active ingredient of Fire, aren't you, General?"

"Sure. The PR is that it's alien royal jelly. Actually, there's more to it than that. It's alien royal jelly, with a drop or two of queen mother extra royal jelly. All that comes from one source, the queen mother who got nuked. Can't get it anywhere else. A minuscule amount of this mixture acts in a positive boosting fashion on the human nervous system." The cigar remained in the tray. It went out. The general ignored it.

"Correct. However, even with a minuscule amount, Neo-Pharm, the manufacturer, found itself running out of the regular jelly. They started manufacturing synthesized stuff, with mixed results. It still needs a few molecules of queen mother royal jelly to work, though."

The general grinned. "Right. I'm not surprised they're running out of jelly. We blew most of the bug bastards straight to hive hell!"

"Absolutely and we did a fine job of it, too—and a *better job* of reconstructing. But that leaves us, as the military, in a bit of a quandary, doesn't it? And I don't have to give you a sheet of facts and figures to prove it. The enemy is mostly defeated, all the governmental money is pouring into rebuilding or into outer space. Now that the military's done its job, it's the same old story. No respect. We get squat in the way of money to develop what we have to develop to stay modern."

The gray eyes sparked with anger. It was a sore subject with all career military sorts. The general had taken the bait. Now all Marshall had to do was to reel him in.

"Public sentiment is also very antiwar machine. I think it's a historical distrust of power. The media tends to think that if the military has too much resources in a time of peace, they get antsy and take over the government. So the other extreme occurs. The military gets weak. And so when the country needs us, we get thrown into the fray, unprepared . . . and get clobbered. *That's* provable history, General."

The general nodded, anger etched into his face. He picked up the cigar, stuck it into his mouth. Marshall happily relit it for him.

"What can we do about it? We're not getting the funds to build new and improved equipment. So . . . why not build a new and improved soldier?"

General Burroughs squinted suspiciously. "What? Synthetics? Cybernetic? DNA jobs? That costs a pretty cred, too, Marshall."

The old boy wasn't following the line of reasoning. That was one thing about Burroughs, he was a little thick sometimes, a little bullish. But like a bull, if you pointed him in the right direction, all you had to do was grab the tail and he'd take you where you wanted to go. That was why Marshall had cooked up his little exhibition. In show-and-tell, the "show" carried the greatest weight.

Marshall smiled. "How about if you could do it for just a few bucks a head, General?"

General Burroughs barked a growly laugh. "Pull the other one, Colonel." He pushed out a stream of smoke and palpable disbelief.

Marshall checked his wrist chronometer. The players in the game would be just about ready. "General, if you'd care to step out on my balcony, there's a little demonstration I'd very much like to show you, courtesy of some of the men in my company."

Burroughs shrugged. "I'm here. I've smoked your cigar. I've listened to your curious nonsense. And I must say, you must have used some of the government money I'm responsible for to throw together this bit of research. So I guess you've put me into a position where I don't have much of a choice in the matter." He took out the smoking cigar and pointed it gruffly toward the colonel's nose. "But let me tell you, Colonel. I'd better see some serious justification for the use of this taxpayer's money."

"Naturally, sir." Marshall got up and marched over to a side wall, hung tastefully with mementos, weapons, and equipment. He pulled out two pairs of electronically enhanced binoculars from rechargers and handed one to the general. Then he pointed toward the sliding glass doors and the open spaces beyond.

"Come on, General. Wait till you get a gander at *this*."

The "balcony" was actually an extension of a cat-walk and stairs system that connected a number of buildings in the newly built assembly of offices, barracks, and warehouses that comprised this portion of Quantico.

Beyond, a bank of obsidian-bottomed clouds hung on the horizon. A storm was brewing. Nothing unusual on Earth now, storms. Marshall shivered a bit at the prospect. They moved fast, those storms. Dark battalions of weather, phantom marchers left behind after the war. But there would be time for the exhibition.

Marshall picked up a walkie-talkie from the desk.

The two officers walked to the edge of the balcony. Marshall leaned against the railing and pointed down at the open yard below. Some yards away, a group of enlisted men seemed to be milling about, up to nothing much more than loitering.

The general glowered. "Looks like a bunch of men goofing off!"

"If you'll just direct your binocs toward that lone private over there in the corner, sir . . ."

General Burroughs harrumphed. But he angled the cigar off to one side of his mouth and put the binoculars up, finger expertly adjusting the focusing vernier. "Looks like just a normal grunt. And a mighty doofy one, come to think of it."

Marshall brought up his glasses and took a look. Yes, there he was, the poor guy, looking a little lost and oblivious as usual. Gawky. Geeky. Big Adam's apple, tiny brain. Colonel Marshall was a collector of mid-twentieth-century cultural remnants and he remembered one of Edgar Bergen's puppets. That was who the guy reminded him of.

Mortimer Snerd.

"That's Private Willie Pinnock. And if I may say so, your assessment is right on the money. Private Pinnock barely made it through boot camp. His reflexes are slow, his IQ is low. He can barely handle latrine and KP duties . . . but he can, which is why he isn't booted."

"So what's so special about this particular private?"

"Just a moment. You'll see." Marshall opened up the walkie-talkie he'd taken with him. "Corporal Glen. Can you read me?"

The walkie-talkie sputtered and spat back. "Roger. I read you, Colonel."

Marshall pointed to where the corporal was standing on a crate, snapped to attention, waving at them. "Our referee, if you will, General." He clicked the channel back on. "Corporal, you may proceed with the exhibition."

"Yes, sir," spat the walkie-talkie.

Up went the binoculars.

Corporal Glen, a well-built specimen who looked good even in fatigues, semaphored to the private off to one side of the courtyard. However, Pinnock did not respond.

Glen signaled again.

Nothing.

General Burroughs arched an eyebrow.

Cripes, thought Marshall. This had better come off or my butt is cooked.

"What's wrong with that soldier?" he barked into the walkie-talkie.

"Off in his own little world, sir."

"Well, drag him out of it and let's get the show on the road. The general hasn't got all day."

Glen "yessirred," then trotted quickly off to where Private Pinnock stood, spinning rainbows. He tapped the nerd on the shoulder, flapped his gums in traditional mad army Drill Instructor fashion, and Marshall didn't need binoculars to see Pinnock jump, flinch, and generally cringe at the chewing out. A bob of head from the private, and then Glen trotted back to his monitoring duty.

Pinnock's shoulders were slumped. He looked quite hesitant and more than a little frightened at the prospect before him. Nonetheless, he slipped his hand into the pocket of his fatigues and drew something out.

"Get a close-up on what he has in his hands, sir," suggested Marshall.

"A bottle of that drug . . . Xeno-Zip."

"Yes, sir, that's right."

Pinnock visibly drew a deep breath. He turned toward a wall, as though he were doing something shameful, and then dragged a shaky hand through his blond short-cropped hair. He opened the bottle of Fire, poured out three tablets, then choked them down, without the benefit of water.

He stiffened, and visibly shuddered.

"Doesn't look like he's having much fun, Colonel."

"No, sir. May I give you a brief personality profile? Pinnock is a meek fellow with a minimal aggression quotient. His adrenaline levels are low;

he doesn't get mad when the other soldiers tease him. They generally just put up with him, since he tends to do the distasteful chores for them."

"With no resentment."

"None that is reported." Marshall looked at his chronometer. The increased dosage in the subject was his order, to increase the speed of release of the chemicals in the bloodstream. The last thing he needed was an impatient general. The results were going to have to be fairly immediate, or Burroughs would just about-face and leave. A minute since ingestion. That would be about right.

"Glen. Next step."

"Yes, sir," snapped the walkie-talkie.

The colonel signaled the milling group of men. They loosely ordered themselves and began marching toward the lone private like a gaggle of surly Teamsters headed for a manager. They were bulky lads, with rock muscles earned by constant drilling and exercises. Marshall could hear a couple of them, joking with one another. They had no weapons, only their fists. Marshall had planned it that way. He didn't want to see Pinnock or anyone get hurt, exactly. Scuffed up a bit, that was all. A little red on the turf was always a dramatic underline.

Besides, these barracks bullies might be in for a little something they hadn't bargained for.

The frontmost of the group, a beefy tower of a man, stepped up to Pinnock, grabbed him by the shoulder, and spun him around. A few obscene motions and words were made. Pinnock did nothing. Another man stepped forward and shoved the private. Pinnock shuffled backward, still not reacting. Not even cringing, which was a good sign.

Then another grunt snuck up behind him and got down on all fours. Big Pecs stepped forward, executed a sharp, swift push. Pinnock tumbled onto the ground. The smallest of the men, a little guy with a rat face, stepped in and gave a sneaky kick to the private's backside.

"What the hell is going on?" said the general. "This is absurd!"

Marshall tensed. There should be some reaction here by now. Was all this going to be a ridiculous fiasco?

The ratty-faced man sneered and went in for another free kick. However, this time, he did not step back after the blow was delivered. And the sneer melted into a look of alarm.

Something snapped. There was a scream, and Rat Face was flung ass over elbows backward. He was slammed into the corrugated metal of a barracks wall and left a smear of blood as he poured onto the ground, out for the count.

The burly bully boys took a step back.

Private Pinnock jumped to his feet.

"Holy shit," said General Burroughs.

The officers' binoculars leapt to their eyes.

Pinnock's eyes seemed to glow.

"Three tablets of the synthesized version of Fire," said Marshall. He brought up his walkie-talkie. "Okay, Glen. Have the boys subdue the private."

The corporal barked out orders. The men stepped forward again, looking quite a bit more tentative now, and probably a damned sight startled. Still, they were good military men and they followed orders.

They advanced, closing in on Pinnock on all sides. There would be a wonderful tussle, but there were a good eight tough boys there and they'd pin the guy down and then they'd get in the restraining leg cuffs and force jacket and let Pinnock burn off his sudden energy.

"We did a genetic workup on the men, and Pinnock proved to be the most susceptible to the effects of the drug," Marshall explained. "Of course no one understands what the hell happens, really, or what's likely to. Sometimes it appears to have no effect at all. Pinnock is a most suitable specimen, don't you think, sir?"

"He's outnumbered . . . but what's happening to him?" said the general. "This is remarkable!"

Up with the binocs. Down with the jaw. It wasn't just the man's attitude and spirit that had changed. His whole physique seemed—altered. Latent muscles seemed pumped up, and the whole face seemed chiseled purpose and resolve. And those burning eyes . . .

Pinnock grabbed the first of the men and with lightning speed lifted him off his feet and hurled him back, knocking over five more Army men.

. . . those burning eyes. His face seemed twisted into a mask of hatred and anger.

From Mortimer Snerd into Superman . . .

"Amazing," said General Burroughs, echoing Marshall's thoughts. He had no idea . . .

Pinnock didn't give the others a moment to rally. He charged in, punching and throttling. Gobbets of blood flew into the air, along with shrill shrieks and gurgles.

Maybe he shouldn't have used *three* pills . . .

Glen's voice erupted over the walkie-talkie, but the device was hardly necessary. Marshall could hear him yelling desperately down in the courtyard.

"Colonel! Pinnock's getting out of hand!"

Pinnock leapt onto the back of Big Pecs, and grabbed ahold of the man's neck. Big Pecs tried to throw him off, but Pinnock was as firmly planted on him as the Old Man of the Sea. The crazed private gripped the head, and wrenched, his tendons standing out from his neck. A loud *snap!*, a pulse of arterial blood, and the big man wilted to the ground, his neck broken, his head almost torn from its mooring.

The other soldiers had watched this, stunned and stuck in indecision. The bloody demise of their fellow soldier sent them racing away.

Pinnock, grinning like a death's-head, caught two and slammed their skulls together. He raced and tackled another, pummeling him into a pulp with fists.

Perhaps, thought Colonel Marshall, I should not have chosen a soldier with such understandable resentment buried in him.

The walkie-talkie spoke again. "Colonel! He's out of control. We need armed soldiers out here. We—"

"Oh, my God!" cried the general. "Behind him!"

The crazed berserker that had been a meek private leapt upon the corporal, grabbed the walkie-talkie, and slammed the hard metal-plastic over and over again into the man's face, until *it* was a bloody mess.

Colonel Marshall did not pause long to watch.

He was screaming into another radio channel for backup. *Armed* backup. There'd been absolutely *no* indication that this exhibition would get this far out of control.

Two soldiers, one with a machine gun, one with a blaster, raced into the courtyard.

Somehow, in the sudden blur and explosion of fire and bullets, and despite a bullet wound and the loss of part of an arm, Pinnock managed to wrest the machine gun away and use it on the backup soldiers killing them instantly.

Amid the decimation, Colonel Marshall watched with horror as the bleeding and burnt chemically charged maniac slowly swiveled around like a gladiator surveying his kill—and seeking out the emperor . . .

"Christ!" said General Burroughs. "He's looking at us!"

. . . and *not* for approval.

"General. Quickly. Back to the office!"

Even at their first step, a hail of bullets splattered over their heads; Marshall was stung with flying cement chips. Ducking, they lunged through the office doors, and the glass windows exploded. Burroughs took cover behind a desk, and Marshall leapt for his wall of weapons. He tore two loaded semiautomatic Hyper machine guns from their racks and threw one to the general.

"I haven't used one of these in *years*!" moaned Burroughs.

"Watch!" Marshall clicked off the safety. He ran to the billowing curtains, took cover, and squeezed off a salvo at the approaching maniac. No hits, but he got the feel of the thing. He dodged as another hail of bullets crashed through the door, tearing up a wall of certificates and pictures. Marshall retreated, letting off two more burps of fire.

There was a moment of silence, and then Pinnock marched in like he was Superman. He gripped the gun and the grin on his face was like an ax wound. One eye was a bloody gouge, but the other gleamed like diamond. Blood rivuleted down his face. One whole side of his body was burned.

He lifted up the machine gun, like a crazed zombie with firepower.

Burroughs had figured out how to use the Hyper and he ripped off a clip. However, only a couple of bullets hit their mark, the others splattering along a wall. Pinnock was knocked off his feet, falling back onto the balcony. But with iron determination and a brain burning with chemicals, he began to get up.

Marshall lifted his gun to fire again, but it jammed. He did not waste time on the weapon, flinging it down and leaping to a rack. The nearest weapon was a bazooka. He tore it off the wall, grabbed a shell, loaded up, and ducked back behind a chair just as a new hail of bullets chunked and screamed into the weapons wall.

A pause. Pinnock was out of ammunition. He *had* to be.

Marshall thumbed off the safety, checked the go-light of his weapon, thanking the Powers That Were he'd kept up on his weapons training. He brought the short barrel of the mini-bazooka up and gave himself only a fraction of a second to aim.

Private Pinnock, smoking and smelling of burnt

flesh, still grinning, walked toward him, death glaring from his one good eye.

Marshall squeezed the trigger.

The shell whooshed out of its pipe and whacked directly into the maniac private's chest, pushing him back through the door into the balcony before it detonated. The explosion of the shell blasted the private and his gun to pieces, not even leaving smoking boots behind.

Marshall gasped and collapsed, dragging ragged breaths into his weary lungs. What a fiasco! A catastrophe of the first order! Support from the general? He'd be lucky now if he didn't get his chops busted, didn't get demoted or sent to deal with some alien infestation in northern Alaska.

General Burroughs cautiously poked his head from behind the desk. His uniform was torn and he had a stunned look to his eyes. He regarded the tattered gore, the remnants of Private Pinnock spread over the balcony like an explosion in a butcher shop.

He smiled slowly. "I believe, Colonel, this drug bears some further investigation. But please—not while I'm around."

4

War is good business.

War is even *better* business after the war is over, especially if there was massive destruction on the order of the kind administered by the alien infestation. When humanity fought off its enemy it found many of its cities ravaged. But like London after the Nazi air blitz of World War II, this was not necessarily a bad thing. Sure, some good buildings were destroyed by bombs in that case—but also destroyed were massive numbers of creaky docks and ancient buildings that should have met the wrecking ball years before.

The result of the devastation: reconstruction and a better city.

Such was the case with the alien infestation.

Take New York City. Manhattan in particular. It had been rotting for years, its roads and subways tottering on the brink of disaster.

The extermination of the aliens had left behind many ruins and much potential. Nothing on the order of Los Angeles, which was still pretty much a smoking ruin with odd nests of the creatures still needing to be wiped out. But the Big Apple needed a big overhaul.

The U.S. government, weak but still there, brought in two traditional weapons in this particular struggle: free enterprise and deregulation. Any entrepreneur, any company that had the stomach for it, were awarded the privilege of going in and wrestling with the wreckage and the building.

A man named Daniel Grant not only had the company and the willpower for such a job, he has a cast-iron stomach and platinum business nerves as well.

Now, Manhattan's towers were shiny again, and majestic bridges spanned the East River and the Hudson. Its subways were streamlined and the aliens were all dead here, though not necessarily all the vermin.

Rats, like Daniel Grant, were survivors.

Although his chic East Side penthouse was only ten blocks away from the infamous Grant Tower, Daniel Grant always had himself driven to work in one of his sleek fleet of robo-chauffeured turbostretch limos.

You had to put on a show.

You needed leverage for business deals. Flash and illusion and glitz helped gain leverage. Sometimes, when the numbers in your bank account were either preceded by negatives or promises, flash and illusion and glitz were all you had.

This was why Daniel Grant always made sure that

he entered his building through the front door, so that the spectacle was available to the local media.

Today was a brisk spring day in Manhattan and Grant had his window open so that he could see his tower as he approached. God, it was gorgeous! A hunk of gleaming obsidian thrusting up toward the sky from the famously firm island bedrock, Grant Tower dwarfed its surrounding midtown neighbors. Of course a lot of these were still in twisted ruins, which gave Daniel Grant's skyscraper the edge. In fact, it looked like a streamlined monument in an urban cemetery. Still, Grant only had to look at it to feel like the Top Dog, the King of the Hill, the Duke of New York.

"Nice day for a skyscraper, eh?" he said to his female companion, tucked away in the plush, dim corner.

Candy (or was it Bambi?) barely looked up from her compact mirror. "*Very* impressive, Mr. Grant." She glanced at the erect structure, nodded, and winked coyly. "Reminds me of last night!" She extended a long, sleek leg and teased his ankle lightly. Grant smiled, glorying as much in his own manly scent as in the mists of perfume and femininity that wafted his way from this choice little bundle of boobs and buttocks and blond hair he'd bedded down with last night, after the *de rigueur* champagne, caviar, and camera clicks. Hopefully, his nightclub antics would make *Spy Sheet* again this month. Let his competitors think he had money to burn—which, of course, he didn't. These days, though, the newshounds checked your clothes and your chicks—not, fortunately, your checkbooks.

"You're the best, honey," he said as the limo

smoothly cruised up to the new permacrete fronting of the G.T.

"You won't forget my number, will you, Danny?"

Grant tapped his sternum. "Your digits are stamped in my heart, babe." He pulled out a microC-card, tapped in a five-hundred-cred-buck limit for the day, and tucked it into her sweet palm. "Go buy yourself something nice, sugar cheeks."

"Oh, Danny, thank you." He got a face full of lips and bosom for his effort.

"Gotta be at Lipshitz and Garfunkel's in Brooklyn Heights, though, sweet cakes. The car will take you there and back to your digs." He puffed up importantly. "But I'm going to need it at twelve-thirty for an important date."

Actually, he had the thing leased out through his car service then, but an important man had to look like he had full use of his limo, right?

"No problem."

"And remember what I told you if you see any signs of aliens?"

She nodded her head importantly. "Call *you!*" Her voice was slightly and unpleasantly squeaky, and as he began to open the door and some sunlight got at her, he realized it didn't flatter her as much as candlelight did.

Unlikely she'd see any aliens. But you never knew. "That's right, darling. Last night was wonderful. I wish our time had never ended. But even billionaires have to work . . . probably harder than most people!" He swept off the seat carefully so he wouldn't crease his trousers. "Ciao, baby!"

She blew him a kiss just as the clatter and flashes of cameras began. Nimbly, he jumped so that a few photographic images would record décolletage and blond tresses (for his ex-wife as much as envious male competitors) and then shut the door.

The robo-limo smoothed off toward Brooklyn Heights and the perma-thrift department store he owned. Fortunately, Candy (Bambi?) was far too dumb to know the difference between new merchandise and restructured merchandise.

Daniel Grant swiveled around to greet the chroniclers of his arrival, trying to looked annoyed.

"Can't a busy man have *any* privacy?" he groused, straightening his power neck jewelry so that it would look right in the pictures. Daniel Grant was sheathed in his usual sartorial splendor. His tailored camel-hair coat hung over his tailored suit perfectly, every angle and nook and color complementing the jut of his square jaw, the tilt of his brain-filled brow, the steely slate of his penetrating eyes. Even the tousle of his hair was folliclecalculated to be photogenic.

Today, even Grant was surprised.

There were usually one or two people here to record his arrival and ask a few questions.

Today, there was a *mob*.

From the corner of his eye he caught a reporter with a new face and an old question. "Mr. Grant. How do you account for your meteoric rise to success? What's your secret?"

Grant paused, lifted his hand like a heckled but patient monarch requesting heed for his proclamation. He went into automatic speechifying mode. Mental tables appeared before his eyes. He chose from column A and column B.

"No secret! I just make a point of proving an old saying: 'You can learn something new every day.' "

Whew. What did *that* mean? Sounded damned good, though.

"Mr. Grant, what led to the recent split between you and your last wife?"

"No comment."

"Can you confirm rumors that you are planning to enter politics?"

"Of course not."

Loved those kinds of questions. You give a definite answer that didn't mean a goddamned thing.

"Who was that young lady you drove up with?"

A slight smirk tugged at the corner of his mouth. "A friend."

"Is it true that your financial empire is in trouble?"

He feigned total astonishment. "Where did you hear *that* one?"

"Mr. Grant, could you comment on the alleged lethal side effects of your new wonder drug?"

Oops. Time to check Column C.

As there was nothing appropriate there, he just had to wing it. "I'm unaware of such reports." A lie. But he honestly didn't think the "wonder drug" actually was lethal. But these impromptu news conferences were no place for complex ethical and biochemical delineations. "I have full confidence in all my employees. Especially those hardworking people at Neo-Pharm."

Yes, that good old tried-and-true method. Head 'em off the track with a statement. In a legitimate question and answer session, Grant could keep up the palaver for so long, a reporter was lucky to remember his *name*, much less his original question.

Still it *was* an alarming question, one that he really hadn't been ready to deal with, despite the news reports.

Time to beat the retreat.

He spun around on the sole of his spit-polished wing tips, again a busy businessman, immersed in the burdens of accruing riches, and stamped away, letting the hail of further questions slip off him. He dodged between two uniformed, sunglassed guards into the building, waggling the finger of command. The thick-necked men stepped between the press and the door, preventing them from further pursuit.

Grant stepped into the marbled halls of the first floor and made a hasty hop and skip for his special turbo-elevator.

He put his face up against a window for a retinal read, even as he placed his thumb into a hole for a quick DNA check.

In this kind of political and economic atmosphere, you just couldn't be too careful.

The car closed behind him and he punched a button. Thus, he was zoomed down to the basement offices and labs of his principal company, the foundation from which Daniel Grant had boosted into the wheeler-dealer stratospheres.

Neo-Pharm.

When he'd sent the message via sub-space to his folks on Beta Centauri colony that he'd used the money they'd given him to purchase a little-known drug company, his old man had thought he'd said "bought the farm"—and thought he was dead. From a friend back on the colony, he'd heard the old fart had just shrugged and poured himself another boost of booze. Fortunately, his mother had

replayed the message and gotten the true gist of
the message before she poured *her*self another
drink. Then, in celebration, they'd bought everyone
at the bar a drink and promptly gotten stinking
drunk.

Of course, with the Grants, that was nothing
new.

They drank so much at the New Town bar, the
old man went ahead and *bought* it to minimize ex-
penditures. Daniel Grant had to convince his father
that the loan was a good business investment by
sharing several bottles of cognac with the man.
Over multiple ounces of the gut-searing stuff, Grant
had pointed out that the alien-torn Earth, now in
reconstruction, was ripe for business opportunities.
A man who had vision there could have *immense*
power. Old Man Grant wasn't so sure of the financial soundness of his son's plan, but he did have
money. Money that he wasn't sure what to do with.
Lend me some of that money, Pop, said Daniel
Grant, and let me show you what I can do.

Daniel Grant had the money transferred to an
Earth bank before his father sobered up, and then
followed immediately thereafter, by a slower route.

The New Earth was violent and exciting and dy-
namic, a phoenix rising from ashes. World govern-
ments bent over backward to encourage growth.
Restrictions were cut. Regulations either forgotten,
ignored, or repealed. It was the freest market imag-
inable, and Grant studied it. He decided that what
Earth people really needed—and would always
need—were pharmaceuticals. Aspirin for headaches. Harder drugs for those harder-to-deal-with
biochemical problems. Euphorics. Other mood-

alterers. And with a crack team of scientists at his bidding, he could map out new directions of bio-chemical technology.

So he bought the Pharm.

Since Neo-Pharm was one of the few drug companies still operating, under the helm of Grant's cunning and ruthlessness, unbounded by law or ethics, it burgeoned. Cash and credit flow were astounding. Grant expanded, buying out other companies, building himself an empire. Real estate, retail, hotels, space shuttles—even gambling casinos. Daniel Grant wanted to make a strong, swift impression.

Unfortunately, his first buy remained his best. None of the other companies did anywhere *near* as well as Neo-Pharm—and often he found himself dipping into N-P's black ink to try to neutralize the other companies' red ink.

If something happened to Neo-Pharm, some financial disaster like a successful class-action suit or (shudder) having to shut down production of Fire, their most popular product, then the whole card castle would crumple.

And he wouldn't be able to make certain personal payments.

Failure would not mean just bankruptcy.

His *ass* was on the line.

Dammit, he thought as the doors shut behind him. He'd paid back the old man. He'd pay his other debts. And he'd still have his cake and eat it, too . . . even if it *choked* him!

The door whispered open before him, and the familiar subdued colors throbbed over him. The acidic smells of the lab assaulted his nostrils.

As always, he could almost *taste* the freaking

bugs down here. At first, he thought the taste was sweet, because it tasted like money. Now, Daniel Grant wasn't so sure.

He stalked across the catwalk that spanned a pit where biochem workers in silvery suits worked over tables and tanks. Along the walls were aquariums filled with pickled bugs—whole bugs, half bugs, bits and pieces of bugs.

And the hellish bug juice—their acid blood—was carefully controlled, the vicious stuff. That was why the technicians worked in the specially lined pit. Anything that got loose, you could sluice it away, and it couldn't get into where it would damage things—or kill people.

"Mr. Grant!" called an alarmed technician from the floor below. "You're not wearing your suit!"

"Well just don't squirt me, guys," said Grant sarcastically. "Is Wyckoff in?"

"Yes, sir. He's in his office!"

"Great. What about the doctor's blood? Does that stuff burn through human flesh?"

"Not that we know of, sir."

"Good. I won't need a suit with him, then."

Helmeted heads swiveled and hooded looks exchanged.

Grant grinned to himself. Let 'em talk. Kept them on their toes!

He finished crossing the pit and entered the bank of offices belonging to the scientists of the firm. Here the air was tinged with a sweetener to clear out the bug stench—but still the stuff hovered.

A door labeled DR. PATRICK WYCKOFF loomed. Grant opened it, not bothering to knock.

The little gnome of a man was huddled among a stack of paper. Paper, paper, everywhere—even covering his computer. Wyckoff liked to figure and doodle on paper. He was a whiz with computers, but for some reason the man far preferred a number two pencil and cheap bond to scratch and fiddle with than one of these overpriced wangdoodles he nevertheless *insisted* was vital to his operation. Wyckoff was so immersed in what he was doing, the shiny-headed, cobalt-nosed little munchkin didn't notice his chief coming in the door.

"Wyckoff! Hey! Look alive. I could be a bug!" he growled in his big, booming I'm-pissed-off voice. *Worse, I'm your rampaging boss!*

The little man did a double take. His round, Coke-bottle glasses flashed in the indirect lighting. Jaw dropped, he stared at Grant for a moment, then recovered his aplomb.

"Good morning, Mr. Grant. I hadn't expected you so early," said the man in a nasal twang.

Grant loped over and slapped a plastic news sheet from his home News Service machine on the desk, featuring a highlighted article about the latest Fire boo-boo. "But you *did* expect me, didn't you, Wyckoff?"

"Ye . . . ye . . . Yes, sir. I knew you'd at least call. The truth is, I thought I'd hear from you yesterday or the day before—"

"Maybe I just trusted my employees to do their job . . . To deal with this ridiculous matter. I didn't realize that I'd have a microphone shoved up my nose as soon as I'd stepped out of my car, and be hounded by news of the lethalness of Xeno-Zip."

Wyckoff shook his head sorrowfully. "No, sir, Xeno-Zip's perfectly fine."

It was Grant's turn for a double take. He blinked, twisted his head around, and examined his scientist from another angle, as though to make sure he wasn't seeing some one-dimensional projection. "People seem to be reacting rather *poorly* to it for it to be perfectly *fine*, Wyckoff!"

"That's just it, sir. As soon as I heard the reports, I did a complete check of our supply. You may not have noticed, but your PR people have been doing their jobs . . ." Wyckoff seemed to be back in control now, though he still was clearly intimidated by his ranting and raving employer. "They've put out the notification that these are counterfeit bottles of Xeno-Zip that are affecting people poorly. Meanwhile, we're exploring the possibilities, and I believe we know now what the problem is."

"Well, why don't you *tell* me, instead of mincing words and hemming and hawing."

"Sir, it's the active ingredient."

"Regal jam, you mean?"

"Um . . . Royal jelly. Anyway, that's what we call it—there are so many equivalencies to the aliens and their nest/hives and the Earthly insect kingdom. Our supply is obtained by free-lance mercenaries who destroy the many hives still around the world. We pay them to take the royal jelly first before they destroy the hive and pass it along to us."

"Yes, yes, I know that—"

"As I said, our main supply of Xeno-Zip is perfectly all right. The effect of a tiny amount of regular royal jelly combined with precipitant molecules of queen mother royal jelly ingested by a human being within the proper biochemical suspension is a safe serotonin booster and nonabrasive stimulant, improving perception and performance in nerve relay. Part of our work here is to either synthesize both or genetically create creatures that will manufacture both types of royal jelly without the less . . . benevolent aspects of the aliens. We have introduced synthesized regular royal jelly already into the market. Even with the precipitant Q-M molecules it, alas, effects a percentage of users negatively. Why, we're not sure yet."

"Because you're a bunch of *morons*, that's why!"

Wyckoff looked chagrined. A pained expression was etched on his face, and he sighed. "There is a possibility that these effects can be controlled by a higher Q-M jelly content. However, doing that would rapidly deplete our supply. Perhaps someone else can explain this to you better." He leaned over and thumbed a toggle. "Dr. Begalli—would you mind coming into my office, and bring some of those charts you showed me earlier. Mr. Grant desires the full scoop."

"Begalli?" said Grant.

"Yes, sir. The researcher you bribed to jump ship from MedTech."

Grant grinned, remembering his coup. "Oh, yes—that bug expert. Cost me a pretty penny . . . but it was worth it, knowing I stomped on Foxnall's nose!"

"You did indeed, and believe me, sir—he's worth it. He not only has the best handle on the genetic makeup of the things, he's got unparalleled field experience and a grasp on the behavior of the things like I've never encountered before. As soon as he heard about this—ah—little problem, he started an amazing amount of work in conjunction with our computers and the other scientists."

Grant, who had felt a tantrum coming on, was intrigued.

He found himself flopping into a formafit chair and allowing himself to be served some soothing medicinal tea concocted by Neo-Pharm—thankfully not derived from anything alien. The scientist who Wyckoff had summoned showed up with surprising speed, not even allowing Grant an edge of impatience.

Dr. Amos Begalli slouched in, as though burdened by the computer-generated charts and diagrams he carried under one arm.

"Morning," he whispered in a hoarse voice to Grant, almost seeming to bow in obeisance. If he didn't have the charts in his hands, Grant suspected that the man might rub his hands together in the manner of Uriah Heep.

Grant grunted and leaned back, the expression on his face clearing communicating "Show me."

Begalli's eyes flicked over to the pot of tea that Wyckoff had just brewed. "Might I trouble you for a cup of that tea?" he said. He coughed, in an annoying phlegmy fashion.

But then, just about everything was annoying about Dr. Amos Begalli. Grant had always found him an unctious, queasy worm, and would never have hired him at all but for his expertise—and the extreme harm it did to MedTech. He was a dark-complected man with limp black hair that looked greasy even when clean. It dropped down over a sloping forehead in ridiculous bangs, emphasizing an almost Neanderthal brow. Dark rings underlined dark, bloodshot eyes. Only in the center of those eyes could intelligence be discerned— intelligence of a searing, sneering variety that even thick-skinned Grant found a little unnerving.

A weak mouth below a long, hooked nose twitched, showing a flash of eellike teeth as he spoke.

"Thank you," he said, accepting the steaming brew. He pulled out a small bottle of Xeno-Zip and took out a tablet, which he washed down with a gulp of tea. "Marvelous stuff, Mr. Grant. I would not be able to perform at peak mental ability for such long hours without it."

"Good to see you putting some of the money I give you back into the firm," said Grant. "But I'm a busy man, Begalli. You want to get on with this show-and-tell?"

Begalli put the tea down and began to prop his charts up on an easel. He spoke in a hoarse, low but audible voice as he did so.

"Mr. Grant, I believe you are aware of my background and many other important things. But I do not believe you are aware of the amazing number of secrets comprised in the genetic makeup of these marvelous xenotropic creatures, so interwound with human experience."

"I'm a businessman. You're a scientist. I have the money, you have your work."

"Indeed, indeed, but you have to understand something of what's going on here in order to have a grasp on not only the essence, but the cutting edge of this business." Slender, snaky fingers were tapping on a chart, which looked like some modern art collage of the alphabet connected by lines and squiggles and the incomprehensible. Grant recognized it as an incredible tangle of genetic code, with some new symbols that had been invented just for the silicon-based segments of the alien creature's makeup. Begalli gazed at it for a moment, absorbed and fascinated.

He snapped out of it just before Grant was about to get mad. "This is the closest we can get to an actual chart of typical alien DNA. There's so much we do not understand—so much to learn." Eagerness and awe crept into his voice. "So much opportunity . . . But look what I have discovered, Mr. Grant!"

His eyes widened and he tapped the edge, where the code performed a curious curlicue.

"A goddamned crossword puzzle?"

Begalli laughed an oily laugh. "The whole DNA is a puzzle, sir—but what this is, is nothing less than a recessive gene!"

Grant did not pretend to understand. "Look, talk in English, will you?"

"Mr. Grant, when we first started getting reports of the hyperactive results of some doses of Xeno-Zip, I was among the batch of scientists who immediately investigated the biochemical reasons. The reason that some people have been reacting in this fashion to the drug is that their biochemistries are sensitive to the unique properties of the synthesized regular alien jelly."

"Yes, dammit, but what else are we going to use? We're running out of the natural stuff, right. We've got to synthesize the jam or jelly or whatever."

"Yes, sir, but if you'll allow me, there's more. Apparently the berserker antics were the result of a batch of Xeno-Zip in which too much of the precipitant was introduced."

"What a waste!"

"Indeed. Nonetheless, normal amounts still affect a portion of the populace negatively."

"So. What are we going to do?"

Begalli shrugged. "I for one would like to study the possibilities in this recessive gene."

"What does that have to do with our problem?"

"Mr. Grant, you're going to have to face up to facts. We need more royal jelly, and we need more queen mother royal jelly. At the moment, our understanding of the genetic makeup of the aliens is not sufficiently advanced to clone either. We need to go to the source. I have reason to believe that the DNA avenues I have been exploring could result in drug breakthroughs far beyond mere Xeno-Zip. At the very least, we could obtain a source of the active ingredient in the cornerstone of your drug empire that would allow you to manufacture safe batches for a long, long time. And I have the feeling that the answer to my questions could lie at the source of what we need."

The man nodded significantly as though Grant was supposed to catch the significance from these words alone.

Grant shook his head, jumped to his feet, and let the frustration out, full volume.

"Look, goddammit! I'm staring at the possibility of lawsuits buggering me from now till kingdom come . . . I'm going to hear from sales as soon as those spineless assholes get up the courage . . . and you know what I'm going to hear? A drop-off of sales for Fire. That will kill the cash flow, which will kill Neo-Pharm . . . And I'm in hock for everything else!" He stalked nearer to the cowed scientists. "And you're telling me I ought to give a rat's ass about a blip in a weird ladder? You're telling me that I've got to spend more money than God owns for a trip to an alien planet?"

Begalli blinked and smiled uneasily. "In every seeming disaster, there is incredible opportunity. And this particular discovery . . . well, sir, it simply *reeks* of it!"

"What, because it makes people as crazy as aliens? I just don't get you guys! I'm running a business here, not a nonprofit research group. I'm in desperate straits! I need help, not homilies! I need—"

The vid-phone chimed. Wyckoff jumped for it, as though for a lifeline to pull himself from the storm.

Curiosity and deep respect for that demigod of the business world, the telephone, caused Grant to stop mid-spew. Begalli watched the proceedings, engaged but more than a bit bemused.

"Yes?" said Wyckoff. His eyes swung toward his employer, still wary and more than a bit relieved by the interruption. "Yes, he's here, but this is a—" He blinked. "Oh. Oh, I see. Well, very well, I suppose . . . Yes. Right away." Wyckoff turned to Grant and handed him the receiver. "It's General Burroughs of the United States Army, sir. Vital communication."

As Daniel Grant reached for the vid-phone volume button, he saw Begalli's lips tilt up into a half smile, as though he'd expected something like this all the while.

5

There was only one thing worse than the nightmares.

The nightmares, plus a hangover.

When the phone kicked Colonel Alexandra Kozlowski out of sleep at 0600 hours in the morning, she was experiencing both.

"Yeah?" she said, fumbling with the vid-phone control. She was covered in a snarl of sheets. She was still dressed in the civvies from last night. From what, for where? Her pounding brain came up empty.

First things first.

"Who is this?" she demanded.

"Colonel?" Unfamiliar face.

"That's right." Inventory. All her limbs seemed intact and still attached. No empty bottle of whiskey on the counter. Even better, no naked body beside her. That limited the possible damage of last night. Shreds of memory and the dinner tray in front of the vid told the story.

Too much video, too much vino.

She hadn't raised hell outside, she'd just raised it inside. Much more discreet. Far more destructive.

"Colonel, this is Burroughs. General Delmore Burroughs." She sat up, ran a hand through her hair. "I'm sorry to bother you this early in the morning, but we've got an important meeting today in Washington. I'm going to have to ask that you get on a jump-skip."

"Yes, sir." Civility and duty won over surliness. Why the hell had she stayed in this stinking profession anyway? Why was she taking this bullshit?

"Good. There will be a plane ready for you at eight hundred hours. The meeting is scheduled for eleven hundred hours, sharp."

"Yes, sir." She struggled for the proper words. "Begging your pardon, sir ... but could I inquire about the nature of this meeting?"

"I'm afraid not, Colonel. Top secret. Priority one. You'll know soon enough."

"Thank you, sir."

"And, Colonel. Wear your dress uniform. Wear your medals ... and some kick-ass boots."

"Yes, sir."

She disconnected. Well, it wasn't any problem getting to the transport. She was living on base at the moment. All she had to do was call up her adjutant and get him to wheel her all of two miles to the airfield.

The trouble was going to be getting out of bed.

Dammit! she thought, groaning. I wait around

for months for something important to happen, and it happens on my day off, hours after I've had a snootful. The karmic balances of the universe were just getting far too hair-trigger for Alex Kozlowski's taste. The stupid Eastern theories were immediately banished for the colder, more mechanistic, and less vengeful rules of Western science. You drink too much, you get sick. Moreover, if you're a career officer, you took it all like a good soldier.

Groaning, she heaved her compact, muscular body out of bed, wishing she'd been working out more lately. Cripes, she felt like a pair of hips with a torso and limbs tacked on as afterthought. She peeled off her clothes, then walked (no, Koz, she admonished, more like *waddled*) to the shower stall, avoiding the mirror. She turned on the water, hard and hot, held her breath, and jumped in. The pounding heat against her neck and shoulders immediately improved things. Suddenly she had an afterthought head, too.

It wasn't like she was an alchy or anything. She'd go for weeks with just a glass of wine or a shot of bourbon and beer with the gang now and then. Every once in a while, though, when she started thinking about Peter too much, she found herself motoring for a jug of wine, gallon size, and just going apeshit.

Peter. Peter Michaels. Lieutenant Peter Michaels.

There had been men since him, just as there had been men before him. Hell, soldiers in foxholes and all that stuff. Nothing like sex to ease the tension. But there had never been anyone like Peter

ever again. No one she cared about. No one she
could love.

Had it been love with Michaels? Hard to say. She
just knew that she didn't have much in the way of
tender emotions anymore. They had got eaten up
with that alien acid. All that was left was guilt and
nightmare—and a large sturdy pile of grit that was
the essential stuff of Alexandra Kozlowski.

The grit. The iron. The hard stuff. That was why
she was a colonel now.

After that nasty business with the Hollywood
nest, she transferred to the Marines. They took her
in a shot. She found herself immersed in space
and the vessels that traversed it. It was a way to get
her brain out of the acid. She was a top student
and her rank just increased and increased. She was
on Camp Kennedy base now, doing some prelims
on a possible space cruise, but it looked as though
her superiors had something different in mind for
her, which was just hunky-dory.

Busy. That was what she needed. To be busy, to
immerse herself in work. When she worked hard,
she slept hard. When she slept hard, she didn't
have nightmares.

When she didn't have nightmares, she didn't see
Peter's dissolving face again.

Dammit! Just shut up! she told herself, pounding the tile of the shower stall, letting the hot water
sluice down her face. Just shut *up*! It *wasn't* your
fault, why are you *torturing* yourself? It was Peter
who'd been getting weird, who had to show his in-
dependence. If he hadn't demanded to go up to
that bulb, if he had *listened* to her, he might still be
alive.

After his death, they'd cleaned the nest out. It was as though all her men had become an extension of her need for revenge. There wasn't much alien jelly. They'd taken the piddling amount out. Not worth the bother, certainly. But no alien bodies, no DNA samples. They slagged all that. It was like a dementia. It was like nothing that Alex had ever experienced before. If the bugs had had half a brain between them, they would have run, because there'd seldom been a killing machine like her and her men, taking revenge for that sneaky little alien trap. Somehow they'd all made it through alive, too, which was a wonder. They'd used part of their extra leave for a wake for Peter Michaels. It should have been enough for her, it really should have.

But it didn't bring back Peter.

The thing about it was that they'd both known that something like that could happen. They'd promised each other that if it did, they'd get on with their lives, not cling to memories and hope. But it *had* happened and now Alex had to live with that and somehow there were always other kinds of pain she'd rather have.

She dried herself off. She put herself together. She made herself some coffee. Then she called her adjutant to pick her up. She found her good uniform, she put on her pants—one leg at a time, as usual. She combed her hair and she had another cup of coffee.

The pounding in her head had subsided, but she still felt weak and weary.

She looked at the clock. Five more minutes to pickup time.

She looked at her hands. They were trembling.

Damn and double damn! What was happening to her? She wasn't nervous, yet she couldn't function. She'd never been like this after drinking.

She took a deep breath, but it didn't calm her. She sighed. Then, wearily, she went to her medicine cabinet. She took out one of the bottles there, opened it, and tapped a pill into her hand.

She took it with a gulp of coffee, and almost immediately began to feel better.

Damn this stuff, she thought. Damn it to hell.

She tucked the bottle of Fire into her carry-bag, and put her face into her hands.

Daniel Grant smiled.

He felt the room lighting up around him from the effects of that wonderful smile, and he reveled in its power.

"Gentlemen, all I ask for are three things." He turned the smile wattage up just a tad higher. "Guns. Grunts. And a gondola. Send my team of specialists and scientists on a little voyage, and I promise to bring back happiness and satisfaction for us all."

The meeting place was a high-level war room, streamlined angles, all polished wood and chrome and underlit attitude. It smelled of after-shave and leather, and was about five degrees cooler than it had to be. Architecture and technology contrived to create a crib of spare power, with acoustics that made the most of monosyllabic speeches.

There was enough brass in the room to supply knuckles for an army of hoodlums. They sat around a black oval table, bracketed by uniform high-backed black chairs, still and forbidding as monuments in a nighttime cemetery.

"To the alien *homeworld* for God's sake?" said Admiral Niles. The old man moved forward in his chair. He was a good-looking man, with a shock of gray hair and a slash of a mustache below an aquiline nose. His face was lined with weariness, but his eyes were sharp as a hawk's.

"Not homeworld, sir," a supernumery corrected. *"Hiveworld."*

"The source of all the aliens that have been encountered in this quadrant of the galaxy, from all signs. The source of the queen mother that was brought to Earth—not of the race," tendered another expert.

The extent of the spread of the xenos had not yet fully been determined. So far they had been found only on isolated planets; all the clues pointed back to this so-called Hiveworld. The Hiveworld had been the source of the Alien-Earth War.

However, naturally, there was great concern. Any newly discovered planet had the potential of being infected. And no one knew if any eggs had been illegally exported from Earth.

Admiral Niles grunted. "Whatever. This place must be hell. I know that the xenos are comparatively well contained here on Earth." He looked at Grant, and it felt like those coal-black eyes were boring into him. "In some ways, perhaps, even *farmed*. But on their own turf, surely—"

Grant snapped his fingers.

The AV portion of this morning's DC festivities.

A holotank eased down into its moorings and lights flickered. Three-D film flashed of brave soldiers and mercenaries in the latest getup, carrying the most modern weapons, slamming through the ranks of an alien nest. He would have enjoyed splicing in some martial John Philip Sousa, but his PR people had talked him out of it.

"Not bad, huh? And lots of these folks are yours. Just crack teams! Crack! And I even understand you've got a real handle on the alien-blood-in-battle problem. Wonderful!" Grant was all enthusiasm.

"I know those films!" said the admiral. "They're from the North Carolina campaign earlier this year. A piece of cake, true—but we're talking about a place where aliens have total sway."

"Not necessarily, sir," an expert's nasal voice twanged. "The Hiveworld may also be inhabited by the alien homeworld original predators—or corollary predators. There's got to be a similar ecology to some extent for them to have developed there the way they have."

"Hmm. So you're saying an expedition there is feasible, and not overly risky," said the admiral, settling back in his seat.

"Any environment containing these critters is going to have an element of risk, sir," said Grant. "But then . . . I know your people can handle it! And the rewards would be spectacular!" He leaned forward confidently. "I mean, it was General Burroughs here who approached me on the subject. And I found it to be not only a fascinating concept—but a mutually rewarding alliance. An expedition into the adventure of free enterprise and the onward evolution of the American soldier! General Burroughs? Would you care to elaborate?"

The black general glared at Grant through slitted

eyes. "The admiral has been thoroughly briefed on the benefits of the royal jelly you can supply." The man was playing poker here, and that was okay, because Daniel Grant appreciated a good negotiator.

It brought out the best in him.

"Yes, but before me I see intelligent eyes, *questioning* eyes!" Grant stood and gestured outward at the assemblage of frowning brass. "And as I am the pitchman here, and you've granted me time—please allow me to properly present my pitch!"

Again, a snap of fingers.

The moving pictures flickered into a different round.

The Baghdad Goodwill Games. Oriander's world record, and his unfortunate demise.

Ratty videos of the horrible slaughter at Quantico.

He heard the sharp intake of breath.

"I'm sure you're aware of these tragedies and others like them that have caused a huge number of lawsuits to be leveled at my company," Grant said gravely, deep into presentation mode.

Then: soldiers, looking noticeably calmer, performing tasks and exercises with sharp precision and sharp eyes.

"Here we have a group of men who have just taken small doses of regular Xeno-Zip . . . which I shall call Fire from now on. This, as I hope you know, is derived from normal alien royal jelly. My company Neo-Pharm has patented the proper methodology of transforming normal alien royal jelly utilizing molecules of queen mother royal jelly so that tiny doses will perk up a normal human's day—and enhance any soldier's performance. A little costly, perhaps—but worth it.

"However, as you no doubt are aware, the supply of normal royal jelly has been dwindling. We have synthesized the jelly ... with mixed results ... however we need not go into that right now. What is significant is that a batch of the synthesized jelly Xeno-Zip was accidentally spiked with extra queen mother royal jelly. In a marked percentage of those who ingested it, the result was quite incredible. Properly modulated, the results of this new drug will create nothing less than a supersoldier."

Another picture appeared on the screen. A gladiator soldier, hammering away at robots with sword and machine gun—but under control. A berserker without a doubt, but with orders and a plan.

"The good general here is already at work experimenting with this new kind of jelly. However, our supplies of queen mother jelly are reaching depletion. And may I also add, we're still not exactly well stocked in regular royal jelly, either, which is our own bread and butter, far preferable to us than our synthesized sort."

He waved away the audiovisuals, and motioned for normal light. He leaned forward emphatically on the table.

"It's very simple. My company needs more regular royal jelly as well as Q-M royal jelly—and a way to get a regular supply of both. Your company—I mean, your armed forces—already staggering under heavy opposition and funding cuts—need to make maximum use of every soldier in conflict. I have the scientists and the talent—you've got intergalactic vessels, pilots, and soldiers. My scientists predict the certain existence of what we both need on the Hiveworld." He smiled. He held his hands up in an eloquent shrugging gesture. "So some of my kiddies go, some of your kiddies go. We get what we want. We make a little pact. You help me, I help you. You scratch my back—I save your butt."

"Pardon me, Mr. Grant . . ." chided the admiral, shaking his head a moment as though to clear it. "Just a moment. I thought it was *your* company that was inundated with civil suits."

"We've got a few legal problems, sure. So sue us!" Grant chuckled. "Besides, I'm sure a few military words in the attorney general's ear will go a long way toward helping the company you'll be climbing into bed with."

"Mr. Grant! This is a lawful assembly," said the general, but with a hint of irony to his deep tones.

"Absolutely. Without a doubt. Unquestionably. But my association with a powerful legal force isn't going to do my legal standing any harm. And by the time people understand why we're doing what we're doing—by the time they see the benefits of our research . . . They will surely not be so vehement in our pursuit." Again, a shrug. "But only time will tell. In the meantime, no skin off your noses, eh?"

He could tell his spiel was getting to them. Everyone loved a rascal, especially when what he was coming up with could do big time good. He might as well get out the victory cigar in his vest pocket and start smoking it.

A new voice sounded from the assemblage. "Pardon me, Mr. Grant, but are you planning on accompanying this proposed mission?"

Grant blinked. "Hell no!" He looked over at the originator of the suggestion. A woman. Short hair, nice chin, scars. She would have been pretty if she wore makeup. Now she was merely . . . handsome. "I've got an important business to run here!"

The woman leaned forward, clasping her hands together. "Mr. Grant, with all due respect, have you ever put on a suit and gone into a hive?"

"Well, no . . . but what difference does that make?" He looked over at the general as though for help. The black man's eyes twinkled with amusement. Let's see how you wriggle off *this* hook, those eyes said.

"We're apparently talking about a whole *world* filled with bugs, Mr. Grant. Glib as your words may be, this assignment would *not* be simple. In fact, I'm willing to bet that stochastic prophecy would predict losses," said the woman.

"Not the ones projected by our figures!" Grant said. Who the hell *was* this woman? What was she trying to do—scuttle his boat?

The woman swiveled her head back and forth, catching each of the assembly eye to eye for just an instant of seriousness.

"Let me tell you all. I *have* been in alien hives. Miracle weapons or no miracle weapons . . . there will be losses. Are you willing to be responsible for that?" said the woman intensely, teeth gritted as though she were in some kind of pain.

Some of the upper brass began to hem and haw. This was entering touchy territory.

"Aw, goddammit," said Grant. "Give us a break. Is there not a war on? Is this not directly and indirectly a mission against the enemy? Casualties are *always* a possibility. But who's to say they're a certainty?"

He stared at the woman defiantly.

Her eyes were ice. She wasn't giving an inch. "I just wanted to ask a question, Mr. Grant. And state a fact that you seem to be trying to avoid. That's all." The lips curled into a private smile. "As for me, the idea of going to this Hiveworld and killing bugs and stealing their life's stuff is . . . rather appealing."

Christ Almighty! Who was this bitch?

The general and the admiral leaned over and privately conferred. The admiral looked over to his other officers and met merely nods and encouraging eyes.

"Well, Mr. Grant," said the admiral. "It seems as though your intriguing proposal has made the first hurtle. I believe we can work something out."

Grant could not suppress an ear-to-ear grin. His muscles unknotted. "Glad to hear it, Admiral. Glad to hear it!" He put out an impulsive hand, pumped away at the plump paw he'd grabbed. He nodded at the others. "My companies have had a long and prosperous liaison with you fine folks in uniform. I'm glad it's taking off for other worlds!"

There were a few embarrassed coughs, and a couple of members of the meeting made excuses and scurried off into labyrinthine Washington hallways. Grant just mentally shrugged it off. He was used to stepping on boot toes in this business, almost reveled in it. He'd never much liked military people, and secretly resented having to work so much with them, particularly in harvesting the precious royal jelly, far preferring to encourage the mercenaries in the business. Money was something that Daniel Grant could understand when it was the bottom line. When you got into the halls of politics, sex, personality, and power, things got a whole lot murkier.

"Now then," said the admiral, "I believe we have the necessary deep-space tactical vessel at our disposal. It will take some time to prepare it for this special journey. And of course we'll want a staff other than the people that Mr. Grant is supplying."

Grant sat back down. "Of course, you'll get me the best men for the job."

"Naturally, Mr. Grant. Naturally. We have some fine veterans and pilots who would be perfect," the admiral said. "What the expedition needs most is a commanding officer with the right feel both for leading troops and dealing with the quite unpredictable alien bugs!"

"That's your call," said Grant. "I'll leave that one totally up to you."

The general and admiral conferred for a moment in whispers and then the general spoke. "We anticipated the need for such a commander, Mr. Grant. So we invited a certain colonel along to this meeting. The youngest holder of the Congressional Medal of Honor, specifically for a pivotal role in the final cleaning up of the aliens in North America . . . and with special training for further work in space, dealing with infestations on other planets and colonies . . ."

"Sounds good to me. When do I get to meet the man?" said Grant.

The general turned to the small, coal-eyed

woman. "You've already met. The question is, will the colonel agree to such an assignment?"

The intense, scarred young woman leaned over, showing small pearly white teeth in a smile.

"I'd relish such an assignment, sir. Thank you."

It was the general's turn to smile. "Excellent. I cannot commend your expedition into better hands, Mr. Grant. May I formally introduce you to Colonel Alexandra Kozlowski, your commanding officer."

Grant's jaw dropped. He was glad he hadn't lit up a cigar. It would have fallen right onto his expensive Italian suit, spilled embarrassing ashes all over the place. He recovered quickly, converted his surprise into a laugh. "Well, well, well! How marvelous. And I thought you were the one who hated the bugs."

"I do," said Colonel Kozlowski. "I want to see every last one of them either cindered . . . or perhaps even harmless, if that's possible. That's why I'm in this business, Mr. Grant. That's why I'm here today." She leaned forward and tapped the table. "Make no mistake, though. I don't believe in the Devil, Mr. Grant—but if there *was* a Devil, I doubt if even he would be evil enough to invent these bugs. This is not going to be a field trip to an ant farm. Tell your people that."

Those smoldering eyes again.

There was something else in those eyes . . . something that looked at him in a peculiar way that bothered Grant. Bothered him intensely. He shrugged it off, turned to the men in charge.

"Well, seems like a fine choice to me. I like a woman with intestinal fortitude." He pulled out a handful of cigars from his breast pocket. "A celebration seems to be called for. Anybody care to join me?" He flashed a handful.

The general took one.

The admiral accepted one.

"Me," said Colonel Kozlowski, holding out a hand.

Grant had one passed down.

He watched as the petite but hard-looking woman accepted the cigar, examined it, sniffed it, then pocketed it.

"You're not going to smoke it with us?" Daniel Grant said, slightly miffed but playful nonetheless.

"Mr. Grant," said Colonel Alex Kozlowski. "Celebration is hardly in order yet. I'll smoke it when the mission is over and my rear is seated safe and sound back in this chair for a debriefing."

The woman asked for and obtained permission to leave from her superiors.

"Well, what do you think of our choice for your commander?" said the general, an eyebrow raised.

Grant let out a gust of smoke.

"I'd say, I feel damned sorry for those Hiveworld bugs!"

6

"**N**ice-looking boat, huh?"

Daniel Grant flashed the cube-shot to his date sitting in the restaurant booth next to him. She was a hot, big-busted brunette with her spangled dress spray-painted on. Long hair, delicious perfume, and foreign territory for the old Skyscraper Man to plumb. He was impressing her with this nightclub, black and white and dazzle all around—and now, for what reason he knew not, he was impressing her with his power that extended Yea! even to the ends of the Universe!

Her name was Mabel.

"Weird! What kinda thing is that?" Mabel spoke with a New Jersey accent, which gave her flamboyant body a certain earthy charm.

"That's a spaceship, babes. That's *my* spaceship. Pretty, huh?"

"Pretty strange. What you want a spaceship for, Mr. Grant?"

"I told you, you can call me Daniel, sweetheart, just as long as your pretty fingers aren't anywhere near a keyboard."

"You're so kind to take me out tonight, Mr. Grant!" Mabel batted long thick mascara at him. "And me, hardly having worked for two days at your offices. And I don't *care* what the other temps have said—you're *such* a gentleman! Such a scrumptious meal, such delicious champagne—and you haven't laid a hand on me!"

Grant mimed a kiss at her. "I know, and it's damned hard, too, make no mistake about it. But Mrs. Grant brought her little boy up right, I guess."

Truth was, you get enough bubbly percolating in those pea brains, display enough dazzle, and blow enough pheromones in their faces, and women touched *you*. A little trick Daniel Grant had learned early on which kept him out of trouble. Oh, well. He had his share of trouble all right, what with *letting* all those women touch him that wanted to, while he was still married to old Iron Drawers and building his companies. But you tread a fine line, and trouble that came your way tended to be the fun kind of trouble, the thrilling trouble, the trouble that made you feel like you were dashing down a ski slope on a power sled, not a garbage-can lid.

"Anyway, really—what do you think of it?"

The picture was of the U.S.S. *Razzia*, hovering in parking orbit above Earth. Right now, it was getting loaded up with supplies, weapons, men, and whatnot for the expedition to the alien Hiveworld.

A trip that would bring back royal jelly, preserved DNA, and other treasures that would spell not only full financial recovery and put paid to any lost lawsuits—but place him, Daniel Marcus Grant, squarely back into the pure honey of wealth.

"I don't know. It's . . . well, it's kind of ugly."

They'd had more than a few glasses of champagne, so things were kind of blurry. Grant examined the picture again.

There it was, a whale of a ship, bubbles and glassine protuberances making it look like some kind of colorful exotic beetle that had been pumped up with gas to the point of bursting. Aesthetically, it *did* look rather odd. Kind of like a strange cross between the jewelry kind of carbuncles and the flesh-bump kind. Of course, that wasn't the way Grant saw it. He saw it as his beautiful, thrilling hope for riches beyond avarice.

"What is it?" said Mabel.

"Never mind," said Grant, tucking the photo back into his jacket pocket. "Just a little business venture of mine. Let's talk about *you*!"

"Oh, but, Mr. Grant! Daniel! I'm fascinated by business ventures!"

"Stick with Grant Industries, kiddo! We've got our share of businesses. Maybe we'll set you up as a special secretary for one of our branches."

The eyes went wide. A slender hand touched his knee. "Oh, but, Mr. Grant! That would be wonderful. I'd *have* to prove my skills to you first—"

Grant plucked up the bottle of Dom Fauxgnon from the ice bucket and poured some more champagne into her glass. "I'm sure you will, my dear."

He winked at her. "And I for one am looking forward to the fruits of your official labors!"

They clinked glasses.

Feeling positively ebullient, Grant tippled.

This fake stuff sure wasn't classic—but it tingled and did the trick.

He was just finishing off the glass when a booming voice almost made him choke.

"Careful! Careful there, my dear, dear chum!" A dim form moved out of the swirling, milling shadows of the hip night spot and clapped him on the back. Grant sputtered, struggled, and recovered, watery eyes blinking.

"Foxnall!" he said, working hard to keep his voice neutral. "What portal of Hades did you pop from?"

"Ah, believe it or not, dear boy," said the cultured voice from the thin and wiry man with affected square spectacles and billowing silk clothing, "I have not come here to torment you. In fact, if you ask any bartender or regular here tonight, they'll assure you that I am not a stranger to Flickers. But this *is* a treat, especially with you in the company of such a charming young lady. Are you going to be a selfish cad and refuse to introduce us?"

Grant felt a distinct leveling of spirits.

However, everything was still well within control.

"Mabel, this is Lardner Foxnall. Principal stockholder and CEO of MedTech. Lardner, this is Mabel Planer, an employee and . . . ah, new friend."

"My pleasure." Foxnall kissed the woman's hand to her obvious delight.

"MedTech! Why, they make Wonder Diet! I use

that all—" Suddenly aware of her diplomatic error, Mabel cringed. "Oh, dear. I mean . . ."

"No problem, Mabel," said Grant. "MedTech makes a quite reputable line of pharmaceuticals. This is a free enterprise system in which we work—and yes, Neo-Pharm has quite worthy competitors and we value them. After all, if there were no other companies, who could we constantly outperform?"

A muscle in Lardner Foxnall's jaw flinched. However, his eyes remained amused. "Yes—quite. And this new enterprise of yours . . . this journey . . ."

Grant felt a thrill of alarm. "Ah, you must mean—" He began groping for some fake enterprise, to put Foxnall off course.

"Oh, you mean the spaceship! Yes, isn't it exciting?" Mabel fairly jounced with elation. She looked over for approval from her boss, her gentleman date—and found cold eyes instead.

She shut up immediately, to her credit.

"Indeed, Neo-Pharm is looking toward colonial expansion . . . but then what Earth drug company worth its salt isn't?" said Grant aggressively.

An artificial tic of a smile from Foxnall. "Absolutely. And may we all prosper!" He winked. "But some, more than others!" A tip of an imaginary hat. "By the way, Ms. Planer. We're always in need of good help at MedTech. Whenever you care for a free supply of Wonder Diet, please remember us!"

"Quite unlikely!" called Grant after him, barely hanging on to his temper.

He waved for a waiter, and a photosensitive robot

promptly smoothed up. "What's riffraff like that doing in a reputable club like Flickers?"

"Pardon, honored guest—but Mr. Foxnall is the new owner." Lights blinked obsequiously.

Grant started, did a double take, then smiled. "Then that must be why the fellow ordered a bottle of Dom Perignon for the young lady here!" He scratched his nose. "And the caviar and crackers for me, come to think of it!"

"I will see to it immediately."

"He did?" said Mabel as the robo-waiter trundled off.

"Oh, yes. A tradition between pharmaceutical rivals, my dear."

"Oh, Mr. Grant. I'm so sorry if I said anything wrong. Is there anything I can do to make it up to you?"

"Well, let's drink this next bottle of champagne and eat our caviar and have a serious discussion on the matter."

The caviar was cold and quite good, and the Dom Perignon turned out to be far superior to the Dom Fauxgnon. However the conversation in the next half hour grew sour in Grant's mouth and ears, unspiked by sensual desire and the urge for sexual conquest.

Dammit!

Could Lardner Foxnall have gotten wind of what he was up to? Could he possibly know the destination of the U.S.S. *Razzia* and the reason for the trip?

If so, that could mean many things, none of them particularly good, several of them very bad.

His mood seemed to grow fouler as he helped

the increasingly drunk secretary finish their late night treats among the wistful smells and pulsing sounds of Flickers nightclub.

"Mr. Grant!" she said, giggling at some stupid sarcastic statement he'd made about some politico. "You are so *funny!*"

"I think we've had a little too much champagne, Mabel."

"But not too much caviar. I never could have believed that I ever would like fish eggs, but this stuff is just delish! I really am enjoying myself."

"I hope you've saved some for friends," said a cold voice from the darkness. A swath of mist swirled away, and there stood a husky man with a scar riding along his bald pate like a bolt of lightning. He wore good clothes and he smelled of good cologne.

"Gee! Another competitor, Mr. Grant?"

Grant froze. "Not exactly."

Fisk. Morton Fisk.

What was this, old home night for demons from hell?

"Good evening, Grant." The man did not even look at Mabel. His piercing eyes just hooked on to Grant and hung on. "I don't usually visit people personally. However I do have a tradition. I like to make sure that my face is branded on the retinas of dying men."

"Fisk. What are you talking about?"

Grant had a suspicion, but he didn't even want to think about the possibility.

"Who is this guy, Mr. Grant? What's going on?" said Mabel.

"I told you, Grant, when you got me to bail you

out, that I was a patient man . . . until I wasn't patient." The scar on the head seemed to glow a livid pink. Pulsing with contained rage. "And I haven't been. You're months overdue, and you haven't even had the dignity to send partial payments. I am truly offended."

"Fisk! I'm not sure what you're talking about. You've been getting regular installments!"

A big fist grabbed a handful of his shirt, lifted him up so that Grant began to gasp for air. "Lie! He lies to my face! You well know that I haven't gotten a penny for months."

Indeed, Grant did know.

All too well.

In the scrabble for solidity and power after the Alien-Earth War, not all of the fortresses of fiduciary control were entirely legal. And often as not, to get the leverage you needed for truly inspired buyouts, you had to go to these underground people for liquid assets.

Unfortunately, they were criminals.

Violent criminals.

Self-confidence was always the antigrav stuff for Daniel Grant, the by-your-bootstraps talent that hoisted him above the rest. Unfortunately, self-confidence could also be a blindfold. He well knew that he personally owed millions to Fisk and company, but since for Daniel Grant mañana was always golden—well, he'd pay them mañana, when he had the money.

Alas, he saw no mañana in Morton Fisk's eyes.

"Look, Morty. Sit down, pull up a glass of the warm south, get to know this delightful creature . . .

and for heaven's sake, let's jaw awhile, huh?" Grant patted a comfortable cushion.

"Sorry."

The big man spun on his heel, and was swallowed up by the stylish mists and the nightclub gloom.

"Mr. Grant ... Daniel ..." said Mabel. "What kind of gorilla was that?"

"*Not* the gorilla of my dreams!" said Grant, scooting over to the end of the booth. "Look, I'll be right back, Mabel. Got to visit the little boys' room!"

What had happened here? Had Foxnall tipped Fisk off to his presence here? That bastard! That must have been what had happened.

Geez! There were such sharks in business these days!

He was at the edge of the booth, when he heard a *click*. Instinctively he dived for the floor.

An explosion of bullets whacked over the top of him like lateral hail. He could feel their heat. He hit the floor and rolled, the sound of the machine gun echoing in his ear, the scream of his secretary joining in.

He got a glimpse of the poor brunette, jerking amid the passion of the bullets, blood yanked from that sweet body, making a mess of her dress. Glass and champagne and caviar spattered every which way, in a fantasmagoric slow-mo fountain.

The will to live turned Grant away from this death dance, and he scrambled away, like a rat from a pack of cats.

7

A month of her life, just getting this show on the road.

Colonel Alex Kozlowski took a swig of her coffee, and watched as the last batch of supplies got loaded into the shuttle. She managed to get down to a quarter capsule a day of Fire, but she'd already taken that now, and damned herself for wanting more. The stuff wasn't like booze, you didn't see creepy crawlies if you went dry. It was like cigarettes. And just as hard to kick. She wanted to kick it, to show her own superiority to herself. Which was why she felt bad now, wanting another hit.

In just a few hours they'd be boosted up to the *Razzia*, stored away with the rest of the stuff Daniel Grant and his scientists wanted on this mission—along of course with the rest of the marines, her own hard ass included.

Alex Kozlowski was sitting on the apron of the ramp, the lip of which sided a wing of the shuttle that would soon trundle out of the hangar and wing up through the atmosphere. To the other side of her was a warehouse-sized security checkpoint and storage room. Dawn had just shouldered through a cloudy horizon.

She slouched in the chair, watching the crates being loaded.

Hell of a lot of stuff going up there.

She'd been in charge of everything her crew was going to need. She'd wanted to be in charge of the whole shebang. Unfortunately, that was not in the cards.

A bored-looking deliveryman walked over and handed her a piece of paper on a clipboard. "Sign please, Colonel."

Alex took the clipboard.

SUPPLIES, said the checklist. That was all.

"How can I check 'em in, if I don't know what they are?"

"Look, Colonel," said the man, "I'm just doing my job. I'd like it a lot if you could just take a crowbar and prize open a couple and have yourself a gander. I'm afraid, though, that it's all pretty insulated and locked up and you'd be pretty hard-pressed to lock the stuffing back in."

The guy was a civvy, probably worked for the government. Kozlowski could tell by his attitude. She didn't like any man she couldn't give orders to, or take orders from, and the man annoyed her. What could she do, though? Make him clean the latrines? He was the equivalent of a third-rate, truck-driving, trolley-pushing bureaucrat.

It hit her then: what was important to bureaucrats?

"Ooops!" she said, and tore the papers she had to sign into shreds.

The man looked at her, stunned. "Colonel. I'm going to have to go and get another form now! Why . . .?"

"File a complaint, toad-breath," she said. "But have some respect next time you give a lady a form to sign . . ."

The man went off, cursing under his breath, to get another form. Kozlowski went off to sniff around the crates.

TOP SECRET, they read.

THIS SIDE UP.

HIGHLY FRAGILE.

One was even fitted with elaborate refrigeration equipment.

"Oh, well," she said, drumming her fingers against a crate. "You can bet I'm going to find out what's going on when we're light-years away."

She was almost sorry she'd signed up for this gig.

Not that she minded going long distance in interstellar space. That would be fun. And the idea of blowing away xenos en masse still tickled her pink. However, all the mystery and bullshit attendant to her duties had not exactly thrilled her, to say the least. She thought that *she* was in charge of this mission—but over the weeks, the fact had gradually seeped through her thick skull that she was only in charge of the military aspects. Neo-Pharm's other operations on the *Razzia*—and there was plenty of extra room for that, which was doubtless why the ugly scow had been chosen—was strictly out of her control.

Which was one of the reasons they'd probably chosen her.

She could hear the old uniformed farts now, gassing. "Kozlowski! Yeah—she's tough, good, but she's a woman. She's got some give to her."

Alex Kozlowski smiled to herself. The preparations were only part of the whole story. She'd taken the shit dished to her, fried it up nice, and put some ketchup on it. When the Neo-Pharm boys were out there among the stars and planets and xenos, they had better just hope they'd brought some condiments along to stomach what they were going to get from her.

Yep. This was going to be an R and R trip for her, if it killed them *and* her, along with those bugs.

It would be nice to get away from the planet where Peter had died. Maybe, just maybe, she'd find the kind of peace—or war—she was looking for.

She was just sauntering back for another pour of coffee when a man whirled through the door. At first she thought it was Mr. Mover, pissed off and running back with that form to sign.

However, it was not the bottom-level bureaucrat at all.

It was Daniel Grant.

He didn't see her. He ran toward the gangplank of the loading car for the shuttle, looking as though he wanted to climb on along with the baggage. He looked really bad, too, fancy duds all tattered and torn, shoes scuffed, and fancy haircut all frazzled.

"Yo!" she called out.

He swirled around, and the first thing that Kozlowski noticed was how bloodshot his eyes were, how baggy. He looked like a man who hadn't slept much last night . . . only worse.

"Look, soldier. Tell me where I get on the shuttle?"

"Grant?" She went closer, eyeing him suspiciously. What, was the Drug King flying high or something?

"That's right, soldier. You want to help me out? I'm in charge of this mission."

"Colonel Kozlowski here, Grant—and the last I heard you were going to keep your oxfords firmly hugging ground." Unfortunately, she was a bit too astonished to be properly sarcastic.

"Oh, yes . . . Colonel . . . of course. I'm sorry. It's been a rough evening." He sighed, looking back at the access room as though half expecting something to be following him. For a moment he looked lost and vulnerable, and quite a different human being entirely than how she'd seen him before. Something troubled her deeply about him . . . There was an aspect here that reminded her . . .

"Rough evening?" But the sun was rising . . .

"Er—yes."

He seemed uncharacteristically at a loss for words. He kept on looking behind him.

"Don't worry, Mr. Grant. Whoever's chasing you can't get through the base's security unless they nuke the perimeter."

"Chasing?" He seemed to shake something off. "Nothing of the sort . . . I just couldn't sleep last night . . . That's all . . . Got a little groggy, fell down a couple times—"

"Shouldn't you see a doctor then?"

"No. No, Colonel, I'll be just fine."

Before her eyes, he seemed to be putting himself back together again. An amazing act of will. Somatic repair: straightening of poise, sucking in of stomach, stiffening of upper lip. Psychological repair: the psychic armor erected. The eyes recovered, and the willpower returned, the arrogance.

"I made a monumental decision last night, Colonel."

"Did you."

"Yes. This mission is far too important to my companies—to *me*—to allow . . . I mean, not to contribute my presence. I called both the admiral and the general last night and made arrangements. I'll be going along with you, Colonel Kozlowski, to help oversee and participate in the effort." He took in another breath, looking stronger by the moment.

"Are you." Oh, this was just peachy keen.

"Yes. Specific orders are even now being sent over. Now, if you'd kindly drive me to the passenger portion of the shuttle?"

"No bags, Mr. Grant?"

"Er—uh—no. The decision was so abrupt, I did not have time to pack. I'll use whatever's on board. However, the admiral assured me that there are communications facilities available aboard the shuttle that I can use to let my people know what's happening—and dub someone to take my place while I'm gone."

"That's going to be a long time, Mr. Grant. Four months at least. A lot can happen to your company while you're gone."

"I trust my officers here . . . just as I trust you

and your people on the *Razzia*. I'm not dealing with amateurs in either case."

"No, of course not. But don't be mistaken. It's going to be plenty dangerous out there."

Whatever danger was "out there" did not seem to phase Daniel Grant. He seemed far too preoccupied with whatever he was running away from here.

However, there would be plenty of time to find out exactly what that was later.

"Fine. We'll put you on the shuttle with your boxes and the last group of marines going up."

"Excellent, Colonel. I'm looking forward to working with you." He could not seem to help himself, looking furtively around. "Ah—perhaps you could bring me some of that coffee and one of your military style donuts . . . oh, and an Alka-Seltzer. That would help a lot."

Kozlowski stepped forward and poked him on the shoulder.

"Look, Grant. You're in my territory now. I'm not your slave." She pointed, cringing a bit. God, he smelled of alcohol. "There's stuff over there in the office. Get it yourself."

Then she stomped off to get on with her work . . . and check on the promised electro-dispatches. Only way she was going to allow Grant on the *Razzia* was if she was ordered to do so.

This little wrinkle in the future did not bode well.

8

When Grant closed his eyes, he could see Fisk's face, grinning at him.

But he was tired. So tired.

He sat in a corner grav-couch of the shuttle, dimmest part, telling himself he was safe, telling himself it was okay, that he was in charge again.

Rest. He needed some rest.

He was alive, that was the important thing, he told himself. Miserable, but alive. Why had he ever gone out last night? He knew that he hadn't made the payments to Fisk. He knew that Fisk's temper got out of control sometimes.

A mistake. A goof. A snafu. It wouldn't happen again, that was for sure. Of course, he had a few months to get the opportunity to high-life it again. By then, hopefully, the money due to Neo-Pharm and thus Grant Industries and thus Grant himself—the financial entity in direst need—would have arrived. He'd just called his CEOs and ordered them to pay Fisk what they could of his blood money . . .

Deal with the whole disaster, weep with poor Mabel Planer's family, and make sure the insurance company paid off as though it had been on company time the girl had been shot . . .

And, above all, do what Grant was doing.

Survive.

He'd come damned close to falling off the edge of *that* state last night.

Even now he wasn't quite sure how he'd done it. When those blasts had ripped through the booth and Mabel, some auxiliary mode in his musculature must have kicked in, because he'd never scrambled and dodged and ducked so well in his life. Some survival node in his brain must have clicked on as well. He'd done exactly the right thing, headed right on down to the dance floor. The wrigglers and flailers there, doubtless thinking that the explosions above were part of the show, were still going at it to the heavy localized pounding. He hadn't dared to stop for the slightest moment. He'd dived to the exit, skipped his limo, sprinted blocks and blocks, falling down a few times, until he felt safe enough hailing a cab.

And still the chase had not been over. He'd spent most of the night hiding behind cans of garbage in an alley, waiting for one of his aides to come and pick him up. Then he'd directed him on a Toad's Wild Ride to the launchport—and thus, he'd made it to the base, after a sleepless night, grateful to be alive.

In the comparative safety of the shuttle, strapped

in above the equivalent of thousands of tonnes of GeligNuke®, Daniel Grant shuddered at the thought. No, he didn't want to think about it . . . not for a while, anyway.

Sleep. Some blessed sleep . . . that was what he needed. Fisk's ugly mug or no . . .

"Hey there. That seat by you taken?"

Grant's eyes snapped open.

There, looming over him, was a Nordic god.

Thor with a haircut.

Well, not exactly. He was big and strapping, with blond hair and blue eyes and a smile above his square-cut chin. He looked not only damned competent, but perfectly content in that state, and perfectly comfortable in the fatigues that snugly fit his muscular limbs and torso.

Now this guy, thought Grant, looked like a leader.

"Ah—no. No . . . please, be my guest."

The blond god secured a carryall bag in a storage bin, and then slid into the couch, not yet buckling himself in. "Name's Henrikson. Corporal Lars Henrikson." They shook hands. "You must be one of the Neo-Pharm fellows."

"Yes. I'm Daniel Grant. I *own* Neo-Pharm."

Henrikson did not react immediately. He took the information in thoughtfully. "Ah. I had been told that you would not actually be on our expedition, Mr. Grant."

"A last-minute decision."

Henrikson assimilated this information and nodded, as though this were the most natural thing in the world.

"I see. Well, good, I say . . . with all respect. It's good to see bosses take a personal interest in important tasks." A slight bend of the mouth. "Get their hands a little dirty, you know."

Grant smiled, the first time for what seemed like millennia. "Maybe I'm just trying to turn over a new leaf, Corporal Henrikson."

He closed his eyes, hoping to give the man a clue that he'd like a little privacy inside his own head, maybe rest his bloodshot eyes.

Henrikson wasn't the clue-taking kind.

"This is a special mission," he said. "I can feel it in my bones. Nine times out of ten a group of marines head out into space, all they come back with are handfuls of boredom. I've had some of that out there, let me tell you. Soon as I got wind of this mission though, special duty entailing a beachhead on the alien Hiveworld . . . Well, I just jumped at the chance. *Jumped*."

"Couldn't get your fill of bug duty on Earth?"

Henrikson shrugged. "I've killed some bugs. Europe, mostly. Special services. That's probably why I got this gig—the experience. No, that's not it though, sir—you see, I've got this feeling that the human race is destined for great things in this universe. *Destined*. And I'd like to do my bit to make that possible. And I guess I'm vain enough to think I'm a talented enough guy to deal with the kind of situation we've got lined up for us."

Granted expected an inner groan of cynicism to echo in his head. Instead, he found the words oddly striking a sympathetic chord within him.

"That's a compellingly homocentric view of the universe, soldier."

Henrikson nodded. "Yes, sir. I'm sorry . . . I've had people tell me that men are just accidents in the scheme of things. I don't think so . . . Why . . . Because we're *men*. We *stand* for something, goddammit. We've got values and order and . . . hell . . . *purpose* to bring to what amounts to a lot of godless space."

"Indeed. Indeed! That kind of feeling would be a wonderful rabble-rouser . . . I mean, that would go a long way to heal the wounded spirit of humanity!"

"I know, sir. I know." Henrikson nodded gravely. "And that's why I'm here."

"Excellent. Well, you know, Corporal, I think we're going to have lots of time to discuss pertinent applications of that philosophy while we're on our mission. In the meantime, I think I'd like to take a little time to compose myself before the blast-off of this shuttle. You know . . . for meditation . . . a little cat nap, perhaps . . ."

Henrikson looked over at Grant. "Ah. Yes, you do look a little tired. How thoughtless of me. Please, close your eyes. Relax. Snooze. I have my own inner warrior's form of meditation. We shall meditate together."

With that, the corporal's eyes trained onto the front of his couch, and focused.

Well, so much for that. Rest and meditation was even valuable to big boy here. He should have tried that tactic before.

Oh, well. He knew he'd have someone of interest to talk to on the mission. He just wished now he'd brought along one of his PR men to jot all these golden thoughts down.

Grant let his heavy eyelids close.

He found peace for perhaps thirty seconds, before he heard the clamor of feet boarding the boat,

closets opening, packs being stored, voices jab-
bering among one another.

"... look, chum. I'm telling you, that was the
way it was ... the *music* was the soul of the beats!
The hot, cool black music of the streets, man.
That's where the streaming ice lava of the poetry
came from to begin with!" The voice was annoy-
ingly adenoidal and high-pitched.

"Look, Jastrow! I make one single comment the
other day that I enjoyed reading the old free verse of
the twentieth century ... and you think I'm talking
about the beat poets! I'm talking about a number of
writers, including William Carlos Williams ..."

Grant cracked his weary eyelids.

Couple of privates in fatigues and caps. White
boy, black boy. White boy was the one carping on
the literary and music themes. Unfortunate, but he
could tune them out.

"Williams! But Williams *was* John the Baptist to
Allen Ginsberg!"

"Sorry. Never heard of him."

" 'Howl'? You read twentieth-century free verse,
and you've never read 'Howl'?"

"Well, come to think of it ... Perhaps I have ...
but I still don't see the connection between free
verse poetry and jazz."

"Sheesh. Not just jazz, budz. *Be-bop!* Here, let
me show you."

The conversation had become detached, as
though Grant were listening to it through a tin-can
telephone as he drifted into exhausted sleep.

Blaaaaat ... !

High-pitched, running hell-for-leather up some
spidery octave.

Bleeet ... BLEEEEET ... !

The sounds were fingernails and Grant's brain had turned to chalkboard.

He jumped up, awake and disoriented. He hit his head on a low overhang and flopped back onto the couch.

Honk ... honk HONNKKKKK!

He looked over. Sitting on the edge of a grav-couch was a black man wearing glasses and a grimace. His hands were over his ears. Opposite him was another bespectacled guy with a pocket-protector face. His thin lips were clamped on the mouthpiece of a big baritone saxophone.

Both had boot-camp bodies, but faces innocent of the heart of war.

Blat ... blat ... Blat!

"Can't you hear it, Ellis?" he said, unclamping. "I have seen the finest minds of my generation—"

The natural force that was Corporal Henrikson reared up like a vengeful statue. "You guys want to give the rest of us in here some peace?"

His muscular hovering said it all. The salt-and-pepper twins blinked, flinching back.

"Gee—sorry, Corporal."

"Just playing a little Bird, man."

Henrikson stood rock-hard. "Well, I'm clipping your wings! This is not a place for *that* thing. Now over your head ... maybe."

Ellis looked as though he agreed, but Jastrow got a hurt-little-boy expression on his face as he put his musical instrument away in its case.

"I could use a few Z's anyway, Jazz," said Ellis.

"Yeah. Maybe you're right. We'll continue this conversation later, though, huh?"

"Whatever." The man sounded resigned.

Henrikson bent over Grant. "You okay, sir?"

"Sure. My ears are still ringing and I'm wide awake. But I'm okay."

"We got a good fifteen before formal boarding, so maybe you should use them."

"I'll try, Corporal. Believe me, I'll try."

Henrikson shot one more warning look at the newly arrived duo and then resumed his gravcouch. Grant found Ellis and Jastrow peering at him curiously, obviously wondering who he was.

Grant could feel it even through his closed eyelids.

"Name's Grant. The reason you're on this mission," he said. "Mind if we meet formally later? I'm trying to get a little rest."

"Oh!"

"Oh, sure, sir. Sorry."

"Yeah. Right. We'll be real quiet." Whisper. "Sheesh. That's Daniel Grant, man! And you had to squeal that sax in his ear."

"How could I know? I didn't even see him!"

The whispers died into uneasy silence and once again Grant found himself slipping into an uneasy coma.

Which ended all too soon.

He'd been having a dream about his parents, and he hated to dream about his parents, so it was just as well. Still, it was all a little annoying.

The *clump-clump* of steps didn't wake him. He barely heard it: background noise.

The shifting of bags, the snap of storage cases. No problem.

However, when a body fell directly onto him—*that* woke him up.

"Ooophhh!" he said.

"Gahhh. Oh, dear ... damned floor! All these knobs and braces. Sorry!"

That the person was prominently female mitigated the hurt and shock somewhat, and not just because of the softer bits. She looked good and she smelled good, even in fatigues. She was a busty brunette with hair about as long as the Marines would let you wear it if you weren't male, and rich dark eyes that now looked thoroughly repentant.

"That's all right," said Grant, flashing on the immediate lady smile. "I was hoping to get some rest before takeoff, but these things happen."

She pushed herself off of him with ease and a great deal more grace than she'd shown in tripping onto him. "I do better in faux grav, for some reason. And null grav? I'm a swan." She shrugged. "I'm just a space babe, that's all there is to it, and I'll be glad to lift off this—" She batted those splendid doe eyes. "Say. Haven't I seen you ... My God! You're Daniel Grant, the big tycoon! I've seen you on the vids!"

"That's me."

"You look awfu—I mean, I guess you could use some rest." She hobbled over to an empty gravcouch, and Grant, despite his weariness, was unable to take his attention off her delightfully swiveling hips. She turned. "I'd *heard* you were somewhere behind this mission. I didn't think I'd get to really *meet* you though!"

"Well, get used to it, Private," said Henrikson. "He's coming along with us for the voyage."

"No kidding! Well, isn't that ... Isn't *that* news." She swiveled back over, unconsciously smoothing her hair, and gave him her hand and a markedly breath-ier delivery. "My name is Edie Mahone. Private First Class—but I'm still young, and I really think I have quite a bright future with the Colonial Marines."

Grant felt a little nonplussed and couldn't help automatically turning on the charm—and wonder-ing at the same time what this particular woman was doing in the Marines ... and on *this* mission in particular. As he studied her though, he got an impression of strength beneath the apparent ditziness. The oh-gosh business was just an act. Beneath it, Grant could tell, was strength, and it turned him on. It challenged him.

"You have an interest in xeno development then?" said Grant.

"The bugs? Oh, no." She shook her head, shud-dered. "Hate 'em. But then, who doesn't? I can see your question coming. What's a nice girl doing in a place like this?" She shrugged. "I'm just a space nat-ural, I guess, Mr. Grant. I wasn't fooling you ... And on top of that, I'm a tactical weapons specialist."

"Weapons specialist?"

"Yes, sir. Top scores." A mischievous playfulness shaded her voice.

"I'm just glad you weren't carrying any grenades when you fell over me."

"Hmmm? Oh, yes ... yes, of course. Mr. Grant, I really am sorry, and it's such a surprise ... maybe this mission isn't going to be such a grim business after all."

"I certainly hope not. Now, Private Mahone—I hope you'll come to my cabin sometime for drinks and we'll have a nice long chat. In the meantime, my sanity could really use a little rest before it gets rattled by takeoff."

"Of course. Of course, Mr. Grant . . . sir. I'll just hop into a couch over here and leave you alone . . . And . . ." She did a double take. "Drinks? Did you say *drinks* with a tycoon! Of course, Mr. Grant. I'd *love* to! I'm a regular media hound and I watch you all the time. I even bought that unauthorized paperback about you—is it true that your wife divorced you when she found you in your marriage bed with four naked women?"

Grant chuckled mischievously. "And a parrot. Don't forget the parrot, Private Mahone."

He was pleased the legend lingered.

The starstruck private shook her head and rapturously wandered back to her couch. Was it an act? He didn't know. And he didn't care.

Drinks with an attractive private who would probably be disappointed if he didn't make a pass at her. After that tragic debacle last night, he was hardly in the mood for romance right now. But weeks into a space cruise with a bunch of scientists and hardened soldiers? The dominant Grant hormones would doubtless trot themselves out into quest-and-conquer mode. A willing female partner with the requisite assets was something that cheered him immensely.

Now, though, to sleep for just a brief sweet moment.

Grant let his head flop down into the cushion, gratified at the silence that the cabin had cloaked itself in. *Respectful* silence.

This wasn't so bad, shipping out on a boat heading light-years away from Earth with a bunch of scientists and marines. It was *his* mission, after all . . . And he seemed to be getting the appropriate obeisance from his people.

This was good. This was very good. A kind of calm descended upon Daniel Grant. His knotted muscles unwound, and a sense of control of his environment began to knit itself around him. Yes, yes, perhaps it *would* work out for the best that he was coming along to supervise, to oversee . . . no, to *control*. The boys in the office knew well enough how he ran things by now. They could do exactly what he would do, whatever the situation. He didn't have to be around. Instead, he should be doing exactly what he was doing. Heading for parts unknown, spreading his influence, his dominion.

Daniel Grant . . . a great man, destined for the stars.

The cadences of his self-congratulations lullabyed him into that blessed relaxed land just short of slumber, where not even his mother was waiting to natter at him.

Ah . . . !

Sweet, gentle peace . . .

WOOOOOOONK!

WOONNNNNNNK!

The Klaxon rang like hell's own trumpet.

"That's the fire alarm!" cried Jastrow.

"Shit! Something's wrong with the shuttle. We gotta get out of here, Mr. Grant!"

"Please," murmured Grant. "Just let me lie here awhile. I'll die if need be. Just let me sleep."

"No can do, Mr. G!"

Grant felt himself being pulled up out of the couch, and physically carried down the ramp.

The cooler air outside was like a slap across the chops. He blinked, felt himself being jounced . . .

And then suddenly stop still.

"Let me down!" he demanded.

"Do what the man says, turkey! Now!"

Henrikson dropped him onto hard sheetcrete.

"Ow!" Groggily he scrambled up to his feet . . .

And found himself staring into the bores of 10mm blasters.

Connected to those blasters were Colonel Alex Kozlowski and a group of marines, travel sacks at their bags.

"Belay arms," said Kozlowski, striding up to them, arms on hips. If we were a group of bugs, you dopes would be bug food now! Emergencies demand emergency measures!" A toothpick stuck out from the side of her mouth. She worked it all the way to the other side of a scowl. "Isn't that right, soldiers!"

The marines, who somewhere in the midst of all this had managed to effect uncomfortable poses of attention, immediately responded.

"Yes, *sir!*"

Kozlowski worked the toothpick.

"Besides, I haven't assigned seats yet, have I?"

"No, *sir!*"

Kozlowski walked over to Grant, and stooped down beside him. "Welcome to your mission, Mr. Grant . . ." She spat the toothpick.

It stuck into the loose fabric of his pants.

"Welcome to *my* command."

Grant sighed and closed his eyes again.

This sheetcrete was actually rather comfortable . . .

9

Darkness.

Darkness and dreams.

Dream logic tangled in its own shreds and chips of reality and magic.

For six weeks, Daniel Grant dreamed or didn't dream, but in the overpowering darkness, the dreams were all he knew.

Moebius strips of dreams. Jump cuts. Swirls of victory and laughter and glory.

The depths of the past, into secret and overpowering fears.

Mostly, though, it seemed a short sleep, for the dreams were only brief releases of hypersleep to allow brain function and REM.

In the glass-case cubicle, embedded like a fly in amber, when the mechanism and gas mix slowly began to gently pry him from his slumber, Daniel

Grant only vaguely sensed the springing of the lock mechanism of his case. He clung to his dreams, clung to the darkness, a sleeper drunk on sleep.

"Mr. Grant?"

A gentle female voice. Whose? It was sweet and kind and understanding. The kind of voice his ex-wife used to use, in their early love, when he gave himself only to her.

She seemed very real now, very much a part of reality in this darkness.

"Daniel?"

Martha. He'd been dating a lot back then, back in the halcyon days of Neo-Pharm, when he'd first bought it and was working on the beginnings of his empire. She was a model his ad company had hired for commercials. He'd swooped down and never come back up . . . not for a long time, anyway. Still, to this day, he was not sure why there had been others, years down the road. Old bad habits? Part of the life-style he'd loved? Pure stoking of an overblown ego?

He wasn't sure, and he wasn't troubled about it.

Except for moments like these, upon waking, when he doubted himself, when he felt vulnerable.

"It's time to wake up, Mr. Grant."

Wake up? Where was he?

"We've got a lot to do."

That voice. It certainly wasn't Martha's. He realized that now.

"So hop to it."

It was a hard voice now, a voice used to being obeyed.

Grant realized that he was cold. He felt quite naked. Shivering, he raised himself.

He pried open his eyes.

Peripherally, he saw the overhanging cables and cold metal of the hypersleep chamber.

In front of him, crouching, was a good eight feet worth of talons, bony notched spars and open, angry jaws.

An *alien*!

He screamed.

He cringed.

Then he scrabbled back, instinctively throwing up his arms in a helpless gesture to protect him from this, the deadliest creature in the known universe.

Even as he squirmed, trying to grapple over the side of his hypersleep cubicle, what shreds of his rational mind that still operated realized something.

The thing wasn't moving.

It was just hovering there, a few feet away.

And come to think of it, couldn't he barely see a *bulkhead* through the murky black of its articulated body?

A shudder, a *zwip!* of light passed through it.

It wasn't real ... It was a ...

From the left a woman in khaki fatigues stepped, holding a modular control unit.

Colonel Kozlowski.

The beast before him was just a hologram.

"Thought you might need to get your juices flowing." She tapped a control, and moved the hologram away. "Welcome to the U.S.S. *Razzia*, Phase II."

"God *damn* you, Colonel!"

She raised a dark eyebrow. "You want to be a

part of the gang, don't you, Grant? Just consider this a very mild hazing. You're a member of the fraternity now!"

He wasn't groggy at all. The adrenaline had managed to kick weeks worth of sleepdirt out of his head. Still, his heart was racing and he was damned angry.

And, what with only a pair of briefs between himself and nakedness, damned near naked!

He hopped out of his cubicle, one of ten spiraled around a central control and supply center. All the duraplas casings were lifted now, like translucent insect wings.

They had obviously let him snooze awhile longer than normal. All the other cubicles were empty.

"Why am I the last to wake?" he said, getting up and out of the thing, steadying himself on the side.

"You seemed real tired when we left, Grant. We all thought you could use a little extra sleep."

"How far are we from our destination?"

"The gravitonic engines are cut off. We've got to use regular impulse engines to cruise among planets. We'll be in orbit around the Hiveworld in four days." She smiled. "Are you ready for some action, Mr. Grant?"

"It would appear I've already gotten some, Colonel."

"What. From Black Fang here?" She smiled. "Just a training hologram. No reason to be embarrassed. Some younger recruits have soiled their skivvies because of Black Fang. Looks like you pretty much did okay."

Grant snorted. "You have quite a warped sense of humor, Kozlowski. I guess we're going to have to talk about that, and some other things in a few hours. Right now, I'd like to get some pants on."

"Too bad. You look so cute that way." She laughed and started walking away. "Come, boy! Come! Fun's over. We've got some work to do."

The holoprojection ghosted along beside her as she walked away toward wherever.

Grant shuddered. He took a deep breath, got his bearings, and headed off in the direction of the locker room where he'd left his clothing.

In the few days aboard the U.S.S. *Razzia* before he was tucked away in hypersleep, Daniel Grant had had very little time to familiarize himself with the full extent of this very large ship. He'd spent some time overseeing the operations of his scientists and he'd spent time getting some natural sleep. That was about it.

However, he did make sure he remembered where he put his clothes.

He wasn't crazy about the immense and metallic coldness of the ship. The liner he'd taken from his home planet had at least catered to *some* human amenities. It gave some feeling of warmth and sociability. Here, aboard the *Razzia*, it was just a pure case of military utilitarianism. There was about as much decor inside the ship as on the outside.

All in all, Grant was just as happy to snore the time away.

What the hell was going on back on Earth now? he wondered. He'd warned his officers to stay inside, to hire security, and to reinforce measures. He'd even had them tender a small payment to Fisk's "company." Nonetheless, he couldn't help but wonder. Still, whatever was going on, there was absolutely nothing he could do out here, light-years distant in some godforsaken quadrant of the half-known galaxy.

The locker room was down a narrow corridor. Showers, toilets, benches.

It looked, smelled, tasted, felt like something out of his high school sports hero's days. Funky, but somehow homey. Oddly comforting.

A tall blond man was in the corner, buckling the belt of his pants. Oddly enough, he was wearing dark glasses. They made him look more like the MacArthur school of officer than a corporal.

"Henrikson? You just get out of cold sleep, too, buddy?"

The corporal turned and looked at him. "Early this morning. Just finished exercising, sir."

"Just kicked my butt out of bed now. Wonder why they kept me down so long?"

"Maybe they just wanted things spick-and-span for you, sir."

"You have a first name?"

"As I told you before, sir. It's Lars."

"Oh, right. That's it. Lars. Tell you what. You can call me Dan."

The corporal nodded. "Thanks . . . Dan."

Grant found his locker. Racked his brain. His memory coughed up the combination. He twirled the dial back and forth. The lock snapped open. Inside were the civvie scientist grays they'd provided him with, since he hadn't brought along any of his own clothes, and the duds he'd come in with were pretty shredded.

He put his pants on.

"You know," said the corporal, "times like these make me wish I could pop a tab or two of that Xeno-Zip you make. Unfortunately, tests have determined that chances are pretty good I'd go berserk even on the regular stuff. Damned skittish metabolism."

"Oh, well," said Grant paternally. "I'm sure you're a damn fine soldier without it." He grew thoughtful. "I'll tell you, Lars. You must be pretty sick of that colonel of yours."

"Colonel Kozlowski. Our commanding officer."

"She had a bug holo waiting for me when I woke up."

"No kidding. She must like you then."

"*Like* me? Scared hell out of me. Said it was some sort of hazing."

"Tough. She's pretty tough all right, the colonel is."

Grant was surprised. "C'mon. We're friends. You don't have to pull that loyalty crap with me. Tell me the truth . . . you've hated her for months, right?"

In a we-men-gotta-stick-together tone.

Henrikson's face was peculiarly immobile. Behind those shades, his eyes were unreadable.

"Mr. Grant. I guess you could say I feel like I've taken you under my wing. You don't know much about the military . . . and here you are on a military craft. There are things you have to understand about the military . . . and I guess it's not that much different from business life. Maybe even simpler."

Grant smiled. "Right! I knew we could be chums." He continued Velcroing his suit. Damned thing! It sure as hell chafed!

"I'm a corporal. I haven't been in the Colonial Marine Corps that long. But I have previous military experience."

"Exterminating bugs?"

"That's not all the military does in this universe, Mr. Grant . . . Sorry. Dan. Sir." He sighed. "Whatever. At any rate, my point is that it's dog-eat-dog, here. Domination, but in a codified, respectful fashion. I've only served under the colonel since she culled me from the ranks to be on this mission. She's earned my respect."

"Oh. But she *seems* to have some kind of chip on her shoulder. Think she's just trying to make up for not having one between her legs?"

"Like I said, Dan. You've got things to learn. There are codes and games. Just like everything in life. You learn the ropes . . ." He shrugged. "Maybe these little attitude snits . . . Well, I guess you've pulled a few in your time at Grant Industries."

Daniel Grant considered. "I suppose I have. In my own charming way. Good point."

"The colonel is totally in command. And she treats every one as an equal. And if she chooses to dump a little extra shit on your ears . . ." A brusque shrug. "Well, then like I said, Dan. She must like you."

Grant thought about that a moment.

"Fair enough, Henrikson. That doesn't mean I have to like *her*, does it?"

Henrikson put a hand on his new friend's shoulder.

"Any woman ever treat you like this before?"

Grant considered. "Yes. My wife!"

"And what did you do about it?"

"I divorced the bitch!"

Henrikson smiled. "Well, you'll have to marry the colonel to do that! I reckon the captain of the ship's got the legal right to do that."

"Marry . . . Henrikson, I wonder who's got the more warped sense of humor. You or me!"

"From what you tell me, sounds like the colonel does. I'll watch for that little holo trick. She hasn't done that number on me—yet."

"She must not like you, Henrikson."

"No, I guess not." The corporal gave a farewell nod and started leaving the locker room.

"You're a lucky man, Lars."

"We'll see, Dan. We'll see."

The big man was gone.

Grant sighed. He Velcroed his ship shoes, and made a pit stop at the head.

Next stop: his scientists, and his little secret project.

That should make him feel back in the saddle again!

10

"**H**ow we doing, Pilot?" asked Colonel Kozlowski.

The man was bent over away from her, obscuring the motions of his hands. Around him ranged a convex field of lights. LCD screens played spectacular spectrum games. Lume-points glittered, waiting for computer input. From this angle, she could see his bald spot, like the top of a hairy egg.

"Fine, Colonel," he said in a monotone. "Almost finished."

His elbow swiveled. His head nodded.

One last telemetry check?

The culmination of a final primary diagnostic of the *Razzia*'s sys/ops and structural integrity after its long cruise through sub-Einsteinian planes of warped mathematics?

One more little flourish of his hand and he

turned to her. "What's up, Colonel?" He'd turned so that now Kozlowski could see that his hand was nowhere near any of the controls. He held a pencil and a book of crossword puzzles. The blocks in the puzzle were all filled now.

"An interesting form of duty report, Captain," said Kozlowski coldly.

The man's lined, pale face remained impassive. He shut the book, slipped the pencil behind a large, hairy ear, and folded his arms together. "You forget, Colonel. You got a nice long snooze. I got to wake up for a few weeks, to check on things. Part of my job. Got to keep something going to prevent the ennui from driving me nuts. Little diversion of mine." He tapped the book. "Got a whole library of them. After twenty-six years in the Marines, I got lots filled, too. Next year I retire. Bought a nice little chicken ranch on the Ulna colony. And then, I don't want to see the inside of another freakin' interstellar vessel . . . or for that matter the inside of another crossword puzzle book again."

"Just the inside of chickens."

The pilot-captain's name was Hastings. Phillip Hastings.

Hastings shrugged. "The ancient Greeks used to study bird entrails to predict the future. Wonder what a split-open one would tell us now."

"A few tomorrows of many spilled bug guts, hopefully. I take it by your inaction that everything is functional, we're on course, minor things like that."

"We got navigators and copilots and engineers to take care of that garbage, Colonel. I just oversee and coordinate." Hastings looked like a good soldier gone to seed. Beer belly. Slack skin that had that waxen look that toned muscular bodies get when they don't get exercised for a few years. He had thinning brown hair and a network of burst capillaries in his nose. From the look of him, he wasn't just going to raise chickens upon retirement. He was going to do some serious drinking.

Nonetheless, she—and doubtless Daniel Grant as well—had been assured that he was the best in the business. That he was a burnout did not seem to be important.

"What can I do for you, Colonel?"

"I'm briefing the troops. I thought you might like to join us."

"I'm not going down to that hellhole. Why should I?"

"I thought you might find it educational. These bugs have popped up all over the universe—and they spread via ships, as you know. Thought you might like to know some tactics against them."

The captain sucked a lip. "Thanks, Colonel. You going to tape the meeting?"

"Yes."

"I'll watch it some other time."

"Miles and miles of crossword puzzles to do before you sleep?"

Hastings scratched his nose. "Something like that."

"I *am* in command, Captain. I can order you to be at that meeting."

"Then you already would have, wouldn't you? You gave me an option and I'm exercising that option." He leaned forward and tapped LCD displays. "Besides, we're in a planetary system now. A strange system can have all kinds of phenomena waiting. Gravity wells, black holes . . . as well as the usual meteor showers, comets, asteroids . . . I like to ride close shotgun at times like this." He tapped his book. "Besides, I've got some more puzzles to do."

She was ticked off at the guy, but he'd rummaged up a good excuse, so she really couldn't pull rank.

She just wished the admiral had given her someone with a better attitude, that was all.

"Just make sure we don't crash into any moons, Captain."

Captain Hastings turned to his left where a miniature holotank filled with blips and sparks and readings hung. "No moons in our immediate future."

He opened his puzzle book and went back to work.

Kozlowski turned and stomped away.

She stopped at her cabin first. She went inside and splashed some water into her face. Had she done the right thing? Should she have made Hastings go to the meeting?

He was right about not really having to, but his lack of interest, his insolence, annoyed her. She had the command here. He should be doing not only what she told him—but what she suggested as well.

Kozlowski wiped her face with a towel, looked into a mirror.

She had a lost look to her eyes.

Light-years from home.

She'd fought for her planet a very long time. She'd learned the basics of space travel so that she could carry the battle against these creatures to their home. Now, though, like some mythological being, she felt cut off from a source of her power.

Nonsense, of course. Foolishness. All just knots and complexes of neural patterns, easy enough to blast apart. She was a fighting machine and she was just taking a ferry to another part of the battle.

Still, why did she feel so homesick?

She'd popped out of hypersleep a full two days before the others, so she could do some work with the tactical computers as well as knock some of the stasis sleep out of her brain. Wrapped up in maps and facts, figures and projections, inventorying weapons and supplies, and rebriefing herself on the armor, she'd been in her own little world.

Now, though, with a day full of the troops waking up, the whole thing was starting to get to her.

Thirty troops were going to jump down right into the thick of thousands, maybe even *millions* of creatures that could give even biblical demons a scare, with only some half-proven experimental weapons to do the job.

Okay, girlie, she told herself. Just knock that look right off your repertoire. Either that, or get it out of your system, here and now.

There was no reason for this kind of doubt. The Hiveworld had been raided before. True, there had been casualties. However, there had been survivors. She'd studied their reports. Wilks. Billie whatshername. Nasty stuff, but compelling.

Kozlowski had no illusions.

You deal card hands from the bug decks, you

came up holding some casualties. Now, though, here on her first big extra-Earth mission, she'd watched the troops get up today, stretch and go through their metaphorical thawing, and when she saw the vulnerability in their eyes, that moment of terror, that oh-shit-here-we-are expression, she felt what they felt.

Even with that asshole Grant.

Ever since what had happened with Peter Michaels, maybe she was just getting soft . . .

Of course there was a reason she'd pulled the holostunt with Grant. He'd been making noises before sleepytime that he wanted to jump down with them for the mission, to see it firsthand. She was just trying to discourage him, that was all.

Maybe, just maybe the meeting would rattle him. When she thought deeply enough about all the implications, it sure as hell rattled her.

She closed her eyes, did some inner self-composure exercises. What came up wasn't calm and a deep peace, though. What came up was Daniel Grant. She didn't feel good about him being here. Not good at all. For complex reasons she didn't care to deal with just right now.

Even though she'd promised herself she wasn't going to do it, she went to her bag and pulled out a medicine bottle full of the reason Daniel Grant bothered her.

She cut a tablet of Fire in half. She'd tried to give it up, no go. Maybe after this fracas was over.

She washed the half-tablet down with a glass of water.

Then she finished getting ready for the briefing.

11

The bug wavered, capered, lunged.

Drool cascaded down its mouth into the shadows.

Its exoskeleton seemed to glow with evil, spikes sticking out of its back erecting.

The thing looked like a dinosaur attempting to shapeshift into the Devil.

"Yum yum," squawked a reptilian voice. "Fee fie fo fum. I smell the blood of a bunch of bums!"

Uneasy laughter rippled among the assemblage.

"Any of you sweethearts want a date with my ovipositors?" it snarled. "Looks like we'd have a wonderful party. You all look like absolutely splendid *hosts*."

Groans.

Colonel Kozlowski twirled the dial of the holoprojector, and the bug program faded. She let her voice assume its normal timbre as she looked out at the group of amused, anxious marines.

"Okay, listen up, people. I promise you right now, this is going to be no party. But we didn't come all these light-years to party, did we? We came to help make this galaxy safe for peaceful, sentient life. As long as these things infest any of our planets or ships or space colonies *anywhere* in an uncontrolled and above all *misunderstood* fashion, the future of humanity is threatened."

The briefing room felt like the interior of a metal egg, subtly lit in the curved corners. All of the soldiers assigned for planetfall sat in rows of comfortable, slanted chairs, as though in some military theater. They sat at a kind of alert attention. Professionals. Damned good people all of them, and Kozlowski should know. She had helped to select every single one of them.

In the front of the room, alongside her podium, was a table where the big shots in the mission sat, ready to support her in her explanations. Grant. A few of his scientists. Some crew members.

"These killers, these reprehensible aliens, have just got their claws and their blood and their teeth and their incredible powers of survival as weapons . . ." She paused for impact. "Our *ignorance* is their primary weapon, and I hope to diffuse a little more of that with you today."

The soldiers all looked entranced. Hanging on her words. These people had been briefed on xenos before, but now they greedily lapped up the information she was presenting. She was familiar with the phenomenon. When you were a soldier, you could act as macho and as confident as you wanted to—but if you didn't listen and absorb every ounce of information handed to you, you could find yourself dead. Smart soldiers learned to listen. These grunts were smart and capable. Quirky, maybe, but she'd gone through the choices with the command herself, and not one of these people didn't belong here.

Too bad about people like the captain, Grant, and his castle of Frankenstein scientists. But then, if she had control over everything, *pfft!* The aliens would be instant slag, and Peter Michaels would be back.

Anyway, she had some interesting information here.

Her theatrics at the beginning had probably not been necessary, but she liked to put a little pizzazz into the proceedings.

She began with the parameters of the mission.

"Quite simply, people, as much as I'd like to say all this is perfect and noble in our mission, it's not. We're going to a planet which is the origin of the xenos in this sector of the galaxy. We'll be using a specially fitted lander. People, we've got the latest in technology at our disposal. Basically, we're going in to do a robbery. Now, ultimately I have no doubt this will be in humanity's best interest so take whatever nobility you can from your participation here. However, what we're up to here is the biggest heist of queen mother jelly in history."

Jastrow waved an excited hand. "Why?"

"Officially, I can't tell you. You're just supposed to do what you're ordered to do. Unofficially, though, I don't give a shit." She grinned. "Xeno-Zip."

An excited buzz sounded in the meeting room.

"*That*'s why Daniel Grant is here," someone whispered.

"Heck, I use that stuff," another said. "It's *great*."

"That's right, people," said Kozlowski. "We're on a glorified drug run. Take my word for it, though. I'm personally assured that it will make someone a great deal of money—"

Laughter.

"And maybe even help the human cause as well. In any case, be assured. We're taking the Alien-Earth War to the source, and we'll most certainly kill lots of xenos in the process. Call it hard-core vengeance if you like. Call it just another job. In any event, we're here together so I can provide you with some information and equipment designed to preserve your sorry lives."

Quickly she rattled off some of the basics about the xenos, their behavior, their attack patterns, individually and in groups. She summarized what was known about the Hiveworld, and what the main hive itself looked like, from the information provided by the previous expedition. It was all like a mantra, and she ticked off the info, point by point.

"Now then. As for the interior of the hive . . ." She thumbed the projector to a prepared setting, kicking in the holotank in the corner.

Like some magician she conjured up a vision from the depths of Hades.

Here was the familiar bowellike tomb, ropey with intestoid projections and ridged with tubing, bumps, and alien growths, organic in the very worst and most frightening sense. All hellishly lit in orange and yellow. In the central portion of this chilly sight squatted a huge bulblike protuberance, like a half-planted flower bulb. However, instead of bright and colorful plumage, from its pustulelike side it sprouted tubings that connected to other, slightly smaller bulbs.

And from its top, like Mephistopheles happily squatted atop a pile of his own excrement, rose a gently swaying royal giantess.

An alien queen mother.

"All right." She snapped on a cursor-blip pointer and guided it over to the central sack. "What we have here is a quite realistic computer animation suggesting what we might find in the alien central chamber, once we locate it.

"This is where we'll find that royal jelly that Mr. Daniel Grant has sent us after," she said.

Grant, seated at the table in a position similar enough to the chairman-of-the-board's attitude to make him comfortable, leaned back, hands behind the back of his neck. "That's right. And if you can trap a queen mother, that would be okay by me."

"Trap?" said Private Jastrow, a little dubiously.

"It's been done before," assured Private Ellis.

"Sounds awfully dangerous!" piped Private Mahone, looking quite doubtful about the whole enterprise.

"Private—this whole trip is dangerous. You knew that when you volunteered. *Anything* involving these things is dangerous ..." Kozlowski stepped up the magnification threefold, focusing in upon the queen. "Alice in Wonderland time, people. Listen up. We're going in the hive, and pulling this stuff out. Along the way, we will not be delicate. In any event, be assured . . . we've by no means come here to preserve the species. Kill all the creatures you want," she said brightly.

Easy laughter.

"So then, let's cook up a little preliminary strategy on how you pry open a bug hive, shall we?"

With the aid of more prepared graphics, she delineated the technology, science, and tactics that would allow a group of marines to storm a nest of the nastiest monsters in the universe.

"So . . . basically—guns, guts, and lots of *luck!*" she said. She paused for a moment as her people tried to assimilate her words.

She let them twist in the wind for a moment as a parade of aliens wilted before the onslaught of cartoon marines. The blasts from the heavy millimeter carbines tore through the heads and carapaces, splashing splinters of alien exoskeleton hither and thither along with gobs of alien blood that fell upon the marines and the scene like cancerous amoebas.

Kozlowski froze the animation.

"What's wrong with this picture?"

Jastrow raised a tentative hand. "Wishful thinking?"

"Yes. Fantasy, perhaps. Only showing the aliens eating marines wouldn't exactly be the best way to raise your morale, would it?"

"Not particularly, no," mumbled Ellis.

"Wait a minute," said Henrikson. "All that alien blood on the troops. It doesn't seem to phase them. That stuff makes toxic waste look like cotton candy."

Kozlowski snapped her fingers. "My *man*! Exactly!"

"What about the acid blood?" said Edie Mahone. "Can you tell us something about that?"

"Some good news for you all there. We do have something special for you. Something that's going to buck your morale right up." She smiled. "But first, let me remind you it's still very important that at close distance you try and avoid the torso. The splatter potential is quite bad. It's best to go for the knees." The cursor in the air flew to one of the strong and knobby alien lower joints. "As many of you have already discovered, a shot to the knee will not only hamper the alien's mobility ... but such a wound also minimizes bleeding and spatter potential. A discreet coup de grace to the head at that point is made possible. But then, of course, if you haven't actually been in battle with the things, you've at least had simulation chamber experience ... save perhaps for Mr. Grant."

"I'm hardly going to exactly participate in the mayhem, now am I, Colonel?" said Grant.

"As you've never handled a gun before, I hope not ..." said Kozlowski dismissively. "Now then ... I've kept you all waiting long enough ..." She pulled out a com unit. "Thank you, Doctor, for waiting in the wings. You may come out now, and by all means bring your assistant with you."

She turned to the audience, most of whom were on the edge of their seats with suspense.

Kozlowski turned quite serious.

... Michaels, his head molten and sizzling, skin sliding from naked skull ...

She suppressed the memory.

"I know the blood issue is of great concern to all of you, so I'm happy to present an innovation that should all but do away with your fears."

Yeah. Right.

Pep talk. Maybe that's what she'd given too much of to poor Peter. Maybe if he'd been properly scared shitless and quaking in his sweatsocks, he wouldn't have had to act like the Big Man and gone to that trap.

She swallowed down a dry throat, resumed.

"For more on that, I turn you over to Dr. Zato."

Dr. Zato, one of Grant's squids.

The man waltzed into the room like a stand-up comedian just called on to do his act. He was a toady little guy, who blinked as though the light was too much. Receding hairline. High IQ dandruff.

"Ladies and gentlemen," he said in a high, munchkin voice, "I give you your next best friend—"

The assistant walked into the room, slowly, clearly a little weighted down by what he wore, but not uncomfortably so.

Armor.

"Here it is, folks. The Z-110 Acid-Neutralizing Combat Wardrobe."

The assistant wore a streamlined, snazzy-looking jumble of plates, silver and blue in hue. A combination of insect and tortoiseshell. On the back was a compact storage unit. A narrow-visored helmet fitted snugly over his head. An antenna angled out of the back.

Kozlowski had seen it before, but the sight of it still impressed her.

And if it could do what Doc Z. claimed—well, all the better!

"Efforts to produce an armor resistant to the intense acidity of the alien blood have proved impractical."

Ellis waved his hand, got called upon. "Yeah. I always wondered about that. We've got the chemical composition of the alien's exoskeleton down cold. That isn't eaten up by alien blood, clearly. And it's light enough. How come its elements aren't used for armor?"

"Well, that would be all very good, Private, if you'd care to be encased in a toxic suit."

"You can't make an alloy . . . or have that stuff as the uppermost layer?" insisted Ellis.

"Incompatible. What we have here in the aliens is a different kind of chemistry. Part carbon-based, part silicon-based—and maybe something else."

"But we're starting to learn to use their DNA."

"Fooling around with genes and chromosomes doesn't necessarily mean we've got everything solved, Private. These things are still mysteries wrapped in enigmas. Believe me, your suggestions have been tried." He shook his head patronizingly. "Just doesn't work."

"So there *was* some kind of armor that wasn't affected by the alien blood?" said Mahone.

"That's right. But it was too heavy. Now if we were working in low-gee environments, maybe. Such is not the case on the Hiveworld. These suits were already in the works when this mission was established. We tailored the batch we brought along just for this occasion—with all your specific measurements in mind."

"No chance to return these, huh?" said Jastrow.

"That won't be necessary, I assure you. What

we've got here *is* a new process, but we've been testing it for years, and we've got it down exactly."

He went over to the suit and poked the side of the
arm.

The surface gave.

"What we have here is a light, effective armor,
covered with a permeable membrane controlled by a
mechanism in the back of the suit. It's kind of like
having the whole suit engulfed by a friendly jellyfish
that will grow back immediately if hit. Its function is
quite useful.

"Before, the suits that worked were too heavy.
Therefore what we have here is a self-contained os-
motic demi-atmospheric suit that does not resist, but
extirpates."

He poked the suit again.

"The moment alien blood touches this wardrobe,
the threat is eliminated altogether."

He took a vial marked ACID from his pants pocket,
twirled it open, and poured drops onto the shoulder
of the suit.

The top layer frizzled, bubbling.

Kozlowski had to make herself watch.

The bubbling was only for a moment, though.

Fluid welled, swallowing the acid.

The membrane closed up the hole within moments, and it was as though the acid had never
been.

"Yeah, but how *tough* is that stuff?"

"It's a form of plastic, and it can be cut . . . but it's
even better than skin . . . it naturally re-forms into
its previous mode within seconds, and chemically
rebonds itself. A healing process, if you will."

"What about inside. I mean, we haven't exactly

been trained in those sort of suits," said another man.

"That's one of the beauties of the things. In all details, the interior, the articulation, and the booster servos of the suits are identical to what you all have been trained to use. The other aspects are self-regulating. Maintenance will be needed, of course, but only after an encounter with the enemy. I should emphasize that this armor isn't perfect. It will wear out, though it should stand up during battle. Nonetheless *try* and avoid any alien blood you can. Don't go wading in it." He nodded to his assistant. "Go ahead. Let them have a close look."

The man strode around the room.

The soldiers poked and prodded the model.

"Goddamn. I'm going to feel like rubber-boy!" said Ellis.

"This is going to give a whole new twist of the saying 'Bouncing back!' " suggested Jastrow.

"Okay," said Kozlowski, after giving them a couple of minutes to handle the merchandise. "You'll all have the opportunity to get used to these suits in special exercises we have planned every day for the remainder of the journey. But for now, listen up! 'Cause this is how we're going to use these things."

And she told them.

12

One drink down.

Two more to go.

"Another glass of bubbly, my dear?" said Daniel Grant, pulling the bottle out of the thermo-adjuster and tilting it even as he asked the question.

"It is awfully delicious—but . . ." said Edie Mahone, holding out her hand.

Glug glug glug.

The quite large glass filled with bright, dazzlingly effervescent fluid.

"Of course you will. You're off duty, you need to relax, and we've got three whole days before your mission," said Daniel Grant. "*Our* mission!"

He refilled his own glass with the double-strength champagne. Damned good thing he was feeling generous with his team on the *Razzia*. He'd fitted them out with his own concept of hardship supplies. Hell, if they had to go to the other side of nowhere to suck some bug juice from some god forsaken planet, at least they should do so in style. Now, he was reaping the rewards of his own munificence.

"Well, if you insist. I know your time is valuable and I hate to take it up by asking you really silly questions. But I *have* been following your career, and I *do* have more questions."

Somehow the alcohol seemed to have unlocked this woman's pheromones. She smelled good, damned good, and Daniel Grant breathed her scent in greedily. Of course she wore no perfume—a ridiculous and foolish luxury for a person on a highly unglamorous journey in a tin can through space with a bunch of males. That didn't make any difference. Hell, he was *tired* of perfume. What he had here before him was the dangling, rounded hair and breasts and lovely limbs of a full-blooded woman.

His last date had hardly been fulfilling. And the gritty details attendant to moving the *Razzia* and himself toward hyperdrive and hypersleep had pretty much put a hold on his appetites. But as soon as the sleep-rheum drained from his head, he immediately became aware of how *horny* he was. The incident on the shuttle made him naturally think of Private Edie Mahone. After Colonel Kozlowski's briefing, he'd suggested that after evening mess she might like to stop by for that promised drink. He always enjoyed talking to fans about his career, and he was quite *upset* about the gross inaccuracies of that trashy book about him, and wanted to set some things straight—

. . . uhm, so to speak.

Two to go.

He'd sized her up. She was a three-drink girl. In two drinks she'd be pliable. Three she'd sit closer, lean those dark eyes toward him, let that sweet, fresh, scrubbed scent of her dart in for a kiss.

Then *snap!* Like a patient angler fish, he'd swallow her up for a delicious hour or so, and then spit her back out. They'd both be happy, sated, and better able to deal with the grim realities before them.

She brought the topped-off glass up to those full, moist lips and drank half the glass in a couple swallows. He was impressed and gleeful at this. "My, but this is wonderful stuff."

"My own special vintage!" said Grant. "You're one of the few people who've actually tasted it!"

"Goodness! Then I shouldn't be so shy, should I? I don't want to be impolite when I'm so privileged!" With that, and a down-the-hatch determination to her face, she took the large glass and swallowed the rest of it.

That had been a very large portion. This, perhaps, would be very short work!

"Yes, right." In a moment she'd probably have to step off to his private toilet and he'd slip the last bit of liquor into her glass. He had to play it cool though now. "You were asking me about my youth?"

Edie Mahone had an odd expression on her face. She seemed not to be listening to him, just in a kind of trance.

"Edie? Edie . . . are you all right?"

"Mr. Grant . . ."

"Daniel . . ." he said. "I told you, you can call me Daniel."

She got quiet. She closed her eyes.

Hmm, thought Daniel Grant.

Maybe *two* glasses of the old id-tickler was all that was necessary!

He scooted closer.

"You know, Edie . . . We're basically just two people . . . a man and a woman with needs . . . out in the middle of nowhere . . . We should *comfort* one another, the way that normal human males and females do . . ."

Edie Mahone snorted. She sniffed, and the straight line described by her lips crumpled into misery. Tears dripped from the corners of her eyes.

"Oh, Daniel . . ." she mewled, and then dissolved into a quivering mess onto him, arms wrapped protectively over her abdomen. "I don't know what I'm going to do . . ."

"Uhmm . . . Edie . . . what's wrong?"

"I made a terrible mistake. I never should have come along on this mission. It just seemed like the right thing to do at the time. I just wanted to be light-years away. Light-years from *him*."

"Him?"

"Chuck!"

Chuck. Oh, yes. A boyfriend. The usual story.

Grant began to stroke her back comfortingly. He could feel her muscles relax. Oh, yes, this was going to be soooooo easy!

"Tell me about him?"

"What's to tell?" she said in a monotone voice. "Love with the wrong guy. He was in my troop. Started sleeping with our lieutenant. No way to compete. Only thing to do is to ship out. Chuck wasn't going to. So I'd tested high in all necessary categories, I've got the skill and the experience. And now the reason. But now that I wake up here . . . Now that I see those pictures, I remember what it was like, the one actual nest experience I had." Grant could feel her shudder. "It's worse than cold and forbidding out here. And those *things*. They're worse than devils."

"There, there, dear. I know how you feel." She was wearing a green fatigue shirt with buttons down the front. He slowly unbuttoned the top one.

"I know you do. I can feel it. You're really a sympathetic man, a good man . . . beneath that hard, caustic surface. I could tell that . . . even in the book."

Another button.

"You're a very special woman, Edie . . . You deserve comforting." Another button. He could see a fleshy swell of bare bosom, held in check by a tan bra. Out here in the harsh and cold of space, it struck him as one of the most erotic sights he'd witnessed.

He slipped his hand inside her shirt. Soft, warm, pliable.

Ah!

She said nothing. She hardly seemed to notice, wrapped up in her own misery.

Maybe she didn't really want this. Maybe she'd just let him have his way, like a trusting lamb, helpless before the slaughter. Maybe he really shouldn't take advantage of this vulnerable soul this way . . .

Bullshit, he thought, remembering his personal philosophy. Plunder while the plunder's available.

"You know, Edie, I can't think of anything more soothing than if we gave each other hot oil massages. You'll feel much better. Now let me just help you off with this scratchy old uniform and then—"

There was a pounding on the door.

Private Edie Mahone jumped about a foot in the air, eyes going wide. "Who's that?" she said, pulling away from his embrace.

"No one! I'll get rid of them!"

She stuffed herself back into bra and fatigues, sobering up in record time.

"Grant!" called a too-familiar voice. "I know you're in there. Answer the damned door. There's something wrong with your comm unit."

"Colonel Kozlowski!" said Mahone, jumping up and away from Grant's grasp for her. Quickly she ran into his toilet to straighten herself out. She turned back and gave Grant a harsh you're-just-like-the-book-says-you-are look. Then, in a rush of indignation and alarm, she was gone.

Pound. Pound. "Grant. We need to talk."

Daniel Grant had to take a deep breath and straighten his pants as much as possible. *Calm yourself. The bitch doesn't need any kind of salute from you.*

Then he got up and hit the door hydraulics. It slid open, and characteristically Colonel Kozlowski just stormed on in. "You know, with only three days to go, you can't expect to just hole yourself up."

"I was having a conference. Getting to know our troops," said Grant, rearing up to every inch of six feet two.

She glared at him, not buying his attempt at dominance for a moment. "Troops?"

"Private Edie Mahone. She's in the bathroom. She was having a few doubts about the mission."

Kozlowski raised her eyebrow. "Oh, yeah—?"

Edie Mahone came out of the head, looking perfectly composed and professional. "Thank you, Mr. Grant. You've been a real gentleman, but I have to go now . . ."

"Mahone. Why aren't you studying . . . ?"

"Free time, sir. I can use it according to my discretion. Permission to leave, sir?"

"Permission granted," said Kozlowski in a disgusted tone. She didn't even watch as the private departed, a study of healing wounded dignity.

Grant felt mightily vexed.

Sexual frustration piled upon a direct intrusion upon his privacy by a woman wearing confrontation over her head like a storm cloud.

Back on Earth, had this situation arisen, so might have the infamous Daniel Grant temper. A rant, a rave, a metaphorical chomping off of the head. Employee or associate, pressman or president, it would make no difference. Grant would have made mincemeat of them.

He could feel it burbling up, steaming through his capillaries. One little vent was all it would take, and the explosion would blast.

However something gave him pause.

Something odd aglint in this feistmeister of a woman's eye. She *did* present a fetching figure in those skintight duds she wore. And if you got past the cropped, patchy hair, the defiant lack of softening makeup, and those scars she wore like medals . . .

If you turned down the lights a bit and smudged

a little with mind and imagination, this Kozlowski
bitch was really *quite* the looker.

He looked at her. He looked at the unopened
bottle of champagne in its cooler slot. He looked
back at her, suddenly oily with cordiality.

"Well, Colonel. As long as you're here—"

The gall!

She looked at him as though he'd just opened
his zipper and wagged his privates at her.

The unmitigated *gall*!

"No, Mr. Grant. I will *not* have a glass of champagne with you!"

Daniel Grant stepped back as though she'd
blasted a breath of fire at him. "You don't drink."

"I drink. That's not what I came here for,
though."

"You don't like champagne. I promise you, you'll
not taste better. Besides, Colonel . . . We're three
days away from Death leering at us. Carpe diem.
Seize the day!"

She wasn't sure why she was so annoyed at his
offer. He was right. She'd pretty much finished
most of her tasks for the day anyway, and the Colonial Marines were unfortunately not a military navy
force known for packing away kegs of rum onboard
for the officers.

She'd been working hard for three days. Her
mouth was dry. And here was some high-quality,
rich man's champagne being offered to her. She
hadn't had a drink in weeks, and she could feel her
tastebuds and her nerves, falling to their knees and
begging her to accept the offer.

She told them to go screw themselves.

"I'm here, Grant, to officially request that you allow me to tour the levels assigned to your scientists on this mission. In the interests of the success of our journey, I feel the need to know everything going on in this ship."

Grant nodded. "Ah. I see. This, despite what your superiors told you. To wit: that is *not* your territory of concern."

"Yes. I have given it a great deal of thought. Any ignorance on my part could spell a danger to my troops and this vessel."

"I thought the captain was in charge of the actual vessel. He doesn't seem to care much what's going on on Decks E and F."

"The captain? He's a burnout. He does just the minimum to get by, counting things out by crossword. I honestly wonder why he was given this particular duty."

"He seems quite competent to me . . ."

Nonetheless, Grant did not say no.

Instead, he pushed a button that depressurized the seal on the champagne. He tagged another switch. Armatures extended and made short work of the cork.

Pop!

Kozlowski jumped despite herself. A brief spurt of white stuff ran down the upright thing. She licked her lips, a sudden tingling running down her spine.

Coolly, Grant went to a cabinet, pulled out two glasses. He poured these glasses full of the drink, and then carefully slipped the bottle back into its frigid place.

"I'll tell you what, Colonel Alex. Have a drink with me, I'll give you the Grand Tour."

He tapped the side of the glass closest to her. *Ting!* The liquid effervesced delightfully.

She made her decision. It was an easy one. She took the glass and drank a swallow, letting it drift through her teeth a moment. It was strong, but it was the lightest, tastiest champagne she'd ever experienced. Fruit vapor, dancing pirouettes on her tongue.

She glowered. A thought occurred to her. "You bastard. You were going to show me anyway, weren't you?"

He picked his own glass up, sipped it. "You'll never know now, will you?"

"Damn you." She couldn't help but sip the glass again. If anything, it tasted better on the second go.

"But here—I happen to have some pâté. Crackers, too. French and English, respectively." His hand motioned toward a tray of condiments. "So why don't you have a seat."

She finished the glass of champagne in one guzzle.

Heaven.

Her toes seemed to curl.

"Okay! If you pour us both another!"

"Absolutely!" He poured. "So nice to have company."

She sat and she sipped. She sampled the crackers and pâté. After what seemed like a lifetime of reconstituted Marine chow, it tasted like ambrosia. More champagne. Ah. Ambrosia and nectar.

"So then," she said, "I have two questions.

"Number one. What the hell is going on down on

those decks? I saw some of the strangest apparatus being boosted off for the *Razzia*."

"You're just going to have to wait until tomorrow for the answer to that," Grant said. "Then, though, I promise that all will be explained."

"Fair enough. Question two—" She drained her glass of champagne. It exploded inside her like a depth charge of flowers. "Have you got another bottle of this stuff around? This is the best alcohol I've ever had!"

Grant grinned widely. "I think that can be arranged!"

Daniel Grant listed. His eyes were half-closed, and his face was mashed against a cushion of the couch.

A half-filled glass of champagne wobbled in his hand.

". . . I should have never let her go," he mumbled.

Clear-eyed and feeling very good indeed, glass balanced on a raised knee, Alex Kozlowski regarded the scene. Totally in charge. Grant had extra champagne, all right. He'd had it trotted on up to his cabin, no problem. A strategy meeting, she'd explained to the surprised ensign sent to deliver it. A tumbled line of dead soldiers lay on the floor.

"Your wife?"

"Yeah. She was . . . she was the only person I ever really loved." He sighed.

An interesting evening.

Halfway through the second bottle of champagne, he'd put a hand on her left breast.

She'd cold-cocked him.

He'd flown across the room and landed on the couch fortunately, then lay semi-conscious for a few minutes, while Kozlowski thoughtfully nibbled at crackers and sipped the champagne, enjoying the silence and the boost to her ego. It had been a while since a man had been arrogant enough to make a pass at her, much less trespass her body. She enjoyed it.

She got some ice, wrapped it up in a cloth, and gave it to him. He thanked her and asked for another glass of champagne. The pain seemed to have leeched the randiness out of him, and the champagne helped with his sore jaw. He apologized and they drank more. Kozlowski finished off the pâté and crackers. Grant just sipped.

She wasn't going to be able to drink any more before the mission. Drinking now was stretching things. But she figured she might as well enjoy it— and enjoy this first-class liquor—while she could. Might as well have some sound effects while she did so, she'd told herself—so she pried Daniel Grant's life story out of him. Easy, since he was really getting snookered.

Pretty queasy stuff.

Cold mother. Distant father. Money the end-all be-all in the family. No love and affection. A football team approach to sex and affection as conquest. Massive insecurities covered over by efforts and dominance, arrogance and control.

All in all, fairly predictable. Textbook even, she'd imagine. She'd not read much psychology. Hell, most books and computer information had been destroyed.

She'd more or less drunken him under the table.

Either that, or her fist had knocked something loose in his brain. Unlikely. Grant looked like he had a pretty hard head.

She'd lifted the rock up and found a mass of worms and nightcrawlers.

The great man wasn't much different, deep down, from her. A few less nightmares, a little more civilized on the surface. But deep down—the usual writhing stew of human troubles.

"So," slurred Grant. "Your full name is Alexandra Lee Kozlowski."

"You did your homework. Yes. My parents named me after two famous generals."

"Grant and Lee. No wonder the antipathy. Hope we can smooth things out."

She shrugged. "We both want the mission to succeed."

"Yes," he murmured. "This trip succeeds, my company succeeds. I'm in the black, debts are paid off, I'm competing effectively against MedTech again, the mob gets paid off, and I get free of their contract—"

"Which you presume you're safe from out here."

He'd spilled the beans on that one under her probing questions, proving her suspicions correct. He'd come along on the mission because it was a convenient way to get off Earth, away from certain deadly factions. Now she knew why. Simple enough and understandable.

Only she honestly wondered if Grant knew that he'd jumped out of the frying pan into the fire. And there were a lot of nasty bugs in that fire, you betcha.

Grant didn't seem to hear her last comment. He

was just rambling on. "I get things *on track*," he was saying. "God, the world is my oyster, I just got to get through the shell. When I get straight with everyone . . . I'll ask her back. I swear I will. *That's* what I'm pushing for . . . Can't live the life I've been living so long . . . So empty . . . So useless . . ."

"Fast track. Candle at both ends. Strive strive strive so you can build yourself a fancy coffin. Dominance and dominoes—both falling-down games."

"Gotta stay on top. Gotta flash the smile. Gotta work, gotta survive," Grant mumbled.

"Gotta drink the best champagne," said Kozlowski. "Eat the best pâté." She downed the last bit of stuff in her glass, clapped it back on the table, and stood up. "I guess that's as good a goal as any. Thanks, Grant. I had a good time. Tell you what. We get back to Earth, we have a little party. You supply the champagne and eats, and we'll have a good time."

He looked up, bleary eyes startled. "Don't go!"

"Right. I'm gonna tippy-toe out of your place in the wee hours . . . or worse, at the beginning of first shift. Won't that amuse the troops?"

"None of . . . their business . . ."

"True, but it's also a good excuse to slip the noose here, Grant."

"I just . . . I just don't want to be alone."

"Yeah. I've heard that one before." She found herself angry for no explicable reason. "Take a snooze, guy. Let your dreams keep you company."

She half expected him to suddenly jump up and

run in front of her, begging her to stop. She made a fist. Yeah. Just let the lecher try.

But he didn't. She stopped at the door and listened.

Peaceful, content snores.

She opened the door and stormed out.

Now she knew why she was ticked off, and it absolutely annoyed the hell out of her.

She was attracted to the jerk, dammit.

13

Daniel Grant didn't look so good.

He was sipping at what passed for coffee when Kozlowski found him on the observation deck, looking out at the specks of stars and planets in the vast blackness of space as though searching for dawn.

"Hey there," she said. "Captain told me I'd find you here."

"I'm trying to soak my head in the Big Dipper," said Grant, gazing out into the vastness.

"I'm here for my tour."

"So you are. So you are, Colonel Kozlowski."

She considered telling him to call her by her first name. He looked so . . . lost and vulnerable, a wisp of steam winding up from his coffee and misting a piece of the view. She decided against it. She didn't want to give him the wrong idea.

Silence slid between them, which surprised her for a moment. Silence didn't seem in Grant's lexicon of communication devices.

She coughed encouragingly.

Nothing.

Finally, she said, "I did earn my tour, Grant."

"So you did, Colonel. However, I wish you'd said you had a hollow leg."

She shrugged. "You were drinking before I got there. Head start. Besides, I really don't care for your sexual preying before a mission."

"All's fair in love and war."

"Foxhole love. I've had some of that, nice if you like watching your partner in the deed die the next day."

Grant nodded. Managed a smile. "You're far too dramatic, Colonel." He shrugged. "Severe hangovers have a way of putting things in perspective. I guess I'm a bit of the predator. I apologize."

"How's your jaw?"

He rubbed it gingerly. "I can still speak and I can still think. However, I believe you've actually improved my looks."

"You've lost me on that one, Grant."

"I think my face was a little irregular before. You appear to have whacked it back into proper symmetry. Doubtless hundreds of nubile young ladies will come to thank you."

"You know, Grant, if I didn't detect a little self-mockery in your tone, I think I'd deck you again."

A flash of alarm in his face. That immediately retreated into an accepting nod. "I'm an energetic son of a bitch, aren't I?"

"I guess there's a reason you got where you got. But now we're just short of our destination, a parsec and some change from home. And I need to see some more of exactly why we're here."

"Very well. Let me scrape some of my brain off my throat and reassimilate." He sipped some coffee.

She had a notion. "Here you go. I think I've got something that will help." She fished a small container from a pocket.

"Oh. How do *you* know?"

"Believe it or not, I've had a hangover or two lately." She did not get specific. She just snapped open the top and displayed the pills, neatly cut into halves and thirds and quarters.

"Pills? What are they?"

"Fire, Grant. Your own poison. Works damned well in this kind of situation. Check it out."

He shook his head. "Thanks, but no thanks. I never touch my own stuff. But please . . . don't let me stop you."

She'd been thinking of taking a quarter but now, instead, she snapped the container shut and stuck it back in her pocket, feeling annoyed, feeling like a junkie getting the brush-off by the pusher himself.

"Just show me those decks, Grant."

"This way, Colonel."

Corporal Lars Henrikson waited for them at the turbolift.

Kozlowski was taken aback. "Henrikson? What are *you* doing here?"

Henrikson remained stoic. "Mr. Grant called. He asked me to meet him here. I'm here."

Grant put a hand on the big guy's shoulder. Patted. "My kind of man, Colonel. Henrikson here's going to get a look at what we've got inside, too. Why? I'm glad you asked that question. Henrikson's probably wondering, too." He punched the button for the 'lift. The door slid open, and they all stepped inside. Whir of lights, compression, off for another level. "I'm not an elitist. I want to show what we've got here, to give you an understanding of what's going on. That knowledge on your part may come in handy later on. Helps us a lot. It also gives you a better idea of what we're going to need down on Hiveworld."

Kozlowski was a bit irked. First, because from the sounds of it, Grant had always intended to show her what was going on here. Second, because of Henrikson. He was a first-class soldier. During training, he'd come up as number one at all levels. His abilities were unquestionable. Plenty of references, and one of the troops she'd had no problem at all deciding should go on this mission. However, now it seemed as though Grant had taken him under his corporate wing—a corporal!—and was squiring him about, giving him the treatment that she as the commander alone deserved. True, Grant claimed that of all the regular troops Henrikson had the most actual combat time with the xenos. But still . . .

Basically, she felt a tad jealous, as though this selection of Henrikson was a *male* thing, some off-handed way of slapping the fact that she was a female.

"One little condition," said Grant as they walked along the catwalk on Deck E, approaching doors that looked like the entrance to a bank vault. "What I'm about to show you two is strictly hush-hush. I don't want anyone to know about this, especially not the other men—or women. That's why I'm just showing it to you two. I feel as though you can handle it."

Without further explanation, Grant cycled open the door and led them through. The lights were more muted here; it had almost a submarine quality. Aquas and red and shadows. As her eyes adjusted, Kozlowski immediately noticed the equipment.

Banks of it, spread along the ways. Tubing and bulking computers and flanges. Cables and glass and blinking lights. A number of men were clustered at the far end in front of a window that looked like something out of an aquarium. Grant's scientists, doing their geeky scientist thing, mystery wrapped in machinery and mundanity.

It smelled in here. Acidic. Oil, electricity, coffee . . . and something more.

Something that made Kozlowski's hackles rise.

She recognized it. Faint, but there.

Bugs.

No, she told herself. That can't be right. What would bugs be doing down here?

"Isn't this supposed to be a storage chamber?" she said lamely, trying to get Grant to talk, trying to get the creepy feeling out of the pit of her stomach.

"Oh, yes," said Grant, leading them down some

stairs. "And in a way, it still is. But the cargo! That's what's a little unusual."

The steps clanged and echoed.

"So, Grant," said Henrikson. "Why all the secrecy? Why just us?"

Nice of him to echo her own thoughts.

They were walking forward, and through the murky light in the glassed tank she was able to pick out a few details.

Cables, dangling equipment.

Something bulky and organic in the very middle.

And by it . . .

An egg sack.

And the discarded shell of a face hugger.

She walked up to the window in a haze, astonished, looking in upon the gruesome scene enclosed in metal and glass.

"Well, Corporal, I know most marines have come to really hate the aliens," said Grant. "I'm afraid that what we've got down here would really hinder the morale necessary for the operation."

A thickset man with a boyish face and a cowlick in his mass of blondish hair scuttled up to Grant, lab coat swaying about his ankles. In whispers they conferred together in the corner. The man produced a clipboarded chart that Grant nodded at and then pushed away. He took the scientist gently by the arm and pulled him over to meet his guests.

"This is Dr. Murray Friel. He's in charge of this project down here—the science part, anyway."

"Yes—I've met the commander, but not the corporal," said the doctor.

Kozlowski remembered now. There had been introductions and handshakes on Earth, and then the batch of docs, including Friel here, had been swallowed up on these decks. Brief glimpses in other parts of the ship—that was all. She'd met a lot of men like Friel. Plump red-cheeked guys, smart, but with no real experience. They all seemed to have the same arrogance as Friel here had. He was in his own little world—and owned every corner of it.

But it wasn't Dr. Friel that preoccupied her now. She was looking at something else.

It looked like a misshapen excuse for a body, but with limbs and head cut off and lengths of esophagus and intestine connecting it with organic machines nearby.

Liquids pulsed through these, feeding it.

"What *is* that thing?" said Kozlowski, recovering her aplomb, overcoming her initial horror.

"Friel . . . care to do the honors?" suggested Grant.

"Certainly. It certainly isn't very attractive . . . but then, neither would your interior bits, awkwardly displayed. You must excuse me, but I feel rather proprietary toward it. You see, in a way, it's a part of me." He stepped forward, a pudgy palm placed up against the glass. He gazed at it with an odd kind of pride. "You see, it's a donor clone, DNA clamped so that it would grow simply the torso, no brain, limited nervous system. A machine regulates it. These things are usually produced for the purpose of organ and tissue donation." His fingers drummed on the glass thoughtfully and then he turned back to look at her. "I'll admit, it isn't the most attractive creature, but it's proved useful." He tapped his arm. "I'm proud to say its cells of origination were retrieved from my wrist."

The odd, smirky fellow who had been introduced before to her as Dr. Amos Begalli sidled up. "We had a little coin toss. We all wanted to be the one . . . Dr. Friel won. He's like a proud father now, waiting for a son to be born."

Friel shrugged. "It's an interesting experience, I must say."

Kozlowski shook her head. She was finally allowing herself to assimilate the evidence presented here to her. She turned to Grant. "I've seen this before," she said through clenched teeth. "You're breeding one of those damn things!"

"Take it easy, kiddo!" said Grant. "First, everything is quite secure here. The torso is in special suspended animation. It can't blow until the right switches are hit. There are reinforced windows. Special alloy cages. Alarms and an automatic laser lattice should something unforeseen happen."

"But that thing in there . . . it's living . . ."

"Only on the crudest terms," said Dr. Friel. "It doesn't feel any pain. It doesn't think. It's just basically a mass of tissue that serves a purpose."

"But if a xeno gets loose on this ship . . ."

"Colonel, Colonel—the dangers are well known and plenty of precautionary measures have been built into the fail-safe system, I promise you!" said Grant. "Believe me, at Neo-Pharm we've been doing this kind of thing for years . . . And that woman Ripley did it years ago successfully. Our technology is far superior now. We know how to deal with it."

"But why are you bringing along something like this when we're going to a planet full of them?"

"An experiment," said Dr. Friel. "Naturally, we'd like to come back with necessary alien DNA and queen mother royal jelly to create our own colony for purposes I've been told you are acquainted with. Also perhaps even captured eggs. But we want to work with the product of our own DNA manipulation. To create our own kind of queen, utilizing the necessary royal jelly from what you good soldiers are going to retrieve for us. We'd like to work with some different material than we've had on Earth."

Dr. Begalli beamed. "Yes! You see we've got *everything* thoroughly regulated here ... Metabolic control. We've got it set up so that baby won't pop until we've got the jelly we need available for her queening."

"Lovely," said Kozlowski. "Just lovely."

"In addition, of course, on these decks we've got the necessary tanks and holding pens for the jelly and captured eggs, refrigerated alien DNA ... Oh, all manner of good stuff, Colonel. But you can see why your troops might be a little upset."

Friel shook his head. "It's understandable why people are so afraid of these things. However, with the proper applied measures of science, Neo-Pharm is proving that what has up till now appeared to be a threat to humanity—can in fact be a great help. We've just begun our work in the area of drugs and medicine ... Heaven alone knows how our understanding of the alien DNA will help us in the future." He sighed happily. "And to think ... I'm to be like a *father* to a whole aspect of what may be the most significant advance in human evolution. Its chemical interaction with xenobiology! Who knows what wonderful new vistas await us!"

"Try horrible pain. Try death. Try species *extinction*!" said Kozlowski.

Dr. Friel flinched with the intensity of Kozlowski's response. "I don't think, Colonel, you appreciate the beauties and intricacies of the alien genetic gifts."

"I don't think, Doctor, you appreciate the *threat* these things are—" She paused, calmed herself down, took a gulp of air.

Grant seemed taken aback. "Colonel . . . Alex. You were there at the initial meeting. I saw you there . . . you heard everything. You're aware of our ultimate goal. You know what you're here for."

She swung on him, outthrust finger just short of his nose. "Make no mistake, Grant. I may be here to head up this mission to facilitate your personal and professional goals. That's secondary to my duty to the armed forces I serve—and my own purpose. Which is, quite simply, to do everything I can to make sure these bugs are either rendered into a threat equivalent to cosmic cockroaches—or thoroughly exterminated." She lowered the finger. "Any bugs crushed underfoot along the way are all the better."

With that, she turned and stalked the hell away from this charnel house in the belly of a starship.

14

Everyone knew that service chow sucked.

You didn't join the Colonial Marines for gourmet food, that was for certain.

Still, as Kozlowski accepted the food dumped unceremoniously on her plate at the cafeteria line, her stomach cringed at the lumps of colorless, reconstituted whatsits her meal comprised. She well knew that all the food groups were represented, that this was vitamin and nutrient rich stuff. There just wasn't much taste or appeal to it, that was all.

Still, the gig was two days away.

Gotta carb up!

She stepped over to push a button that would put a dollop of what the machine claimed was mashed potatoes on her plate. She positioned the plate under the nozzle, still not quite there . . .

She'd been a bit preoccupied ever since she'd seen that cloned torso down on Grant's deck. The merging of alien and human to her had always been the height of obscenity. Eradicating that threat had been what her life had been about now for over twenty years. Her use of Fire she'd rationalized as an exercise of dominance over the aliens . . . Now, though, she wasn't so sure. Unfortunately, she suspected she was hooked on the stuff. She'd been okay this morning, no bad champagne headache, just a chemical pall of gloom riding her. A quarter pill wouldn't banish it. A half pill didn't give her the buzz she realized she wanted to get through the day. She'd taken what amounted to an entire pill, something that she'd only done before in battle exercises and war itself.

And the stuff had unwound in her, like the talons of a bug, zapping her neurons . . .

She shuddered, tried to forget about it. When this mission was over, she was going to throw her pills in the garbage. Clean up her act. Live clean and healthy. But she knew that she needed the Xeno-Zip to deal with what was coming up in her life—and it pissed her off. Especially with her conflicted feelings about Daniel Grant. Especially after what she'd seen down there.

She tried to tune out the chatter in her head, to focus on getting some of this food down, despite her lack of appetite. She took her tray and sat down, alone, at the side of an unoccupied table.

In another corner of the room, Jastrow was noodling on his saxophone. The man didn't play well, but he didn't play badly either. At least, if it wasn't exactly melodious, it wasn't that grating either.

However, his buddy, who was sitting beside him as usual, didn't seem to appreciate it.

"Could you give it a rest, Jastrow?"

"What's wrong, Ellis? I thought you liked music."

"I like music fine. But not blaring in my ear while I'm eating."

Kozlowski listened to them bicker. Better than concentrating on this crap that she was stuffing into her face. Jastrow stopped playing and they talked. They talked about Henrikson, who had just come in, walked through the cafeteria, taken his food, and was walking out again.

"Hey. Check it out," said Jastrow. "Henrikson's doing it again. He's taking his food to the room. Oh, man, the bet's still on here . . . I say he's a synthetic!"

"Gimme a break," said Ellis. "They make models that eat, you know."

"It's not just that. He won't shower with us. I've never seen him shave . . . And from the way he talks in briefings, I'd guess he's never seen combat."

"Yeah. That is odd."

"I say he's a company plant. And I don't like it. Bad things happen to Marine ships with synthetics on board!"

The next thing Kozlowski knew, Henrikson was by the table.

"Jastrow. Why don't you just say what you've got on your mind—to my face."

He lifted the private off the chair. The sax banged onto the floor.

Kozlowski shot up to put a stop to this.

"Shit, man! Let me go!"

"Sure." The big corporal threw the private across the room.

"Henrikson!" screamed Kozlowski.

Henrikson froze. He turned around and looked at his commander, his face impassive. "Sorry."

Ellis was leaning over, attending to his buddy, who seemed okay, just dazed.

"We're all under pressure here, Henrikson," snarled Kozlowski. "Take it out on the bugs." She swiveled on the privates. "And that means you two. We're all working together on this. No divisiveness."

"You know, Corporal," a voice said behind her. "I admire a man who doesn't take any crap. I honestly do." Grant's voice. He came up to them, and his easy-going arrogance seemed to cut through the tension. "But the truth is I need every last one of these troops for this operation." He looked over to the fallen Jastrow, who was just getting up. "You don't have to kiss and make up, but please don't mash his skull, okay? Thanks."

Henrikson nodded. Kozlowski dismissed him. He took his food and went off again toward his quarters.

Kozlowski turned to the others. "All right. Back to the chow. I don't want any energy-deficient troops when we get down to work." As an example, she went back to her own plate, which had gone cold. Nonetheless, she began to stuff it in her face.

Grant came over to her.

"Colonel," he said in a low voice. "Can we talk a moment, please. Alone?"

"Pull up some vittles, Dan. If I've got to work my way through this stuff, so do you."

He didn't even try to argue. He went off, got a minimum order of gruelish reconstituted stew, and spooned it down, trying to look cheerful as they made chitchat. The sucker looked much better now. Probably had himself a cocktail and a nap and a good hot bath. He even smelled good. Oddly, Kozlowski enjoyed the small talk. She was still annoyed at her attraction to the asshole, but she didn't have to let him know about it—and she could enjoy the warped sex appeal he presented on her own terms. He probably sprayed on pheromones, the conscienceless bastard.

Finally, when she was satisfied the last morsel was gone from his plate, she agreed to go with him to somewhere they couldn't be overheard—but a meeting room, not his room.

"Look," he said. "I didn't know you'd react the way you did down there. Corporal Henrikson took it well. He's even volunteering to double-check security. I just want to make sure I'm still getting the best out of you on our mission, Colonel."

"There was never any doubt of that, chum. You asked for the best, you got the best—but I want to tell you, I'm not real crazy about your methods."

"What I'm doing is for the benefit of mankind!"

She laughed in his face. "You don't have to try and pull that one on me. You're doing this for the money."

"Ultimately, it will save lives."

"What are you talking about? You're risking good Marine lives for this damned jelly and what-all . . . For profit, pure and simple. You're a ruthless bastard. At least my superiors honestly believe they're doing what's right."

"I'm risking my own life here, too, remember."

"Only because you're too scared to face up to a souped-up loan shark back home."

He cringed. "Ah. I told you that, eh?"

"You bet. I'd pretty much guessed something along those lines anyway."

"Nonetheless. We figure a source for this—a safe controlled source—we can finance a full erasure of the aliens on the planet Earth. Studying them, we'll be able to know how to deal with them when we encounter them on other worlds."

"All sounds good. Doesn't change anything about what I think about *you* though."

"You'll honor my concerns about the others, though . . . Not letting them know."

"You think I want to undermine their morale by letting them know that a xeno's going to be prowling in some cage below them while they're helpless in hypersleep? They're my people, and I'll take care of them . . . You watch out for your own crew. Understand?"

"I'm glad we're clear on this, Colonel. I really don't quite understand your hostility, though . . . I think it's best for both our sakes if we got along much better."

"Don't push it, Grant. And most of all—don't push me."

She got up, and she got away from him.

If she hung around the handsome goon much longer she didn't know what she'd do—kiss him or kill him.

She wasn't sure which she'd enjoy more.

• • •

In the dim lights of the Cargo Bay Nine, shadows moved.

Padding past open doors, feet paced over to controls. Fingers pushed, pulled, tapped. Status quo alarms were turned off. Serums were released and rheostats adjusted.

Inside the ghost-lit tank, the hanging torso jerked.

Satisfied that the necessary measures had been taken, the figure hurried back out of the room, door shushing closed behind it.

In the tank, the hanging torso jerked again.

In the hanging torso, the alien embryo, already formed and at full term, but previously kept dormant by electronic and biochemical means, shivered into full life over a matter of mere minutes.

It shook. It gasped. Sparked by the energies that had been shot through it, and the instincts that had been ignited, it flailed in its seating.

Membranes tore, muscles were yanked from their mooring.

Still it was not yet free.

Instinct activated.

With a preternatural power, it pushed up against the diaphragm, up through the tangle of lungs and heart and arteries.

Up against the rib cage.

Then, with its hard equipment prepared for just this moment, and every bit of its energy, it plunged through the bones, through the skin into the freedom of gaseous atmosphere.

The torso exploded.

Blood spattered. Bronchial tissue splattered up

like the eruption of a volcano. Bits of broken bone spanged against metal and glass.

Like a worm with a head of all teeth, the alien chest-burster reared up above the carcass of its birth, weaving in a sensory dance. Sensing no danger, it began to scuttle for the darkness of a corner.

The hands that had nudged the obscene delivery forward had not removed the precautions against just such an event.

Delicate motion detectors reacted to the scuttling, heat-seeking alien. Spectrographic readings determined its nature, double-checked, and then implemented the next step. Should the thing be born in unsupervised circumstances, there was no other alternatives.

Servomotors hummed as coaxial cables controlled three separate particle beam weapons, aiming toward the source and form causing the spectrographic abnormalities.

Had it not had to pause for a moment to attempt to get through the glass of the tank, the alien might have survived longer, rendering the mission an entirely different affair.

However, it did pause.

And the weapons did fire.

The beams converged into a fulcrum of energy.

The alien blew apart, adding its gore to that of the torso it had already scattered. The force lifted its little head up and off and through the hole it had smacked in the glass, followed by charred bits of its tail.

The teeth gnashed. The tail twitched.

Then both stilled, surrendering their last signs of survival to the alarm that blared to life.

15

When she reached the cargo bay of Deck D, and she successfully convinced the flustered scientist by the door that she had Daniel Grant's permission for access (a little determined pushing helped greatly), she found the cause of the alarm waiting for her, bathed in emergency light.

Hovered over the dead infant alien, wearing their acid suits, were the science team.

Daniel Grant paced beyond the reach of any acid, punching the air and cursing. "Goddammit. Goddammit! What the hell went wrong! I'm looking at a million-dollar loss here, minimum!"

He did not notice Kozlowski come up behind him until she put a calming, restraining hand on his arm. He jumped away from her, looking startled, then sighed and folded his arms. "I don't understand. I just don't understand."

Dr. Friel knelt the closest to the wreckage. Tears were streaming from his eyes. He looked as though he would have liked to have gathered the bits and pieces of the alien baby and cradled them in his arms. Acid-neutralizing liquid had automatically been splashed, but there were still pocks and holes in the floor.

Dr. Begalli stepped up beside Grant and Kozlowski.

"Looks like someone diddled with the equipment. Took off the safeguards. The baby bug popped early. The good news is no alien running amok in the sewage pipes. Bad news: damage, no alien baby on hand to queenify ... and a little heartbreak, it would seem."

"Christ," said Grant. His face was white. "A saboteur."

"Who would *do* such a thing?" sobbed Dr. Friel. "So young ... so very young ... And she didn't even get to see *me!*"

"Uh—I trust you checked your doctors' psychological profiles," said Kozlowski. "Friel looks a bit on the edge here."

"He'll be fine, he'll be fine," muttered Grant. "Just a little too wrapped up in his work."

"No wife, no kids ..." said Begalli. "Looks like Friel wanted to be a daddy. Bad."

The stricken scientist spun on the assemblage. He swung an arc with an accusing finger. "Which one of you monsters was it?" Tears runneled down his cheeks. "Which one of you killed my baby?" The finger stopped on Kozlowski. "Was it you, Colonel? You despised it the moment you saw what was going on here. I could tell!"

"No, it wasn't me, you fool," she spat back. "Would someone get a shot of something for this hysteric? Something strong? And maybe a strait-jacket." She motioned to the wreckage. "And douse this stuff in some more acid neutralizer fast, in case the blood wants to eat through the deck any-more."

"I trust you'll help me establish better security here for the return trip," said Grant.

"Of course," she said. She spun around and started away.

Grant caught up with her. "Colonel . . . Alex . . . Could I ask for a moment of your time? Alone."

She was going to spit back a curt no, but his eyes implored her. They looked frightened and haunted. The part of Daniel Grant that she'd seen when he was drunk was there, and she was startled by its humanity.

"Meeting room. Five minutes. I'll brew the tea," she said.

"Thank you, Colonel."

The meeting room was secured, peripheral sound dampers down, communications off.

The two sat across from one another, sipping a soothing herb tea.

"So," said Kozlowski, breaking the grim silence. "Who do you think it is? An emissary of the organized crime boys you owe money to. Or one of your drug company rivals, like MedTech."

"I don't get it," said Grant, shaking his head. "I can't believe I overlooked this possibility. Everyone knows that if this mission fails, I'm history."

"If you ask me, it's better this way," said

Kozlowski. "Something tells me you would have gotten more than you bargained for with Dr. Friel in control of a queen alien."

Grant sighed. "You're probably right, but that isn't the point. This sabotage will continue, and a lot more than money could be lost next time."

Kozlowski shrugged. "It's hard for me to be frightened of a corporate spy or even of the mob when I've been fighting drooling monsters for years."

"Yes, but how often have you run into infiltration? Don't you see? You and your soldiers have always been united against an obvious threat. Take it from someone who knows—nothing is deadlier than the enemy within."

"You have any suggestions?"

"That's why I asked you here. Have you any clue as to who the saboteur could be?"

"You didn't set up your systems to safeguard against one or to detect the activity of one. I suggest you do so now. I haven't the vaguest. I can only tell you . . . it isn't me."

"No. You think I'd be talking to you if I thought it was you? No, Colonel. We'll take precautions. But we'll have to take precautions and remain vigilant. If you note unusual activity in any of your people, please report it to me."

"I could say the same about your people."

"Oh, you can be sure I'm going to check them *all* out." He sipped his tea. "Nonetheless, this is going to be one hell of a mission . . ."

"It's already that, Grant. But then, I've been to hell before, so I'll put in a good word with Beelzebub."

"Thanks, Colonel."

"Strikes me that you're getting awfully self-involved here. We're all in this mission together, and we're committed to its success. Remember that, Grant. The mission comes first. Everything else, later, including your narcissistic moans."

"That's all well and good, Colonel. Just pop a couple of pills and all *your* troubles go away."

"Bastard."

She got up to go, then had a second thought. She reached into her pocket and pulled out a medicine bottle. "Just a warning, Grant." She tossed it to him. "That's my supply of the shit that you make. I'm swearing off, so I'm going to be in a pretty bitchy mood."

Grant looked down at the bottle. "Okay, Colonel." He stuck it in his own pocket. "Maybe I'll take it along myself. A dose of my own medicine might be in order."

"I wouldn't suggest it," she said, turning away so she wouldn't grab it back. She regretted the gesture already, but she'd see the bastard in true hell before she took his poison anymore.

She did, however, take the tea.

The U.S.S. *Razzia* locked into orbit around the planet dubbed Hiveworld.

Hiveworld, of course, was not its official name. That would be G-435, for obscure classification purposes. It was the fourth of ten planets orbiting Achilles Two, a GO star. It was a class M planet, with a great deal of seismic activity that rendered it generally flat and comparatively barren.

Huge banks of clouds obscured the surface, but analysis sensors had already scouted out the geographic area that was known to be the location of the alien hive visited previously.

Zero hour approached.

The mothership, naturally, would not descend.

A class 9 lander would perform that duty, bearing with it the complement of marines who embarked upon the mission. The marines all knew their jobs, but there was a palpable pall of tension and dread in the lander's interior as the soldiers, already garbed in their special acid-neutralizing suits, began to file in and strap into their grav-chairs.

They all carried their carbines and the array of other special weapons in which they specialized.

Private Jastrow carried something a little extra.

His saxophone.

"So what are you going to do, Jastrow?" said Mahone, attempting a smile. "Scare the crickets off with free-form? A little late Coltrane?"

"Shut up, Mahone," said Jastrow. "You never know when I'm going to need to unwind."

"Yow! Just having a little joke! Gimme a break!"

"Cool it, Edie," said Ellis. "We're all a little on edge huh? These suits don't douse acid words."

Edie Mahone nodded. "Sorry, guys. I'll get off your case. How about some knock-knock jokes?"

Ellis grinned. "As long as they're dirty."

Nervous titters.

Dr. Amos Begalli walked in, and slouched onto a chair, looking a little preoccupied.

Ellis nudged his friend. "Hey, Jazz. I didn't know that old Big Nozzle was taking the plunge."

Jastrow shrugged. "I don't know. Something big went on down in Mysteryville Deck. Nobody got killed or hurt. I've been keeping track and I've seen them all. But from what I saw on the down list, that Dr. Friel guy was supposed to take the plunge. Looked a bit forlorn yesterday. Freaked out, I guess. Couldn't deal with it."

"Probably smart."

"That's okay. That Begalli seems to know his stuff."

"Yeah, but I get the creeps from him."

"You get the creeps when I play Sun Ra tunes."

Jastrow lifted his horn up to blow a few notes, but Ellis stopped him. "Look. These guys are all hyped up to kill things, Jazz. Don't make them practice on you."

"Okay, okay. So where's Grant and the colonel?" He looked at his chronometer, featuring dials and sensors capable of all manner of odd things.

"Humpin', you think?"

"Come on . . . I think dear Koz dug her gonads outta herself with a rusty spoon."

"I don't know, man. I feel some heavy vibes between them."

"Yeah. Hostility. Just be glad she's directing it at someone else and not us."

Jastrow shook his head. "You know, I've trained for this. I've killed bugs. I know everything by heart. They say I'm about as ready as a marine can be mentally and physically. Spiritually though?" He shook his head. "I ain't ready."

"Who is, buddy?" Ellis said. He shuddered. "Who is?" He looked around and saw his shudder echoed in the eyes of his fellow troops.

Colonel Alex Kozlowski entered the ship. She'd already stowed her personal weapons and

supplies in the appropriate cubicle earlier that day,
just before she ran through the checklist of the
Mark Nine Planetary Surface Lander, dubbed
U.S.S. *Anteater* by some wag. Now she carried a
large steaming cup of coffee and a grim smile.

"Ready to waste some bugs, folks?"

A roar of approval greeted her words.

"Good. But remember, that's incidental to our mission. Our priorities are inside that nest . . . our appointment with the queen mother!" She sipped at
the strong black coffee. The caffeine helped her
cope with the downer she was experiencing from
withdrawal from Fire. She'd put some regulation
pills into her suit, things her system was used to.
She didn't want to jeopardize the troops or the mission by lack of performance. She did not, however,
want to fall back on Fire. Although the decision put
her on edge, the boost in spirit and self-
determination more than made up for it.

"Anybody see Daniel Grant around?" she asked.

"Last I saw him, he was talking to Hastings
about something," said Corporal Henrikson.

"He'd better get his tail down here, or it's going to
get left on the *Razzia* . . . and no big loss." She am-
bled over to Fitzwilliam and Tanarez, the lieutenants
who'd been pegged as pilots for this boat. They were
huddled over their banks of controls, doing final di-
agnostics of their system arrays. "How's it doing,
guys?"

Fitzwilliam grinned at her. "I'm telling you, Colonel. We've got one mean machine here. Backup
systems galore . . . Lovely and elegant."

"Yeah," said Tanarez, not looking up from a

screen he was reading. "War with the xenos has given us a boost in technology. We've got some pretty stuff in here. Gives me a huge boost of confidence, I'll tell you that."

"Too bad this thing can't just do the dirty work," said Fitzwilliam.

"What . . . robot-controlled? And miss all the fun?"

Laughter from the troops. A good sign. Ever since she'd shown them the acid-neutralizing suits, they'd seemed to perk up quite a bit. Without the big threat of the alien blood eating through you, this was a much less dangerous mission, and the troops seemed to realize that.

As though he'd taken it as a cue, the last passenger hurried on, lugging a sack closed by a zipper. He quickly stowed it where the other stuff had been placed.

"All right, people," Daniel Grant said. "You can close the access port."

The door closed behind him after a touch of a pilot's finger.

"Thank you. I just want to say quickly that this is the most exciting day of my life," he said, in a voice that had been clearly exercised much at after banquet speeches. "Down there," he said, pointing out a port toward the pearl and cerulean clouds swirling above a continental mass. "Down on this strange world are the secrets that will strengthen our country . . . Perhaps even point us all toward a better future. Down there are the brethren of the creatures that not only are a threat to humanity— but who devastated our beloved homeworld." He paused for dramatic impact. "It's in our hands now. In our power. Let's do our mission and do it well."

A roar of approval arose from the ranks.

Grant, smiling like a politician, took his grav-chair and belted himself in.

Kozlowski gave him the thumbs-up signal.

Well, Grant you goat, she thought, get ready for the panty raid of your life.

16

Docking struts released, the half-million-ton lander first parted from the mothership *Razzia* on retros. When it was at a safe distance, its powerful impulse thrusters in, pushing it down and away, deeper into the hold of the Hiveworld's gravity.

The U.S.S. *Anteater* descended.

This was still the part of space travel that Kozlowski had never gotten used to: planetfall.

She remembered when she was a little girl, before the aliens came, she had taken a ride on a roller coaster at an amusement park. She'd thought for sure, despite the strong and reassuring presence of her father, when the coaster took a long angled dip that she was going to fall out. Now, as the lander tilted down and began its powered descent, as her heart filled her throat, that was the way she felt here.

Only if she fell, she knew it would be forever.

She desperately wanted a tab of Fire. Maybe she was going to need it, she thought. Maybe Kozlowski now, without her drug, would be a crippled foot to the mission.

Later, she told herself. She'd make that decision later.

Initially, parted from the faux gravity of the *Razzia*, there had been the heady feeling of null gravity. But then, as the ship descended, she felt the butterflies flutter into her stomach and then chute up the back door to climb her spine.

Then the gees started kicking in.

The retros roared, slowing them down. Ablation reddened the hull slightly before a force shield kicked in. Landers went down much too quickly for Kozlowski's taste. She much preferred the mollycoddling you got on a passenger shuttle. A slow, smooth descent. Friggin' Marine landers, though, acted like sperm charging out of the gate for an appointment with a pretty egg.

They were still well above the clouds, but the atmosphere started buffeting the lander, shaking it like a toy. Kozlowski gritted her teeth. She looked over. The other troops looked intent. Some just had their eyes closed. Daniel Grant looked a bit green at the gills. Kozlowski suspected that she didn't look all that great herself, but there was no place to powder her nose now.

The suits had temp controls, but they were open now and the air-conditioning wasn't on. The cabin's air control wasn't working well, and it was a bit hot and humid. Kozlowski could smell her own sweat. It was a comforting smell. What she didn't like much was the sweat from the others.

"Turbulence!" called Fitzwilliam, up in the pilot blister, with the best view. She'd chosen Lenny Fitzwilliam herself. He was a top expert at this kind of planetfall, a ranging muscular guy with a Texas accent who could have been the reincarnation of one of those crazy pilots who broke the barrier between Earth and space back in the twentieth century. His wife had just died, and this was his way of getting back some life in himself, in what he knew best.

"No shit, Sherlock!" said Tank Tanarez. He flipped on the PA. "No smoking. No trips to the can. Fasten seat belts. All that stuff. It's going to be a rocky one."

"*Going* to be?" said Grant weakly.

Tanarez never exaggerated. He was a short, stocky guy with a buzz cut and a two-dimensional way of looking at the universe, which made him a gem in this kind of piloting situation. With his fierce concentration branded in those dark eyes of his below that sloping brow, he cut straight through problems to the solutions. He could drink everyone under the table but herself. Kozlowski knew. He'd tried. He had a mordant sense of humor that was just what Kozlowski needed to hear now.

"I'm reading some pretty fierce mid-atmospheric activity. This place ain't exactly paradise."

The lander began to rock and jerk violently.

This continued for some minutes. Kozlowski suspected that there were going to be some gouges in the armrests after this from the digging in of fingers. Including hers. Nobody puked though. That was something.

The twirling lengths of gray cottony clouds seemed to reach up like an ocean of mist and absorb them. The rattling and rocking continued, and then calmed down.

"Okeydokey, folks," said Fitzwilliam. "We're through the worst of it. We should be done in about thirty-five minutes. So sit back and enjoy the flight." Fitz was clearly from the Chuck Yeager school of pilots. Fly by the seat of your pants, but even if your wings had sheered off and your ejector was jammed, at no time abandon your laid-back Texas accent.

Kozlowski took a luxurious breath of bad air. It tasted good through slightly less constricted lungs.

"Can't see a goddamned thing," said Argento, the dark-haired mustached sergeant who sat behind her. Argento's brooding eyes and bushy eyebrows and bushier mustache made Tanarez look like the Blue Boy. He was like a Neanderthal with all that hair and stolid attitude. But there wasn't a man in the Corps who knew his way around artillery, light or heavy, better. Kozlowski had worked with Argento the year before, and when the possibility of his coming along arose, she grabbed it. He had a rich, deep voice that inspired confidence in him from the git go. He was a man's man and a fine poker player, too.

"Do you really want to?" said Jastrow, suddenly talkative. "If ignorance is bliss, let's enjoy it for another half hour, huh? Me, I'm just going to rest my eyes."

That seemed like a good idea to Kozlowski. Unfortunately, she was too high-strung to give herself even that much of a treat. She had to see it all. Somewhere, in this hellish cloud cover, might be something she needed. In the first break, when she got the lay of the land—that might make a change in her strategy that might save lives, might give this mission the edge it needed for a thorough success.

So, for long minutes she watched as the lander pierced the cloud cover.

Occasional comments arose from the troops, but generally there was silence.

Finally, the cloud cover started to break up.

Kozlowski peered out through the port.

As far as she could tell, they were still a couple miles up, but she could make out some of the landscape below. She'd seen pictures of it before of course in her studies of this godforsaken planet.

Like Mars, the report had said. A few mountains, lots of volcanoes, but for the most part flat and pocked. More atmosphere than Mars. Breathable even. Not nice, though. Not nice at all.

The pictures had clued her in to the starkness, the hellish wasteland quality this place had. There was something stricken about it, something *unholy*. Kozlowski wasn't a religious person, but that was the first word that came to her mind.

Unholy.

Damned, was the second.

Shakespeare could have used it for his "blasted heath" in the play *Macbeth*.

"Still can't see much down there through the cloud cover," Fitzwilliam was saying.

"Anything coming through the telemetry topography scan?" said Tanarez.

"Hey. What do you know? Calculations totally correct. The sucker's down there!"

A thrill of elation filled Kozlowski.

The moment the *Razzia* had entered parking orbit, its heavy-duty sensors, on full power, had gotten to work. The coordinates of the original alien hive were known. And sure enough, it didn't take long to locate the ugly hive, poking up from the flat land like a huge unlanced boil.

"What the hell is this?"

"What?"

"Just take a look, will you!"

Begalli's eyes grew bright with excitement. "I *suspected* as much!"

About a hundred miles away from the original hive, there was another hive. A hive shaped differently from the original, according to the sensors.

Sure enough, up close, the sensors were showing it was indeed an alien hive. So far so good. Now they just had to determine if it was the flavor alien they wanted.

The misty clouds swirled away from the ship, and they got a better view.

Somehow, even from way up here, Kozlowski could tell that things weren't quite right.

"Jeez," she heard Tanarez say. "This unit checks out. So this reading must be correct."

"Yeah? So what's it say?" Fitzwilliam shot back.

"Well, judging from the surface activity." She could hear the slight gulp in Tanarez's voice, breaking up that Yeager effect. "There's some kind of *war* going on down there!"

"Let me look!"

Grant's eyes were suddenly open and eager. He strained forward on his belt, his hands frantically scrabbling at the catches.

"Grant!" she barked at him. "We haven't landed. Keep your goddamned butt parked. We don't want your brains all over the ceiling."

Grant halted his efforts to release himself. Nonetheless, his desire to see what was going on down there had not diminished. "What's going on? Begalli! Talk to me! How does this work into your high-flown theories?"

Begalli was wearing a shit-eating grin. "Couldn't be sweeter, boss."

"We're looking at aliens swarming like ants around a hive and that's supposed to be sweet?" said Grant.

Kozlowski wasn't too worried. They had the technology to deal with this. Just a detail. The brass were going to like this—they were going to be able to check out how well the new stuff worked.

"You bet. You ever hear of the xenos fighting among themselves wholesale, Colonel?"

"Nope. Not the batch that came to Earth."

"Exactly. Because they were all the same breed, the same race. They smelled the same to each other. They worked together. The fact that there's conflict down there tends to prove that what we suspected would happen, has."

"Like *what*?" demanded Jastrow, eyes round and a little protruding with fear.

Kozlowski didn't blame him. Looked like a goddamned African ant war down there. Hundreds and thousands of the bastards, swarming, swarming . . .

"Okay, okay. Classified material. Sorry. Shouldn't have brought it up in front of the troops," said Grant.

That pissed Kozlowski off, but she didn't say anything. Wouldn't do the soldiers any good anyway. Would just take their minds off the job at hand. Nonetheless, she knew what Begalli was talking about, and dammit, it did make sense. She just hoped it wouldn't complicate things, mucking over the mission beyond redemption.

The theory was, of course, that aliens without a controlling queen would branch off into different packs. Breeding might (and apparently did) give rise to bugs with recessive traits. If these bugs were allowed to continue to breed, the result would be a new race . . . and hurry over to start up a new hive, complete with a new queen.

This was a new hive here.

Call them the Democrats.

But apparently, the old fart bugs had gotten things together and spawned a new queen mother . . . and millions of workers. And although the new Democrat hive was a long way away, eventually they'd located it. Their queen mother had sent off her armies to destroy the interlopers into the genetic xeno broth.

Call them the Republicans.

She looked out at the troops. There were naked questions beside the fear and misgiving in their eyes.

"What are you assholes looking at! Plan C takes this kind of situation into account." She smiled grimly. "Just look at it this way . . . We're going to be able to kill more bugs."

"Pardon us, Commander . . ." said Fitzwilliam. "Plan C starts the same way they all do . . . Land as close to the hive as possible. There are thousands of aliens down there now."

Colonel Kozlowski grinned. "And hopefully there will be thousands there when we land—only *burnt* aliens."

Grant shook his head. "Well, I guess those bugs aren't the only specialists in genocide."

They continued their descent.

17

When they were a mile above the hive, the mist had cleared enough to use optical magnifiers to good effect.

Sure enough, there was a war going on down there. As vicious a war as Alex Kozlowski could imagine. Thousands of struggling bugs going at each other.

Fangs and talons.

The ruddy landscape was running with alien parts, alien blood, spasming monsters.

How long had this been going on?

Kozlowski's best guess, offhand, was that this was just the latest of many attacks. She saw alien skeletons littering the landscape. One more battle.

That wasn't all the crew of the *Anteater* saw, though.

"Run this over with me again, Begalli," said Grant.

"Very quickly, sir, the creatures have had a freak genetic offshoot. Normally a queen mother would stamp this out immediately. With no queen mother, though, another colony has been allowed to take root and thrive. As for the possible difference caused by the recessive gene theory . . . we'll just have to examine them closer, won't we."

The most important thing the magnified view on the screen pointed out was that Begalli's theories were entirely correct.

One set of bugs had a vague reddish cast. The rest—the defenders, it could be seen, because they were the ones streaming from the portals of the huge hive below—were the usual dark color that Kozlowski was accustomed to.

Begalli whooped. "What did I tell you. And ten to one, they've got unpredictable internal differences. I can't wait to find out. There's also got to be other kinds of life on this planet that have learned to survive the xenos. If possible, I'd like to check on them."

"Celebrations later, fella. For what I'm not sure. They all look nasty as ever. And as for other forms of life—yeah, I guess the critters have got to eat something. But that's not why we're here, is it?" Kozlowski unhooked her belt and hurried up to a place beside the pilots. "Okay, fellows. I've got this wonderful idea. You usually use force impellers as well as a few retros to land, correct?"

"That's right."

"Anything to stop us from using the thrusters to land? That should cook a lot of them pretty good."

"Sure. Lots of fuel consumption though," said Fitzwilliam.

"We just need enough to get back."

"We've got plenty to spare for that," said Tanarez. "I could do a configuration of the primaries and tertiaries that would do the trick."

"Good. Then do it. Burn the bastards, and make sure they're well done."

"Okay. That looks like the main entrance to the hive. Not as close as we'd like, but it's the only option," said Fitzwilliam.

"That'll be just fine," Kozlowski said after studying the computer schematics that the pilot had called up on the screen to illustrate the lay of the land.

"You'd better sit back down, Colonel, and buckle that seat belt. Rockets are a little bit rougher than force impellers . . ." suggested Fitzwilliam.

"So I've noticed."

The craft was rumbling and rocking like a son of a bitch. Kozlowski stumble-walked back to her chair, strapped herself in again, and watched the action, eyes gleaming.

The *Anteater* slowed down.

There was a mighty wrenching as the rockets cut in. Fitzwilliam was right. It felt like they were riding a jackhammer down. She had to clench her teeth to keep them from rattling.

She looked up to the magnification screen. The bugs had stopped fighting. Some were waving their heads, as though attempting to look up, to make out the source of the terrible rumbling in the sky with their primitive photosensors.

"I hope the bastards don't have the sense to run," she said under her breath.

"Unfortunately, the instinct for survival is paramount in the creatures," said Begalli, above the roar. "They're disoriented, but as soon as they sense the presence of the ship, they'll start to scatter. Fortunately, there are enough of them clustered that they can't scatter fast."

"Can we go down quicker?" said Kozlowski, excited.

"Not and get the effect you want!" screamed Fitzwilliam.

"Besides, we want 'em good and crisp! We don't want any of that blood eating away at the hull or support struts," said Tanarez.

True. Very true. C'mon, Koz. Use your head ... not your hate and bloodlust.

She looked up again at the screen.

The shadow of the craft showed now, spread like a blot on the land and the mass of aliens.

Who began to scurry.

The shadow narrowed, darkened.

"Shit!" cried Tanarez. "That outcropping over there!"

"Yeah. I see it," said the other pilot. "I'll take her another twenty-five meters away. Tight fit, but I can land this baby on a dime."

The confidence in Fitzwilliam's voice encouraged her.

She could feel the shift of the ship. It slewed sideways, and started down again.

Catching a bunch of the bugs by surprise.

The tongues of intense puce and orange and

ocher shot down to the ground, licking across the arid ground.

Lapping at the creatures.

Unable to take her eyes off the scene, she watched as the rocket flames covered and consumed hundreds of the beasts. Hundreds more not directly in the fires nonetheless burst into incandescence at the horrible heat.

Fried.

"Incredible," she whispered.

She watched as long as she was able as the aliens were immolated. A black swath of alien ash . . . lovely. The *Anteater*, in just a minute, had wiped out enough to fill a couple of nests back home.

Unfortunately, it looked like there were plenty left to take their place.

"Hold a moment. Scorch the ground a little more before we land," said Fitzwilliam. "We've got about all we can. I just want to make sure these below are properly cooked."

"Sure."

The craft jerked, and hung for just a few seconds.

Smoke was curling up now past the viewports, obscuring the scene. Kozlowski closed her eyes. Afterimages of the skeletal demons torching up flickered across her vision.

Then the ship descended again, this time landing on its struts with a wobbling jolt. It swayed, then stilled.

A red light shifted on.

"All right, grunts!" snapped Kozlowski. "We've

got ourselves an emergency combat landing on our hands. It's *showtime!*"

Now everything was in the hands of an Irishman named Seamus O'Connor—and the marvelous new technology at his fingertips. O'Connor was a guy she didn't know that well. He was a technician who'd helped develop the procedure he was about to use, a sandy-haired gentleman with a soft voice and a twinkle to his eyes in social situations, but a rock-solid attitude of concentration during briefings and exercise. He looked like the kind of person who got a job done, and then went off to the pub to play pipes and whistles and have a few pints.

She looked out at the heaving mass of aliens, outlines in the soot. And if that didn't work, they might as well just take off again out of here!

"All right, O'Connor," Fitzwilliam's voice crackled through the 'lobephone. "I've cut the engines. The smoke is pretty much dissipated. "Do your duty before any of the things put on their boots and stomp back in."

"Roger, Skipper."

Corporal Seamus O'Connor scratched his beard. He adjusted his grav-chair for a better view of the control panel. He'd been training for this moment for months in virtual reality sims. Unfortunately, somehow it wasn't quite the same here. He'd never had xenos crawling all over the place before. He'd never had a field of dismembered and burnt bugs to negotiate before.

What O'Connor operated were the PEHs—the Perimeter Extension Harpoons. The marines had learned pretty damned quick that in dealing with hostile life forms—i.e., bugs—force fields were quite useful. They'd been in use to a certain extent in the routine humdrum of company galactic life, but as soon as the nasty things with a penchant for destruction were discovered, necessity became the mother of invention yet again. Power was increased, but in landings like this one it was rapidly discovered that the Fields could only be beamed out a short circumference around the ship. In situations involving the need for expanded territory, their reach had to be expanded.

Some kind of fence had to be constructed, utilizing force-field generating devices. However, in a theoretical hostile situation, neither men nor robots could be expected to trundle out and erect these posts.

Hence the harpoons.

They'd been tested before in the field, of course. Out in deserts and plains, among rocks and what have you. You just played Moby Dick, and shot them out to likely-looking spots. When they thunked in properly, you pressed a button for remote control and—ZAP. You had yourself a wide but snug little force-field cap within which to work.

O'Connor's job now was to get those harpoons out.

He touched a button and the ports opened.

He did a quick analysis, adjusted the aim, said a prayer . . .

And fired.

Four harpoons—each seven meters tall and two thick—burst from their ports, sailed out into the alien atmosphere, trailing their power cables like baited hooks tossed from fishing rods.

They sailed majestically and gorgeously.

C'mon you beauties, thought O'Connor.

Hit your marks.

The sharp points, capable of boring into rock, struck the surface of the alien planet and—marvel of marvels—stuck.

"Bull's-eye!" O'Connor cried.

The radio crackled. "No time to rest on your laurels. Looks like those bugs haven't been discouraged much. They're coming back in!"

"No problem!"

O'Connor leaned over and pulled the switch.

The posts sparked. A shimmer of power traveled down the lines, and then spread like electric coloring in water, connecting the posts, the cables, and swirling along the ground.

"Outwall activation has been initiated," O'Connor reported, a note of triumph in his voice.

Dozens of aliens caught in the power grid were simply sheered in half. Others heading back in toward the lander simply bounced off the field, limbs and heads bent or smoking.

O'Connor grinned to himself, and put the field on automatic. He'd done his job.

Now the troops were going to have to do theirs.

This was why they had worn their suits:

So they could go into action at a moment's notice.

"We've got some cleaning up to do, people," said Kozlowski, motioning for the troops to hurry along into the hangar deck. "This is what we came to do."

The rest of the crew already had their helmets on, so she couldn't see what their faces registered.

"It's why we're drawing a salary."

She put her own helmet on, tongued on communications.

"Gentlemen," she said. "I do believe we're ready."

"Roger, Colonel. Hatchway opening initiated."

The carbines, plasma rifles, and other automatic weapons of the assembled rattled upward, positioning themselves for firing.

No depressurization was necessary. However the PSIs were not the same, so there was a distinct escape of air as the hatchway opened. A chiaroscuro of dark colors and smoke wavered between them and distant jagged rotten-tooth mountains. Before her oxygen-rich mix started to whisper through her suit's ducts, she fancied she smelled the land beyond.

Burnt carbon.

Burnt silicon.

Alien acid.

Never-ending death beneath an eldritch, evil sun.

She had a regulation upper-pill in her hand, ready to take it. Looking out, though, she realized she didn't really need it. She threw it away.

A surge of victory ran through her.

"C'mon, people," she snapped through her microphone, staccato calling of a parade into a battle on shores not made for humans. "Let's earn some money."

18

The operation was basically a clean-up proposition.

The landing had cindered hundreds of the bugs. The force-field perimeter had locked out the remainder. Only about twenty-five of the aliens had made it past the harpoons before the field crackled on.

These were the current targets.

These were the bugs that had to be crushed.

Vague colorings or internal differences didn't seem to matter. From the way these things acted, all were every centimeter the crazed berserkers their cousins were.

The lip of the ramp had not been touched down, and one of them leapt on it, scuttling up toward them, slavering and tearing away at the air.

"Simultaneous!" she cried and lifted her own rifle and fired.

The blast of weapons was so strong converging on the bug that the force lifted the thing up a good meter and slammed it back another ten. Damned good thing, too. It disintegrated into a splatter of parts and blood in midair.

"Keep that shit off the hull!" Kozlowski cried. "Okay now, move it!"

As practiced before, the troops moved out, plasma weapons first. A robo-wagon trundled out after them, bearing extra weapons, supplies, and automatic support keyed from the *Anteater*. As soon as the first four marines cleared the bottom of the ramp, they started blasting. A wave of fire, like a manic flamethrower on amphetamines, roared out, whacking into a group of five bugs scampering into the melee.

They all fell apart in the hellish fire.

Kozlowski and the others were out in a flash, bringing up the rear and selecting targets. Kozlowski felt as though she'd just downed a couple tabs of Xeno-Zip. Adrenaline? Yes, and bliss, too. It had been a long time since she'd fought real xenos, and there was nothing like the satisfaction of the prospect of one's slugs putting out the lights on a bug to get a gal's heart to thumpin'.

"Fire at will!" she said.

She jumped off the ramp and swiveled over to cover the underside of the lander. A space of about seven meters existed between the base of the lander and the ground. All in shadow. Unlikely that any had scuttled under here, but you never knew.

She nudged the correct com switch. "Turn on the bottom lights, Control!"

"Roger."

The lights started to blink on, but even before they were up, through the heightened "ears" of the suit, she heard the telltale hissing.

"Damn!"

One was coming toward her.

They had descended to Mission Control, to stand and watch beside Corporal Seamus O'Connor as the monitors flashed the frenetic details of the conflict.

Daniel Grant felt giddy victory turn his skin to goose pumps.

What a spectacle!

Whatever doubts he'd ever felt about the competency of this batch of marines disappeared within seconds as the group fanned out in perfect formation, their weapons efficiently blasting away. Out in the open, the alien strategy seemed simple: charge and destroy. The Marine strategy seemed equally simple: blast the things to bits.

The marines acted like precision-sensored robots. Their aims were deadly. Like a phalanx of destruction, they performed this grisly, pyrotechnic ballet. Grant suddenly wished for some appropriate music. Sturm und drang!

O'Connor was clearly equally impressed. "Wow." He turned to Dr. Begalli. "Those suits you produced are working great. Used to be, you couldn't fight these things in such close quarters."

Indeed, Grant noted.

As the radium bullets, the plasma blasts, and the

tossed explosives struck the aliens, rupturing the chitinous material of their exoskeletons, they tended to burst apart like ripe tomatoes atop M-80s. Their "blood"—a viscous green ichor— hurled every which way, slapping across the white armor and helmets the marines wore.

The skin of the suit ruptured, fluid leaked out, instantly neutralizing the horrible full-bore effects of the acid. Then the skin "healed." And voilà—no harm done to the marine. Nonetheless, the troops seemed to be trying for the knees and the heads, as Colonel Kozlowski had instructed them, waiting till the aliens were prone before they blasted the torso apart.

Whatever they were doing, whatever the plan had been, it seemed to be working just fine. True, the alien blood was leaving pocks and craters in the ground, but the soldiers were trained to deal with them.

Particularly impressive in his efforts was Corporal Henrikson. Like some military juggernaut he moved over the battlescape with fierce speed and agility, his plasma rifle snuffing out aliens and putting them to fiery deaths in what seemed like speeded-up film.

"Man," said Grant. "Look at Henrikson go!"

"Quite something," said Begalli. "He's a regular one-man army."

"I've heard rumors. Some of the troops think he's a synthetic," said O'Connor.

"What the hell does it matter?" said Grant. "He's doing his job and damned well!"

Dr. Begalli shook his head. "True. True. With soldiers like that, we're going to get into the nest."

Grant looked up just in time to see an odd look
pass over Begalli's face. A squinting feral look, like
a rat considering the implications of a maze—and
looking forward as much to shitting in the passage-
ways as to getting to the cheese at the other end.

But then, Begalli had always struck him as one
odd customer, and so he just set the observance
aside and turned back to this marvelous bloody
sport up there on the screen.

All he needed now was a beer and some pea-
nuts!

It was a big one.

The alien under the lander scrabbled for Kozlowski like some frenetic dinosaur closing in for the
kill on what it considered a soft-bellied mammal.

"Just try, asshole," said Kozlowski, whipping her
gun up.

The lights came on full bore, stopping the thing
not one stride, but illuminating it thoroughly.

She fired.

The burst of bullets from her semiautomatic rifle
fanned out perfectly. Textbook. The explosive slugs
caught the thing in the kneecaps, exploding them.
The beast went down, snarling and hissing, scrabbling for her without missing a beat.

She drew a bead on its bananalike head and
squeezed off another burst. The thrill of competency seized her as the head burst apart. The blast
kicked back a dollop of blood onto her suit.

Her reaction was knee-jerk terror. Experience
had taught her that a burst of xeno blood on armor
meant trouble.

Then her brain kicked in, salving her trained reaction with reality: this was a special suit.

Time to see if it worked. The guinea pig: herself.

The junk immediately sizzled and bubbled through the plastic lining. Like oozing pus, the neutralizing agent flowed out, and swallowed the acid.

Sizzle.

Bubble.

The plastic shell moved back over the hole and the suit was whole again.

Unfortunately, there wasn't a lot of time to feel good about it. Already three more aliens were running her way underneath the lander. She picked off the right one. Knees. Head. Torso. The weapons these days were so *good*. The shells just cut through that damned exoskeleton like it was the thinnest of tin. So *satisfying* just seeing them *burst* like that.

Overripe gourds in a shooting gallery!

Another soldier was beside her.

The nametag read MAHONE.

No discussion. Just quick efficient drawing of a bead, and then her gun coughed off, dealing amazing damage to the beast to their left.

They swiveled as one, and their fire converged on the central alien, only five yards away now.

The strength of their blasting shattered the thing, and its blood blew back as well, among the tumble and tatters of its wasted body.

"He looked like my last boyfriend!" said Mahone over the radio, her voice sounding immensely satisfied.

"No," said Kozlowski. "Seems to me the others look more like boyfriends."

"Yeah. I think you're right. Let's waste 'em!"

Mahone's grin showed through her faceplate.

However, before they could go and look for any more, a voice crackled over Kozlowski's radio. "Colonel. We got one on the ship!"

"Damn," said Kozlowski. "Not good!" She turned to Mahone. "Stay here and cover me. I have to check this out."

"Roger."

She turned and started running for the other side of the ramp to gain a vantage point on the situation.

Intellectually she'd been aware that the gravity here was only .9 of Earth Standard. However, she was shocked at how quickly she was able to move. True, these suits were a little lighter than she was used to . . .

She didn't complain at all. She just had to adjust herself accordingly.

"Okay, hotshots," she said to a soldier she immediately recognized as Jastrow. "What's going on?"

Things looked pretty well contained. The rest of the bunch were killing either the last standing alien, or raking their weapons across the remains of ones already shot down, making sure they were dead.

Jastrow pointed. Sweat dripped down his temples and forehead despite his suit's air-conditioning. Kozlowski followed the direction of his forefinger.

The xeno had somehow leapt up to one of the gemlike pilot blisters. Its talons were scratching along the structural spokes and its tail whipped hard against the material, attempting to break through.

Even as she stood, considering, Private Ellis puffed up, raising his rifle.

"Hold on, soldier," said Kozlowski, holding out a halting hand. "Shoot the thing with that, we'll have bug blood all over the hull."

Bang! Bang! The tail whipped the blister. Probably giving the pilots fits.

"Jastrow! Haul the wagon over here," she commanded.

Speedily, the private obeyed, grabbing hold of the robo-wagon. Kozlowski punched open a latch, lifted the lid, looked.

Selected what she needed.

The thing was like a squarish grenade launcher, with various tangly things extruding. She picked it up, put it up against her shoulder, aimed at the offending alien, and fired.

The projectile that shot out progressed half the distance in a blur, but then at the top of its trajectory bloomed out into a net drawn by three guided bolos. Expertly directed, they whacked past the bug, scooped it up in the net.

Electricity arced and zapped.

The bug was pried off its hold, and carried off meters away to bounce hard upon the land. It rolled, and lay there, just a faint hiss and crackle emerging.

"Dead?" asked Jastrow.

"No way," Kozlowski said. "I doubt it. The electrical charge in the mesh is probably just enough to stun it."

"What should we do?"

Kozlowski considered.

Her first inclination was to just kill it. Quick. However, she well knew that Grant was watching the proceedings, and may want to imprison it with a force field in order that his scientist could examine it. She tongued her com unit, hating having to do it.

However, like a bolt out of the blue, before she could do a damned thing, a plasma blast fried the bug and the net.

She swung around to see the perpetrator of this, wondering whether to chew the soldier out or thank him.

Standing there, looking totally competent and unfazed, was Corporal Henrikson.

"It looked like it was about to break free, Colonel," the man said.

The colonel shrugged. "Yeah. Next time, though, check with me."

"Sure."

She looked around the field of devastation.

The bugs were squashed here, totally.

She took her helmet off and sniffed.

"Ah. What a stench," she said. "Nothing like it in the universe."

19

Soldiers, still helmeted and suited up, were carrying burnt and destroyed bodies of the enemy to collect them in a single pile. A vehicle was building a border of dirt around this pile, to prevent any possible spread of lingering acid.

Although he wore no suit, Daniel Grant *had* taken the precaution of donning acid-neutralizing boots. What with the lower gravity, though, he did not notice the extra weight or bulk.

On alien soil.

Grant had been born on a colony, but his own homeworld had not been that much different from Earth. His years on Earth had made him feel like a native. So it was an odd sensation indeed to actually be walking on ground so far from home, and so distinctly different in taste, touch, smell, and general atmosphere. Too, there could be no doubt that he was walking over a battlefield now.

Or that another war entirely was going on beyond the background buzz of the force-field perimeter.

Tune that out for now, man, he told himself. Take it a step at a time. Right now you're a lot safer here than you were back on Earth with that gangster Fisk breathing down your neck!

A couple of the troops were standing by the edge of the encampment, looking out past the clear shimmer of the force field to the events beyond.

Swarms of bugs were moving, dodging and sparring, occasionally dashing out and tearing one another to bits. Not exactly a melee, and the oddest battle that Daniel Grant had ever witnessed. Flashes of green and black. Fillips of splashed blood. Limbs flying and occasionally crackling into the field, bouncing back off in a spray of sparks, singed.

"Sun's up. Clouds are off," said Private Jastrow. "Feels good."

"What, you're enjoying a nice sunbath?" said Private Ellis, sarcastic. "God knows what kind of deadly radiation is coming down from that sun!"

"Like this whole planet is a health spa! Look, Ellis. You take your pleasure where you can get it! I'm taking mine here! Right now!" He held his arms outstretched. "Ah! Wonderful! I may come back with a tan."

"Just be happy if you come back."

"Actually, Ellis, I gotta tell you. I'm feeling relief. Great relief."

"Heaven's sake, *why*?"

"Everything is working great. That last bit wasn't so bad. Not too bad at all." Jastrow smiled. "Hell, this operation's going to be a cinch."

Ellis looked out at the mass of bugs, the hive, the stricken panorama. "Yeah . . . right."

Grant stepped up to them. "Hello, gentlemen. I just wanted to tell you how much I appreciate your work today."

They spun around, slightly alarmed. "Mr. Grant!" said Jastrow.

"Sorry to creep up on you like that. I didn't mean to, really. I just want to personally congratulate you. I was watching you guys. All of you. On the screens. You operated like a well-oiled, absolutely brilliant machine. It's good to be working with such fine people like you."

The two could not help but break out into broad smiles. "Thanks, Mr. Grant," said Jastrow.

"You know, you two may not be in the marines all your lives. Whenever you're out, Grant Industries is probably going to have positions for guys like you."

"That's *wonderful!*"

"So just keep up the good work!"

He moved away, to go have a look at what was going on at the side of the *Anteater*. That little speech should help boost the morale. Those two would probably spread it among the others, and he would be happy to repeat it. It wasn't bullshit, either. He really meant it. He'd be happy to hire all of these people.

First thing he'd do was set them on that maniac Fisk.

On the side of the lander, a huge portion of

metal had flipped down on hinges, exposing a bank of gleaming guns. A regular arsenal.

Grant felt a lilt to his step, a bounce to his walk as he approached.

In the command control area behind this array of weaponry, Sergeant Argento was doing a double check to systems.

"Looks like some mean machines here, Sarge," said Grant.

"That they are, Mr. Grant!" Argento said from beneath his drooping black mustache.

"What's the plan?"

"Pretty simple. We've got about seventy more yards to go before we can start thinking about getting into the hive entrance. Unfortunately, there's a lot of activity going on out there, what with alien species war going on."

"So I've noticed. Lovely to see them going at each other, instead of at us."

"Yes, sir. Well, we synchronize openings in the field to allow for explosive discharges. Then we bomb the territory between us and the top of the entrance, to clear off as many bugs as possible. Once the things are either dead or scattered, we blow out another PEH. Sink it in, turn it on— extend the force-field perimeter. Little trickier on this kind of rock but nothing harder than what we've just accomplished, really."

"And then we go for the gold."

"Exactly."

The silvery weaponry gleamed in the alien sun, sparkling with promise.

Grant gave the sergeant a thumbs-up sign.

"Here's to a campaign without a hitch."

"Yes, sir." Argento returned the gesture. "Without a hitch and then back home for the biggest party in one of your best casinos."

"You've been to one of my casinos, Argento?"

"Yes, sir. The Beach Blossom, last year. Lost my shirt, but I had the time of my life!" Argento was grinning, showing even, white teeth.

"You don't know how happy I am to hear that, my friend. Yes, an excellent concept. A party for you all . . . At my casino, the Beach Blossom at New Atlantic City!"

"Without a hitch!"

"That's right, soldier! That's pretty much what I promised your commanders before we started this trip—and now, thanks to the wonderful technology here, look where we are!"

He walked over and stood just meters away from a red and a black alien, slashing at each other.

It was like watching a movie.

He felt totally safe.

He put his hands on his hips and laughed.

Piece of cake!

They were playing horseshoes outside the lander.

Alex Kozlowski wasn't quite sure where they'd gotten the stuff. Probably fashioned it in the metal shop on board the *Razzia* for just such a possibility, and then stashed the stuff on the *Anteater*.

Clang!

Private Ellis's throw was a ringer, twirling around the post.

"Good shot!" said Jastrow.

Cheers arose from the audience.

Those two! What a pair! When they'd asked permission to set up the game, Kozlowski's first inclination was to say no. However, the pressures were so much that she not only assented, but went the next step.

Why not a picnic? The clouds had cleared and there was a sun shining through. They'd done the first part of the mission extremely well, and there was still a few hours till the rest of the operation could be properly set up.

So, instead of making her marines eat their meal inside the cold and antiseptic *Anteater*, she'd allowed the sandwiches and sodas to be set up on a folding table just outside the ramp. You had to be a little careful—if something went wrong with those force fields, you wanted to be able to make it back into the hold of the lander ASAP.

Jastrow finished his game, then moved to stand by the force field of the perimeter with his saxophone. He serenaded the aliens with John Coltrane-like free form squawking, with an occasionally more melodic passage thrown in for fun.

She was eating a tasteless sandwich layered with energy-rich Vit-C sauce for a boost, listening to Jastrow's jazz, and along with some heavily carbed macro-drink, when Daniel Grant sidled up, chomping confidently on his sandwich.

"Regular holiday."

"A bit bizarre, I agree," she said. "They need it though. There's worse ahead. Much worse."

"What? Things are going great."

"Grant. This is a war. Already we weren't quite expecting conflict on this level. Me, I would have preferred to wait until these things killed each other, then moved in."

Grant shook his head. "Not in the schedule. Things like fuel involved . . . money . . . time . . . Most especially time." His jaws worked thoughtfully around a mouthful of sandwich. "I don't have much time, back on Earth. Can't waste any hovering above this Hiveworld. Wonder what's going on back there, anyway."

"Maybe you better concentrate on this particular hellhole."

"Yeah right. But I came here because I need to talk to you a moment."

"You are talking to me."

"Alone, I mean. Not in earshot of the troops."

"Ah." She examined her wristwatch. She was out of her suit, taking the opportunity for a little bit of freedom. She didn't know how long she was going to be in next time she donned the thing. Probably *too* long. "How about inside the ship?" She wasn't that crazy about it out here now, anyway. Sun or no sun. Those bugs crawling and lumbering and fighting out there *bothered* her, dammit.

"That will be just fine."

She took another bite, another sip, nonchalantly gestured for him to follow.

Even as she walked into the locker room, she felt a little better. There was the smell of B.O. and gym shorts, sure, but at least it was human and familiar. The whiff of those bugs out there triggered all her inner alarms.

She spun on him, slapping her fingers clear of crumbs. "What's up, Grant?"

He sat down on a bench. "These troops . . . they're good."

"You're telling me something I don't know?"

"I'm sure they're going to pull this mission off, just fine."

"I sure as hell hope so. You dragged me in here to tell you *that*?"

Grant got up and began to pace.

"I don't know. That sabotage thing has got me worried."

"Consider yourself reassured. I think if they were going to strike, it would have been by now. Besides, think about this one, Grant. Right now, the numbers are down. They're in the same boat we are. We sink, they sink." She shrugged. "Besides, if there is a saboteur, I'd be happy to lay odds that it's one of your scientist bozos. Now there is a collection of premium losers."

"We do have a scientist along, remember. Begalli."

"Rat-face. Yeah. I'm watching him, don't worry. I'm watching everybody. But take it from me. I'm watching my own ass most of all."

"Me, too! It *is* a nice one."

She laughed out loud. "You're a hard case. Even while you're sober, and I smell like a horse after the Derby."

"You smell fine."

She nodded. "That's what Michaels used to say."

"Michaels?"

"Peter Michaels. Old lover. We used to fight together. Hell, we used to *waste* those bug hives, he and I. What a team." She shook her head. "God, we got into this incredible habit. After a gig, we'd come back. We'd be so hot, we didn't even bother to shower. We just stripped our suits and screwed. Sheesh. Couple of crazy horny kids."

She looked over at him. His face had turned a bright pink.

"Something wrong, Grant."

"Nothing. Nothing, Alex. Only . . ." He smiled. "I know women. Sorry about the old drunken stupor the other night, but you know, you're not bad-looking . . . And you're pretty damned tough and not exactly the most feminine creature I've ever encountered . . . I like you. Moreover . . . I think you like me. I can sense these kinds of things, kiddo. So I was wondering, once this is all over . . ."

"You touch me, you asshole, and I'll cut your genitals off and stick them up your nose."

He shrugged. "Just thought I'd try." He got up to go. "Well, off to my possible death."

She stepped over, spun him around, yanked his head down, and devoured his mouth with hers.

Just as the surprise wore off and Grant warmed up to the osculation, she pushed him away so hard he almost tumbled over the bench.

"God!" he said, catching his balance. "What was *that* all about?"

"Just don't let it go to your head, okay?" She smoothed her mussed hair and stormed from the room, enormously upset at herself.

She'd liked that a lot, dammit.

20

The troops were lined up and ready, their helmets back on and properly secured, their weapons cocked, primed, fully loaded and hungry for action.

A silence descended upon the troops, bordered by the buzz of the force fields and the snarling tumult of the fighting aliens between them and the entrance to the blacks' monolithic hive.

Kozlowski could feel their tension.

Or was it just her *own* tension, multiplied by twenty-five? This was going to be the make-or-break of the mission.

Thankfully, the ranks of the bugs had thinned somewhat. Whether many of them had simply been killed or crawled into holes somewhere she didn't know. She just hoped they hadn't gone into the hive.

She tongued her comm. "Troops ready."

The bounce-back from Control Central. "All set here." O'Connor's brogue. "Sergeant Argento?"

She looked back to where the sergeant sat, behind his banks of big weapons.

"Guns are sighted and ready," said Argento, fingers playing expertly across the controls. "I don't see a more optimum time."

Kozlowski looked up. She could have wished for a little more light. The clouds had closed back up, tight.

Oh, well, it didn't really matter that much. They had a good five hours till darkness. That would be more than enough time.

"Right," came O'Connor's voice. "Opening force-field apertures."

Kozlowski looked up toward the top of the force field. The field looked like a thin wavering skein of gray normally. It would open just—

There!

A wide hole sphinctered, and Argento wasted no time.

The big guns thundered.

The many millimetered shells sailed out perfectly, hammering onto the landscape. Whole clusters of bugs were destroyed, even more thrown back in the explosions.

More shells, differently directed, hammered out of the guns, exploded on the landscape.

When the smoke cleared, Kozlowski saw that a wide swath had been cleared. A trail of craters lay in the valley that led up to the opening of the hive.

"Harpoon away!" called O'Connor.

The appropriately aimed gun on the side of the lander thumped. Amid an explosion of gases, the harpoon launched. It sailed over their heads swiftly and majestically, trailing its cable like a kite caught in a gale. It threaded the hole in the force field easily and whooshed toward its target.

Even back here, many meters away, Kozlowski could hear the large harpoon thunk into place, burying itself in the ground right on target.

A hearty "Hurrah" sounded from the troops.

"We have a successful landing!" chirped O'Connor's voice. "Prepare for perimeter extension."

The troops grew quiet. Kozlowski braced herself, getting her rifle ready. Theoretically, when O'Connor pushed the right combination of switches and levers, the force field would move out like an arcing gate— only expanding as it did so.

Whacking all bugs en route.

However, in the activity, there was always the possibility that one of the aliens would slip through unharmed. That alien would have to be dealt with, immediately, hence the preparedness of the troops.

She could see the force field flicker erratically as it moved.

"Take it a little slower," she instructed.

"Can't," replied O'Connor.

With a whoosh, the force field was patterning out and then—*snap!*—was in place.

Leaving behind a scattered handful of aliens, in various states of disrepair and shock.

"Kill 'em," said Kozlowski.

The troops moved forward, bullets and plasma leaping out to smack into the survivors. It was all over in a matter of moments, bug pieces scattered to the winds of destruction.

And the force fields were buzzing away, the tunnel within easy striking distance.

"Yes!" Private Ellis's fist smote the air.

Cheers broke out among them all as they broke ranks and several broke out and headed deeper into the newly taken territory.

"Wait a minute, you assholes!" screeched Kozlowski. "I didn't order you . . ."

The force field wavered.

The troops all stopped in their tracks.

Kozlowski could *feel* something wrong before she saw anything.

But when she saw it, what was wrong was pretty obvious.

The newly planted harpoon was starting to list.

"What the hell—"

"Shit, what's going on—?"

"Oh, my God! We couldn't see it when it struck . . ."

"The thing landed on a couple of intact bugs."

That was the only explanation, and the veracity of it, and its implications swept through Kozlowski like electricity.

"Fall *back*!" she cried.

The alien acid must be eating through the base . . .

The upright harpoon shifted more, and the force field flickered again.

Then the thing toppled, its extended antenna breaking up.

The southern force field went down.

For a terrible moment she felt like an EVA astronaut with her suit ripped off.

"Get back to the original lines!" she screamed.

At first the surrounding bugs didn't seem to notice. But then, with the damnable speed of their breed, they perceived that the strange almost-invisible wall that had kept them from new prey had evaporated.

A few tentatively began to straggle toward the troops.

The soldiers who had gone the farthest out turned to run back. The aliens coming through seemed to sense their fear. They loped forward in the attack.

"Cover them!" screamed Kozlowski. She fired a volley as close to the troops as she dared, catching a couple of the bugs in their thoraxes, stopping them cold.

But others took their places.

"Okay!" she said after chinning her com. "They're past the original wall. Get that back up."

"Trying," said O'Connor. "Something's short-circuited!"

"*Do* it, dammit!"

"Argento!" said O'Connor. "Get that other harpoon off. That will do the trick."

By this time, Kozlowski had her hands too full to make commands, let alone comments.

The bugs were starting to come in.

Not the whole horde, thank God, or they'd be as good as dead.

She started blasting, just hoping her people had the sense to come in out of the storm.

"Shit!" said Daniel Grant. He pounded his hand hard against a bulkhead. "Shit shit *shit*!"

"Steady, Mr. Grant," said Dr. Begalli. "I'm sure they've got alternative plans."

O'Connor was leaning forward, stabbing at the controls. "Goddammit, Argento. Fire the thing! Manually!"

A voice crackled over the radio. "Can't. Can't find an opening. The things are swarming back into the crater."

"Then *make* an opening!" said O'Connor. "That's what you've got the starboard guns for. Blow 'em off!"

Grant watched disbelievingly.

Without a hitch.

Falling apart. Right before his eyes. If those troopers came out of this one without a casualty, it would be a miracle.

The point man—the one the farthest out—had to turn and blast with his weapons.

Grant watched with helpless horror as a bug scuttled up the backs of two of its fellows and leapt high into the air, landing directly on the man's back.

The soldier fought.

Grant had never seen such a fight.

Even though suddenly the aliens were all around him, like ants around a lump of sugar, they quaked and blew apart from the plasma blaster.

Then the havoc there stilled, and Grant could see the things scrabbling away, carrying bloody bits of suit, and pieces of the soldier, like trophies.

He had to turn away.

Without a hitch.

He'd never before seen his optimism turn to sewage, right before his eyes. His stomach turned, and he felt as though he was going to throw up. He contained himself, though. He reached down deep for strength, found it.

"Hell with the perimeter. Just have him blast those things! Cover the retreat!"

"I'm sure Argento is doing what he can."

"Look, can you get at least a *partial* up. Use what you got, man! Give them some time!"

He'd come light-years with these people, eaten with them, come to respect them in an odd but compelling way. And now they were being torn apart before his eyes.

O'Connor nodded. "I can try, sir. I can try."

Sergeant Argento cursed.

How the hell was he going to kill all these bugs alone? Should he start blasting, like O'Connor seemed to want—or should he clear out a crater and send off a harpoon?

He decided to do both. He blasted away with all the guns, making sure he didn't hit any of the troops. The shells streaked out, scattering whole swaths of bugs, and making craters.

Not exactly as far as they would like, not as close to the entrance of the hive as they needed—

But it would have to do.

He sent off another volley.

Excellent! It was giving the troops a fighting chance.

He swiveled the guns slightly to the right, concentrated on aiming—

And then heard the hissing.

Damn!

He reached down for his hand weapon and spun

around, but it was too late. The bug jumped down from the hull of the *Anteater* like a spider pouncing on its prey.

Its secondary set of jaws rammed through Argento's neck, speckling his guns with rich arterial blood.

They were moving back.

She'd watched Rodriguez go down. Go down bravely and well, taking a lot of bugs with him and maybe giving them a second or two extra to retreat. No time to grieve now, Kozlowski knew.

It was time to fight.

And she'd never fought quite like this before in her life.

Her rifle was discharging so quickly she could feel the heat come off the thing even through the gloves of her suit. With skill and precision she didn't know she had, she slammed away at the monsters, blowing them apart as fast as they came at her.

The thing was, she didn't have to think about what she was doing, it was all coming automatically. Because of these suits, the acid-splatter factor was not significant. She didn't have to aim at the knees, and then finish with their heads. She could just keep the rifle level and rip off fire at precisely the moment her instincts and skill dictated.

All the rest of the soldiers seemed to be doing equally well. The aliens were going down in huge numbers. The problem was that their numbers kept on getting replenished.

Sensing something on her peripheral vision, she wheeled around and found one of the bugs almost on top of her, its gooey saliva dripping as though in preparation for a feast.

She fed it a blast of plasma.

The thing's head lifted up off its neck in the gout of fire and flipped back like some obscene rocket aborting in its takeoff. She ripped off another round of fire to give herself some breathing room, and then took stock of the situation.

They'd all made it back to within the original perimeter . . . all but one.

Private Jastrow was just outside the area, his rifle blasting away.

"Jastrow!" she said. "Step back, dammit! Step back so we can put the field on!"

The man's radio apparently was not working. He did not respond. He just kept firing away at the things.

She was going to have to go out there and *drag* him back in, dammit! She started wading through the pile-up of dead bugs, firing away, then stopped dead as she looked back in the direction she was going.

The bugs covered Jastrow.

One was blasted away, but another took its place.

The radio screeched. "Ellis! Ellis, I need some backup! Ellis!" There was a muffled scream, signaling the end of a jazzman's military career.

"Argento! Start pounding the perimeter wall!" Kozlowski radioed.

No response.

What had happened to the guns, dammit! What was going on!

"Argento! Push them back with the guns!"

Another voice on the radio: "Argento's down, Colonel. There's a bug up there!"

Shit. Only one recourse now.

"O'Connor! Reactivate the southern wall! ASAP!"

Another bug charged her, dripping with human blood.

For some reason, Daniel Grant could not take his eyes off the gory demise of Private Jastrow.

He was stricken by grief, an unfamiliar emotion. He'd actually liked Jastrow, he suddenly realized. He hadn't realized before that he could *like* anybody. That concept just didn't seem appropriate to the kind of businessman he was.

He felt helpless. If only he could do something!

Then he heard Colonel Kozlowski's command come in.

At least she was still alive.

"Will do, Colonel," said O'Connor. "I've got the thing rerouted, and I think it's possible."

No more from the colonel. Grant watched as she swiveled and her plasma rifle shredded an approaching alien.

O'Connor leaned forward, hand outstretched toward the switch that would effect the renewal of the force field.

Dr. Begalli reached forward and stopped him. "Wait!" he said.

"Wait my ass! What's going on?" said Grant. "More and more of those things are starting to notice the breech. You've got to close it up. Lives are being lost down there!"

O'Connor reached for the switch again.

Begalli said, "No!"

Grant stood up and pulled Begalli back. "What are you trying to do, Doctor?"

But O'Connor paused as well. "He's right!"

"Right? What are you talking about?"

"Marines!" said O'Connor through his headset. "Get someone up on those guns!"

"What are you doing?" demanded Grant.

"Dr. Begalli's right, Mr. Grant. There are too many of those bastards down there. Only thing that's going to kick them out is that gun array. First off, there's going to have to be someplace to go to. Second place, using those guns with the force field up full is damned dangerous to the lander. *That*'s what Dr. Begalli means."

Begalli looked furtive about the whole thing. "Uhm . . . Yes, of course. That's what I mean."

"Does the colonel know that?"

"Yes, sir," said O'Connor. "They *all* know that."

When she killed the alien that almost got her, Kozlowski didn't have time to enjoy its death throes.

"Get that bug off those guns! Get 'em going again, dammit, or we're *cooked*," she said, surveying the situation. "Private Mahone! You're the closest. *Do* it, dammit!"

"But, sir—"

Mahone was on one knee, spraying charging bugs, keeping them at bay.

"We'll keep them at bay. Do it—"

A pause . . . and then Private Mahone was up. She sidled on, and Kozlowski got a look at her face through the mottled faceplate. She looked uncertain and scared.

"Mahone. That xeno squatting up there by the guns. Looks an awful lot like that old boyfriend of yours, doesn't he?"

"Yes, sir. He kinda does."

Immediately the private began to hustle. She moved up the steps on the side of the lander. The alien hunkered over the remains of Argento. It hissed at her, wobbling like a spider guarding its prey.

"Don't let it bleed on the guns, Private."

Two steps forward.

The private dropped to the steps, avoiding a lunge from the alien. Brought her plasma rifle up at just the right angle.

Fired.

The force of the fiery discharge impacted on the thing's torso, pushing it over the edge even as the blast cindered it. The thing wilted to the ground and dropped, a flaming husk, not even giving a good heartfelt spasm.

"Good show, Mahone. Now, you think you can fire those guns?"

"Yes, sir." The private clambered up the stairs and over the body of Argento. "They're all starting to look like somebody's boyfriend!"

She jumped into the seat.

Immediately the guns started to swivel, pointing downward at the bugs already inside the force field, and those still crawling through.

They spoke.

The shells came hot and heavy . . . and well placed.

"Okay, guys. Let's get out of the rain, before we get blown up as well," said the colonel, motioning an ally-alley-in-come-free.

The troops seemed all too happy to obey, retreating and contributing their own fire.

The result was a rout. Between their concentrated wall of blasts and the powerful guns above them, those aliens not smart enough to retreat through the opening of the force field were obliterated.

Soon, all that moved among their ruins was smoke.

"Okay, O'Connor. Give it a try now."

The force field shimmered back into place.

"Okay, people," Kozlowski said. "Fan out and finish off any still alive!" She sighed. "Then we can count our dead."

21

The task was grisly, and it took a while, but the remains of the dead were placed in body bags, zipped tight, and then lined outside the ramp to the *Anteater*. All it would take was the okay from Kozlowski and they would be carted back into the freezer inside the lander.

When the bags lay in a row beside the lander, Colonel Kozlowski called for a moment of silence for the dead. When that was over, she spoke.

"I'd better say something now, because I might be the next one to go into one of these things. These were good people. There will be plenty of time to honor them properly and grieve later. They gave their all to the mission. Others may not recognize their contribution later. But we always will. Argento, Jastrow, Rodriguez, McCoy, Lantern, Chang. Their shells may be zipped up, but their spirits are still with us, and will be as long as we do our jobs with dedication and sincerity."

She bowed her head and observed her own moment of silence. In her mind, she heard a sweet snatch of some tune that Jastrow had played once. It sounded like hope, even now.

"Okay," she said, keeping herself stern and businesslike.

The bags were put on a wagon and taken up the ramp.

A raucous squawking made Kozlowski jump.

She turned around, hand going to the sidearm she was wearing.

Sitting on the edge of a folding chair that had been used for lunch was Private Ellis, lips around the end of Jastrow's saxophone. He moved the mouthpiece. "Sorry, Colonel."

"That's all right, Private. I'm just a bit on edge."

"Think I can ever learn to play this thing?"

"Why would you want to?"

"Jastrow. He always wanted me to try. I always told him I had no musical ability and besides, there was spit all over it." He sighed. "That part doesn't seem that important anymore."

"Sorry about your friend."

"Yeah. I figure we've gotten about a thousand or so bugs for every man killed here."

"It's not worth it, is it?"

"No. It's not."

She felt someone looking at her. Turned.

Daniel Grant was walking down the ramp.

She was about to get on her soapbox and rant at him, but then she noticed his face. It was white. In his eyes were the beginnings of tears.

She turned away and let him come up to her.
Let him start the conversation, if he wanted to.

"I want you and your people to know how sorry
I am," he said finally, after a long silence. "I guess
when you see life turning into death so abruptly, it
puts thing in perspective."

"Some business we're in here, eh, Grant?" she
said.

"Some business." He nodded thoughtfully. "My
problems . . . they can't compare with this." He
sighed. "We can't quit now, though, can we?"

"No. My country sent me here to accomplish
something. It's my duty to do that. You'll get what
you came here to get, Grant."

"And maybe more than I bargained for."

"Definitely."

"Colonel. There's going to be a linkup with the
Razzia in ten minutes. We're going to confer on
the situation and decide a course of action. Naturally I want you to be there."

"Yes. I'll be right there."

She turned and continued to do what she could
in the time remaining to her to give her the confidence and grit that she herself felt rapidly escaping
from her.

It was a makeshift conference table at best, but it
would have to do.

"I've just finished a full transmission to Captain
Hastings of the events that have just occurred
here," said Corporal O'Connor. He swiveled and
turned a switch. "He's waiting to join the conference. Permission to let him in?"

Grant nodded.

"Permission granted," said Kozlowski. "We'll need all the input we can get."

Captain Hastings bid his regrets at the turn of events. His voice sounded even more subdued than usual.

"Now then," said Grant. "We've got a situation on our hands. I'd like to say, why don't we just give it another try with the perimeter extension harpoon. However, after what we've just been through, I don't think so."

"It's possible we're going to have to," said Kozlowski. "But that doesn't mean we can't explore other possibilities. Dr. Begalli ... you seem to be the resident expert on the present situation with the aliens. What's your prognosis?"

"Clearly our projections were quite accurate," said the man, after scratching his large nose. "There is a genetic offshoot of the aliens, and the originals are attempting to eradicate them. Only we never anticipated this kind of scale ... Or that it would hinder our actions to this degree."

"Not quite true," said Kozlowski. "We've got the technology. It's just not working as well as we would like."

Begalli's ferretlike eyes flicked back and forth over those assembled. "Despite our feelings of loss and frustration, I cannot forget just how correct my projections were about the recessive gene. Something that was quite unlikely. Naturally we're sorry for the loss ... But after years and years, my science seems to be correct." He tapped his finger emphatically. "What we all want is in that hive. It's the answer to our dreams ... Maybe, ultimately even to the whole alien conflict."

"Why would you say that?" said Henrikson.

"We came here to get the queen mother royal jelly and we've got to do that. Do you know how much we've been working with in these last two decades? About two hundred gallons' worth, that's all. Our tank here can go up to well over two thousand gallons, and I'm sure we can fill it. With that amount to work with, all kinds of possibilities will open up.

"We can learn something, I suppose, from this red and black alien business. Still it's all academic curiosity. There are no practical applications yet. With the jelly, those applications may be possible."

"Oh. Like what?"

"The key to the genetic control of the aliens! It could be in the queen down there and her royal jelly! Sorry, Mr. Grant, but there's a lot more at stake here than money for your company, and hyperspeed for the armed forces." He tapped the table emphatically. "Why do you think the red aliens are attempting genocide on the blacks?"

"Isn't it the same old story? They're different?"

Begalli shook his head. "You've got to have a certain amount of intelligence to be bigoted. The xenos aren't that smart. No. It's because on a very real level, the *existence* of difference threatens each other.

"Eradication is programmed into the species. I would daresay that in hives every once in a while red eggs are laid—and immediately destroyed by the queen or the queen's guards. When we removed the queen from the black hive and killed her guards, it probably allowed time for these freakish red eggs already laid to develop and grow . . . And then escape and build their own hive."

"Look, this is all very interesting," said Kozlowski. "But how is it going to get us past the *war* going on down there, and into the hive, where we can do our job? And get out with our butts intact, I might add!"

"Yes," said Grant ruminatively. "A definite priority."

"Let's look at it this way then," said Begalli. "What we have here is warfare on a grand scale. Each of these alien races would like to eradicate the other. Annihilate. This mission is deeply embedded in their chromosomal structure." He shrugged. "Now if we just tilt that warfare in the favor of the blacks, that would be to our definite advantage. We don't want mutant jelly. We want the black jelly, the stuff we know something about and can use."

Hastings's voice crackled over the radio. "I got lots of great weapons up here, folks. If you want, we can just nuke the red hive."

Begalli nodded. "Excellent! That might just work."

"How?" Grant asked.

Kozlowski nodded. "Well, it would kill off the red queen mother for one thing and with her any psychic control of her drones. Which would send the red army into disarray."

"More than that," said Begalli. "Without that control, instinctively the red army would retreat toward their hive. Equally instinctively the black army would pursue!"

Grant snapped his fingers. "Leaving the black hive wide open!"

"That would be the theory, yes . . . It's the best choice, in my opinion," said Begalli. "We'd still have to deal with the black guards, and they will be bigger and fiercer. But they would be limited in

number. What we're facing out there is a problem
of sheer oppressive volume."

Grant smacked the table. "Yes. We're going to
have to do it, I think! Opinion, Colonel?"

"Sure. Why not. At the very least we're going to
kill a lot of bugs!"

"Captain. How soon can you have those war-
heads ready?" said Grant.

"Couple of hours," came the voice.

"Excellent. We can accomplish this well before
nightfall," said Kozlowski. "Get started, Captain.
We can always postpone till morning if necessary."

"I don't think that will be necessary," said Hastings. "I'll get right to it."

Grant was nodding, his face intent. "One more
thing, Colonel. I'd like to come with you when you
go into that hive."

"What for?" said Kozlowski. "You're a civilian.
You're not trained for this kind of work."

"I feel responsible here. I feel a moral obligation.
You need extra people. I can aim a gun and shoot
it. I—"

"Okay," she said.

"I want—" He blinked. "What?"

"I said you can go. There's a spare suit about
your size down in the holding tank in the locker
room. We'll go over the situation here in a few
minutes, I'll brief you on a few things you'll have to
know . . . And then you can suit up."

Grant's mouth flapped for a moment like a fish
out of water.

"It'll be good to have you along, Grant!"

Henrikson and Begalli excused themselves to
start preparations for the next assault.

"All right, people," announced Kozlowski. "Now that we've got a plan, let's chew over some details."

She felt charged again.

Those bugs were going to pay.

Big time.

Kozlowski was letting him go along!

A few minutes after the hour-long meeting, Daniel Grant was making his way down to the locker room, brain buzzing with the "briefing" that he'd just received. He felt beat up with facts and instructions, as though somehow Kozlowski had put him through a brief but intense boot camp under the whip of Drill Instructor Koz herself. Not fun!

Not that he wasn't *sincere* about wanting to go along.

He just hadn't really expected for her to agree to his volunteering.

Well, nothing for it now, old man. You're in for the full nine yards now. Play it out, do your job, and this will turn out fine! Just fine!

He entered the familiar smell of the locker, particularly ripe now from the recent press of ripe bodies that had just passed through.

Where was it that Kozlowski had said the spare suit was? Oh, yes, over in the cabinet yonder.

No lock, no latch.

Sabotage was the last thing on Grant's mind, he was so preoccupied with the lessons he'd learned about alien killing.

He opened the door and saw the suit, and reached for it.

What he did not see was the alien egg pod sitting in the shadows.

22

The thing stood like an ob-scene, fleshy orchid bulb.

Grant smelled it before he saw it.

That now-familiar, intense acidic blast of stench.

As he reached for the suit, his foot stubbed against the growth. It gave like a stink cabbage.

He looked down.

At first, he didn't want to believe his eyes.

Then he saw the tangle of talons, wiggling at the opening of the bulb, like the beginnings of a sand crab, emerging from its shell.

He froze.

He'd seen alien larvae before, of course. He'd seen them prey on test animals plenty of times. Only they had been behind thick glass at the time . . . Now this one was mere inches from his face.

It hissed at him, and began to come out faster, bending the petals of its deadly flower as it came.

"Screeeee!"

It launched.

Directly for his face.

Sheer desperation somehow prized the freeze lock off his muscles. Off to his right was a hanging suit. He reached out, grabbed it, and pulled it between himself and the face-hugger.

It bounced off it and flopped onto the floor.

Grant had just enough time to let off a yelp and take a step away from the thing before it animated again, leaping up toward him as though its legs were spring-loaded. As though his face were metal and the thing were a magnet, it headed straight for his eyes.

He reached out and caught it.

The talonlike claws tore at his skin. The pain shot up his arm, causing him to throw the thing down. It hit the floor, but it had clearly discovered its mission. It jumped around and was about to leap back up at him, when a blur flashed off to the left and a suited foot kicked it square in its crabby ass.

The thing hit the wall like a hockey puck smacking the sidelines, sluiced along the floor.

A rifle went up, tracked, sighted.

Energy sizzled out.

The blast smacked it like the finger of God, smushing a demon. Some of its acid came out, bubbling a small hole in the floor . . . But most was consumed in the incendiary blast.

He stepped back, his legs hit a stool, he sat down hard.

"Thanks," he said.

"Just my job," the person said, with bite.

He looked over to his savior.

It was Colonel Kozlowski.

"Looks like one of your pets wandered off the beaten track," she said, already going for a bucket. She put it in a shower stall, started filling it with water. "I'm losing count of the screwups in your 'harmless' project, Grant."

Grant shook his head. "I don't understand. I only authorized *one* creature for incubation." He drew in a breath, savoring it. "Take a look in the armory closet there!"

"In a moment."

She took the bucket and sluiced the water in the small crater. Hissing steam rose up, and that was that.

"The closet."

Grant nodded. "That's where the thing came from."

She looked and grunted. "Yep. You got yourself a pod here, Grant."

"I was the only one not armored, so it's obvious this thing was planted to get me when I came back here." He smacked a fist into a palm. "It's got to be Begalli. He must still be working for those scumbags at MedTech. I want you to put that bastard under arrest—hang him . . . keelhaul him . . . something."

"Yo! Rein yourself in, Grant. Then come here and take a look at this."

Grant walked over reluctantly. He looked in the closet. Kozlowski was pulling something off the side of the pod.

She pulled it into view.

"You know what this is, right?"

In her hand she held some kind of metal clamp, attached to a bottle-shaped thing.

"Of course," said Grant. "It's a timer clamp. It's used to hold the lips of an egg shut to ensure the creature can't escape during transportation."

"And it automatically falls off when the timer expires," she continued for him. "The planter is nowhere near the eggs when it activates. Looks like it's got a motion sensor on it, too. Anyone could have walked into this trap."

"So."

"So anyone could have planted this egg." She stood up. "Even me."

"This is just a regular chest-burster. I did not authorize this to be shipped out. Just that larvae queen." He shook his head. "I still don't feel good about that guy Begalli. He's been acting strangely."

Kozlowski sighed. "He seems clean to me. Anyway, he's the only alien expert in the landing party, and he's been giving us *good* information, by my lights."

"I don't know."

"Maybe you don't know this, but all radio signals are scrambled by the content of the shell in those hives. Once inside, we'll have no communication with the lander. We're going to need 'that bastard' in there more than any other crew member. Without him, this operation is dead in the water. You still want me to bust him?"

Grant thought about this.

He didn't like it, not at all. MedTech could very well be behind this whole sabotage business, and most certainly Begalli had been purchased from MedTech.

Had they purchased him back?

Was Foxnall back on Earth rubbing his hands with glee, waiting for the news of the demise of this mission, the death of Grant . . . Or would they just act when the mission got back? How could they possibly hope to pull off something like that?

At the same time, he well knew that Kozlowski was right.

Begalli knew his stuff, and they needed someone with knowledge of the inner workings of the alien queen's chambers, and what any change in the norm might mean.

"No. I guess you're right."

"Good. I'm glad we're agreed on that." She started out of the room. "I'm going to get the team ready for our push. Take a break, have a cup of tea—but if you're coming with us, I want to see you out there in an hour. *Capische*?"

"Yes. And Colonel Kozlowski . . . Alex." He tipped an imaginary hat. "Again, thanks."

She stopped and turned around. "Mr. Grant . . . Daniel . . ."

"Yes?"

"This isn't exactly the kind of mission you had in mind, is it? I know your type. The enduring optimist under fire. The sturdy campaigner who uses ignorance as a positive. Overconfidence, Grant. That's what I think it's called."

"Sounds like a defect, Kozlowski. Why are you letting it into that hive?"

"Because it's also called 'spirit,' Danny boy. It's infectious and it might just put us over the top here in a very ticklish situation." She winked at him. "Besides, it turns me on like hell, and your goddamned Fire has got absolutely nothing on good old-fashioned hormones to get me in the mood for action."

Grant found a grin coming to his face. "You going to save some of those hormones for me, Alex?"

"Sure, Danny. Next time I get PMS."

She turned and strutted away.

Grant shook his head.

What a woman. He wasn't sure if he could handle her.

But he sure would like to try.

23

The tactical nuclear weapon struck the red alien hive dead on.

Kozlowski watched the event inside the lander on the screen from the *Razzia*'s perspective. These tactical strikes had an extremely limited radius of effect, with minimal fallout and radiation, but nonetheless they had carefully ascertained the weather conditions beforehand. Everything had been perfect for the strike. The execution had been precise and professional.

"Good shooting!" she told Hastings.

Then she went outside where the troops were waiting for her.

They'd heard the news on their radios and were cheering.

"Just the start, people," she said as she strode into their midst. "The uphill road is ahead." She'd already noticed that the ranks of the battling aliens had thinned out somewhat. "What's going on out there?"

"Just seconds after detonation the reds just kind of stopped whatever they were doing and started spasming. Lots got killed, I think, and lots more are starting to take off," reported Mahone.

"Whatever psychic link they had with their queen mother must have been broken when the bitch got wasted," said Henrikson, nodding.

Kozlowski visualized that moment of intense destruction, the impact as that multimegaton nuke tore through the chambers of the reds, decimating all in it, shrieking caroming nuclear wind.

Had queenie gotten off one final scream of agony, one bitter nasty farewell to her evil crew?

Kozlowski hoped so. She hoped that bitch knew who'd been responsible. She was only sorry the thing didn't have a little picture of her to take down to bug hell with her.

Kozlowski turned to where Grant stood, looking uncomfortable and anxious in his suit. Doubtless, he was regretting his volunteering for the move into the hive. He'd be okay, though. He had the stuff.

"There it is!" said Henrikson, putting down the pair of binoculars and pointing. "You don't need glasses to see that baby."

Sure enough, off to the east, she could see the telltale mushroom cloud, rising up past the horizon of this flat, bleak landscape.

Black and poisonous.

"They're taking off in droves!" someone shouted.

Kozlowski swiveled. Sure enough, the reds

seemed totally disinterested in the conflict now. They were taking off in waves. Racing away back toward their blasted hive.

Why? Instinct? Whatever the reason, it wouldn't do them much good. Still, Kozlowski was pleased. They wouldn't be hanging around here.

The blacks hung back for a moment, perplexed.

Then, as though the thunderbolt of realization had hit them, they started after the enemy who had attempted to destroy them.

Totally ignoring the interlopers behind the shielded vessel from another planet.

"Yes!" said Kozlowski, stamping the ground with unalloyed glee.

Just as planned.

"It worked," she said. "The reds are retreating to the other hive. This one should be clear in a few minutes."

Grant was fidgeting. He clearly wanted this all to be over. "Then let's get moving! Who's going in?"

"Everyone but the technical crew," said Kozlowski. "And Ellis."

"Makes sense," said Grant. "He's taking Jastrow's death pretty hard."

"Yeah," said Mahone. "They grew up together, joined the Corps together, and fought for years in the same unit."

"He's a good marine," said Kozlowski. "He'll be okay in a few days. But I'd rather not have him in close combat right now. Besides, someone has to man the guns." She walked over to the bank of guns poking out the side of the lander. "How are you doing up there, Private?"

"All set, Colonel."

Luckily they'd trained all the troops to use these things.

"Right. I'm sure you'll do just fine." She turned back and walked toward Grant. "How about you? You sure you want to do this."

"No. But I'm *going* to."

"Good. It'll be good to have you along.

"All right then, helmets on." She fitted her own on above her suit, clicked in the radio, waited for the rest of the troops to check in. When they did, when it was all finished, she chinned her radio again. "Okay, O'Connor." The troops lifted their guns, released the safeties. "Drop the southern border."

They moved out.

There were still a few red aliens lingering about, and these charged in when they got a whiff of the intruders.

But this was the kind of operation that the marines had expected, that they had trained for. The blasts of their rifles easily dealt with the charging aliens. It was like a shooting gallery.

Meanwhile, Ellis and O'Connor were doing damned fine work with the PEHs. They spiked a few home to either side of the hive's opening and moments later the marines had a nice tunnel of force field to make their way through, cleaning up the couple of xenos left over and not having to worry about the ones who'd been excluded from the party.

Kozlowski turned to see how Grant was doing. She'd put him in the back, to guard the rear so he wouldn't shoot any of the troops.

He was doing a damned good job of blasting apart the fallen aliens, making sure they stayed down.

When they reached the opening of the hive, Kozlowski put a hand up, halting the party.

"What's the reading say, O'Connor?" she asked through the radio.

"Sensors show they're still on the run. No party's coming back."

"Good news." She turned to the group. "I don't know how long we've got in there before the three bears come home . . . but I do know we're going to go in there and get us some porridge."

Laughter. Cheers.

"However, let's be quick about it, okay? No sight-seeing, no rubbernecking. We picked up enough DNA from dead reds already, so we don't have to pack anything in ice. Moreover, we don't have to take 'em back alive. Now as we discussed before, what we're going to be up against in there are some pretty nasty bugs, bigger and smarter. Take this into account."

"Kozlowski!"

She turned and found herself helmet to red face with Grant. He'd undone his top and was holding it at his side, getting himself a breath of fresh air. "Well, Colonel!" His eyes were gleaming with excitement. He looked like a Boy Scout who'd just fired his first BB gun. "Were my combat skills satisfactory?"

Kozlowski granted him a patronizing scowl. "Pat yourself on the back later, Grant. And put that damn helmet back on!"

She got back on the radio.

"O'Connor. Send up the cargo drone."

That was what they were going to be using to carry the royal jelly back up with.

"When it gets up here, we'll drop the southern border and head out. We all ready?"

She surveyed the covered faces, knowing already they were about as ready as they were ever going to be.

"This is the last radio contact till we get back out," said Kozlowski. "Open her up, O'Connor. Over and out."

The skein of force frizzled off.

Perfect.

O'Connor was getting really good in his manipulations. The tunnel of the force field that led from the rounded entrance of the hive back to the bubble around the *Razzia* was still intact.

There weren't too many of the blacks left out there, but they couldn't get in.

Unless, of course, there were other entrances . . .

Likely, but the things didn't seem particularly interested. They seemed more interested in the cargo drone that had crawled up the slight incline. It was an automatically controlled vehicle with eight thick wheels. Omni-terrain. One of the marines took over the controls when it reached them.

They started down.

The tunnels were recognizably of alien origin. Kozlowski had seen plenty of hive tunnels, that was for certain. Nonetheless, these were a little larger than usual, with a different consistency of building material.

"I've never seen an alien nest so empty before," said one of the soldiers.

"I have," said Kozlowski grimly. "And it was a trap."

The nest on Hollywood and Vine.

It was flashing back on her.

The walls, like inside a tumorous colon . . .

The prickly fear, the sick-in-the-stomach . . .

Having people with her she respected, cared for . . . smack dab in the vat of trouble and fear . . . Along with someone special, for whom she feared the most.

She remembered her feelings for Michaels. It welled up inside of her, and she had to push it back down, along with her fear.

This time would be different, she told herself.

She shut out the memory and went into her automatic "competent" mode.

Nonetheless, she could feel the memories crowding in on her.

About forty meters down it became apparent that things were different in other ways as well.

There was a convergence of tunnels.

Three separate ways to go.

"Okay, Dr. Begalli. Get your butt and that machine up front."

Dr. Begalli shuttled forward. In his hand he held a device with a pair of green sensor extensions. A pheromone detector. Begalli tapped a few buttons and pointed the device in each of the directions in turn, scrutinizing the results carefully.

"Well, Doctor," said Kozlowski. "Which way to the buried treasure?"

The helmeted head bobbed eagerly. "Well, the

pheromone readings seem to jibe with what I expected." He pointed to the left. "Let's try that way."

They started down the corridor.

"This is why we need Begalli," she told Grant. "The tunnels of this hive are much more mazelike than any I've encountered on Earth. Without him, it might take a *long* time to find the queen mother."

Grant shook his head. "If you say so, Colonel. But I'm still keeping my eye on him."

"That's it, Grant. I've found the perfect job for you. Begalli watch. Sounds wonderfully exotic," she said.

"Sure. That's what I'll do." Grant's helmet turreted back and forth. "Where *is* the little creep, anyway?"

"You're not doing your job . . . But don't worry, there's a curve just up ahead. He just went around that. We've just lost sight—"

"Colonel," said Private Mahone. "The motion detectors show significant and sudden activity up ahead."

"Begalli!" Kozlowski yelled. "Get your ass *back* here!"

Just then, the suited Dr. Begalli returned around the bend where he'd disappeared.

Kozlowski could hear him screaming without benefit of the radio.

24

She didn't know the little guy could move that fast—let alone that fast with the hindering weight of a full battle suit on.

"Yaaaaaaaaaaaa!" screamed Dr. Begalli as he ran for all he was worth around the corner. He ran past them, toward the cover of the cargo drone carrier.

"Begalli!" said Grant. "What the hell is it?"

Kozlowski didn't have to ask.

She could pretty much guess.

"Arms!" she yelled.

She needn't have bothered. The others were ready, angling their weapons down.

However, ready as they were, all the preparations were pretty much in vain.

The first of the queen's guard came around the corner and Kozlowski had to stop herself from gasping.

It was big and it was fast, and it was mean.

The blasts caught it full in the chest, and it kept on coming for what seemed like a full second before it was lifted up and slammed against the wall. It tried to scrabble back up and tackle them again, before a final plasma stream knocked its head apart.

"There's more," yelled the point man. "There's—"

The next one was even bigger, and even faster. Before they could swing their weapons away from the first and onto the new arrival, it was on the first soldier.

Horrible claws tore the man's chest apart.

"Jesus!" cried Private Mahone as she was sprayed with blood. She swung her gun around and let off a spurt of plasma, but missed. The beast was incredibly fast. It finished one more ripping shake of the point man and then leapt toward the rest.

Lesser soldiers might have lost it right then, so horrific was the sight. But they kept their cool, aimed their weapons, and let the thing have it.

Two more "guards" attacked.

Another soldier was torn apart before the guards were subdued, blasted to pieces.

In all her time fighting inside hives, Kozlowski had never seen such an intense battle conflagration. The queen's guards were incredibly quick and agile, almost imbued, it seemed, with superpowers. Fortunately, this crew was also the best she'd worked with, and they'd half expected something like this.

Within violent minutes, four aliens and two humans lay smoking and quite dead upon the ground.

"God," was all that Private Mahone could say, lying slumped against the wall, gasping for air and still grasping her weapon, ready if another bug should care to call.

"No, I don't think God's around here," said Henrikson. "This is more like the Other Place."

For her own part, Kozlowski was just numb.

"Okay, we'll pick the bodies up on the way back. Take a quick moment for a breather, because that's all the time we've got if any of us wants to get out of here."

Two more dead. She couldn't believe it, even when she looked down at their twisted and torn remains. This wasn't worth it. But she had her orders, and she had her duty, and she knew nothing more than that she had to complete this mission, or their lives and the lives lost earlier and the months spent on this project would have been for naught.

A suited figure peeked around the corner of the cargo drone. "Is . . . is everyone all right?"

Dr. Begalli. Apparently, his head had been well stuffed in the sand.

Daniel Grant, who had been leaning on the side wall, exhausted, pushed himself off and walked over to the man. "No. Two more dead. You couldn't have warned us this would happen?"

"We knew about the guards. What we didn't know was that they'd come charging up at us like that," said Kozlowski. She got her second wind, went over to have a look at the only xeno head that had survived the mauling. "Ever see anything quite like this, Doctor?"

Begalli gave the angry and suspicious Grant a

wide berth in coming around to look. "Oh, heaven, what a mess—No, Colonel, I had no idea . . . Loathsome beasts. I don't recall the report from the last visit here giving them full justice. We knew they were bigger, but not this nasty. This is fascinating." He looked up from the dead beast. He took a small piece of blasted "skin" in a bottle. "I'll have to do a genetic workup when I get back. The queen mother may equip her guards to continue to evolve." He shook his head, mystified. "Or could the things have *devolved* rather than evolved. What a fascinating mystery! So much is down here!"

"Let's get a roll on."

"Yeah, Begalli. And you go first," said Grant. "Let's see a little courage for a change."

Begalli nodded, picked up his pheromone meter, and they were off again toward the depths of the alien hive.

"The queen's chambers should be down there," said Begalli.

The electric torches stabbed down into the darkness—but beyond their reach, Kozlowski saw the beginnings of what appeared to be some kind of bioluminescence.

"Okay," she said. "This place has had a few surprises that we weren't prepared for. There still might be more. Dr. Begalli, Corporal Henrikson, Daniel Grant, and myself will head on down to the chamber. Dicer, Clapton, and Mahone, stay here and guard our backs. I don't expect the radios to work, so let's just say if we're not back in an hour, get back to the lander and get out of here."

Private Dicer was a skinny guy with big eyes that

seemed about to pop out of his head. He'd put on an excellent display of bug killing, but clearly the pressure was getting to him. Sweat pasted his long stringy hair down over his forehead. Private Clapton was a little more poised. He was a thickset easy-come, easy-go sort with a ready humor that he'd somehow lost now. Private Mahone looked as though she simply could not even believe she was here. But they were all good soldiers. They'd been good soldiers up above and they'd be good soldiers down here.

"Yes, sir," they chorused.

Kozlowski took the controls of the drone from a trooper and motioned the party onward.

It took another ten minutes to get down to a place where the lamps were necessary to see. Still, Kozlowski kept the side lights of her suit on, just in case things suddenly went dark.

The tunnel went around a bend.

Suddenly opened up.

It was the biggest chamber that Kozlowski had ever seen.

Eerily lit by the bioluminescence was the scene that the scientists had more or less predicted.

The four huge pods, radiating around a larger pod, above which the queen towered, a true giant, like a devil tilted atop her evil throne.

Only the sketchy holograms could never have hinted at the textures or the colors, the bizarre organic geometry here that threatened to drive a mind mad if concentrated on too closely.

The queen's pod glistened and oozed with what Kozlowski knew to be royal jelly.

The stuff that would make Grant an incredibly

rich man, that would give the armed forces what they wanted, that would spell a success to this bloody campaign.

"Incredible," said Grant.

However, his eyes did not glow with avarice.

"Amazing," said Kozlowski. "We've hit the motherlode of royal jelly here." She looked at Grant. "You're going to get your tank filled, I think."

She patted the metal, and it echoed hollowly.

"Little problem," said Grant. "What about queeny?"

The gigantic creature perched atop the center mound did not even seem to notice they were even there. Its attention seemed focused off into space, as though it were meditating.

"I'm sure it's psychically directing the rout of the reds," said Begalli. "Must be. It's so absorbed, it didn't even notice the death of its guards." He quickly scanned the room again. "Four pods. Four guards. Excellent correspondence. Looks like we've got this place all to ourselves. All we have to do is to deal with the queenie, and she's just a sitting duck!" He smiled broadly, skipping a little closer to the gleaming, gooey treasure hoard. "Looks delicious, doesn't it? Ah, what wonders that stuff must hold. I can't wait . . ." He cut himself off suddenly and looked furtive.

"Can't wait?" said Grant. "This is *my* expedition. What *exactly* can't you wait for?"

"Uhhmmm. Nothing. Nothing, sir . . ." He drifted closer to the pod. "Look at it all. I never thought I'd see this much up close. God, it's beautiful."

The queen mother was as still as a statue. As still as death.

Beautiful? Was fear beautiful? Dread? Terror? All the primitive juices battled now at Alex Kozlowski's barrier.

Michaels's beautiful head boiling apart with acid.

His scream.

Her guilt.

She wanted to turn and run from this place. It was worse than she had ever imagined it. The dead body of her lover seemed superimposed over everything.

She calmed herself. She'd known that she would never get the trauma of that dreadful Hollywood day off her mind, that she'd have to live it all over again in her head.

She just never realized she'd have to live it over again in reality.

And this time it could be *her* skin bubbling off, to expose the grinning skull beneath.

"Beautiful?" said Grant. "I'm not so sure anymore. People have *died* for this stuff. I feel . . . responsible."

"No time for self-remonstration," said Kozlowski. "Glad to hear you've got a conscience, but we really should finish this mission up. Begalli, get away from there. We can't take any chances. I want that thing up there dead, and I'm going to do it myself, right—"

Grant, though, was on a jag. Apparently the deaths of the other three soldiers, so close, had really shaken him up.

"I don't know," said Grant. "I just don't know."

"Mr. Grant! You started this whole thing rolling."

"Yeah, and I'm going to have to live with it for the rest of my life, too. I'm paying for my ignorance. But you, Begalli—" He brought his gun up. "You've been sabotaging this mission from day one, haven't you?"

"What?" said Begalli, turning back to him.

"Come off it! I've been watching you, Begalli, and I know damn well you're up to something," said Grant. "You're still working for MedTech, aren't you?"

"Okay, sure . . . I have been up to something." He took a breath. "I'm doing research, independent of Neo-Pharm. I'd planned to publish articles on my findings."

"Articles?"

"A new kind of alien. I'd go down in history. I'd be famous . . . forever!"

"Articles?" repeated Grant.

"I've got more than enough money, Grant. And I always hated MedTech—what I want is to be acknowledged for my scientific efforts. *That's* why I wanted to come down here. Maybe I'll even write a book . . . Yes, a bestseller!"

"You heard it, Grant," said Kozlowski. "The only thing he's guilty of is scientific greed. Now back off . . ."

"So how do you know he isn't lying . . . ?" Grant started to say, before a sudden hissing shriek froze his sentence.

Without warning, the queen mother jumped.

It sailed through the air, and it landed just short of Dr. Begalli. Stunned and disbelieving, Begalli tried to turn.

A long set of secondary jaws streaked out from the alien's mouth, slicing and hammering into the back of the scientist's head, boring through and pushing his eyes out of their sockets like red Jell-O being squeezed through cookie cutters.

Kozlowski was stunned. The thing wasn't supposed to be able to do that. Wasn't its ovipositor fastened to the pod? But then wasn't that just something else they didn't know about these aliens?

Only a flicker of a second of thought, though. Already her rifle was going up, aiming, squeezing off a round.

Henrikson fired at the exact same moment.

Their fire converged upon the exact same spot on the queen. It hissed and wailed, a hole blown in its thorax. Its blood rained down upon Begalli's head and boiled his face away. The alien started toward them, forelimbs clutching and seeking.

Kozlowski lifted her rifle and aimed at its head.

It still came forward.

Henrikson's blasts joined hers, and the thing's head burst asunder like a ripe melon.

They backpedaled to avoid the spurting acid, and the great queen mother writhed and spasmed in its death throes.

Kozlowski stepped forward, looking down at the massive thing.

Fortunately it had come far enough that it hadn't spoiled its own jelly.

"Right," she said. "Too bad about Begalli. Let's get this tank loaded out of here, quick."

She jumped over to the vehicle and pulled out

the vacuum tap. This bit was going to be the easy part.

Only when the cargo drone's tank was topped off, did Kozlowski pull the tap out of the membrane. There was lots more jelly, but they just couldn't take it.

"I hope this will be enough," she said sardonically.

"Yes," said Grant. "Yes. It will have to do, I suppose."

"Something wrong, Grant?"

"I think you know what's troubling me." The man sighed deeply. "Besides, I don't get it. Only a few people knew about the alien incubation project. If Begalli didn't sabotage it, who did?"

Casually, Alex Kozlowski grabbed ahold of her rifle. She'd been thinking about that very same thing.

And she didn't care for what was floating up on her mental screen.

She was about to turn when Henrikson's voice sounded behind them.

"Thank you, folks. That looks just fine," he said. "Please drop your weapons. This close, one blast of this rifle can deal with you both."

25

"**H**enrikson?" said Grant. He knelt and put his rifle down behind him. "You?"

"That's right, Grant. MedTech pays a lot better than the marines. Damned interesting ride, too. Been enjoying myself." He motioned with the tip of his rifle. "Come on, Colonel—sir. Get that pretty finger off the trigger and set your gun down."

She obeyed. "You're going to kill us and leave us here, aren't you?"

"Absolutely. And no one will be the wiser. And by the time we get back to Earth, a goodly part of this royal jelly will be siphoned off—and some of the DNA samples will be gone as well. Just in case . . . I daresay, once it's been announced you've been killed in action, your creaky empire will be up for grabs. And the Neo-Pharm scientists will pretty much disperse . . . The best ones bought up by MedTech."

"I checked your credentials, dammit. They were spotless!" said Kozlowski. She knew there was somebody giving them trouble, but she'd always felt that she could contain any problems. She thought she'd read this guy, that he was straight as an arrow. He'd given absolutely no previous sign of disloyalty.

"Hey! You've got an eminently corruptible bunch you're working for, Kozlowski." The man was grinning maliciously now, savoring his victory.

"What! Are you really a synth, Henrikson?" said Grant, clearly just as shocked as Kozlowski at this turn of events. And no wonder. Henrikson had been Grant's main man, his apple polisher. He'd brought him down to show him the alien incubation. There'd been a trustworthiness about the guy. A big brotherness.

Why hadn't they seen *through* him, dammit, she thought.

"C'mon. I'm no synth! If I were a synth, I could have taken those Xeno-Zips with absolutely no effect!" He nodded over to the royal jelly. "I avoid the crap."

"But . . . but I *trusted* you." said Grant. "I've got such a good nose for this kind of thing."

The grin got broader. "There's where MedTech has got your company beat all to hell, Grant. Every day I douse myself in a special pheromone, designed specifically for leader types to sniff. Makes you trust me, gives type A's like you confidence in big guys like me. That's why the other grunts didn't care for me . . . they weren't the kind that like this pheromone. You guys bought it!"

"But you've risked your life with all the rest of us . . . You've been a damned good soldier!" said Grant.

"Yes, I have, and I've had a good time, too, folks, let me tell you. I am a soldier. A soldier of fortune. I raid alien nests with buddies for money. I'm an independent and damned good at it. Only there's more money in this for me than I'd ever dreamed of—and I get to see the stars, too." He shrugged. "Don't look for anything deeper here. That's all there is."

"But the death of the alien baby . . . that pod . . . the sabotage . . . it just doesn't add up."

"Sure it does, Grant. I caused confusion. I hurt the program, and I pretty much framed poor old Begalli. Fact, when I get back with this liquid gold here, that's what I think I'm going to tell them. Yeah. 'It was Begalli, guys. He's dead now, though, along with poor old Grant and Kozlowski. Boo hoo. Mission complete. Now let's get the hell out of here.' You see. Piece of cake."

He started laughing.

Unless she acted, they'd be dead within seconds.

However, since they'd all taken off their helmets, there might be a shred of hope here.

Without a further thought, Kozlowski dived for her rifle. She scooped it up, put her finger under the trigger.

And was blasted by the quadruple barrels of Henrikson's weapon.

Grant watched in horror as the blast hit Kozlowski's left thigh. She spun around and fell hard onto the ground.

The next thing Grant knew, he was on top of Henrikson. The man had been swerving his rifle for the coup de grace—but Grant's fist sailed into the man's bare face with a solid impact before he could pull the trigger again.

Where that had come from, Grant didn't know. But it felt so good that he found himself doing it again.

The attack surprised Henrikson so much he clearly wasn't sure what to do. To defend himself at close quarters he'd have to drop the rifle. But Kozlowski wasn't dead yet, and to give up the weapon meant certain defeat. He lifted his other arm—but Grant countered.

And nailed him with another punch.

Thank God he'd worked out regularly! He hadn't done it for fights. He'd done it for his self-confidence and for the ladies. But his reflexes were good, and it had all paid off.

The blows had opened up Henrikson's face. He bled from the nose and from the mouth, and he went down like a fighting suit full of potatoes.

Grant kicked the rifle away from him, and then booted him in the head again. Hard.

"Unnnh!"

The lights in those bright blue eyes dimmed.

"You don't smell so good to me anymore, Henrikson!"

A groan from behind him. He picked up Henrikson's weapon, and then went over to Colonel Kozlowski.

"Ooooh," she said. "I think my hip is broken."

Indeed, there was a smoking hole in the overplating of the hip area of the suit, exposing underpart beneath.

"Yes," said Grant. "The underplating of this armor is designed to withstand severe concussions.

Still, you're probably right about that hip. You're going to need some help."

He helped her up. "Yeah. Thanks." She cringed. "I'll make it."

"Good."

"Looks like you did a number on Henrikson there. Surprised you didn't take his rifle and blast him."

"Don't think the thought didn't enter my mind. No, if we can get him back, I'll be able to use him to string MedTech up by its dangling prescriptions."

"Sounds good. We go now?"

"We go."

They revived Henrikson with a few slaps across the chops, and then they made sure that he knew which direction their rifles were pointing.

Grant propped Kozlowski up on the sideboard of the drone. She could walk, sort of, but he figured he'd better save that for later.

The suit was getting too heavy for him, so he took off the top.

"Helmets?" she said.

"Forget the helmets. We've got enough weight to slow us down as it is."

"At least stick them up here on the drone, dammit."

"Yes, sir."

He had Henrikson do that. The traitorous corporal performed the task grudgingly, without comment.

"The creatures should be miles from here," said Grant.

They started trudging back the way they'd come, with him keeping a bead on Henrikson while Kozlowski controlled the cargo drone.

They were just at the tunnel opening at the end of the chamber when they heard the rumbling.

"What the hell . . ." said Henrikson, looking behind. "It's coming from that other tunnel, on the opposite end of the chamber."

"Oh, shit," said Kozlowski.

Grant watched, disbelieving, as an alien ran into view in the dimly illuminated distance.

Followed by another.

Followed by three . . . four . . .

A clot of the monsters burst out of the tunnel.

"They must be coming back through another entrance!" said Kozlowski. "They must have sensed the death of their queen, dammit, and started to head back."

"And took a short cut! Well, let's get a *move* on here. I—"

He'd taken his attention off of Henrikson for one moment—one short moment!—and had been rewarded by the big man, big time.

Henrikson's body plowed into his, knocking Grant down, bashing the rifle from his hands. It clunked down beside him, and Grant grabbed it up again.

Henrikson jumped on top of him and they wrestled for the gun. They were on the other side of the cargo drone, away from any chance of Colonel Kozlowski interceding immediately.

"For chrissake, you asshole," said Grant. "They're almost on top of us."

"I'm gonna make it out of here, Grant," said the big man. "I'm going to be the only one who does."

As they struggled, the bottle of Xeno-Zip fell out of Grant's pocket, cracking open on the alien floor beside him, spilling its contents.

Henrikson was distracted.

Grant used it.

He wrenched the rifle away from the man's hands and whacked the butt across the man's chin.

Stunned, the man fell back.

Kozlowski was limping around at that point, holding a rifle. "Stand back, Grant. I'm going to kill him!" she said, nostrils flaring with anger.

Grant took a look at the groaning Henrikson and the fallen bottle of Xeno-Zip and then at the approaching aliens.

"No," he said. "I've got a better idea."

He scooped up a handful of the pills, and he stuffed them into Henrikson's mouth, holding his hands over the man's lips so he was forced to automatically swallow them.

"Get yourself on the front of that drone, and let's get the hell out of here," he said.

"What . . . ?"

"Let's just say that it's a far, far nobler thing that Corporal Henrikson is going to do today than he's ever done before."

Grant put the rifle down between the Corporal's arms and then he grabbed Kozlowski's arm and helped her over to the lander.

The man's eyes popped open.

Inside he felt as though an atom bomb had just gone off in his brain.

He rolled his head, and saw, just meters away, a horde of charging, hissing aliens.

In his arms was a rifle.

Fire raged through his bloodstream and nervous

system. He felt the familiar flight-or-fight response, only flight didn't seem necessary.

Henrikson, after all, was God!

And in his hands was a fistful of lightning bolts.

Grinning, he got up as the aliens approached.

"C'mon, you bastards!" he screamed. "Let's play!"

He'd kill them all.

Then he'd go back up and nail that bastard Grant and that bitch Kozlowski.

Yeah!

The gun in his hand started blazing.

Something was going on down there. Something huge. The motion detectors were going nuts in Private Mahone's hands. And her own internal warning system, her instincts, told her that it was danger, pure and simple.

"Cripes," said Private Dicer, his eyes bulging, a tic working at his mouth. "I can even feel it in my feet!"

Sweat had broken out on the brow of Private Clapton. "Shit, man. What are we going to do?"

"Colonel says if they're not back, we should cut and run. I say we obey orders."

Every cell in Mahone's body agreed. She wanted to run and hide. She was exhausted in every respect but for the terror that had filled her from the very first. This mission was worse than she'd ever imagined.

Something deep inside her though surged up. Something strong inside of her took ahold of her, and she realized that it was as much her as her fear.

"No."

"Say *what*?" said Clapton.

The rumbling was building.

"Shit, Private, those idiots down there are probably getting torn to pieces. We wait here, and that's just what's going to happen to us," said Dicer.

Dicer started moving away toward the exit, eyes rolling with terror. Clapton started following him.

"You assholes move one more step, I'm going to blast you," she said.

Dicer kept moving and she put a blast a yard short of him, and then aimed in a fashion that they well knew could take them both out with a simple tug of the trigger.

"Jeez, Mahone? Are you crazy? Our asses are in a sling here!" whined Clapton.

"Well then rock in 'em, guys. We're going to stay right here and give aid and succor." Her eyes blazed. "And you know what! I've half a mind to go in after the others."

"You're nuts!"

"I'm looking at my watch here. We've got a good ten minutes to wait this out. I'm just following orders." She grinned. "Just doing my job."

Sweating and fidgeting, the others stopped.

Private Mahone smiled to herself. She was getting something out of this crazy jellybean hunt. She was getting her soul back.

She just hoped she was going to have a future to use it in.

"What happened?" said Mahone. "What the hell's going on down there?"

The three soldiers were still waiting for them patiently where Kozlowski had placed them. Seeing them there was a great relief, a testament to her ability to judge people.

"No time to explain," said Grant. "We've just got

to get *out* of here. There's a batch of aliens coming up through the tunnel."

That was all it took.

The cargo van kept going, rolling along with a few more guards.

Behind them, she could still hear the echoes of Henrikson's blazing gun.

Then it stopped, and there was a shriek the likes of which she'd never heard before.

"If we're lucky, enough of the dead things piled up that they're going to have to clear them out first," said Grant. "C'mon, can't we get this beast to move faster?"

"It's flat out," she said.

Running speed. It would have to do.

It seemed to take forever, but finally they saw the lip of the tunnel's entrance.

They rolled out, and there, like a delightful promise, was the *Anteater* patiently waiting for them.

With her excitement, Kozlowski could almost ignore the pounding pain in her hip.

She chinned her radio on. "O'Connor! Drop all walls of the perimeter and tell Fitzwilliam to start the engines!" she gasped a breath. "Prepare for an emergency lift-off!"

"Yes, sir!"

"Ellis. Get those guns ready. We're going to have some visitors coming out of that hole too damned quickly. Try and stop them, if you can!"

"Yes, sir."

They hightailed it.

They were halfway there when the aliens started gushing out of the tunnel.

"Now, Ellis!"

"Roger."

The private started blasting. The shells devastated whole sections of the emerging aliens. One blasted the side of the hive, sending down clumps of stuff to crush a few.

But there were so many of the things that they just kept on coming, regardless.

And coming too damned fast.

"Hurry it up!" called Grant.

Fortunately they hit a decline, and gained some speed.

They were almost there.

The ramp had been lowered for them. All they had to do, thought Kozlowski, was make that ramp. Roll up. Get in, and nip off.

That was all.

Grant was running alongside her. "Alex . . . how's the thigh?"

"Better. Why?"

"I think we can run faster than this drone. We might have to abandon it."

Kozlowski shook her head. "No freaking way, Grant. We came all the way to get this stuff. We're taking it back with us. Do you hear? I for one want to see you take a bath in the shit!"

Grant grunted. "Only in the nude, and only if you'll join me."

"If we're both lucky, Grant. If we're both lucky."

Somehow, they made it to the ramp.

The drone rolled up like a champ.

"Fold up shop!" cried Kozlowski. "Ellis, get your butt in here."

The hydraulic struts of the ramp started squealing up, hauling up the platform.

Through another door Private Ellis raced in, still clutching his dead friend's saxophone.

"Closing up the guns."

"Damn. We've got nothing to shoot them with now," said Kozlowski, hopping off the cargo drone, letting the side serve as her crutch.

"Engines firing."

"The damned hatch has got to close first!" she cried.

Then, a flicker of nightmare:

Talons, scrambling for a hold on the ramp, coming up now like a castle drawbridge in the face of vandals.

The too-familiar banana-shaped head, the drooling fangs . . .

A hissing insinuated through the sound of the hydraulics.

Guns raised to shoot the alien scrabbling in.

"No!" cried Kozlowski. "The blood will eat through the door. We won't be able to lift—"

"Hell," said Ellis. "I can't play the stupid thing anyway."

With all his might he threw the saxophone.

Its metal base bashed directly into the alien's head. *Bonk!*

The creature was knocked off the door, and it closed, tightly and firmly, no alien blood acid eating through it.

The lander rumbled and throbbed, and Kozlowski could feel its rockets kicking off this foul planet's dust with fiery disgust.

Epilogue

She was lying in bed, with a beautiful view of the stars through a viewport window.

She was safe and sound, and a few simple, nonaddictive drugs were running through her system, killing the pain of the fractured thigh.

She was off the Fire. The mission was complete. The Corps was going to be happy, and maybe she'd even get a promotion. She felt the loss of her troops heavily, but then she'd lost people before. Old hat. The emptiness went away. Eventually.

She felt no imminent sense of danger. She had some books to read, and some vids to watch.

Why, then, Colonel Alexandra Kozlowski asked herself, did she feel so bored and antsy?

This should be a time to celebrate.

After they'd gotten the *Anteater* safely back on the

Razzia, and off-loaded the tank, they realized they had twenty-five hundred gallons of the stuff. Grant's scientists were totally blissed. It was enough to work with, and absolutely top quality, no sign of that red strain whatsoever. There was a good chance now they could even create their own queen mother.

They'd nuked the black hive as a parting shot.

There were probably xenos left on the planet. But it would take a long, long time to regroup. Kozlowski imagined one playing a soulful sax as its hive burned.

Yeah!

Turned out, according to Friel and others, this whole "red aliens" thing was a fluke. The queen mother and the queens were dead now, and all their eggs. They'd never come scratching on their door again.

The generic brand though . . .

They'd be around. They were the universe's cockroaches, with a vengeance.

And she'd helped step on her share.

A time for rest and relaxation and recuperation. A time for peace and meditation and—

Whatever.

So it was that when Daniel Grant came to see her later that day, she was overjoyed at his visit—though she'd be damned if she'd let him know how much.

"Hello, Colonel. How are you feeling?"

"Okay. Not an extreme fracture. The machine set it, and it should heal while I'm in hypersleep. A little physical therapy on Earth, and I'll be right as rain."

"Good. I'm pleased. Very pleased." His eyes

seemed to drift toward the stars and into abstraction.

"You come here to talk about something?"

"Nothing in particular. I just wanted to make sure you're all right."

"I'm fine. Nothing more?"

"Well, everyone seems to be on the emotional mend. Lot of people are just sleeping . . . I guess in reaction to all that stress."

"And you. What are you doing? Taking any baths in your royal jelly yet?"

"No. No . . . Waiting for you." He laughed. "The scientists are just tickled pink. They've already started to work on it, along with the samples of the red alien DNA. They say maybe they really have got something here."

"I hope so. We had to dole out a few lives for it."

"I'm going to make sure that those lives were not lost in vain, Alex." He looked down at the bed, smoothing the linen thoughtfully. "Actually, you know, maybe there *was* something I wanted to talk to you about."

"Shoot. I'm not going anywhere."

"I was impressed by your work here. When we get back, I'm probably going to need someone to head up a security team for Grant Industries. The job is yours, if you want it."

She laughed. "And leave the marines? No way. I've got a mission in life, Grant. And it's not to guard your butt."

He shook his head. "I don't understand, Alex. How much longer can you do things like this mission? How long do you think you can survive?"

"I don't know any other kind of life . . . except . . ."

"Except what?"

"Except for maybe when I was a little girl. Yeah. I had a real good life when I was a kid, Grant. Perfect. And then a bunch of monsters came down and destroyed that life and destroyed a lot of lives." She shook her head. "Think about it, Grant. Think about it while you're sitting up there in your ivory tower when you get back. This may seem like hell to you. It's pretty rough, sure . . . That mission was one of the roughest. But chew on this—most wars get fought between people arguing over some relatively silly matter . . . usually involving money or land or possessions. People kill people. It's stupid, senseless, and a waste. History is drowned in the shed blood of martyrs for meaningless causes." She shook her head. "I don't know if I'm even going to make any history books, Grant. But I do know that whatever I accomplish against . . . against this *plague* against decent life . . . this *evil* that has infected the galaxy . . . It's not meaningless." She took a deep breath. "Now how many people can be positive . . . absolutely feel-it-to-their-toes sure . . . That their lives mean something. That as full as foibles as they are, they're living and fighting for something *good*."

Grant seemed to consider that for a moment.

"I can't argue much about that, Alex." He slapped his knees and stood up. "But we can't all be Joan of Arc. Somebody's got to get the engines of commerce running. And somebody's got to be in charge of those engines."

"Well, maybe you've got a different view of things

now that you've looked at life through the jaws of one of the monsters coming at you?"

"Sure. Sure. Of course, now I've got to figure out how to look at life without worrying about mobsters or MedTech."

She laughed. "I'm sure the generals and admiral back home will be so pleased, you'll have no problem, Grant."

"I don't know . . . I just hope that what we've done on this journey *does* make a difference."

She smiled. "I've been watching you, Grant. I think it already has, jelly or no jelly."

"Thanks. I guess maybe you're right." He started to leave, then paused and turned.

"Alex?"

"Daniel?"

"If you won't work for me . . . Maybe you'd like to have a little bubbly, a little caviar, a little gourmet dinner with me sometime?"

"Hell no!"

He sighed, nodded, and turned to go.

"But if you want a beer and some pretzels sometime, Daniel—I keep my larder well stocked with those."

He seemed confused for a moment, looked at her.

She winked at him.

His face flushed and he laughed.

"Count on it, Colonel. Count on it."

He blew a kiss at her and turned.

"Oh. And, Danny boy," she called after him.

He turned. "Yes?"

She'd pulled out the cigar he'd given her, along

with a lighter. She puffed the thing alight. "Thanks for the smoke."

"Anytime, Colonel. Anytime."

He left.

She looked back out at the stars.

She hadn't seen stars as beautiful as these, she thought, as filled with wonder and awe—

Well, since she was just a kid.

Suddenly, unaccountably, she found herself craving pretzels and beer as she blew thick puffs of smoke at the bright points of light.